MIDNIGHT SURRENDER

Allyson was tired of being strong all on her own. She felt as if she had been doing that most of her life.

"Will you . . . hold me for a little while?" she asked.

Ethan gladly obliged. He put his arm around her and held her close, letting her cry against his shoulder. "Hey, this isn't the Ally I know."

"I needed that stove," she wept. "It isn't . . . fair."

He thought about how his mother had died and how Violet died, taking the baby with her. "A lot of things in life aren't fair, Ally, but we have to put up with them anyway. We just have to keep going."

Ally breathed deeply of the smell of him, a manly scent of leather and out-of-doors. Here was a man who knew how to get by on almost nothing, and tonight she needed his strength.

He struggled against the urge to do more than just hold her. "What am I going to do, Ethan?"

"That's your decision to make. I told you I'd take you to Fort Supply if you want to give this up. You'd be protected there until you decide what to do next."

She closed her eyes. "I can't give in to somebody like Nolan Ives. I know it could work, if I could just get started right. I've never given in to anybody in my whole life."

With his free hand, Ethan touched her cheek. "Maybe it's time you did," he said softly. "But not to Nolan Ives."

Unforgettable

Rosanne Bittner

Zebra Books
Kensington Publishing Corp.

http://www.zebrabooks.com

ZEBRA BOOKS are published by

Kensington Publishing Corp.
850 Third Avenue
New York, NY 10022

Zebra and the Z logo Reg. U.S. Pat. & TM Off.

First Printing: January, 1994
10 9 8 7 6 5 4 3

Printed in the United States of America

Love is a light, in darkened ways;

Love is a path, in pathless lands;

Love is a fire, in winter days;

A staff, in chill, unsteady hands.

Speak to your heart, my own, my Dear,

Say: this is love, and Love is here.

from *Diversi Colores* by Herbert P. Horne

1

April, 1889 . . .

Ethan Temple squinted through a stinging wind to make sure he was seeing straight. On the trail below, several Indians tied loosely together, were walking behind a man and his horse. Farther ahead, six white men on horseback herded several head of cattle and the Indian ponies.

Ethan removed the glove from his right hand. He would need his fingers free in case there was any shooting. He cursed the miserably damp, cold weather as he pulled his rifle from its boot, his hand almost sticking to the cold steel. He knew he could expect trouble, and he wanted to be ready. Ever since whites had started coming into Indian Territory under permission from the Federal Government, there had been problems, especially here along Deep Creek Trail and the Cherokee Outlet. There was little enough land left to the many tribes who had been forced into this territory, and every new treaty they signed seemed to result in their being shoved from one area to another.

He pulled his hat a little farther down on his forehead to help keep the wind out of his eyes, then started his horse down the embankment. "Easy, Blackfoot," he said softly to the animal, a big buckskin with black tail and mane, all four feet black to the knees. He guided him around thick undergrowth, man and horse partially hidden from the men below by thick stands of trees.

He well understood Indian resentment of more whites

coming into Indian Territory. He was half Cheyenne himself, his white blood his father's, his Indian blood his dead mother's. He still lived in both worlds and had grown up for a time among the Cheyenne, but spending most of his adult years among whites. He supposed he had the only reasonable job for a man of his divided heritage—army scout, his primary goal to keep the peace between white ranchers and the Indians. It was certainly not an easy job, especially in the summertime, when cattlemen from Texas started herding their beef north through Indian Territory into Kansas. That was when the really big trouble always began, when cattle strayed onto Indian lands; the drovers sometimes lost their way, not always sure which trails were legal and which were not. The Indians certainly knew what belonged to them, but some cattlemen didn't have an ounce of respect for land that was not legally their own.

He finally reached the clearing below and kicked Blackfoot into a hard run. When he got closer he could see there were ropes tied around each Indian's neck, linking them together like slaves, their hands tied behind their backs. He fired his rifle into the air to stop the procession—the gunshot sent the cattle ahead of them into a run. Three of the cattlemen took off after them, while the other three turned to see who had fired the shot. Ethan saw one of them draw his gun to shoot back. A bullet whizzed past him, and he drew his sure-footed buckskin to a sliding halt in thick mud and took aim with his Winchester, shooting the man's hat right off. Now that he was closer, he recognized the culprit as Cass Andrich, who worked for a local rancher, Jim Sulley. Andrich was a troublemaker, a man who hated Indians simply because they existed. "All of you halt right there!" he shouted into the wind. "Drop your weapons, or the next bullet goes right through your head, Andrich!"

All three men hesitated a moment, and Ethan shot off another man's hat.

"Sonofabitch!" the man shouted, taking out his handgun and throwing it to the ground. The others followed suit.

"Rifles, too!" Ethan demanded, easing Blackfoot forward. He let the reins dangle so he could keep his rifle steady, depending on the well-trained horse to obey signals from his legs and feet. "Cut the ropes on those Indians!" he demanded.

"Ethan!"

He glanced at the Indian who had shouted his name. It was Red Hawk, one of his cousins who lived on the nearby Southern Cheyenne reservation.

"These are Jim Sulley's men!" Red Hawk told him. "They say we stole the cattle! We were only bringing them back after we found them grazing on reservation land!"

Same old problem, Ethan thought. "You men know Sulley's damn cattle are always straying," he shouted louder to Sulley's men. "What's the idea tying these Indians like this? You aren't supposed to take these matters into your own hands! They're for the *army* to settle!"

"The army ain't gonna do a damn thing!" Andrich complained. "The damn Indians get away with murder, all in the name of peace!"

"We aren't talking about murder here," Ethan shot back, still aiming the rifle. "At least not *yet*! We're only talking about a few stray cattle."

"Bullshit! We had cattle missin', and when we come lookin', we found these Injuns here roundin' 'em up," Andrich answered.

"And you know damn well they were only herding them together to chase them off reservation land! The Indians need that land for their own grazing." Ethan wished he could shoot them all out of their saddles. He watched Sulley's men look at each other, not knowing what to say. He did not recognize the other two. "What were you going to do? *Hang* them when you got them back to Sulley's ranch?"

"That's no more than they deserve, Temple," Andrich answered with a sneer. "We caught them red-handed. I don't give a damn what they say; you might be an army scout, but you ain't the law out here."

"I'm all the law you've got right now, and I'm telling you to cut these Indians loose and take your cattle back to Sulley's ranch! If you're ignorant enough to start a war over a few head of beef, then you deserve to be the first one to die, Andrich! I guarantee if that's what it comes to, I'll be riding with the Cheyenne, and I damn well know where to find you! Now cut them loose!"

Andrich eyed Ethan a moment longer, cussed under his breath, then ordered one of the other men to free the Indians. By then some of the men who had gone after the stampeding cattle were riding back toward the confrontation. "Tell them to back off and keep their guns in their holsters," Ethan ordered Andrich, "or you'll go down first!"

"You half-breed sonofabitch!" the man grumbled. He turned and signalled the oncoming men, waving his arms. "Keep your weapons holstered!" he shouted. He looked back at Ethan. "Our day is comin', Temple," he sneered. "I don't like takin' orders from no half-breed scum."

Ethan ignored the insult. He had heard the same words many times and had come to accept the fact that he couldn't spend his whole life hitting people who insulted him. He had learned that in many white men's eyes, being a half-breed was worse than being a full-blooded Indian. If that was the way they wanted to think, there wasn't much he could do about it. "You'll either do what I say or come back with me to Fort Supply and face charges," he answered.

"Charges! What kind of charges?"

"Trespassing on Indian lands. It's still a crime in this territory, whether you're looking for strayed cattle or not!"

"*Stolen* cattle!" one of the other men barked.

The third man finished cutting loose the four Indians, who moved closer to Ethan.

"Go empty all their weapons," Ethan told his cousin.

Red Hawk gladly obeyed, grinning with a feeling of victory as he spun the cartridges of six-guns and opened rifles. When he was finished, Ethan ordered Sulley's men to pick up their weapons and take their cattle and go. "And leave the Indian ponies," he added. "Maybe I *should* bring all of you up on charges, for stealing Indian horses!" he added. "Stealing horses is a hanging offense, even if they *do* belong to Indians!"

"Go to hell, Temple!" Andrich sneered. He and the other men picked up their weapons and mounted up, glaring at Ethan.

"Jim Sulley is a fair man," Ethan reminded him. "He won't like hearing what you've done here. This kind of thing just keeps the hatred going. You know damn well how important it is to stay on good terms with the Indians in these parts, especially here along Deep Creek Trail. The cattlemen from Texas have to use this trail to get to Kansas, and their beef stray all the time. They need the Indians' cooperation to get them back without trouble. You ought to be fired, Andrich, and I intend to talk to Sully about it!"

"You get me fired, and I'll come lookin' for you, Temple."

"I'm not hard to find. Just ask around at Fort Supply."

Sulley's dark eyes narrowed with rage. "You bastard," he muttered. He turned to the other men. "Let's get these cattle back to the ranch!" With one more glance back at Ethan, he rode off, he and the rest of the men whistling and waving their hats to get the cattle together. They all made their way along the trail, riding into a rising wind that brought with it a cold mist.

Ethan shoved his rifle into its boot and dismounted. "You all right?" he asked Red Hawk.

His cousin's dark eyes glittered with hatred. "The next time I see that white bastard, he is a *dead* man!"

"You know you can't kill him, Red Hawk. I'll report this to the army and to Sulley. Just settle down and leave these things to the law."

"Law!" Red Hawk spat on the ground. "*White* man's law! That is all we have around here! This is supposed to be *Indian* land! Men like Andrich have no right attacking us and calling us thieves!"

"*Did* you steal the cattle?"

Red Hawk held his chin high, took a deep breath, and tried to look hurt. Then he grinned, the cold wind blowing his long, black hair over his eyes. "Whatever comes onto Indian land and eats our grass *belongs* to us!"

Ethan sighed in frustration, tying his wolfskin coat higher at his throat. "You know you can't think that way, Red Hawk. Whether you like it or not, some whites are going to be allowed to settle around here, and cattlemen are going to keep coming through from Texas. If you try to fight it, they'll win, not you, because the government will get behind its settlers. Haven't you learned that from past experience? How in hell do you think the Cheyenne and the rest of the tribes ended up with only this little bit of land in the first place? The war is over, Red Hawk. I don't like it any better than you."

"It is easy for you. You live among them. The army is your friend."

Ethan shook his head. "It isn't easier, Red Hawk. I'm

only *half* Indian. You know what I've been through because of my mixed blood."

Red Hawk nodded. "You are *all* Indian . . . in here." He put a fist to Ethan's chest, then grinned. "*Most* of the time."

Ethan smiled in return. "You aren't making my job any easier, Red Hawk."

"I did not start this one. Andrich and the others did."

Snow began to batter their faces. "I know," Ethan answered. He shook Red Hawk's hand. "You'd better get yourself home."

"When will you come and see us? You spend too much time at the fort now, Cousin."

Their eyes held, and Ethan felt the old longing to go and live with his Cheyenne relatives again; but since losing his Cheyenne wife . . . "I've got a job to do," he answered. "I'm helping all of you more this way than I could if I came back to the reservation to live."

"And the white man in you keeps you away."

Ethan nodded. "Sometimes."

Red Hawk smiled sadly. "Go then, Running Wolf," he said. "I am glad you came along when you did. You are probably right. It is good, what you are doing. Come and see us when you can."

"I will."

"Do you have a blanket we can use? Andrich threw our blankets and winter jackets to the ground. We will have to ride back and find them."

Ethan felt renewed rage when he realized Sulley's men had forced Red Hawk and the others to walk in the cold wind wearing only their deerskin shirts. "Sure." He turned and took three blankets from his gear, taking note that at least Red Hawk and the others had been allowed to keep on their winter moccasins. "Here." He handed out the blankets. "These are all I have."

"You might need at least one of them yourself."

Ethan shook his head. "I'm headed back to the fort. I'll be all right." Wind whipped at his jacket, ruffling the fur and making him shiver. "What about your fourth man?"

"We will take turns with one of the blankets until we find our own."

Ethan nodded. "You go straight back, Red Hawk. No more trouble. Promise me."

Red Hawk, who at twenty-four was four years younger than Ethan, flashed a handsome smile. "No more trouble." The three Indians with him had gathered their painted ponies and were mounted and ready to ride. One of them handed Red Hawk the reins to his own horse, and the young man leapt onto the animal's back in one swift movement.

Ethan thought how sad it was that proud young warriors like his cousin had no pathway now, no idea of where they fit into the scheme of things. They could not live the old way, and could not quite adapt to the new. They were caught between . . . and he well knew that feeling. "I'll come for a visit after the cattle drives," he told Red Hawk. The other man nodded, a sad look in his eyes. Ethan watched him ride off with the others, headed toward reservation land. Mounting Blackfoot, his heart was heavy as he thought of things that might have been . . . and his own torn loyalties. It would always be like this. "Let's go, boy," he said, kicking his horse into a gentle lope toward Fort Supply.

"We have to get off this train somewhere, Toby." Allyson Mills held the collar of her faded and frayed woolen coat over the side of her face, partly to warm her cold nose, and partly to keep her near-whispered conversation with her brother private. "If we don't, they'll separate us. Mr. Bartel says they won't, but you know he's lying."

"We ain't got a choice, Ally."

"Sure we have a choice," Allyson answered, her blue eyes glittering with daring. "We can get off now, before the train leaves the station, and go live on the streets again. It would be hard to go back to that life, but at least we'd be together."

Toby sighed, scowling. "Henry Bartel has both ends of this railroad car being watched," he reminded her. "He's got goods to deliver to families out west—*human* goods—and he means to make sure we get there. I expect he'll be real glad to get *you* off his hands, what with all the trouble you've caused him the last four years."

"He *deserved* to be reported to the priest," Ally sniffed. "He's an evil man, and me being sixteen and you seventeen, you *know* he thinks we're old enough that we should go to separate homes. Once he gets us out there in uncivilized country, he'll separate us, just to be mean. He'll leave you with one family and take me a thousand miles farther before he dumps me off, maybe with some horrible old farmer who needs a wife or something dreadful like that. You know people don't adopt kids our age out of love and goodness. We'll be used like slaves!"

Allyson's heart ached at the desperate hopelessness in her brother's eyes. She thought how, when they were younger and she kept her red hair cut short, people used to think they were twins. That was when she and Toby used to run in the streets and alleys of New York, stealing for their drunken father just to keep food on the table. For two years after their father died, they had continued to live by stealing and rummaging, until the police finally put them in a Catholic orphanage. Soon after, Allyson's body began to betray her

attempts to pass herself off as a boy. It infuriated her to remember how, not long after the police took them to the orphanage, the boys' supervisor, Henry Bartel, had beat her
with a paddle when he realized she was a girl, calling her all
sorts of names for "living in sin" in the boys' section just so
she could be near her brother.

She had only been twelve then, and she hadn't even
known what "living in sin" meant. She had been sent to the
girls' wing of the orphanage, and was expected to behave
like some wilting flower. For the past four years she had not
even been allowed to cut her hair. Now it fell to the middle
of her back, and when the nuns helped brush it out for her,
they always remarked on how beautiful it was. Allyson wondered why, if it was so beautiful, she always had to wrap it
back into a twist around her head. To wear her red mane
brushed out long was another act considered sinful, but she
decided that was fine with her. She didn't like fussing with
it anyway.

She wished with all her heart that she *was* a boy. Then
Mr. Bartel wouldn't have found ways to frighten and humili-
ate her by making suggestive remarks and grabbing at her
breasts whenever he found her alone. She had already made
the plans to run away when she and Toby were surprised
with the news that they were being sent west by train to be
adopted. They were "getting too big" to be wards of the orphanage, they were told, but were still too young to be sent
out to survive alone. They had been given only one day's
notice, not enough time to plan an escape.

Being separated from Toby in different wings of the orphanage had been bad enough, but now they faced total
separation. She knew Toby was just as frightened as she
was, maybe more. Her brother was a slow learner, a quiet,
reticent young man who often depended on her, even

though he was a year older. Allyson was convinced he could not possibly survive without her, and although she hated to admit to any weakness, deep inside she was not sure she could survive without Toby. It was for his sake that she masked her own fears. She had no one else, and certainly no one else was going to love her the way her brother did.

"Ally, even if we could get off this train, what's out in the streets has to be worse than where we're going," Toby reminded her. "It would be harder for you now. You can't be running the streets anymore. You wouldn't last a day before you'd be dragged off by some gang of hoodlums who would take advantage because you're a girl. If you were caught stealing, you'd be put in jail, or sent to one of them factories where they work you near to death. We got away with stuff when we were little, but it's all different now. Maybe this is a good thing. Maybe we'll end up on some nice farm, where it's safe and the people are good. *Anything* is better than the orphanage, or the streets and alleys of New York. You know that."

Allyson forced back tears. She hated crying more than anything she could think of. "I just don't want us to be separated. You need me, and I need you. Each other is all we've got." She snuggled a little closer, keeping her voice even lower. "We're getting off this train, somehow, somewhere. Maybe you're right about there being a better life for us farther west, but we'll make our *own* way, and we'll do it *together*. Bartel is not going to separate us." She kissed his cheek, which sported a mass of freckles and still did not need shaving. Her own freckles were limited to a few over her nose, the rest of her skin *smooth as porcelain*, as the nuns put it. *Not like your brother, freckles from head to toe.*

Toby's hair was even a brighter red than her own, and his eyes a paler blue, not the deep blue of Allyson's. Now that they were older, they did not look so much alike. Toby was tall and gangly, but fast filling out into manhood. To her chagrin, Allyson had remained tiny, couldn't seem to get past five feet and a couple of inches. If not for her full breasts, one would think she wasn't even sixteen yet, and that angered her. She was going on seventeen, a grown woman, and she did not belong on an orphan train. Oh, how she wished she was a boy—no, a man! She would have so many more rights and privileges. She wanted to be big and strong, so she could sock Henry Bartel and march right off this train and fend for herself!

The orphan train—that's what people called it. She and Toby and twenty-two other children, most of them younger, had been ferried across the Hudson River to New Jersey, where they were herded all together into one train car. The locomotive pulling that car would take them to places west, and none of them knew just who they would be living with once they got there.

Ally had watched the looks on people's faces for the last half-hour as they walked past the coach, staring up at the windows and shaking their heads. One would have thought the car in which she rode was packed with some kind of strange, pitiful creatures. How many of those people knew the pain she and the others suffered? Why did they look at these children as though their predicament were their own fault? Did being orphaned somehow taint you? She felt a deep anger at their attitude, their unwillingness to take any of these children and give them a nice home, give them the love they had so long been without.

It was Toby who needed that love and protection most of all. He was too willing to accept things and let people walk all over him. Who would be there to protect him if they were separated? He needed the security of his sister's love.

Maybe it was because he needed to know at least one person cared, at least one person forgave him. He had caused the fire that had killed their mother, but it was an accident. Allyson had never blamed him, but she knew he blamed himself, and their father also blamed him. The man had taken to drinking after that, beating her and Toby often, always reminding poor Toby it was his fault their mother was dead.

Ever since then Toby had been a frightened, hesitant young man who considered himself worthless. She could not let him struggle alone with that. It might not be so bad if their grandparents had forgiven him, but they treated him like a murderer, and had allowed them both to live in the streets.

She realized it was mostly her fault they were being sent west. She had caused the most trouble, tried to run away several times, complained to the priest whenever Henry Bartel abused her. It didn't do much good, but at least it embarrassed Bartel and made her feel better. Lately she had been counting on their ages to mean she and Toby would soon be freed. She had not expected to be carried off into the Great American Desert, where they would both surely be forever forgotten, maybe captured and eaten by Indians or sold to outlaws. Who could say what would happen to them?

She grabbed her brother's arm tighter when the locomotive whistle startled her with three loud shrieks. Ahead of them were two cars full of regular passengers. Then came the car full of orphans. It lurched, and the train began to slowly leave the station. Allyson watched out the window as the train rumbled past the platform where people still stood, some just staring, others smiling at the "poor little children." One woman had a rather pious, judgmental look on her face, as though everyone in the orphan car were some kind of criminal. Allyson squiggled her face into a hideous contortion and stuck out her tongue, then laughed when the woman's eyes widened and she appeared to gasp as she pointed at her. She wiggled her tongue a little longer until the woman was out of sight. There came a sharp, painful rap on her shoulder then, and she quickly turned to look up into Henry Bartel's dark eyes, which glittered with retribution.

"What do you think you are doing, young lady?"

Allyson glared back at him, keeping her chin raised in defiance. Oh, how she hated this man who often took privileges with some of the other younger girls, then threatened them with terrible punishment and embarrassment if they dared to tell the nuns or the priest. Allyson had told anyway and suffered often for it, but she didn't care how many beatings she took or how often she was forced to stay in a room alone for days at a time with hardly any food. She had managed to make it difficult for Bartel to get away with things he had no right doing, and she gladly made the sacrifice. She hoped the fact that he had been given the assignment of accompanying the orphans to their various locations was in turn a punishment for him. The man did not seem to like this job one bit. He had grumbled constantly about having to accompany a bunch of "restless brats" into "wild Indian country." The nuns had said they were sure there were no "wild" Indians left, that they were all tame now and living on reservations. Allyson hoped they were right. After all, this was 1889. The Indian wars were supposed to be over.

"I was just smiling at the nice people on the platform who were waving to us," she answered Bartel, keeping her voice firm and her eyes steady.

Bartel took the cane with which he had hit her and poked it against her chest. "I saw what you were doing, you little troublemaker! I want no problems from you on this trip, young lady. We are away from the orphanage now, and you are under my complete authority."

Allyson studied the man's long, thin nose, set in a thin face. Everything about him was thin—his lips, his build, the hands that held the cane . . . even his eyes were small and beady. Of all the mean, lawless people she had come across in the back alleys of the city, she hated this man most of all. She studied the bony hand that held the cane, felt sick at the memory of that hand touching her breasts.

"Go to hell, Henry Bartel," she sneered defiantly. She could hear the gasps of some of the other children around them, sensed the wide eyes and open mouths, but she kept her eyes on Bartel, whose face was beet red. She knew that if he could get away with it he would give her a good thrashing, but two volunteers who were active in the church that supported the orphanage had come along to help transport the children, and Bartel had been trying to present a picture to them of a kind, generous, caring superintendent. He knew his job was on the line because of allegations Allyson had presented to the Church over the last two years. She was glad to have made trouble for him.

"Leave her alone, Mr. Bartel," Toby spoke up. "I'll make sure she minds her business."

Bartel turned the cane to Toby, touching his cheek with it. "You do that, boy. And you remember that if it wasn't for your sister, you would still be in the safe confines of the orphanage and not being shipped off to strange people in a strange land."

The man walked away, and the train began to chug along faster, steam billowing up past the window where Allyson sat. She put her head on Toby's shoulder. "We're getting off this train and away from Bartel," she told him. "We'll make a new life for ourselves out there somewhere, Toby, but it won't be with people who adopt us. We'll do it on our own, just you and me, like it's always been."

Toby reached over and patted her hand. "If you say so, Sis."

"I say so." Again Allyson blinked back tears. This was no time to cry or worry about Henry Bartel. For the next few days she had to think hard, plan their escape. Surely the terrible dangers of the wild west couldn't be any worse than the dangers that lurked in the streets of New York City . . . or in the dark hallways of the orphanage whenever Henry Bartel was on duty.

2

A weary Ethan Temple halted Blackfoot in front of civilian quarters at Fort Supply. The gelding shook a cold, wet snow from its black mane as Ethan dismounted. "I know what you mean, boy," Ethan grumbled, removing his floppy leather hat and knocking it against the hitching post to get the snow off. "I hate this weather as much as you, but it's a spring snow that'll probably turn to rain by tomorrow. Won't be long before warm weather is here."

He tied the animal, hoping he was right. It was unusual to have any snow this time of year in Indian Territory, and this sloppy, damp weather made his job more difficult, especially when it came to finding a dry place to make camp. It felt good to be back at the fort, where he could go inside and sleep in a dry bed for once.

He patted the horse's neck, looking over at a teenage Cherokee boy who was always hanging around talking about being a scout some day. "Jack, come on over here and tend to Blackfoot, will you?"

Jack turned up the collar of his wool jacket against a stinging wind, grinning as he ran toward Ethan. He wore no hat, and his straight, black hair was wet from the mixture of rain and snow. The cold did not seem to daunt his youthful eagerness as he approached Ethan, ready to help.

"I haven't slept for a couple of days," Ethan told him. "I'd appreciate it if you'd take Blackfoot here over to the livery and get him fed and brushed down. I'm too damn tired."

"Sure, Mr. Temple. You have any trouble this time?"

"Just the usual. Those ranchers never seem to learn they've got to keep their cattle off Indian lands. I expect it will get worse this summer again."

"Maybe we'll have another big Indian war, huh?"

Ethan laughed lightly, patting his horse's rump. "I don't think things will ever get that bad again." He turned to pull his Winchester from its boot, then removed his saddlebags from Blackfoot and headed inside. The mention of Indian wars brought painful memories to mind, memories of a place called Sand Creek and a three-year-old Cheyenne boy hugging his dead mother, who had been viciously murdered by soldiers. That boy was a man now, a half-breed, with no family left except his white father, whom he hadn't seen in several months. He felt the recurring stab of pain at his heart remembering he'd had a wife once, had looked forward to the birth of their first child; but that happiness had ended four years ago when Violet died, taking their unborn baby with her to the grave. She was buried on the Cheyenne reservation.

He strode on long legs into the building that held several cots for single civilian men who lived at the fort, most of them scouts. Only one, an old, full-blood Cherokee scout named Hector "Strong Hands" Wells, was inside. He sat on his cot, leaning against the wall and smoking a pipe.

" 'Bout time you got back," Hector said with a scowl. "What'd you do, get lost? You Cheyenne, you don't know how to find your way around."

Ethan grinned, his tall, broad frame blocking the doorway. He had to duck to come inside, then closed the door and walked over to a potbellied stove, leaning his rifle against the wall and hanging his saddlebags over a peg. "If it wasn't for the government, us Cheyenne wouldn't even *be* in Indian Territory. We'd be up in Colorado and Wyoming where we belong."

"Yeah, and us Cherokee would be back in Tennessee and Georgia," Hector answered. He gave his pipe a few quiet puffs. "But there ain't no goin' back, is there?"

The picture of his dead mother again flashed into Ethan's mind. "No, there sure isn't," he answered. He removed his hat and wolfskin coat, revealing a fringed buckskin shirt beneath it. His pants were also of deerskin, and he wore fur-lined, knee-high moccasins, preferring them to leather boots in winter. He unbuckled his gunbelt, throwing it and the six-gun it held over onto his cot. He still wore another raw-hide belt that held his hunting knife. He rubbed his hands together over the top of the stove, thinking how much more of his mother's blood was in him than his father's. His skin was nearly as dark as any Cheyenne's, and he had never had the desire to cut his hair like the white man. It was a deep brown, not as black as his Cheyenne relatives', and he wore it pulled back in a tail.

"Any trouble?" Hector asked.

Ethan shrugged. "Some. I caught some of Jim Sulley's men trying to drag my cousin, Red Hawk, and three other Cheyenne back to Sulley's ranch. I have a feeling they might have tried to hang them, accused them of stealing some of Sulley's cattle. You know the story. Sulley's cattle strayed onto Indian land, the Indians herded them together, and then they got caught. I managed to settle it without any bloodshed, but it was touchy."

"They probably *were* stolen," Hector teased, a sly grin moving across his face. "You Cheyenne are just a bunch of thieves anyway."

Ethan chuckled, walking back to his saddlebags and reaching inside. "You're wanting trouble, aren't you?" He pulled out a pouch that held tobacco and cigarette papers.

"Just enjoy gettin' under your skin, Breed."

Ethan walked to his cot, perfectly aware that Hec's use of the word *breed* was in jest. "If you weren't so old, Hec, I'd show you what a Cheyenne can do to a Cherokee."

Hector laughed lightly. "In my good days there wasn't *nobody* who could beat me." He studied Ethan a moment. He was a handsome man with a nice smile. He liked Ethan. He was an able scout, good with his fists and his guns, but he was of an age when he ought to be settled with a wife and children. Too bad that wife of his had to go and die on him. Hector looked at Ethan almost like a son, and he owed him his life. Two years ago, while out scouting, Hector and his horse had taken a tumble down an embankment, leaving the horse with two broken legs and Hector with several broken bones of his own. They were in one of the most remote areas of Indian Territory, hidden in a ravine, where Hector was sure he would die of wounds or starvation. It was only because of Ethan's uncanny skills at literally sniffing out trouble that he was found. When others had given up the search, Ethan kept on until he finally found him.

"There's gonna be more trouble this summer, and not from the trail herders," he told Ethan as the man rolled himself a smoke.

Ethan had already pulled off his moccasins and leaned back on his own cot. He lit the cigarette and took a deep drag. "What kind of trouble?"

"Settlers. I'm told it's all set. That Indian land they're opening south of the Cherokee Outlet will be up for grabs come April 22. They'll be mixin' land-hungry whites with Pawnee, Sac, Fox, Potawatomi, Shawnee, Cheyenne, Arapaho—hell, the army will be wantin' us to go keep watch, make sure the land-grabbers don't go claimin' sod that ain't theirs, keep them off reservation land that still belongs to us Indians. Pretty soon there won't be any of that left. For years we've been chasin' out squatters as criminals, and now they're gonna let thousands of them come in here and take what they want."

Ethan took another drag on his cigarette, then just stared at it as he held it between his fingers. "The way things are going, the entire Cherokee Outlet will be opened in a couple more years. The government is doing a good job of practically forcing it on every tribe involved."

"Hell, we're all used to bein' pushed from here to there. It ain't never gonna stop, you know that. Pretty soon it will seem silly to call any of this Indian Territory. It will be white man's territory. Trouble is, there ain't no place else to send us. We been squeezed right down to nothin'."

Ethan nodded. "The white man calls it *progress*."

"Your pa, he shouldn't have give up his tradin' post along the Outlet. With these whites comin' in, he'd do good."

Ethan leaned forward and crossed his legs, resting his elbows on his knees. "I guess it's the same for whites as Indians. Pa missed his own people. He's getting old and was feeling poorly, thought maybe he should go back to his relatives in Illinois and see them again before he dies."

"He ought to be with his son."

Ethan grinned against the pain. "I don't belong there. Pa told me several times over the years that my uncle still thinks it was wrong for him to marry an Indian woman. I don't expect I'd be too welcome in his house. But I don't really blame Pa for going back. He hadn't seen his brother in nearly fifteen years. According to his last letter he's not been too well, so it's good he's got people to take care of him. I expect I'd better go see him later this summer."

"Hope you get the chance." Hector took a handkerchief

from his shirt pocket and wiped his nose. "All those new settlers comin' in, it's gonna be a busy spring and summer.
Them people are gonna come swarmin' in here like flies to
horse dung, and you know how greedy the white man can
be. Them that don't get the best spots are gonna go tryin' to
take a little of what don't belong to them. Then the Indians
are gonna get hoppin' mad. We'll be busy, all right."

Ethan scooted down and rested his head against a pillow.
"Right now I don't want to think about it. I need to sleep, so
quit your talking, old man." He reached over to a stand beside his bed and put out his cigarette.

Hector chuckled, rising from his own cot. "I'm goin' to
the commissary, get me a new razor."

Ethan opened one eye and grinned. "Your old one getting
dull from scraping over all those wrinkles?"

Hector pulled on a deerskin jacket. "Wrinkled skin
means a wise man. From the looks of you, you don't have
much wisdom yet."

"Yeah? Well, don't get lost between here and the commissary. I'm too tired to go looking for you."

"You ain't gonna let me live that down, are you?"

"Hell, no."

"You're a mean man, Ethan Temple, pickin' on an old
man like that."

Ethan studied the man's short, stocky build. Hec Wells
was as strong and ornery as any younger man. "Get going,
and let me sleep."

Hector smiled and nodded. "I know. You Cheyenne ain't
very strong. You need your rest."

Ethan reached over and grabbed a pillow from a nearby
cot, throwing it at Hector. The man laughed and went out,
and Ethan could see the snow had indeed already turned to
rain. He lay back down with a sigh, thinking about the com-

ing land rush. Hector was right. They would be kept busy this summer.

He closed his eyes, thinking how nice it would be if Violet's soft, brown body were lying next to him, her long, dark hair tangled in his fingers; how nice it would be if the Cheyenne could live in the old way; but those times were gone. The white man was invading the Indians' last stronghold.

The orphan train slowed to a crawl as it made its way into the station, and Allyson could feel the excitement of the crowd outside. Every kind of wagon imaginable lined the streets beyond the depot, and hardly one open spot was to be had as far as she could see. "This is our chance," she whispered to her brother. "Just think how easy we could get lost in that crowd!"

Toby scowled, leaning over to look out the window. "It's because of that land-grabbing thing Henry Bartel was talking about with Mr. Harrington yesterday."

"The crowds have been getting bigger at every stop on our way here," Allyson told him. She read the sign over the depot. "Arkansas City," she muttered. This was the town Mr. Harrington had called the "jumping off" point. From here, all these people would join the race for land. "Toby, if we could get out in that crowd, Bartel would never find us."

Toby watched the throng of people. "I don't know." He ran a hand through his hair. "If we do get away, what do we do then?"

"We join those people in the land rush," Allyson answered in a near whisper.

"But we don't have a wagon or any supplies and no money to buy them with. All we've got is the clothes on our backs. And what do we know about riding horses or driving a wagon?"

"I'll get the money. We'll worry about the rest later."

"How will you get the money?"

"Like I used to get it when we stole for Father."

"Ally, that's wrong. You know we decided we shouldn't do that anymore."

"This is an emergency. God would forgive us."

"Ally—"

She squeezed his hand. "This is our only chance to get off this train, Toby. You be ready."

"The conductor says that we will be here a while, children," Bartel announced, walking slowly up and down the train car. "Most of the passengers on this train came here to join in the land rush. They'll have a lot of supplies to unload. I am told that there are facilities behind the train station for those of you who need to relieve yourselves—two at a time now—Mr. Harrington will accompany you, and I will go and see about getting some biscuits and perhaps a can of milk or water that you can pass around. I was not given much money to feed all of you, so biscuits is about all I can do."

Allyson glared at the man, sure he was lying. She suspected the Church had given him much more than he let on and he was just keeping the extra for himself. They were all half-starved, eating only twice a day and then usually just soup and biscuits at the train stops. Her whole body ached fiercely from sitting for days on her hard seat, sleeping in the seat or on the floor of the car at night. She wished she could find a way for all of them to escape, but for now she had to think of herself and Toby. She could only pray that the rest of the children would end up in good homes.

Clyde Harrington, a much kinder escort than Henry Bartel, began leading children off the car and through the crowd to take care of personal matters. She waited for Henry to leave to see about food, then turned to Toby again. "When Mr. Bartel comes back, we'll make our move," she whispered. "I'll get the money while his arms are full. Be ready to run with me."

"I don't know, Ally—"

"This is our last chance. Do you want us to be separated? We're in Kansas now, Toby. It won't be long before they start dropping us off here and there. For all we know one of *us* will be the first!"

"What about Miss Emmy?" Toby turned to look at the only woman who had come along to help watch the children. Miss Emmy was an old maid who helped at the orphanage and was truly kind but easily befuddled.

"You know Miss Emmy. She won't do a thing. Get your bag ready."

Toby rose and took down both his and Allyson's worn carpetbags, which held their few belongings, including a stuffed doll Allyson had kept with her since childhood. Her mother had made it for her.

"You don't need those bags, Toby," Miss Emmy spoke up.

"There's just something we want to look for, Miss Emmy," Allyson answered with a sweet smile.

The woman nodded, and Toby placed Allyson's bag on her lap and sat down again beside her. "You'll have to carry both bags at first," she whispered to Toby. "I'll be busy getting the money and keeping Bartel off guard."

Toby nodded, and both waited with pounding hearts. Finally Henry Bartel came out of the train depot carrying a large, round tray stacked with biscuits in one hand and a can in the other. Whether the can held water or milk mattered little. The point was, his hands were full, just as Ally had hoped. She quickly slipped on her woolen coat, even though it was too warm now for it. She didn't want to have to carry anything. She waited until Bartel climbed back into the car and started down the aisle before suddenly jumping up and running toward him.

"I have to go bad, Mr. Bartel!" she exclaimed. "I can't wait for Mr. Harrington to come back."

"What—"

Allyson ran into the man, who held the tray up and concentrated on keeping it balanced. Allyson scooted past him, relieved to know she had not forgotten how easy it was to pick a man's pocket. In one swift movement the wallet of money Henry Bartel carried in his inside coat pocket was in her hand and slipped under her own woolen coat. She dodged past him then and darted off the train. Bartel struggled to balance the food when Toby, taller and taking up even more room than Ally, suddenly burst past him carrying the bags.

"Hey! Stop!" Bartel managed to set the tray and milk can on the floor and turned to chase after them. Several of the other children began swarming around the food, and those between Bartel and the entrance to the train car deliberately joined them, blocking Bartel's path so that he could not immediately chase after the two runaways.

"Hurry! Hurry!" Allyson called to Toby. He kept hold of the bags as they both ran, their stomachs growling with hunger, their legs stiff and aching, but fear and desperation giving them the energy they needed. They quickly melted into the crowd.

"Stop! Stop those two kids!" they heard someone yelling in the distance, but by then people weren't sure who the man was talking about. The throng in the streets was so heavy that it was easy to get lost. Finally Allyson ducked into an alley, and Toby followed, both of them out of breath.

"We did it!" Allyson rejoiced. "Bartel can't follow us. He doesn't have time! The train will pull out pretty soon."

"Did you get his wallet?"

Allyson looked around, moved farther away from the crowds, then turned away so no one could see her pull the wallet out of her coat. "I'll bet Bartel doesn't even realize yet that I took it. By the time he does, they'll be miles away." She opened the wallet, her eyes widening. "I knew it! I knew they gave him a lot of money!" She fingered through the bills. "There must be three hundred dollars here! We can buy us a couple of horses and some supplies and join that land rush, claim ourselves a spot of our own!"

"And do what? We don't know anything about living out here."

"We'll learn. And we have enough money to buy extra supplies, maybe enough to sell some once we get where we're going. We'll open our own little store, maybe just in a tent at first, but we can do it. Maybe a restaurant! I helped cook at the orphanage. Out in new places like this, I'll bet there will be a lot of hungry men willing to pay a pretty penny for a good meal!"

"And what will you cook it with? Where will you get a stove?"

"We'll worry about that later."

"Later? Well, what about *now?* You said we'd pick up a couple of horses to carry our supplies. What do we know about horses? All we've ever done is ride behind them in a trolley car."

"We aren't going to *ride* them, Toby. We're just going to *lead* them. We'll have to walk." She opened her carpetbag and shoved the wallet into it.

Toby grasped her wrist. "Ally, that money was supposed to be used to feed the other kids."

Her smile faded. "The Church gave Mr. Harrington and

Miss Emmy some money, too. Besides, Bartel can always wire back and have more sent out, and most of the others are getting close to their destinations anyway. You heard Mr. Bartel say that from here on children would be dropped off at just about every depot. Come on! Let's go see about buying some horses and supplies. Then we'll find out when everybody will start moving into Indian Territory."

Toby frowned. "We'd better put on hats. If Bartel *is* looking for us, our red hair will make it easier to spot us."

Allyson agreed, pulling a wide-brimmed bonnet out of her bag. Toby put on an old, frayed helmet hat he had stolen out of someone's trash long ago. "Do you think there will be trouble with the Indians?" he asked.

"Of course not. The government wouldn't open up their land if they thought that. The Indians *sold* it. Why would they make trouble when people start settling on it?" She headed for the other end of the alley. "Get the bags!" she called back. She hesitated, walking back to where he stood. "We'd better buy a wedding ring first thing—just a cheap band. We'll get by a lot better if we pass ourselves off as husband and wife instead of sister and brother. People will wonder why a sister and brother would be wandering around out here alone, but husband and wife—that makes sense. We're off to start a new life together. And we'd better not use our own names, just to be safe." She removed her coat as she thought, the spring day growing even warmer. "Jane. Jane and Robert—Bobby—Harrington. We'll use Mr. Harrington's last name. Remember those names."

"Jane and Bobby," Toby repeated.

Allyson held her chin proudly as she tied her bonnet. "Shall we go buy some supplies, dear husband?" She kept her coat over her shoulder and picked up her bag, slipping an arm into Toby's free one. They moved back into the crowd, asking where they could find the closest supply store, making sure to keep themselves between the crowds of people on the boardwalks and the buildings themselves so it would be more difficult to spot them. Allyson turned when she heard the train whistle at the now-distant depot. "Do you hear that? All the stops we've made, I recognize that whistle. It means the train is ready to leave. Once it's gone, we're free!"

Toby breathed a little easier, thinking how brave and daring his sister was. For such a little thing, she had more courage than most men. It wasn't that she didn't get scared. She just went ahead and did something anyway.

A couple of men came stumbling out of a saloon nearby, and when Toby saw how they looked at Allyson, he grabbed her arm defensively. "Let's get away from here." He glanced across the street. "Come on. I see a supply store."

"We'll be lucky if they have anything left, with all these other people here stocking up on things." Allyson darted into the street, Toby right behind her.

"Whoa! Watch it!" someone shouted.

Allyson felt the bump, not even realizing at first that it was the chest of a buckskin-colored horse that had run into her, knocking her to the muddy street. Its hooves barely missed stepping on her.

"Ally!" Toby quickly helped his sister to her feet.

"Take a look where you're going before you run into the street, little girl," someone warned in a deep voice.

An angry Allyson tried to brush mud from her faded calico dress, one of the many hand-me-downs given her by the orphanage. "I'm not a little girl!" she fumed. "I am Ally—I mean, I am Jane Harrington, and I am a married woman! This man with me is my hus—" She looked up into the face of the owner of the horse. He had dismounted and picked up her carpetbag. He handed it back to her. Ally's blood ran a little colder. The rest of the words she had intended to spout at the man caught in her throat, and Toby was also left speechless. Was this a real *Indian?* He certainly looked like one, his long, dark hair hanging tied into a tail at the back of his neck, his skin a deep brown. He was dressed in white man's clothing—denim pants and leather boots—but he wore a fringed buckskin shirt. A red bandana was tied around his forehead. Allyson thought him a most handsome man, even if he *was* an Indian, and it surprised her to even think such a thing. She had never before been attracted to or fascinated by any man.

When the young, freckle-faced woman in front of him did not take hold of her carpetbag right away, Ethan Temple just set it down beside her and stepped back, looking her over. "You hurt?"

Allyson shook her head.

"Are you an Indian?" Toby asked unabashedly.

Ethan was accustomed to the question. "Only half." He frowned. "You two are *married?*"

"Yes, sir!" Toby answered, pretending pride as he put his hand to Allyson's waist.

Ethan watched them carefully. The girl, or rather, woman, looked barely old enough to *be* married. If it wasn't for the way she filled out that well-worn dress she had on, he'd have his doubts. He noticed she wore no wedding band, but he decided whether or not they were telling the truth was none of his business. This crowd of land-grabbers contained more kinds of people than he'd ever seen in his life. A young couple running off together would be no surprise.

"I'm sorry my horse knocked you down, ma'am," he told Allyson, "but you darted into the street before I realized what was happening. You sure you're okay? He didn't step on you or anything?"

Allyson realized she was still gaping at the man. She closed her mouth and straightened her dress. "I . . . I'm not hurt. As far as the mud, it will dry. It was my fault for not looking."

Ethan pushed them both a little more aside as a troop of uniformed soldiers rode past. "You getting these people organized, Ethan?" one of the officers called out.

"I'm trying. It's not easy," Ethan called back.

The officer just grinned and shook his head. Ethan turned to the young married couple he had just met. "You two heading for Indian Territory?"

"Yes, sir," Toby answered, trying to sound confident. "We were just going over to stock up on some supplies."

Ethan nodded, wondering what the truth was about these two. Jane Harrington and her husband looked more like brother and sister than husband and wife. And why wasn't the woman wearing a wedding band? On top of that, he was sure the young man had called her Ally, not Jane, when he first helped her up. Even she started to say the name when she introduced herself. They were both damn young, and they apparently had no possessions except a couple of carpetbags full of clothes. They sure didn't look like people who had enough money to buy what they needed to settle in a new land. Had they both just run away from home because their parents didn't approve of them getting married?

"Once you get what you need, come to the train depot tomorrow," Ethan told them. "That's where we're gathering everyone to lead them through Indian Territory to the borders of the land that's being given away. You'll be under army escort."

In Allyson's eyes, this wild-looking man represented all

she had pictured about the West—ruggedness, a dark Indian, danger, probably bravery. He wore a pistol at his side, as well as a big knife. She had never seen anything like him. "Do . . . do the Indians out there still kill white people?" she asked.

Ethan could not suppress a smile, but he managed not to laugh out loud. "Oh, sometimes they skin them alive, scalp them, who knows? My own people enjoy torturing a captive before finally ending his life. You just have to stay off their lands, and you'll be all right." He saw a hint of terror in Jane Harrington's eyes, and he smiled. "I'm just making a joke, ma'am. You don't have to be afraid of the Indians. Fact is, they're most likely to stay as far away from the white settlers as possible."

"How come *you're* here," Toby asked. "You said the army would be escorting people into Indian Territory tomorrow—said it like you'd be along."

"I will be. I'm an army scout, kind of a go-between for the whites and the Indians—try to keep both out of trouble, settle grazing disputes, that sort of thing. Name's Ethan Temple." He put out his hand, and Toby shook it, impressed by Temple's strong grip. "I don't think I got your first name."

"Robert," Toby answered. "Most call me Bobby."

Allyson watched Ethan Temple's dark, discerning eyes. She had a feeling this Indian scout wasn't fooled at all, prayed he wouldn't do any investigating.

"You two watch out for yourselves," Ethan told them. "There are a lot of people in this crowd who'll take advantage of your youth if they can. You can bet this land-grabbing won't take place without considerable trouble and bickering, and there are a lot of gamblers, drunks, and thieves among this bunch."

Allyson reddened a little at the word *thieves*.

"It might not hurt to buy yourselves a gun and learn how to use it." Ethan glanced from Allyson to Toby. "You've got an awfully pretty wife, Mr. Harrington. Out in these parts, pretty women sometimes need protecting."

"Yes, sir. I'll take good care of her."

Allyson wondered why the words stirred such an odd longing deep inside, a special pride in being a woman that she had never felt before. This wild, handsome Indian man thought she was pretty! She watched him remount his horse, a big buckskin for a big man. He got into the saddle with ease and grace.

"Keep that bonnet on," he advised her. "That fair skin will burn real quick out here. Either that, or you'll end up with a lot more freckles."

He gave her a grin, and Allyson had never seen a more handsome smile. She watched him ride off.

You've got an awfully pretty wife, Mr. Harrington. She picked up her bag, and in spite of her plain, faded dress and the mud on it and on one side of her face, she felt beautiful. "Let's go get our supplies," she told Toby.

They hurried across the street, and in the distance they could hear the train whistle again. Then came the sound of a locomotive chugging as it picked up speed, carrying the rest of its orphans, and Henry Bartel, to places farther west. Allyson breathed a sigh of relief, but it was also frightening to realize she and Toby were on their own now, in a strange, new land that was unlike anything they had ever known before.

3

For the last four days since leaving Arkansas City with his human caravan, Ethan deliberately stayed close to Jane and Bobby Harrington. His curiosity and suspicion about their true reason for being here were getting stronger every day. It was obvious the young couple was innocent of survival in this kind of country, and he worried about Jane, had noticed how several of the single men and even some of the married ones looked at her. Her husband did not strike him as being capable of fully defending her, and he was surprised at his own protective feelings for her, the secret desire she aroused in him. He fought those feelings and wished he could keep his distance, but the couple's ineptness was both touching and humorous.

He'd had to help them put up their tent the first night, and the two of them could hardly handle their packhorses. He had taught them the correct way to put on a bridle, the proper commands, how to load an animal so that the weight was evenly distributed. Whoever had sold them the horses in the first place had taken advantage of their youth and ignorance of horse flesh. Those horses were a couple of old nags that could hardly keep up, even though the Harringtons only used them to carry their supplies.

He had agreed to take some time this evening to show them some pointers on how to use a handgun. The hordes of settlers were nearly at their destination, and once the actual land rush started, he feared Jane and Bobby would have need of such defense. They had already bought themselves a gun back in Arkansas City, but neither of them knew how to use it. He approached their camp on foot. "You two ready to do a little shooting?"

Allyson looked up from the fire she had built, over which sat a pan that held some leftover stew. "Yes, Mr. Temple," she answered. "Would you like something to eat first?"

"Smells good, but I already ate, thanks."

"Jane's a real good cook," the young man spoke up proudly. "She learned back at the—"

"My mother taught me," Allyson interrupted, casting Toby a look that made Ethan wonder. He wished she would have let her "husband" finish the sentence. What would he have slipped and said? The young man's face reddened a little.

"I don't doubt your cooking abilities," he told her, "but now it's time to learn something else."

She just smiled, and again desire swept through Ethan's body, but he kept it hidden. "And by the way, call me Ethan."

"Then you call us by our first names, too," Toby said. He took a handgun from his gear, then put on his hat. "Let's get to it."

"We don't have a lot of time," Ethan told them. "It's getting late, and anybody here with children won't appreciate the noise. I imagine a lot of these people want to turn in early. Big day tomorrow."

"Do we really get to go into the promised land and see it for ourselves before the rush?" Toby asked.

Ethan wanted to laugh at the term *promised land*, as though they were all on some Biblical mission. "That's the plan. We go in, come back out, then at noon the next day everybody scrambles for what they want. I have a feeling it won't be a pretty picture. You two had better be ready. Let me see your gun."

Toby handed him the pistol, and Allyson watched Ethan as he studied the gun. He seemed so dark and dangerous in those buckskins, looking so "Indian," yet the sight of him made her heart rush so that sometimes her chest hurt. She hated deceiving him, after all he had done for them, but much as she had come to look forward to his presence, she realized that somehow over the next day or two, she and Toby had to find a way to avoid Ethan. They had the slowest horses of anyone there, so weak they couldn't even be ridden. Come the day of the land rush, they would never make it to the best spots ahead of everyone. The only answer was to find a way to sneak in tomorrow night, but they could never do that as long as Ethan was watching.

She had talked to Toby about finding a way to cheat the others, but he was afraid to try it, sure Ethan would discover them. *He could find a needle in tall grass*, Toby had lamented. Ally figured he was probably right, but they had to think of a way to get past the man.

"At least you got a better buy on this gun than you did on those horses," Ethan was saying. He spun the cartridge. "This is a Colt .38 double-action pistol. Just pull the trigger and it automatically cocks and fires. It's a good weapon, but with a handgun an amateur should wait until his target is close before firing. It's not easy for even an experienced gunman to hit something far away with a pistol."

"I'll bet *you* never miss," Toby said with a note of admiration.

Ethan smiled. "Oh, I've had my bad days. One secret is to get used to your own guns. They all fire a little differently, and some hit high, some low, some to the right or left.

That's why you have to practice. It's too bad you don't have more time for this. All you can do tonight is get the feel of it, how it kicks in your hand, how loud it is. That way you won't be startled if you do end up having to use it, which I hope you don't." He took a leather bag full of ammunition Bobby handed him. "Let's go. I've got some targets set up."

He led them to a clearing away from the camp, wishing Jane didn't look quite so fetching. In spite of the fact that she was married to someone else, he was drawn to her, fascinated by her porcelain skin. Tonight she had already brushed out that long, auburn hair, and it was tied into a tail at the base of her neck and hung nearly to her waist. He wondered how soft it must feel in a man's hands, how it looked draped around her white shoulders, hiding her full breasts. Surely a woman with skin so white had nipples as pink as flowers.

He felt like an ass having such thoughts about another man's wife, let alone the fact that a half-breed had no business having fond thoughts for any white woman. He cursed himself inwardly as he led them to a spot only about eight yards from a row of stumps. On top of each stump sat a can or a bottle, with more "targets" lying nearby, things he had collected that the travelers had carelessly thrown by the wayside, littering the land with no consideration for how it looked or what animals it might harm. The trash these people left to scar the land was just one of the things that enraged the Indians about white settlement. They seemed to be the most wasteful people ever born.

For a half-hour he tutored Jane's husband, getting behind him at times to grasp his wrist and show him how to steady the weapon. When the young man hit a few of the targets, he gave out a yip and laughed. "Show Jane!" he said eagerly. "She should learn, too!"

Ethan reluctantly did the same with Jane, a little surprised that Bobby so eagerly let him. Most husbands would want to show their wives something like this themselves, just to prove they were masters of their household and to keep from being shown up in front of their wives by another man. On top of that, most white men he knew would not allow an Indian to stand so close to their wives, touch them the way he had to touch Jane Harrington.

Bobby's behavior just did not fit that of a husband, but Ethan didn't have time to try to get these two to admit who they really were. Besides, he didn't mind stooping down behind Jane and having her hair brush his lips. It smelled nice, in spite of there being no bathing facilities these last few days. Her skin was soft to the touch, her wrist feeling so tiny in his big hand. It was warm now and coats were not necessary. Her luscious body seemed to fit perfectly against him as he pressed behind her to support her wrist while she fired the gun several times. When she hit a target, she gasped and smiled, turning her face so that it was only inches from his own.

Never in his life had Ethan been so tempted to kiss a woman just for the hell of it, and never would he have thought he'd have such urges for a *white* woman. He had just always figured he would and should be attracted only to Indian women. This was a new feeling for him, and he straightened, declaring that was all the practice they could get in. They both begged to try a little more, and he allowed it, but told them they were on their own. They had to learn to shoot without him standing behind to guide them.

They each hit a couple more targets, and their interaction as they celebrated learning the "ways of the West" did not at all appear to be that of a man and his wife, or even lovers. Ethan found himself hoping there was no such relationship between them, that Jane Harrington, or whoever she was, was a free woman.

Frustrated by his own desires, he finally declared it was getting too dark to practice any more. "Watch how you handle that thing when you go back," he told them. "Remember you don't have to cock it first by hand to fire it, so it can easily go off. On most expeditions like this, more people get hurt from gun accidents than anything else."

"Yes, sir, we'll be careful," Toby answered. He checked the gun to be sure all the chambers were empty.

"Thank you for helping us," Allyson told him.

Ethan watched her eyes. Was she feeling some of the same forbidden emotions he had felt for her? Something in those big, blue eyes made him wonder. *Damn her*, he thought. If only she wasn't so pretty, or so mysterious, or so brave and determined. He would be glad when this whole thing was over with and he could leave "Mr. and Mrs. Harrington" to their new life and not have to set eyes on Jane Harrington again.

"You two watch out for yourselves from here on," he told them. "I'll be busier than ever." He tipped his hat and left, his disturbing thoughts for Jane interrupted when he heard men shouting back at camp. Obviously another fight had broken out, over cards or who should get a position "up front" in the morning. Ethan wondered how much worse the arguments would get once this crazy mixture of people began scrambling to claim their land.

Allyson sat down in the grass, her feet aching so badly that she began unbuttoning her shoes. "We'll never get back here in time tomorrow to get the best lots," she complained to Toby. "Somehow we've got to find a way to stay close by tonight instead of going all the way back. If that one family hadn't offered to let us ride part way, we'd still be way back behind everybody."

"Ally, watch how you talk," Toby said quietly. "And I still say you're crazy to think we can sneak through tonight."

Allyson sighed, rubbing at a stockinged foot. "Well, my feet can't take walking all the way back and doing this again tomorrow." She looked over at a group of well-dressed men, all milling near the railroad tracks, not far from the watering station. "See that big, fat man over there wearing the fancy suit and smoking a cigar?"

Toby looked. "What about him?"

"It's men like that who will get the best pick, and it isn't fair. They can afford to come in on the train. They're the ones who'll get here ahead of everybody. It took us five hours of walking since before sunrise to get this far. Now we'll have to walk all the way back to the border and do this again come tomorrow noon. Do you realize how much walking that is, Toby? By the time we get back tonight we'll be wishing we were dead, and these old horses of ours might *be* dead. Even if we ride them, we'll be behind."

Toby glanced around at the hundreds of people who milled about just in the immediate area. As far as he could see, thousands more were inspecting the land, plotting their strategies to claim the choicest spots. In the distance he could see Ethan Temple riding among them, keeping an eye on everyone. Throughout the crowd soldiers kept watch. "Ally, this is the best we can do. We'll never get away with trying to do anything illegal."

Allyson glared at the men standing near the tracks, the fat one pointing at the ground as though to show where he would build something, all of them laughing. She supposed the laughter was over their joy at thinking about the money they would make claiming land near the railroad. One of them began walking off several paces, as though to judge how much room a building would take.

"That's where we want to be, Toby," she said, a determined look in her eyes. "Right where those fat, rich men are standing. They know the best spots to take, and they'll be here lickety-split tomorrow afternoon to claim them. We've got to find a way to get here ahead of them." She removed her other shoe and began rubbing her foot again. "I'm not making this trip all over again tomorrow, just to get here last and find nothing left. We're going to claim a couple of lots near the railroad, and before you know it we'll be rich. There's a reason we got on that orphan train, Toby, and this is it. Most of our lives other people have taken advantage of us. Even our grandparents wouldn't help us. I'm ready to show them all, especially Henry Bartel, that we can do just fine without *any* of them. This is the best chance we've had to never again depend on other people."

"Ally, we can't—"

Toby left the sentence unfinished when he saw Ethan riding toward them. Ethan grinned when he saw Allyson sitting and rubbing her feet. "Quite a walk, wasn't it?"

Allyson looked up at him with a scowl. "We're all right." She resented the humor in his eyes, but she could not quell the way the sight of him stirred odd, new feelings deep inside.

It was obvious to Ethan that Jane Harrington was in pain; both she and her husband looked bone-weary. He noticed the shoes Jane had taken off were well worn, the soles probably so thin that she felt every little stone along the way. The toe of one of her socks had a hole in it, which she tried to keep her hand over as she rubbed at her foot. Wherever these two came from, it was obvious they had been poor.

Jane's faded blue calico dress was a little big on her, as though it had been given to her by someone instead of being made just for her. Her long, red hair was twisted clumsily into a bun, and there were dark circles under her eyes. Her slat bonnet hung at her back, and the fair skin of her face was turning red from the sun.

Ethan couldn't help feeling sorry for her, and the ache the woman stirred in him simply would not go away. He wished he could do something to help these two find their dream. He admired Jane's determination to be strong and uncomplaining, but from here on he dared not show any favoritism. His job was only to make sure everyone knew their boundaries and to keep them all from killing each other once the land was opened. He did not look forward to any of it. "Have you decided what lots you want?" he asked.

Allyson nodded toward where the men in suits were standing near the train. "Right over there, near the railroad. You can't go wrong opening a restaurant and a boarding house right by a railroad depot."

Ethan struggled not to laugh. Such big plans these two had. Considering their age and what they had to start with, it was almost comical; yet it was equally sad. He felt an odd ache in his heart at the look of hope and determination in Jane's eyes, and he also felt alarm. She actually seemed to be serious about claiming land near the railroad. "Jane," he spoke up, "I hate to tell you, but railroad lots are going to be the first to be taken. A lot of these people can afford the high fares to have a train bring them in. It's businessmen from the bigger cities, like those standing over there, who will grab up the railroad lots. By the time you and your husband get here, those places will be gone."

"Wherever we make a claim, we'll do just fine," Allyson answered. "It isn't fair that those with more money should get the advantage of using a train. All this new land should be for people just starting out. Those men over there probably already own all kinds of businesses someplace else."

"Most likely. That's the way life is. Those who have the most seem to get the advantages."

"Well, someday my husband and I will be in the same position." Allyson began pulling a shoe back on, her mind whirling with confusion as to how she was going to somehow slip past this eagle-eyed scout after dark.

"There's a wagon full of supplies back over there behind you," Ethan spoke up, pointing to a huge supply wagon that a traveling salesman had driven into the new district from the eastern border. "Maybe he has some shoes along that would fit you. Looks to me like you need a new pair. You ought to go and see him. Maybe he can see about getting you a cookstove. He claims he's got a lot more supplies coming in by train after tomorrow. Get your order in early. He's going to be a busy man pretty quick."

Allyson put on her other shoe, then tied on her bonnet, glancing over at the supply wagon. She looked up at Ethan, who still sat on his horse. "I'll go talk to him. Thank you, Ethan." She suspected he knew something wasn't quite right about her and Toby, but she didn't dare tell him now. She and Toby might not be allowed to claim their lots if people knew they had lied about their names and relationships. She stood up, avoiding his all-knowing gaze.

"Thank you again for teaching us how to use our pistol, Ethan," Toby said. "And for helping us with everything else. We'll be fine from here on."

"Yes," Allyson put in, seeing an opening to get rid of the man. She finally met his eyes again. "I know you'll be terribly busy come noon tomorrow, so you just forget about us and do whatever you have to do. We'll be all right, won't we, Bobby?" She smiled, slipping an arm through Toby's.

"Sure will," Toby answered.

Ethan felt like shaking them until they told him the truth. This could be dangerous business for two people so young and inexperienced. The strange thing was, their inexperience seemed to apply only to how to handle horses and pitch a tent and live off the land. He couldn't help feeling that they were not totally innocent or inexperienced when it came to other forms of survival. There was a hint of hardness about them, especially Jane, something that shone through in her dogged determination to make this work. That first day or two he'd known them, they both seemed nervous, always looking back, as though worried someone might see them. Were they running from the law? Now they seemed to want to avoid him, too, hinting that he could quit looking after them. Neither he nor the soldiers he rode with were foolish enough to think that none of these people would try to break through the lines tonight and beat the others to the best land. Did Jane Harrington have something like that in mind? He leaned down from his saddle, giving both of them a stern look.

"You two abide by the rules. Things are going to get nasty once this thing is opened up, so keep your .38 ready. And don't try something stupid, like trying to get a head start on someone or trying to take lots away from somebody else. Once this thing is opened up, I'll have my hands full, so if you make trouble for yourselves, I might not be able to help you."

Allyson's grip on Toby's arm tightened as she tried to hint to him to keep a casual appearance. "We'll do everything by the rules, Ethan. We'll be fine."

Ethan glanced over at the men in suits. He had not missed the look of envy and resoluteness in Jane's eyes when she was watching them. "And stay away from men like those over there. Remember, there's no law out here.

Men like that make their own laws. Same goes for the gamblers and con men who'll try to move in and take what you've got."

We know all about gamblers and con men and thieves, Allyson thought. "We'll be careful," she said aloud.

"Ethan!" someone shouted.

Allyson looked past Ethan to see a man riding toward him who looked even more Indian. His long hair flew in the wind as his roan-colored horse charged up to Ethan. "Big trouble with a couple of Cheyenne over on the west end. You better come. One of them is Red Hawk, and he's been drinkin'. You know what that means. You're the only one who can talk to your cousin when he's like that. He's sayin' the Indians shouldn't ought to have sold this land—says he's gonna shoot any white man who settles on it."

"What's wrong, Hector? Can't a Cherokee warrior handle a Cheyenne?" Ethan answered with a sly grin. "You always end up needing my help, don't you?"

"If the damn Cheyenne wasn't so drunk and worthless most of the time, there wouldn't be no trouble like this," Hector answered with a quick smile. "Your people just ain't civilized like us Cherokee."

"Yeah, and not as soft either," Ethan shot back. He pulled a cheroot from a pocket on his deerskin shirt and stuck it in his mouth, then lit it.

"Hurry!" Hector chided. "You wait much longer, that cousin of yours is gonna kill somebody and then there will be a fine mess for all of us."

"Red Hawk is more mouth than action, you know that."

"All I know is with this many whites comin' in, the way he's actin' is only gonna cause big trouble. He sure as hell ain't gonna let no Cherokee put a stop to it. It's gonna have to be you."

Ethan turned to Allyson and Toby. "You two remember what I told you. If I don't make it back by tomorrow, good luck to you."

"Thank you, Ethan," Toby answered.

Ethan glanced at Jane once more. *Who are you—really*, he wanted to ask. "Take care of yourselves." He turned his horse and rode off.

Allyson felt a growing excitement. "God has just given us our chance," she told Toby. "It sounds like Ethan Temple will be gone all night!"

Toby sighed, shaking his head. "I don't know, Ally. You heard what Ethan said. If we try to pull something—"

"I've got it all planned. We can do it, now that Ethan isn't around to watch us like a hawk. Don't you see? It's like God *made* him leave." She grabbed his hand. "Come on. Let's go see that supplier. Maybe he can order us a cookstove. We'll stock up on food and get to work as soon as we claim those railroad lots tomorrow! That big fat man in that suit over there is going to get a surprise."

"Ally, it's too dangerous."

Allyson dragged her brother toward the supply wagon. "Be quiet, Toby, and have faith. We haven't failed yet, and we aren't going to. God means for us to have that land." She walked briskly to the supply wagon, feeling more confident all the time. A piece of red hair fell from under her hat, and she wondered how terrible she must look, needing a bath and all; but those things didn't matter right now. She had a plan, and she had to talk Toby into going along with her scheme. Ethan Temple was not here to stop them now.

"Come on, Red Hawk." Ethan picked up his cousin and managed to fling the young man's sturdy body over his own shoulder. By the time he had reached the place where Red Hawk had been threatening a group of new settlers for hours with his rifle, not allowing them to leave, his cousin had already passed out.

"It's not fair," Red Hawk mumbled. "The land . . . belongs to us," he slurred.

Ethan carried him to his horse, ignoring the curses and mutterings of the settlers, who had plenty to say about "drunken Indians." One man had declared that when more white settlements were established in Indian Territory, there would be strict laws for Indians caught drunk on white men's property. Several others had agreed, voicing the opinion that they were glad liquor was not allowed in the territory and wondering how Red Hawk had got hold of some.

"You scouts and the army need to do a better job of keeping out the whiskey traders!" one man shouted at Ethan. "The army shouldn't ever *use* Indians for scouts. It's probably men like you who let the whiskey peddlers in!"

"Why don't you shut up?" Hec retorted. "Maybe you'd like it if all us Indians got together for a good ol' slaughter, like the old days," he threatened, enjoying the look of fear that came into the eyes of the man causing the most trouble. "You folks strayed too damn far onto Cheyenne land. Get the hell back with your group and get some rest. You've got a big day ahead of you tomorrow." The Cherokee turned to help Ethan position Red Hawk over his pony. He knew how Ethan felt about the white man's remarks, knew why Red Hawk had decided to get drunk today; and he made no teasing remarks to Ethan about drunken Cheyenne. This was a day when all Indians *needed* to get drunk. Tomorrow the Indian Territory would be changed forever. Their last stronghold would be gone. "You want some company taking him back?" he asked Ethan.

"No, thanks. You go on back to your assigned post. We all have a big day coming tomorrow."

"Ain't *that* the truth! I'm sorry to take you away from your own assignment, Ethan. If I'd known he'd pass out like this, I wouldn't have bothered."

"It's all right. Thanks for your concern."

"Think you can make it back in time for the rush tomorrow?"

"I'm going to try. I want to buy a couple of good ponies from my uncle first. I know a young couple back there that could use them."

Hec frowned. "We ain't supposed to be showin' no favoritism."

"I know. There's just something about these two . . . I don't know how to explain it."

"The woman's pretty?"

Ethan grinned, although inside he was aching for Red Hawk . . . for all his people. "Yeah. She's pretty."

"Single?"

Ethan took hold of the reins to Red Hawk's mount, then eased up on his own horse. "I'm not sure."

"Not sure? What does that mean?"

"Exactly that. She and the young man she's with are supposed to be married, but I think they're lying about that and even about their names."

"Why are you helping them then?"

Ethan stuck a cheroot between his teeth. "Damned if I know. I guess because I'm a damned fool."

"Damned is right, if she's white. I tell you, you Cheyenne ain't got an ounce of sense." Hec slapped him on the thigh. "Get your cousin home before he gets himself shot. And stay away from that pretty white woman, you hear?"

Ethan grinned sadly. "I'll do my best, but I'm still taking

her and her supposed husband some fresh horses. The two old nags they've got can barely carry their supplies."

Hec shrugged, mounting his own horse. "See you somewhere in the mess tomorrow. Good luck, Ethan."

Ethan nodded. "Same to you." Their eyes held in mutual understanding. "Things sure do have a way of changing, don't they?"

Hec nodded. "They sure do."

Hec rode off, and Ethan lit his cheroot. It was already getting dark, and in the distance he could see the dim light of thousands of fires built by the new settlers. The sight brought a sick feeling to his stomach, but he knew there was no changing what was happening.

Red Hawk groaned and suddenly vomited, and Ethan just shook his head. He took a few puffs on the cheroot. "Let's get you home, Red Hawk." He rode in the direction of the Cheyenne reservation, hoping he could get back with the fresh horses in time to help Jane and Bobby Harrington, totally confused himself as to why he should want to aid anyone in taking this land. If not for that red hair and those fetching blue eyes . . .

"We've done it, Toby!" Allyson moved out of the ravine where she and Toby had waited half the night. They had mingled with the thousands of others earlier in the day when they were all herded back to the border by the soldiers, then had quietly drifted away on the pretense that Allyson had to relieve herself. They had headed into a ravine until they and their horses were hidden by heavy overgrowth along the creek, and they had simply never come out again.

Allyson buttoned her woolen coat tighter against the cold

night air. They had not dared to light a fire for fear of being seen, or even put up a tent because of the noise it would make. The dark ravine was frightening, owls hooting, a soft wind causing odd noises in the brush. Toby kept his pistol ready as they both sat against a bush hanging onto the bridle reins of their horses.

"I won't feel good about this until we claim that land tomorrow without any trouble," Toby spoke up.

"We can do it. There are a few others out there. You heard them same as I did. We aren't the only ones who held back or sneaked through the soldiers. Those lots we want aren't far away. We'll wait right here until we hear the sound of everyone coming, then we'll just charge out of here and look like we just got here quicker."

"On *our* horses? Nobody would ever believe it!"

"Toby, you have to think more positive. We can do this. There are going to be others doing the same thing. With all the confusion here tomorrow, we can hold our own. If there's trouble, you just let me handle it. Maybe I can smooth-talk us out of it, or soften them up by crying. I'll think of something."

Toby fingered his pistol, hoping he wouldn't have to use it. "You just be careful. I don't know what I'd do if something happened to you. None of it would matter any more."

Allyson touched his arm. "Nothing is going to happen."

He turned to see her in the moonlight, kissed her cheek. "If this works, we'll really be free, won't we? We'll have something that's all ours, and nobody can take it away from us." He laid the pistol aside. "You sure are brave and smart, Ally, I'll hand you that." He rummaged in one of their supply bags. "I'm hungry. What can we eat?"

"There's some of that jerked meat in there that the man at the supply store back in Arkansas City said was good for eating when you couldn't make a fire. Here, I'll find it for you."

Toby handed her the bag and leaned back again. "I'll sure be glad when we get settled and you can get to cooking real meals."

"And with any luck, hundreds of single men settling here tomorrow will think the same thing and will pay good money for a woman-cooked meal."

"Well, it's a good thing those single men think you're my wife. I've seen how some of them look at you. We would have had some problems if they thought you were available."

"Saying we're married will help in a lot of ways. For some reason it brings us more respect. If we have any trouble tomorrow, it's going to help for the land agent to think we're married. At our age, if they know we're brother and sister, they might toss us out as a couple of kids who have no business here. Besides that, somebody might find out how we really got here."

"Where do you think Mr. Bartel is by now?"

"Who knows? Maybe he's on his way back to New York. Even if he stops to look for us back in Arkansas City, he'll never find us."

"He could trace us here. If he does, people will find out the truth."

"He won't find us. I told you to think positive, remember?" Allyson shivered and pulled her skirt farther over her legs. "Let's eat and try to get at least a couple hours' sleep." She handed him a piece of meat. "Just be patient a little longer, and you'll see I'm right about everything."

They both sat quietly then, biting off the tough meat and chewing it slowly to make it last. An owl hooted again nearby, and Allyson scooted closer to her brother when she heard another rustling in the brush.

"Probably just the wind again," Toby spoke up, "or maybe a small animal, a rabbit or something."

"It's no rabbit," came a deep voice. A tall figure loomed in front of them, and for a moment their hearts pounded with fear and dread at having been discovered. Toby scrambled for his pistol, but a big, strong hand reached down and grasped his arm with just enough force to let Toby know he could break him in two if he wanted. "Don't bother," the man warned. "It's me . . . Ethan."

4

"How did you find us?" Allyson exclaimed.

Ethan reached down and grabbed hold of her arm with his free hand, still holding Toby's arm. He jerked them both to their feet. "The better question is, what the hell are you *doing* here!"

"I *told* you he could find a needle in tall grass," Toby told his sister angrily, his breath coming almost in pants from the shock and fright of suddenly being found. What would Ethan Temple do? Arrest them? Take them to a fort? Have them sent back to the orphanage?

Allyson was scrambling to think of a way out. They had come so far. It was almost dawn. She was not going to lose what she had sat here freezing all night to have.

"Please, Ethan, we'll do anything to be allowed to stay." He had an eye for her, didn't he? Could she soften him up because of that? She touched his chest. Memories of Henry Bartel made it difficult for her to act submissive to any man, his hideous assaults on her making any man's touch seem ugly. Still, if she could convince Ethan Temple she was soft on him . . . "Can't we go a little bit away from here and talk about this? Just you and me?"

"Ally! I mean . . . Jane!" Toby exclaimed.

"It's all right, Bobby." Allyson gave her brother a gentle push. She threw her arms around Ethan and rested her head against his chest. "Please, Ethan. My husband knows . . .

about our attraction to each other." She brought on the tears
then. "I know it's wrong . . . and we've talked about it. I
know you only want what's best for us . . . and we appreciate
your watching over us. But it has to end, Ethan." She looked
up into his face. "If you let this go, we won't say anything to
your commander about . . . about how you've been hanging
around us, upsetting my husband. They must have some
rules about Indians messing with white women, and I
wouldn't want you to get in any trouble, after all you've
done for us."

Ethan didn't know whether to laugh at her or hit her for
the insulting remark and her childish attempt at seducing
and then threatening him. "You little wench!" he growled,
deciding to give her a good scare. He had already heard part
of their earlier conversation, knew these two were no more
married than he was. He let go of Toby and grasped both
her arms, pushing her away from her brother and leaning
close to her. "*You're* the ones in the most trouble here," he
sneered. "You do right by me, and I'll let you both go."

Allyson gasped when he suddenly turned and whisked
her up in one arm, her feet dangling as he walked off with
her. "Your husband hasn't got the guts to stop me yet. Let's
see him do it now."

"What are you doing?" Allyson squealed. She pushed at
him, but to no avail.

"Exactly what you've been asking for." Ethan carried her
behind a bush, then got to his knees and plunked her back-
wards into the grass. "I'm taking my payment for being
quiet," he told her. Before Allyson could answer, he met her
mouth in a savage kiss, angry enough to want to frighten her,
maybe even to take what he'd been wanting since the first
day he'd set eyes on her. This little liar had teased him long
enough, and her remark about white women and Indian

men had infuriated him. He grasped her hair, put his full weight on top of her, held her head so that she could not turn her mouth from his. She didn't seem to know how to kiss. He had to force her lips apart, and experience told him that this little woman had never been with a man in the fullest sense.

Allyson's heart pounded wildly, and her mind rushed with a mixture of hatred and desire. It was impossible to push this big man off of her, and part of her did not want to. The wild and dangerous-looking Ethan Temple was kissing her! He *wanted* her! This was a new and different feeling. More than that, if she went along with this, maybe he really would let them go. She considered doing just that, but as the heated kiss lingered, her reasons for allowing him his pleasure changed from plotting to have her way, to just plain enjoyment. One of his hands left her face then, trailing down over her body and under her coat to find her breast. Flashes of the way Henry Bartel had humiliated her brought her back to reality, and she began fighting him harder again.

"Don't! Please don't!" she whimpered.

"Why not?" a still-angry Ethan answered. "Isn't this what you were offering me?"

"You don't understand—"

Ethan ached to do more, but instinct told him she was more child than woman when it came to men. "You little fool," he groaned. "Do you really think I would force myself on you? I just wanted to see how far you'd go with your lies!" Suddenly Ethan froze as he heard the click of a gun hammer.

"Get off my sister," came Toby's shaking voice. "I've never killed anybody, but I'll shoot you if you don't leave her alone."

Ethan stayed on top of Allyson for a moment, watching

her eyes in the moonlight. "So, finally the truth comes out."

Allyson studied the strong, dark figure hovering over her. To her surprise he leaned down and gave her another kiss—this one was quick, sweet, gentle, as though to apologize. He got up and helped her to her feet. In one quick movement, he grabbed Toby's wrist and pushed his arm up, then wrenched the pistol out of his hand.

"When you point a gun at a man, son, you'd better be ready to use it!" He backed away. "Now, how about the truth? I already know your real names are Ally and Toby. I heard you talking to each other. Did you really think a man who's been scouting this territory and lived here all his life couldn't find you?"

"We didn't think—" Toby began.

"You didn't think I'd be back at all last night," Ethan interrupted. "You figured with me gone, you could sneak down here and hide, then wait for the others to come and join them as though you just got here when the land is opened up this afternoon."

Toby hung his head. "Something like that. It was Ally's idea."

Ethan looked at Allyson. "I'll just *bet* it was!" He shoved Toby's gun into his own belt. "Now, how about telling me who you two really are? You running from the law?"

Brother and sister looked at each other, and Ally was the one to answer when she looked back at Ethan. "Not exactly. We came out here on an orphan train from New York. We were supposed to be taken to families out here somewhere to live, but we would have been split up. Toby and I have never been apart, and we were afraid. We figured we'd just be used like slaves to help on somebody's farm. I didn't want to go live with some strange man, and I didn't want Toby to be away from me. He needs me."

Ethan could not help feeling sorry for the fact that they were orphans, if, indeed, they were telling him the truth this time. "What are your names?"

"Allyson . . . Allyson and Toby Mills," Allyson answered. "I'm sixteen, almost seventeen—just another month. Toby is eighteen. Our mother died ten years ago, and our father . . . he was always drunk, so he couldn't keep a job. We had to steal to keep food on the table. Father died when we were ten and twelve. We lived in the streets and alleys for a couple of years until the police took us to a Catholic orphanage."

"How'd you get off the train and end up here?" Ethan asked.

Allyson shivered, holding her coat tighter around her neck. She could still taste Ethan Temple's kiss, wondering if she was shivering from the cold or from the memory of his big hand touching her breast. Had he just been trying to scare her, or did he truly have feelings for her? "We just . . . ran off the train. We saw the big crowd back at Arkansas City and figured we could easily get lost in it."

"Why do I think that, too, was all *your* idea and not Toby's?"

Allyson shrugged. "We had to do something or be separated. It was worth the chance we took."

"Mmmm-hmmm. And how did you get the money to buy the supplies you needed for this trip?"

Allyson swallowed, and Toby kept looking at the ground, shuffling his feet. "*I* got it," Allyson answered, deciding she might as well tell it all. "Off a mean old man who was in charge of bringing us out here. He *deserves* to lose his money. When Toby and I worked the streets back in New York, I learned to be real good at picking people's pockets. I got three hundred dollars off of Mr. Bartel, and I don't mind saying so. After the things he did to me, stealing from him is nothing compared to what I *should* do to him. I'd have *shot* him if I could get away with it!''

This time her voice broke, and real tears wanted to come. She wished she could fight them, but she was so tired she wanted to die. There had been no sleep tonight, and tomorrow was the big day.

"Please don't turn us in, Ethan," Toby spoke up. "Ally wants this so bad. Things happened to her back at the orphanage. That Mr. Bartel, he beat her a couple of times, and he tried to do other things to her. That's the God's truth. Now we've got a chance to make a life for ourselves, earn an honest living, stay together. We can't go back to New York. It's too hard for somebody our age to find decent work there, except maybe to slave away in some factory where you work such long hours you never see the light of day. We decided with this new land opening up and all, maybe we can have something of our own."

Ethan sighed deeply. Considering the hell these two had been through, it was amazing they were both still alive and full of such spirit and determination. Allyson Mills had guts, and that attracted him as much as her fair skin and red hair and the way she filled out a dress.

"I don't like being lied to and made a fool of," he grumbled. "I rode all the way back to the base camp last night— got no sleep at all—just to bring you a couple of good horses so you could have something faster to ride in on this afternoon. I was going to give you some quick riding lessons this morning. I felt sorry for you having to walk in and finish last." He shook his head, sighing and walking a few feet away from them. "Do you think this Henry Bartel is after you?"

"He wouldn't know where to find us now," Allyson answered. "He had to go on with the others. He might not even be through yet delivering the other children to their adoptive families."

Ethan stood quietly for a moment. Now he understood why these two dressed so poorly—probably hand-me-downs from the orphanage. "Why in hell did you try to pass yourselves off as husband and wife?"

"Partly to protect Ally from other men," Toby answered.

"And we thought we'd get more respect and fewer questions if we said we were married," Allyson added. "It would also be easier to lay claim to a couple of the town lots. If they know we're brother and sister, they might think we're too young or something, or maybe that we're runaways. They might start asking a lot of questions, maybe even send us back to New York if they find out who we really are. If they do, we could get sent to prison! Please don't tell, Ethan. Please!"

"You know how terrible that would be for Ally," Toby put in.

Ethan took a cheroot from an inside pocket of his deerskin jacket. He walked even farther away to light it, wishing he could erase the memory of how Allyson Mills's young body had felt beneath his own. He'd never kissed a woman like that before, one with such fair skin and blue eyes, alone against the world. It gave him a feeling of possessiveness and desire. Now that he had tasted those lips, now that he knew she'd been abused, how could he let some other man be the one to show her about men and making love? How could he ignore her strengths, her courage? She was a hell of a woman in the making, a woman any man would want at his side, in spite of the fact that she was a little thief. He could understand her reasons. Wild, she was. Wild and proud and brave . . . and he wanted her like he'd never wanted another.

He took a couple of puffs on the cheroot, then turned to face them. "I'm risking army punishment if I let you go. On top of that, I'm allowing you both to put yourselves in great danger. Does either one of you understand what's going to happen here tomorrow afternoon? When people are told something is free for the grabbing, they seem to temporarily lose their minds. Normally passive people are going to turn aggressive. There will be fist fights, gunfights, you name it. It's bad enough for those who get here the legal way. Those suspected of moonshining are going to find themselves in a lot of trouble."

"Moonshining?"

Ethan stepped closer, directing his gaze at Toby. "That's what some back at the base camp call the ones who tried to sneak through, 'by the light of the moon,' they say. You aren't the only ones. A few were dragged back to the camp while I was there. I have no idea how many others are out there waiting to cheat on the rest. My main concern was you two, and I care a lot about you." He moved his eyes to Allyson. It was easy to see her in the bright moonlight. "I admit you were right about one thing. I *am* attracted to you, and I'm not going to let you get hurt over this."

Allyson folded her arms, pretending not to be concerned about his feelings. She wanted nothing to do with a man that way, so she decided she might as well not give Ethan Temple any hope that there could be anything between them, even though his kiss did still burn on her lips. He had forced that kiss. He was just as much an animal as Henry Bartel. She could just imagine what this crude man would be like if she gave him any encouragement. She had long ago learned that she could depend on no one but herself, and Toby. Most men were worthless brutes, and this one was part Indian besides. Just how savage could he be if a woman was willing?

"You needn't be concerned, Ethan," she told him. "We would certainly not hold you responsible for anything that happens to us. This is our decision, and if you really care like you say, you won't try to stop us. If you turn us in and we lose those lots, I don't know what will happen to us, where we'll go."

She kept her voice and stance firm, but never had her emotions been so confused. Everything would have worked out perfectly if Ethan Temple had not taken an interest in them. He was about to ruin all her plans. She wanted to hate him, but other feelings overwhelmed that hatred, feelings that frightened her.

Ethan walked off, returning with the two sturdy ponies he had bought for them. "Here. They're yours." He took the pistol from his belt and handed it to Toby. "You keep that handy. You're going to need it tomorrow." He turned to leave them.

"Ethan—" Allyson called.

He stopped for a moment but did not turn around. "Thank you," she said. "We . . . we'll never forget you . . . what you did for us."

Ethan wondered if he had ever done anything so foolish as to fall for a sixteen-year-old, virgin white woman, let alone going completely against his principles in allowing these two to sneak through the lines and cheat on all the others waiting at the borders. In all the years he had worked as a scout for the army, he had never gone against the rules. Was he losing his mind . . . or his heart? "Good luck," was his only reply.

Allyson watched the scout disappear around the bushes, and moments later she heard a horse trot away. Toby breathed a big sigh of relief. "You were right. He let us go."

Allyson wondered why her chest hurt so much. "We'd better try to get a little sleep," she answered. "The sun will be up in an hour or two."

* * *

Ethan rubbed his tired eyes, realizing the sun had been up for at least an hour already. Every part of him seemed to ache from weariness as he got to his feet, and he cursed Allyson and Toby Mills, as well as himself, for his miserable condition. He had determined to forget about her, to ignore his temptation to protect her and let her and her brother face whatever they would end up facing alone. That was what they wanted, and that was what they'd get! If he'd had any sense, he would not have left them those horses. What they both really deserved was a swift kick in the rear.

He gathered a little broken, rotted wood from around the patch of trees where he had made camp and added them to some smouldering embers from a fire he had built several hours earlier. Angrily, he took items from his supplies, more coffee grounds, a little bacon. He had only slept perhaps three hours at the most. If he was going to have any strength for the strenuous day ahead, he at least had to eat. He plunked a tin coffeepot on the fire once he got it going again, poured in some water from a canteen, then put some ground coffee beans into a gauze drawstring sack, tying it shut and dropping it into the water. He wished he had fresh coffee beans instead of just the half a sack he'd had ground at Fort Supply several days ago. The stale beans would probably make terrible tasting coffee, but right now any coffee was better than none at all. He just wished there was some way to make it boil quicker.

He scratched at a stubby beard, wishing there was time and a place to bathe and shave, but he intended to ride as close as possible to the border area this morning before the expected stampede after twelve o'clock. He had already ridden a few miles the night before, just to get far enough away from Toby and Allyson to keep from being tempted to go back and help them. Let them help themselves! He would do what he was supposed to do—accompany the rest of the crazy people who would soon be heading for this area, and do what he could to keep them all from killing each other.

He poured some water into his hand and spashed it onto his face. He figured that with a couple days' growth of beard and eyes probably bloodshot from lack of sleep, he must be a hell of a sight, but who cared? Allyson Mills certainly didn't. He rinsed his mouth, scrubbing his teeth with baking soda, wishing there was a way to physically wash away the memory of the taste of that woman's lips. He'd made a damn fool of himself through this whole thing, especially last night. Somehow he had lost his ability to reason, but after today that was going to end. He was getting the hell back to Fort Supply, maybe take some time to go see his father in Illinois. Little Miss Allyson Mills and her brother could proceed with their dream of getting rich in Guthrie, if they even managed to hang onto the lots they planned to claim illegally.

He walked off into the bushes to relieve himself, then got some clothes out of his gear and changed into a clean pair of longjohns and denim pants and pulled on a blue calico shirt. Although the night had been chilly, he could tell that today would be plenty warm. He ran a brush through his hair and tied it back, then threw a sliced-up potato and some bacon into a fry pan. He walked over to Blackfoot and began resaddling the horse. "Sorry to get you up and going again so soon, boy, but at least you had a little rest. Once this day is over, I'll give you a good brushing down and a couple of days off. That's a promise." The horse whinnied and turned its head to nudge him in the side, as though to protest. "I know, boy. Life's a bitch sometimes. Just suck in that gut and accept it."

He finished strapping on the saddle, then rolled and lit a

cigarette. He took a long, deep drag, walking a few feet away to study the northern horizon. In a few hours it would be black with dust from thousands of horses and wagons. Everywhere, east, west, north, and south, people would descend upon one of the last pieces of ground that was once promised to the Indians forever. So much for government promises.

He turned to walk back to the campfire, hoping the coffee was ready. He needed more than coffee to face what lay ahead, but it would have to do for now. He didn't doubt that by tonight, a shot of whiskey would taste mighty good.

5

The silence was eerie, like the calm before a storm. Ethan allowed Blackfoot to walk slowly, man and horse ambling toward the northern border, waiting to be met by the hordes of people and wagons that would be headed his way in the mad rush that had begun at twelve o'clock. Soldiers were to fire shots into the air as the official signal to proceed, and he was sure he'd heard those shots far in the distance over an hour ago.

He slowed Blackfoot, not only hearing a distant rumble, but also feeling it. "Here they come, boy. Take it easy."

Even Blackfoot sensed what was coming. The horse whinnied and tossed his head. Ethan took a chain watch from his jacket to see it was one o'clock. He heard a train whistle in the distance, and he knew the Santa Fe locomotive was on its way, probably packed with people hanging out the windows and clinging to the steps at the end of packed railroad cars. He was not far from the truth. By the time the train came into view, he could see it was just barely ahead of a thundering mass of horses, wagons, buggies, stagecoaches, carriages, mules, carts, every kind of wheeled contraption a man could name. A cloud of dust on the horizon rolled high into the air, and he felt sorry for those who were behind the ones in front. They were most certainly caught in the choking dust. Blackfoot edged sideways nervously. Ethan patted his neck. "Just relax, boy. We'll have to keep up once they get here."

Much as he wanted to quit thinking and worrying about Allyson and Toby Mills, he could not. Watching the approaching mass of land-hungry fiends only made him more concerned. He smashed out a cigarette against his canteen, then urged Blackfoot into a gentle lope. Soon the charging land-mongers were at his heels. He kicked his horse into a faster run and found himself caught up in the excitement. Blackfoot seemed to think he was in a race. Two horses passed him, and the big buckskin took off at a mean gallop, mane flying into Ethan's face, Ethan's hat popping off and bouncing at his back as its string tie remained caught around his neck.

Never had Ethan heard such near-deafening noise. The air was filled now with the sound of thundering hooves, the clatter and banging of wagons bouncing over holes and rocks, men yelping like wild Indians, here and there a scream from a woman who thought her husband was driving their wagon too fast. Somewhere in the distance he could hear another woman cussing her husband out in language he'd never even heard come out of men's mouths. A few soldiers charged past him, one whistling and calling out to him. It was Sergeant Adams. He hoped the man never discovered he had found "Mr. and Mrs. Harrington" and had let them go.

Within an hour he and most of the others reached what was once just a little watering hole called Guthrie. Tents were already springing up in every direction. People had charged in a mad dash for prime lots. The train had arrived, and arguments were already underway. He could see a fistfight to his left, and he rode his horse between the two men involved, forcing them apart and knocking one of them to the ground.

"If you have a dispute, go see the land agent or you'll both get kicked out!" he ordered.

The fallen man got up and dusted himself off. He clenched his hands into fists, but decided not to challenge the big Indian.

"I was here first!" the other man shouted.

"Says who?"

"Says *me!*" A third man joined the argument, and the first man waved them both off and stalked away. Ethan wondered if they realized how childish they looked. He heard a scream, then turned to see a woman crying and holding her injured baby, who had been thrown from the family's wagon when a wheel came off at the last moment.

The air was filled with the sound of sledgehammers pounding stakes into the ground as even more thousands of tents were erected. More arguments could be heard, and far off in the distance he heard a gunshot. Nearby a man stood pointing a rifle at another man and his wife and children. Ethan rode closer, pulling his own six-gun and aiming it at the man with the rifle. "Put it away, mister. You aiming to shoot a man down in front of his wife and kids over a piece of land?"

"If I have to."

"You try it, and you're a dead man."

The man pouted, looking up at Ethan. He lowered his rifle when he realized the wild-looking Indian probably would not hesitate to shoot him. "Who the hell are you?"

"You saw me back at base camp. I'm an army scout, and I'm here to keep people from doing anything stupid, like commit murder over a piece of ground."

"Only reason these people beat me here was because my wagon broke down. They probably loosened a wheel bolt on purpose while I slept last night!"

"Sir, we are a Christian family!" the woman retorted. "We would never resort to such underhanded measures!"

"First come, first serve, mister," Ethan put in. "That's the way it is, no matter what your excuse for not getting here."

"I claimed these lots yesterday," the man answered.

"You didn't claim *any*thing yesterday," Ethan reminded him. "Nobody could. You just saw the lots you wanted, but you got here too late. Now get going!"

The man's face was red with rage, but he finally left. Ethan thought he was prepared for this, but the behavior of these supposed adults still surprised him. Didn't they understand a man couldn't really *own* land? It was put here by a Higher Being to be used and shared by all. The Indians knew that, but the whites were bent on cutting out a little piece of it and saying it "belonged" to them. It was sights like this that made his Cheyenne relatives sick to see, whites swarming in like bees, tearing up the land, putting up their fences, declaring that they owned this piece or that. His Indian side felt guilty for being a part of the whole mess.

He rode on ahead, shocked at how fast a new town was being born before his very eyes. He broke up two more fights, all the while trying to ignore what might be going on near the railroad tracks several hundred yards to his right. It was another gunshot that finally drew his attention in that direction. A woman screamed so loudly that it was easy to hear what she was saying. "Toby! Toby!"

Ethan's heart tightened with dread. He turned Blackfoot and headed toward the tracks at a dead run. He quickly reached the lots Ally and Toby had claimed, his horse shuddering and prancing sideways as he dismounted before the animal even came to a full halt. Ethan's blood ran cold at the sight of Allyson sitting on the ground, holding her brother's limp body on her lap. Blood covered the front of the young man's shirt and was beginning to stain Allyson's clothes. The heavy-set man Ethan had seen eyeing the railroad property the day before was standing nearby with two other men. One of them still held a smoking gun.

"What the hell happened here?" Ethan demanded, walking toward the fat man.

"Who are you?" the man asked haughtily.

In one swift movement, Ethan's pistol was drawn and laid against the well-suited man's blubbery neck. "Right now I'm about all there is in the way of law around here, mister. You tell your two hired guns here to lay their weapons on the ground until we've had a little discussion!"

It was difficult to concentrate, with the sound of Allyson wailing Toby's name in the background. "He's dead! He's dead! Oh, my God, he's dead!" she sobbed.

"Go ahead and put your guns down, boys," the fat man ordered. "We've done what we needed to do." He held Ethan's eyes. "What's your name, Indian?"

"Ethan Temple. I'm an army scout, one of the men sent here to keep things in order; and until Guthrie gets organized and elects their own law, I'm it! Now, you talk fast, mister, or my Indian blood just might take over and I'll kill me a fat white man!" He jammed the gun a little harder, making the man wince. "That kid lying dead over there is just that—a *kid!*"

The man sniffed. "He was man enough to point a gun at us."

"That doesn't mean he was going to use it!"

"How did we know that?" one of the gunmen asked. "Our job was to come here with Mr. Ives and make sure some moonshiner didn't jump the land he had picked out for himself. Somebody sneaks through illegally, he'd better be ready to face the consequences."

Ethan backed away a couple of feet, still holding his pistol on all of them. "Ives, is it?"

"Nolan Ives, from Chicago. I'm a lawyer, so don't go preaching to me about what's legal and what isn't," the fat man answered, grasping the lapels of his suit with a look of authority. He struggled to pretend he was unruffled by having the barrel of Ethan's gun buried in the folds of his double chin, but he could not keep the sweat from breaking out on his face. *Damn, stinking Indian,* he thought. *How dare he go ordering around a man like me!*

"Mister, out here we don't live by the same rules as back in Chicago. We *make* the rules as we go," Ethan answered. "I know these two kids, and they came here with the rest of the land-grabbers this afternoon, *legally!*" he lied.

Allyson looked up at Ethan in surprise. He was covering for her! If only this had not happened to Toby, everything would be wonderful. Now her dream had turned into a nightmare. If Ethan had not come along, she wondered, would Nolan Ives's gunmen have shot her, too?

"You know damn well those two snuck through last night!" Ives fumed.

Ethan stepped forward again, holding his .44 Colt Peacemaker against the man's chest. "I say they got here legally. For the next few days it's the *army* who decides these things, mister, and I don't care if you're the richest man in Chicago! This is *Oklahoma! Indian* Territory, and the army is the law, which makes me part of that law!"

"You got trouble, Ethan?"

Ethan recognized the voice of Lieutenant Michael Sand. He kept his eyes on Nolan Ives. "I've got a man here willing to kill to try to steal a claim."

"I wasn't stealing anything!" Ives growled, his fat eyelids leaving only slits for his eyes, eyes that glowed now with anger and insult.

"Mister, my advice to you is to go find yourself a different piece of land," the lieutenant advised Ives.

Ives straightened, keeping his eyes on Ethan. "You know that by now there's nothing choice left!" He looked over at a still-sobbing Allyson. "That little bitch over *there* is the thief!" He moved his eyes back to Ethan. "You know damn well I'm right!"

"All I know is you'd better get off these lots and be on your way before I decide to have you arrested."

"It was self-defense!" the shootist spoke up.

Ethan kept a close eye on all three men, he and the lieutenant both holding guns on them. A small crowd had gathered, and a woman was bent over Allyson, trying to soothe her. "Get moving," Ethan ordered.

"Better do what the man says," the lieutenant told Ives and his men. "Ethan here has a little trouble with his temper at times."

Ives looked over at Allyson. "You tell that bitch that she hasn't heard the last of this! Let her claim the lots! The land between here and the railroad tracks belongs to the *railroad*, and I own a great deal of stock in the Santa Fe! I'll just make a deal with the railroad to let me buy that land. I'll choke her right out, buy the lots from everybody around her, build my warehouses and hotels right up to her back door so she can't even see out a window! I've got the money to buy out half the people here, and one day I'll buy *her* out, too! By then we'll have our own law here in Guthrie, and I'll have this town in my pocket!"

Ethan rammed his gun into its holster and walked up to grab hold of the front of Ives's fancy vest. "You make more trouble for that girl, and you'll answer to me!" He gave the man a shove so that he stumbled backward. When he fell, he was so fat that he actually rolled over twice before landing on his back. Panting and puffing, his face beet red, Nolan

Ives managed to get to his feet only with the help of his two gunmen. "You mark my words!" he shouted. "This isn't over!" His gunmen picked up their weapons warily, Ethan watching them like a hawk. They turned and left with their boss, who was still panting as he stumbled away and climbed onto the steps of his private train car, cursing vehemently.

Ethan turned to look at Allyson, who sat rocking with Toby's head in her lap, stroking his hair gently.

"What's the truth, Ethan?" the lieutenant asked. "Those two moonshiners?"

Ethan rubbed his tired eyes. "No."

The lieutenant backed his horse. "If you say so." He knew damn well Ethan was lying, also remembered that Ethan had helped this young couple for several days before they got here. Was the Indian sweet on that woman? He could make more trouble for all of them, but he liked Ethan Temple. How could he *not* like him? Ethan had saved his neck once when some young, drunk Cheyenne men cornered him after he'd got himself lost along Deep Creek. The mood those angry young men were in that day, he couldn't help wondering if he'd even still be alive if Ethan Temple hadn't come along when he did and calmed the situation. "You need me to do anything?"

Ethan watched Allyson sadly. "Yeah. Go find a land agent and get him over here. I want these lots recorded right away, in the name of Mr. and Mrs. Toby Mills." He thought of using the fake names Toby and Allyson had used up to now, but Allyson had said Toby's name so many times over by now that it wouldn't do any good to go calling him Robert. A lot of the people around them had come in from the other borders and were not familiar with the young couple, so they would never know the difference. At the moment, he didn't recognize anyone familiar.

The lieutenant rode off, and Ethan walked Blackfoot over to a hitching post near the watering station several yards away. He noticed Toby and Allyson's two horses, as well as the two he had bought them, were tied there. Brother and sister had already started pitching a tent on their lots, and Ethan figured Ives must have come along before they were through. One side still sagged, waiting to be staked. He walked back toward Allyson, his heart heavy for her. Life had been hard for this young woman, making her stubborn and determined. He supposed she had managed to get through it all because she at least had her brother at her side. Toby was all she had, and he could understand how his death would devastate her.

He had meant to forget about this red-headed spitfire, but how could he turn his back on her now? What the hell was she going to do, only sixteen, trying to do something she had never done before, and now no brother to help and protect her? He came closer, knelt down beside her. The woman who had been consoling her was called away by her husband. "Everybody takes their own chances, Rita," the man yelled, obviously feeling no concern for Allyson. "Get back over here with the kids and help me set up this sign!"

The woman frowned, looking at Ethan. "Do you know this poor girl?"

Ethan sighed. "I know her. Go on with your husband. I'll look after her. I'm an army scout. It's my job."

"I saw how you handled those terrible men. I'm glad you got rid of them."

"Rita! Come on!"

The woman rose. "I'm sorry. My husband is anxious to get his carpenter business set up. Heaven knows he'll be plenty busy for the next few weeks." She patted Allyson's shoulder and left.

Ethan leaned over Allyson's shoulder and checked Toby's neck for a pulse.

"He's dead," Allyson sobbed. "What am I going to do? It's always been me and Toby."

Ethan put a hand on her arm. "We've got to get him buried, Ally. I've sent for a land agent to come over here—said you and Toby were husband and wife. Is that the way you want it? You can just give this whole thing up right now and I'll see you get settled somewhere safe."

Her body jerked in a sob, and Ethan ached to hold her. She leaned down and kissed Toby's cheek, stroked his hair. "He died for this. It's partly my fault. After all this, I'll be damned if I'll give it up! I'm staying right here, for Toby!"

Ethan rubbed at his eyes again. "Ally, this is really no place for a sixteen-year-old girl. All the single men around here are going to look at you now as a lonely widow."

"I'll manage. If I could survive in the alleys of New York and hold my own against Henry Bartel, I can make it here." She wiped at her eyes and nose with the sleeve of her dress. "Thank you for standing up for me against that Mr. Ives."

"He's another reason you should consider giving this up. He's not through trying to get this property. You can bet on it."

"He can't do a thing, once it's recorded in mine and Toby's names. And he wouldn't dare try to hurt me to get it. There are too many people who witnessed what happened today." Her voice choked, and she took a couple of deep breaths, wiping at her eyes again. "If anything happens to me, they'll know who to blame. Once the property is mine, Nolan Ives will *never* get it, because I'll never *sell* it!"

Ethan studied her sky-blue eyes, red and swollen now, so full of stubborn determination. What did it take to get this excuse of a woman to give up? "Ally, you could have a lot easier life—"

"I'm doing this for Toby, and there's no arguing it!" she answered, wondering if Ethan could read the fear in her eyes. She had never been afraid before, not like this. Now she was truly alone. Even when she and Toby were separated at the orphanage, she at least knew he was nearby. She had always been the strong one, the one to make the plans and give the orders. It surprised her to realize how much she had needed her brother after all, just to know someone was there who loved her. "Will you help me bury him? Help me find a cookstove and a supply of food? That's all I need from you."

You need much more than that, Allyson Mills, Ethan thought. *Some day you'll understand that.* "You know I'll help you. I told you I've already sent for a land agent. I was just hoping you'd do the smart thing—change your mind and let Nolan Ives have these lots—let me take you back to Fort Supply with me. You could decide what you want to do after you've had time to get over losing Toby."

Allyson scooted out from under her brother's body, studying the blood on her own dress. "I already know what I'm going to do. I'm on my own now, and that's that." The pain in her stomach cut at her like a knife. She shivered and got to her feet, looking up at Ethan. "Toby has always been there to defend me, the only one to care about me. Even *you* tried to threaten me last night."

"Ally, I was just trying to get the truth out of you."

"It doesn't matter! What matters is nobody is going to stop me! You want me to give up, but I'm not going to! I appreciate your help, but once I get settled here, I don't need you either. I don't need anybody but myself!"

Ethan felt like dragging her off and tying her up until she realized the foolishness of what she was saying. Never had he felt so trapped in his own emotions. He wanted to stay here and take care of her, but that would mean falling even deeper into these feelings he had no right experiencing, and right now she was in no mood to accept his help. He had thought for a brief moment . . . last night . . . maybe there could be more to this than just a casual friendship between a settler and a scout; but it was obvious she had forgotten that kiss. More than that, she had had some bad experiences with men that left her feeling she didn't even want one in her life. Her brother was the only male she loved and accepted, but now he was dead, by another man's cruelty. He looked past her to see the lieutenant returning. "The land agent is coming," he said.

Allyson looked down at her dead brother, finding it difficult to comprehend what had just taken place. Toby was dead! Suddenly there were so many decisions to make.

"Let me do the talking," Ethan told her, leaning close so he could keep his voice down. "You're in too much of a state to think straight. You've got to be eighteen to hold title to these lots, and you're probably right about letting them think Toby was your husband. It will get you more sympathy. Just remember you're eighteen, not sixteen. Toby was twenty. You're claiming the land in your husband's name. He took hold of these lots before he died, so they were his, fair and square."

Allyson hardly heard him. Her brother's death hit her all over again, and she collapsed in tears, crumbling beside him again. She was vaguely aware of Ethan talking to the land agent. "Lots A-6 and A-7," someone was saying. "Mr. Tobias Mills and his wife, Allyson. Where from?"

"New York City," Ethan answered. "Mrs. Mills is eighteen. Her husband was twenty."

"They got birth certificates?"

"Do you ask everybody else around here for birth certificates?"

"No, but—"

"Just make out the damn papers and let her sign them!" she heard Ethan saying angrily. She knew good and well she could never have got through this without the Indian scout who was being so patient with her. Still, she hated having to depend on anyone. No matter how she felt about Ethan Temple, he was an Indian, and certainly not a settling man. Besides that, a feeling much stronger than anything she felt for Ethan had welled up in her soul, a terrible need to show everyone, even Ethan Temple, that she could do this. She had thought for a moment she might like something more from Ethan, but when he touched her breast, the shivering revulsion had hit her all over again. Was that all men wanted? If that was so, she didn't need one. Never again was any man going to take advantage of her.

She turned then when Ethan shoved some papers under her nose. "Sign these—two copies. Sign for Toby, too. I've convinced the land agent to make these out as though Toby signed them and took hold of the land before he died. That will make it even harder for Nolan Ives to give you trouble."

Ally looked into his dark eyes, again feeling drawn to him in ways she did not understand. "How did you get him to do that?"

"Never mind. Just sign." Ethan wondered where his mind had gone. He just spent a good deal of his savings bribing the land agent, money he'd meant to use to go and see his father. He didn't doubt that for the first few weeks, it was the land agents who would be the richest men in these parts.

Allyson signed the papers, and Ethan gave one to the agent, keeping the second copy for Allyson. "Keep that in a safe place. I'll finish raising your tent and put up a couple of stakes on these lots with your name on them. Then we'll bury your brother." He walked off, returning with a blanket, which he laid over Toby's body. Allyson felt faint from lack of food and sleep, combined with the shock of watching her brother die in her arms and feeling as though it was mostly her fault for insisting they try to claim the lots Nolan Ives wanted.

Ethan saw her eyes rolling back, and he quickly grabbed hold of her, picking her up and carrying her over to the tent. "Sit down here and keep your head bent over your knees for a few minutes," he told her. "I'm going to bring you something to eat. Once we bury Toby, you're going to lie down in that tent and sleep for a good long time. I'll keep watch outside. You're in no shape to be looking out for yourself right now."

"I can do it," she said weakly. "You don't need to—"

"You don't have any choice right now." He left her there, walking back to his horse to get out some food and water. The sounds of a new city mushrooming from land that only a few hours ago was quiet and barren filled the air. Whistles and shouts, horses whinnying, mules braying, pigs squealing, chickens clucking. Sledgehammers hitting metal stakes rang in every direction, and as far as Ethan could see, tents already decorated the landscape. Not far away a gambler had already opened up a game, and beyond that he saw a questionable-looking woman prancing around a group of single men. This land was supposed to have been opened for honest settlers, but half of these people were gamblers and prostitutes, shady businessmen and opportunists.

He looked back at the tent, thinking how tiny and helpless Allyson looked sitting there. Still, in spite of her size, he figured she had more guts than most men. It was just too bad she didn't have any common sense to go with it. "Damn," he muttered. How in hell could he go off and leave her alone here? Yet to stay was too dangerous . . . for his heart.

6

Allyson emerged from her tent rubbing her still-puffy eyes. The last two days had been miserable, as she struggled against her wretched grief and loneliness. So far she had managed to keep back most of the tears, but it made her stomach ache fiercely. She had always found crying a useless endeavor, but watching poor Toby's crude, wooden coffin being lowered into the ground . . .

She breathed deeply. No. She couldn't think about that. Time. She just needed time. For now she would have to get through each day the best way possible, which was to keep busy. Two days ago she had claimed this land and buried her brother. Yesterday she had visited a supplier and had given him a list of items she needed to get started; and today she *would* get started, even though it would be a few days before her ice box would arrive. Her cast iron cooking stove was to arrive today by train, or so the supplier had promised. She could at least get started baking bread and pies. Already supplies like flour and apples were plentiful, as merchants had descended on Guthrie with a vengeance, hawking everything imaginable.

She gazed at a new, waking city, thousands of tents sprawled everywhere. Activity around the tents, mostly gambling, never ended. All through the night one could hear the voices, laughter, sometimes fighting. Tents and booths for gambling were erected right in the middle of what was supposed to be streets, and already people were complaining and plotting to get rid of them. Guthrie was in need of law and order, but she would leave that to the men who had already begun appointing themselves in charge. It was rumored that before long meetings would be held to elect officials and set rules.

She had decided she could not worry about that right now. Her job was to start making money, as soon as possible. Ethan had promised to watch for the stove and find a man to haul it to her. She was not sure what she would have done without him these last three days, yet she worried she was growing too dependent on Ethan Temple, not just for the physical help, but emotionally as well. She didn't like being dependent on anyone, nor did she totally trust Ethan's intentions, not after that kiss the other night and his admission that he cared about her. She had no room in her life right now to bring a man into it, nor was she ready for the physical aspects of such a relationship.

She picked up a bucket of water and poured some into a wash bowl. She wondered how long it would be before Guthrie would devise a well and water tower of its own, or if she should see about having someone dig her a well so she could pump her own water. Their first day here, the railroad's water tower had become the supply for most people, and it was soon empty. Yesterday two huge tank cars full of water had been brought in by the Santa Fe, paid for by the government. They were moved to a side track, and people had to carry their water daily from the tank cars to their homes and businesses, which were still mostly made of canvas. The air was filled with the smell of fresh lumber, also brought in by train; and with the sound of pounding hammers, as wooden structures sprouted everywhere, replacing the tents.

Today another government-supported train would arrive with a freight car full of blocks of ice, as well as tons of goods being shipped in by various suppliers who had set up tables along the tracks to take orders. She had already presented a long list of necessary items. Besides an ice box, she needed a couple of tables and many small items, like a pastry board, rolling pin, an egg whisk, potato masher, dishes, bowls, pots and pans. She had just enough money to pay for all the supplies, which meant she needed to get started right away, at least selling bread and pies. She would buy what food she could and cook at least a few meals. She had to start earning money so she could continue buying other things and pay for more coal for her new cookstove, which she would have to set up temporarily outside her tent.

There was so much to think about, and that was good. It kept her from dwelling on Toby's death. She just wished he was here to see what was happening. Just a few days ago she never dreamed she would be part of such an adventure, but Toby's death had taken any joy from it. She missed him terribly. Now her dream had become a matter of stubborn determination, a way of making up for what happened to Toby, and a form of revenge against Nolan Ives.

She carried the bowl of water inside her tent, wishing there was a better way to wash, aching more from emotional than physical weariness. She took a clean but well-worn dress from her carpetbag, thinking how wrinkled it was. That was another thing she needed—an iron. She wondered when she would ever have enough money to buy herself some new clothes. The business had to come first.

"Hello in there!"

It was Ethan. Why did her heart rush so at the sound of his voice? She wasn't supposed to feel this way about a man. She wondered where he had been. For the last two nights he had camped near her tent in case Nolan Ives tried to give her more trouble, but there had been none. When she first peeked out of the tent in the morning, she noticed Ethan had already been up and gone. She pushed some of her hair behind her ear, thinking how terrible she must look after several days without a real bath, let alone how her face must look after nearly three days of crying and hardly eating. Whenever she was distraught about something, circles appeared under her eyes. Besides that, her face had gotten sunburned and was already peeling. She moved to the tent entrance and looked out. "Good morning."

"How would you like a real bath, a place to sit in a tub of hot water, wash your hair, the works?"

She squinted against the morning sun. "Where?"

Ethan ached at the way she looked, wishing he could do more to help heal her broken heart. He knew he was getting in way too deep, knew damn well there was no future with this woman, if she could even be called a woman yet. He had been determined to leave today, but the poor kid was still so inexperienced, still needed so much help. He had tried to tell himself that was *her* problem—she had brought all of this upon herself. The stubborn woman was determined to stay and make a go of it, and if he had any sense, he would get the hell out of Guthrie and let her succeed or fall flat on her face all on her own. So, why was he still here? He knew the answer. He just didn't want to admit it yet, not even to himself.

"I found a man who's already set up a bathhouse. Right now it's just two big tents, one for men, one for women, but he's got water boiling, plenty of soap and towels." He held up a package. "I bought you a new dress. Hope it's the right size."

"Ethan, you shouldn't—"

"It's just one dress. Come on. Climb up here in front of me and I'll take you over there."

Allyson hated continually depending on this man, but the fact remained that a hot bath sounded absolutely wonderful. "Just a minute." She ducked inside the tent to gather her underwear, a comb, and other personal belongings, throwing them all into a pillow case along with a clean dress, in case the one Ethan brought her didn't fit. She left the tent and walked up to Ethan's big buckskin horse. He reached down and hoisted her up in front of him, and she could not ignore the shiver of strange desire that moved through her at the feel of his strong arm around her, the closeness of his body as she leaned against him, the warm feeling of safety she always felt when he was around. How could she ever repay him? It was as though he could read her thoughts. Here she had been wishing for a real bath and a new dress, and along comes Ethan Temple offering both.

He left her off at the bathhouse, and minutes later she was enjoying the most luxury she had known in weeks. It felt wonderful to soak in the hot suds, even more wonderful to wash her hair. Each person paid ten cents for their bath and had to carry their own hot water. There were three bathtubs in each of the two tents, with blankets hung between them for privacy. The set-up was rather primitive, but it served the purpose. With the lines outside the tents, Allyson did not doubt that the man who ran the bathhouse would be rich in no time. It made her even more anxious to get started with her own venture. Excitement grew in her soul as she dried off and put on all her underclothes. She heard a train whistle in the distance. Surely some of her supplies were on that train, maybe her cookstove!

She combed through her damp hair and let it hang loose to dry, pushing it behind her ears, then unwrapped the brown package that held the dress Ethan had bought her. Her heart rushed with delight at the lovely bright calico garment, a sky-blue color, accented with little yellow flowers. It seemed too pretty to wear for a hard day's work. She held it against herself for a moment, vowing someday to be able to afford to dress in lovely clothes. She carefully folded the dress again, rewrapping it. She put it into her pillow case of supplies and took out the faded but clean dress she had packed earlier. She put that one on instead. Someone yelled that her time was up, and she quickly left, as the wife of the man who had opened the bathhouse came inside to drain her tub for the next customer.

When Allyson emerged from the tent, Ethan was waiting. She saw the disappointment in his eyes at the fact that she was not wearing the dress he had bought her. "It's beautiful, Ethan, too nice for what I have to do today. I want to save it for something special."

Ethan had looked forward to seeing her in it, but then he thought perhaps it was better this way. Just being bathed, that long, red hair hanging damp down her back . . . That made it hard enough to think of leaving her. He pictured her sinking her naked body into the hot water, wished he could have gotten right in that tub with her. She was beautiful, even when she wore her plain, frayed, too-big hand-me-downs. It was probably better he didn't see her in that pretty blue dress that he was sure would fit her every curve just perfectly. "Just so you liked it," he answered, reaching down to help her onto Blackfoot again.

"It's so pretty, Ethan, but you shouldn't have."

"I just thought it would boost your spirits to have a new dress." God, she felt so good against him. Now she smelled sweet and clean. He was falling in love, and he damn well knew it. He also knew it was wrong. "Soon as we get back

I'll go check on your stove. A train arrived just a few minutes ago. With any luck, the stove will be on it."

"I thought the same thing when I heard the train whistle."

"Well, I hope it's there so I can get it set up for you. In a couple more days I'm going to have to leave. I'm already overdue at Fort Supply. I should report in. After I finish whatever it is they want me to do next, I'll be going to Illinois to visit my father."

I don't want you to go. Allyson could not bring herself to speak the words. Of course she wanted him to leave. He had done too much for her already, and she must not let herself grow so dependent on him. Besides, wasn't it wrong for a white girl to be seen so much with an Indian? Somehow she didn't see him as Indian anymore. He was just a terribly kind and handsome man for whom she had feelings she must not allow to be revealed, even to herself, nor could she allow herself to admit how afraid she would be once he was gone. She was going to be on her own, and that was that.

They rode to her tent. Ethan dismounted, then reached up for her, lifting her down with ease. Allyson ignored the pleasure she felt when his strong hands grasped her around her small waist, ignored the little wave of desire that enveloped her when she grasped his arm for support and felt its hard muscle through his cotton shirt. She even forced herself to ignore how good he looked this morning, cleanshaven, his smile bright. He wore a red shirt, and it was a wonderful color on him. His denim pants fit his slender hips snugly, and his six-gun spoke of a man who knew how to take care of himself. She would never forget how he had stood up to Nolan Ives and his men, how he had helped and protected her since then . . . all the more reason it was a good thing he was leaving. She was not sure how much longer she could fight these feelings.

"Right now there are long lines at the train," he was saying. He had to raise his voice to be heard over the sound of thousands of pounding hammers and scraping saws. A wagon clattered by, and the noise of the crowd gathered by the supply train was getting louder. "I've already been over there, and it's a mess. We might as well have some coffee and let the lines go down a little before we go see about your supplies." He started to build a fire outside the tent.

Allyson brought her belongings into the tent, then came back to join Ethan, who had put on some coffee and bacon.

"I'm going to start right away this afternoon making my bread dough. I decided that until I get an ice box and can store more food and make bigger meals, I can at least bake bread and pies and sell them. I've got to start earning money right away. I have almost none left."

Ethan poured them both some coffee. "You're really going through with this, aren't you? No changing your mind?" He handed her one of the metal cups.

"No." Allyson met his dark eyes, and felt a flutter in her stomach when his fingers touched her own. "I have to do this, not just for Toby, but to prove to myself I can be someone important, that I can make my own way without having to steal. If I leave now, Toby will have died for nothing. Besides, it would also mean Nolan Ives has won, and I'm not ever letting that happen. I didn't let my father break my spirit when he used to beat me. I fought off boys in the streets of New York, and I outwitted Henry Bartel. Now I'll show Nolan Ives that just because I'm young and a woman doesn't mean I'm weak or that he can scare me away. He doesn't realize that by killing Toby, he just made me stronger."

She sipped her coffee, and Ethan watched her, smiling and shaking his head. "Whatever you say." He wished he could get his hands on every man who had abused her and had made a sweet, pretty girl into a calculating, determined female who seemed to have no room in her life for emotions or plain old common sense. He knew damn well she was afraid, but the brave little thing was going to charge ahead anyway. He watched her reach over to the fry pan he had set aside and take out a piece of bacon with a fork. She laid it in a tin plate. "Ethan, you can't go away without telling me more about yourself. I just realized this morning that I don't know anything about you except your name and that you're an army scout. You must lead a very exciting life. As long as we have to sit here and wait, you might as well tell me a little bit about it." She bit off a piece of bacon. "Don't you have an Indian wife waiting for you somewhere?" Yes, that was the way to put it. Let him know gently that he belonged with an Indian woman, not a white girl. Still, the pain she saw in his dark eyes when she mentioned a wife made her feel guilty for asking. She had touched on a sore subject. "I'm sorry if I said something wrong."

Ethan set down his coffee cup and took a cheroot from his pocket. He had not missed her direct hint that he had better have no romantic interest in her, but he had a feeling she wasn't at all sure that was what she really wanted. "It was an innocent question." He lit the cheroot and puffed on it a moment. "My wife died four years ago. She was Cheyenne . . . died of pneumonia when she was only about six months along with child. She was about your age."

Allyson felt a surprising rush of jealousy at the thought of him lying with a woman. He had made another woman pregnant. Why in the world did that suddenly bother her? And if that woman was her own age, then he must look at *her* as a woman, too. She seldom thought of herself that way, but Ethan Temple had awakened that part of her. She wished he had let it lie. Immediately the memory of that long, intimate kiss the night before the land rush came vividly to mind, and again her curiosity was aroused. "I'm sorry."

Ethan picked up his coffee cup again, holding it in his hands and staring at it. "Her name was Violet. There hasn't been anybody else since. I've just kept myself busy doing whatever the army sends me to do."

"You must have family. I heard that Indian man the other day mention your cousin. What about your mother and father? Which one was white?"

Ethan met her blue eyes. "Which do you think?"

Allyson shrugged. "Probably your father."

"And what makes you think that?"

"Well, you almost never hear of an Indian man marrying a—" Allyson felt heat coming to her face. She could tell by his eyes that she had inadvertently insulted him, and she wanted to kick herself. "I mean . . . I've always heard stories about white trappers and men such as that going west and marrying Indian women. I've even read about them."

Ethan decided to ignore her insinuation that white women never married Indian men, at least not willingly. He figured it was an innocent remark, not aimed at him directly. He finished his coffee. "Well, you're right. My pa was a white trader, my mother Cheyenne. Pa is still alive, with white relatives in Illinois. My mother was killed back in '64. You ever hear of Sand Creek?"

Allyson shook her head. He wondered why he had even asked. Sand Creek had happened before she was even born. "A bunch of soldiers, Colorado volunteers, attacked a peaceful Cheyenne village in southeast Colorado, raped and mutilated women, murdered children . . . it was a massacre, and with no cause. I was there."

Allyson envisioned soldiers and Indians going at each other with knives and tomahawks. "Did you fight?"

Ethan smiled sadly. "I was only three years old, but I remember quite a bit. Some people can't remember that far back, but when you're ripped from your mother's arms and then you stand and watch her being . . ." He saw her reddening again, and he decided not to go into all the gory details. "Suffice it to say, when they were through with her she was lying in pieces on the ground. I remember standing over her and crying, begging her to get up and put her arms around me. Some other Indian woman grabbed me then and that was the last I ever saw of my mother."

True sorrow came into her eyes. "Oh, Ethan, how awful. Where was your father when it happened?"

Ethan fingered the cheroot. "He was at a fort buying more supplies. He figured we were safe." He sighed. "After that my pa was never the same. He left me with Cheyenne relatives up in the Dakotas for a while, went back to Illinois, where he came from. He didn't take me because he knew his white relatives there wouldn't show me the love my Cheyenne relatives did. I was ten when he came back. He worked as an Indian agent here on the Cheyenne reservation, made sure I got some decent schooling through some missionaries. That was when the Cheyenne had more land than they do now . . ." He waved his arm to indicate the new surge of whites in Guthrie. "Thanks to land deals like this."

He smoked quietly again, and Allyson waited. This was the most Ethan had talked about himself. Since he was normally a man of few words, she did not want to spoil the moment.

"Pa lost that job because the government said he was too prejudiced on the side of the Cheyenne to effectively carry out government mandates," he finally continued. "They were probably right, but it caused Pa to turn to drink. When I took a wife I let him live with us, but not long after Violet died, Pa was caught smuggling whiskey into the reservation. He had Indian friends who liked it, and he was drinking heavily himself then. He was ordered to stay out of Indian Territory completely. I had gotten myself involved by then in scouting for the army . . . needed to stay busy to keep from thinking about Violet, a lot like you're doing right now to keep from thinking about Toby."

Allyson glanced at her lap. "How else do you get through something like that?"

"I don't know." Ethan rose and stretched, watching the crowd near the train. "At any rate, I couldn't leave. Pa went north to see if he could do anything for my Cheyenne relatives up in the Dakotas. My cousin Red Hawk lives on the Cheyenne reservation here. He's the son of my mother's sister, who died a few years ago. My mother's brother, Big Hands, lives up on the Standing Rock reservation in North Dakota with a Sioux wife. My maternal grandmother also lives up there. Her name is Sky Dancing. My Sioux grandfather is dead, but she chose to continue living on the Sioux reservation rather than come down here. The Sioux and Cheyenne used to run together. There was a lot of inter-marrying. Fact is, there were just about as many Cheyenne at the Little Big Horn as there were Sioux."

"Really? Were *you* there?"

"I was only fifteen then. My pa had come back and I lived with him down here on the Cheyenne reservation. Those were really restless times, though. Indians everywhere were afraid of some kind of government retaliation. Things are still real tense and unsettled up in Sioux country."

Allyson studied his magnificent physique when he turned away. Why did it pleasure her so to look at him? She felt so torn. He was indeed a brave, handsome man, but he was an Indian. She shouldn't have these feelings. Besides, whenever she thought of what being involved with a man led to, the sick feeling always returned to her stomach. No. She could never let a man touch her that way. She had not minded Ethan Temple's kiss, but when his hand touched her breast . . .

She looked back down at the pan of bacon, embarrassed she had even thought again about that. How often did Ethan think of it? Had he really just been trying to scare her, or would he have done much more if she would have let him? They had not talked about it since, and she preferred to leave it that way. They were just good friends.

"Back to my father," Ethan was saying. "I didn't see him again until about a year ago, when he came back here to tell me he was returning to Illinois. I guess whiskey had gotten him in trouble up at the Standing Rock reservation, too. He just figured if he couldn't live near his wife's people, he'd go back to his own. I got a letter from him not long ago, and I have a feeling he's not well. I've got to go and see him as soon as I can."

"Yes, you should. And be glad you had a father who loved you, as well as your Indian family." Allyson picked up another piece of bacon. "What about your scouting duties? I'll bet you've had some close calls, been shot at, maybe wounded."

Ethan sat back down on a log across the fire from her. "Oh, I've had my run-ins, with whites and Indians both. I've got the scars to prove it."

Allyson smiled, enjoying the way he looked when he was smiling. "It must be hard being part of both races. Don't you kind of wonder sometimes where you really belong, with Indians or with whites?"

His eyes moved over her strangely then, and Allyson felt a shiver. Had she insulted him again? Or was he wanting something he couldn't have?

"All the time," he answered. "I've always lived like a white man, but my looks, and in here—" He put a fist to his heart. "I'm more Indian. The reality is, no matter how Indian I am, I can't live that way. Even *Indians* can't live like Indians any more, thanks to the government. It's all different now. Things like Sand Creek put an end to the old ways. Right now I'm kind of living in both worlds, I guess. Maybe that's how it will always have to be." Ethan noticed the lines at the supply train were thinning a little. "I'd better go check on your stove. Give me that list of yours and I'll see what else I can find."

Allyson rose, picking up a small towel to wipe bacon grease from her fingers. "You've done too much already. I can go myself."

Ethan stomped on the cheroot. "All right. How about if you go get in line, and I'll find someone to haul the stove. We'll need three or four extra men. Those cast iron stoves are damn heavy."

She smiled. "Good. I can't wait to get started. I'll bet I won't be able to bake bread fast enough for all my customers." Again she felt a shiver at the way his eyes raked her body.

"I'll agree with that. You just remember you're going to have a lot of men for customers, and they won't always be coming here because they want bread. They think you're a lonely widow now. That could be dangerous."

"I have my six-gun."

Her hair was drying to a beautiful red luster, and he wanted to grab her and beg her to give this up, marry him, and let him take care of her. How could he know so soon he felt this strongly about this daring little thief from New York City? He hadn't wanted a woman so badly since his wedding night with Violet, and part of him couldn't help wondering if that was desire he sometimes saw in those blue eyes that were so innocent of the woman in her. If he could stir that woman, as he was sure he had done that night he kissed her . . .

He turned away. What was the use? "Whatever you say," he answered. "I'll go round up some help."

Allyson watched him mount his horse and ride off, thinking how very different he was from anyone she had ever known. She told herself to be glad he would be leaving soon. She could sort out her feelings then, get her feet on the ground, learn to understand these strange new emotions. She was sure she didn't know her own mind right now. If she did, she wouldn't feel desire for an Indian man—for *any* man, for that matter.

She turned away and went into her tent, tying on a bonnet and picking up her handbag. After today most of her money would be gone, but she would at least have what she needed to get started at her business. She forced aside all thoughts of Ethan Temple and marched toward the train. She had more important things to think about now, like finding a sign painter. There was every other sort of tradesman in the new settlement—she could surely find someone to make her a sign to post. *Ally's Place.* She had already been thinking of what to name her establishment. That sounded as good as any. It was simple and to the point.

She reached the train, and on a flatbed car she saw a

new, black, cast iron stove that had just had a canvas cover removed from it. Her heart raced with joy and anticipation. There it was! That stove was going to help her become one of the richest women in Guthrie, in spite of Nolan Ives, and without Ethan's help. This was something she had to do on her own, and personal grief, personal fear, or personal emotions over some forbidden man were not going to stop her. For the next few months that big, black cookstove would be her friend, her most prized possession. It didn't do a person any good to depend on other people. Somehow those people either failed them or hurt them, or died on them. The only thing to depend on was one's self . . . tools of their trade . . . and money. She was on her way to being one of the richest ladies of Guthrie, and she would do it all by herself.

She waited patiently, her eye on the stove the whole time. She was almost to the supplier's table when she saw men begin unloading the stove from the flatcar to put it on a cart with huge wooden wheels, a contraption apparently designed for hauling a lot of weight. She supposed that it was the men Ethan had hired who were taking the stove from the car, but then she saw a fat, well-suited man giving the men directions. It was Nolan Ives!

She pushed her way past several people to reach the supplier. "That's my stove!" she declared. "You're letting those men take my stove!"

"What?"

Allyson pointed frantically to the cookstove being loaded onto the cart. "That's the stove I ordered! You said it would be in today. Don't you remember? I ordered it just four days ago, the day before the land rush."

The man searched through a pile of papers lying in front of him on a makeshift table of wood and barrels. "What's the name, ma'am?"

"Allyson! Allyson Mills!" Allyson's heart beat so hard that her chest hurt. It was bad enough to see someone hauling away the stove she so sorely needed, but to have it be Nolan Ives made it all the worse.

"Sorry, ma'am, I don't have any record of your order."

"But you have to! You're *lying*, aren't you? How much did Nolan Ives pay you to let him take the stove?"

The man glared at her, his face dark red with anger. "I'm no liar, girl! Now, if you want to reorder, I'll place the request right away. You'll have your stove within a week."

"A *week!* I need it right now!" Allyson fought to keep from crying.

"That's the only one that came in, ma'am, and it's first come, first served. I do have an order for a Jane and Robert Harrington, but they never came to claim it. Mr. Ives was here asking for a stove, so I let him have it, since the Harringtons hadn't paid in advance."

Allyson's heart fell. She realized she had ordered the stove under her fake name. To admit it now could cost her her lots, claimed under her real name. She realized she was actually lucky the supplier didn't remember her well enough to connect her to the fake name. He'd seen so many thousands of faces over the last few days, it was probably impossible for him to remember them all. "Please! Whatever that man paid for the stove, I'll pay you more!"

"Sorry, ma'am, the transaction has already been made."

Allyson just stared at him a moment, until someone behind her asked her to please move out of the way so he could get his supplies. She struggled to keep from breaking down completely, then turned and stormed toward Nolan Ives. "Get that stove off that cart! It's mine!" she shouted, ignoring the stares of the others.

One of Ives's men walked over and put an arm out to stop her. "Go order yourself another one, lady," he exclaimed.

"This one's bought and paid for. Mr. Ives has come here to build a house for his wife, and he needs the stove."

Allyson backed away as though touched by something horrible. The man who had pushed at her was the very man who had shot Toby. She looked from him to Nolan Ives. "How much did you bribe the supplier to let you have my stove!"

Ives grinned. "Whoever ordered this stove, they never came for it."

"Look at the line! A *lot* of people haven't been able to get their supplies yet! The only reason you got that stove was because you probably paid twice what it's worth!"

"Give it up, little girl. Sell out to me now, and you won't lose much. You're a woman alone and barely a woman at that. You don't belong in a place like this." Ives turned away and left, walking alongside the others who led the oxen pulling the cart.

Allyson glanced up at the brute of a man who had stopped her. "You're a coward and a bully! Lower than an earthworm!" She turned away quickly so he would not see her tears, knowing he would only enjoy the sight and also knowing she was not going to get her stove from Nolan Ives. She trooped back to the supplier, shoving her way past others while she pulled money from her handbag. When she reached his table, she plunked down a wad of bills. "You get me another stove, and quick, or I swear I'll get my pistol and use it on you!"

Others grumbled about the way she had pushed her way to the front of the line, and the disgruntled supplier scowled at her. "Look, lady, if you want to order a stove, I'll place the order and put a rush on it. But I can't guarantee anything before five or six days."

"I can't wait that long! I need it *now!*"

"That's the best I can do! Take it or leave it!"

Allyson looked over at the cart in the distance, watching her precious stove roll toward the northern end of the tent city. Nolan Ives was riding on it, his big belly bouncing every time the cart hit a bump. He was still watching her, and she felt almost as though she had been physically attacked. She turned her attention back to the supplier. "Do you have any Dutch ovens?"

"Yes. I can sell you one."

"How kind of you," Allyson sneered. "I'll take *three!* And please fill the rest of this list the best you can." She handed him a piece of paper listing the items she needed. "Someone will be here shortly with a wagon to carry everything. And go ahead and order another stove! I'll pay you for the other things now and give you a down payment on the stove, and I want something in writing from you promising that I get the very first stove that comes through!"

The man's eyes glowered with rage. "Whatever you want, Missy." He began writing. "Why isn't your husband here to do this for you?"

"I don't *have* a husband! He was killed the first day of the land rush." Her voice broke on the words, and she said nothing more while the man continued writing.

He handed her the paper. "I'll need five dollars down on the stove. I'll figure up the other items once your list is filled."

Allyson rummaged through her handbag, handing the man the money. "Fine. I'll be back shortly." She picked up the order he had written out for her and turned away, hurrying back to her campfire, fighting tears all the way. She told herself she must not let this latest setback get her down. She would have to make do with the Dutch ovens. She had used them before, when she helped in the kitchen at the orphan-

age. Over an open campfire, she could still bake bread, as long as she could keep the fire going. If Nolan Ives thought **taking** her stove away was going to stop her, he had another **think** coming!

7

Inside the tent, Allyson wept into her bedroll with such intensity that her head and stomach ached. Thunder rolled in the distance and the rain came down harder, every drop that beat on the tent reminding her that she might not be able to realize her dream after all. Things could not have gone worse. Outside the heavens had opened up in a torrential rain that made it impossible to build a fire. Bread dough sat rising in her Dutch ovens, but there was no way to bake it. She had kneaded it twice already, separated it as it continued to rise, enough for several loaves. It would not be much longer before the air in the dough would be lost and everything would go to waste. At the moment she did not even have a way to chill it.

It seemed silly to cry over bread dough, but at the moment it seemed the most important thing in the world to her. If she'd had her iron stove, she could have had Ethan and some other men build a temporary shelter around it and could have kept it hot in spite of the rain. She could have baked bread and pies all night. She had made all the dough, even the pie dough, had peeled apples all day long. Then came the rain. The apples sat turning brown, and her big plans for starting to sell food tomorrow were dashed. The little tragedy seemed to have brought on a torrent of emotions, even made Toby's death more intensely painful again. She had been so determined not to give up, but now she wondered if maybe she should after all. Who was she, a city girl and soon to be only seventeen, a girl inexperienced in this kind of living, to think she could come here like these other rugged pioneers and make a go of it?

Lightning flashed, and thunder cracked loudly overhead, as though to tell of her fate. This was all she had. Somehow she had to make it work, but tonight she was just too tired and too disappointed to care. Tonight she needed to cry as she had not cried since Toby died; to feel sorry for herself; to rant and wail and physically feel her grief. Oh, how it hurt to remember seeing Nolan Ives taking that stove away.

"Ally?"

She sat up at the sound of her name.

"Let me in. It's pouring out here! I know you're crying."

Allyson recognized Ethan's voice. She untied the flaps and he ducked inside, removing a slicker and his hat and throwing them in a corner. The tent was big enough for at least four people, but not big enough for a man like Ethan to stand up. He remained bent over as he moved closer, then sat down near her.

"I couldn't sleep because of the storm. My damn tent is leaking. Besides, I couldn't stop thinking about you. I had to come by, knowing how disappointed you were about everything." He reached out hesitantly and touched her hair. "I could hear you crying even with all the rain and thunder."

All her inner warnings against anything more than a casual friendship with this man left her. Tonight she needed his company, needed to be held by someone stronger. She was tired of being strong all on her own. She had been doing that most of her life.

"Will you . . . hold me for a little while?"

Ethan gladly obliged. He put an arm around her and pulled her onto his lap, holding her close and letting her cry against his shoulder. He still wished he could kill Nolan Ives. "Hey, this isn't the Ally I know."

"I wanted . . . that stove so bad," she wept. "It isn't . . . fair."

He thought about how his mother had died, how Violet died, taking her baby with her. "A lot of things in life aren't fair, Ally, but we have to put up with them anyway. We just have to keep going."

Ally breathed deeply of the smell of him, a manly scent of leather and out-of-doors. Here was a man who didn't cry just because he didn't have a cookstove. Here was a man who knew how to get by on almost nothing, and tonight she needed his strength. "Thank you for coming," she whispered.

Ethan struggled against the urge to do much more than hold her. He had not been with a woman for a long time, and this one had haunted him since he met her. He wanted to hold her forever, wanted to take care of her. It had seemed impossible, but tonight she was so soft in his arms, so vulnerable. Maybe if he had the chance to show her the pleasures of being a woman . . .

He chastised himself for the thought. "You could use a shot of whiskey," he told her. "I have a small flask in my slicker. I think you should take a swallow. It will relax you and you can sleep. You haven't had enough rest for five or six days now, maybe longer. God knows it couldn't have been comfortable for you riding that orphan train."

He gently set her off his lap and moved to get the whiskey from his slicker.

"I've never drunk whiskey before," she answered, taking a handkerchief from under her pillow and wiping at her eyes and nose. Her slender shoulders shook in a lingering sob.

Ethan returned to sit beside her. "Well, one shot will cure

your crying," he told her. "The burning sensation will make you forget your troubles for a moment." He grinned, taking a cork from the small flask and swallowing some himself.

Allyson watched, wondering if tales she had heard about Indians and whiskey were true. Was she in danger, allowing herself to be alone in such close quarters with this dark, experienced, maybe dangerous man? She felt different tonight, a new longing in her soul to eradicate the child in her, the lingering, youthful innocence that made her vulnerable to men like Nolan Ives. She had noticed how tough some older women talked, mainly the prostitutes who plied their "wares" in the streets, hanging around the gambling tables. They seemed so strong, knew how to handle men, never seemed afraid. If she was more like them, maybe she could have gotten her stove back. Maybe there was some kind of secret to being a full woman that she didn't know about, something missing in her quest to be independent that she still hadn't learned, in spite of living in the streets of New York.

Ethan handed her the flask. "Take a quick gulp. Don't just taste it first or you'll be afraid to take a big swallow."

She watched his dark eyes. Was he trying to trick her? Seduce her? She had to be careful. Still, if she was going to make it on her own, she had to know about life, about men. Maybe they were able to take advantage of her because there was still something she didn't know about how to handle them, something the painted ladies of the streets seemed to fully understand. All she knew was that some men were cruel, like Henry Bartel and Nolan Ives; and some were totally good, like Toby. Ethan Temple was neither all good nor all bad, and one thing about him made him different from any of the others: he was Indian.

She took the flask from him, and with all the daring and

determination with which she did everything else, she tipped it up and took a huge swallow. Immediately she gagged and coughed, pounding at her chest and gasping for breath. Ethan laughed lightly. "What did I tell you? Kind of makes you forget your other troubles, doesn't it?"

She nodded, unable to talk. She reached for the bucket of drinking water she kept in the tent and dipped out a ladle full, quickly drinking it down to cool her throat. She took several deep breaths then, wondering how on earth some men could drink the stuff like water. "Ethan Temple," she finally gasped, "what are you doing with whiskey in Indian Territory? You know it's not allowed in Guthrie or anyplace else south of Kansas and north of Texas."

"Oh, I get around. Where there's a will, there's a way. I just don't generally let anybody know I've got it, especially my Indian friends or relatives. See how privileged and trusted you are? You're one of the few who knows I have any of this stuff on me." He took another swallow, then corked it. "Feel better?"

She watched him carefully. "How much does it take to get you drunk?"

He chuckled. "A hell of a lot more than two swallows. All that did was warm my bones against the cold rain." He studied her pretty face, glad to see she seemed to have forgotten some of her troubles already. "On the other hand, it wouldn't take much for a little thing like you who's never drunk any before."

Allyson felt a little light-headed, figuring it was because she had eaten hardly anything all day. She smiled. "You're right about it making you forget other things for the moment. Maybe I should have another swallow."

Ethan handed her the flask. He couldn't help wondering if a little more firewater might soften her up enough to awaken the woman in her. He knew damn well it was wrong, but he wanted her, and if this was the only way to have her, then so be it. Maybe with a little whiskey in her, she could get over the fear she felt for all men. Maybe once he showed her the pleasure of taking a man, she would realize they could and should be together. Maybe then she would forget this crazy idea of trying to make it alone. And maybe . . . just maybe . . . she would realize that she loved him, Indian or not.

He watched her take another swallow, followed by more choking and panting. He took the flask from her. "That's probably enough."

Allyson quickly drank a little more water, wondering why Ethan's smile looked more handsome than usual tonight. Was it because of the soft lantern light? She watched him remove his gunbelt, his boots. Why was he doing that? His hair was worn loose tonight, and she thought that if he were shirtless and painted, he would look like some warrior out of the books she had read and pictures she had seen about Indians. She leaned her head against his shoulder then. "What am I going to do, Ethan?"

He put an arm around her. "That's your decision. I told you before I'd take you to Fort Supply if you want to give this up. You'd be protected there until you decide what to do next."

She closed her eyes, suddenly feeling as though she was lightly floating. "I can't give in to somebody like Nolan Ives because of Toby, if for no other reason. I know it could work if I could just get started right. I've never given in to anybody in my whole life."

With his free hand, Ethan touched her small face. "Maybe it's time you did," he told her. "But not to Nolan Ives." He wondered why he had said the words, wondered why suddenly it all seemed so right when he knew damn well it wasn't. How else was he going to convince her to give this all up and let him take care of her, without showing her the wonders of being a woman? He had felt her attraction for him, knew she was fighting a battle on the inside over her feelings.

"I don't know what you mean," she answered.

He held her chin in his hand, gently forcing her to meet his eyes. "I think you do. Ever since that night I kissed you, you've been wondering about it, and I've been in near-pain wanting to kiss you again. You *do* have a power over men, Ally, and you don't even know it. If you were a full woman, you'd know what I'm talking about, and I can't stand the thought of any other man showing you the way but me."

She watched his eyes. Was he right? Would she discover some secret power if she gave in to the woman inside her that she held back only because of bad memories? Was it possible for one man to erase those memories and make them sweet? It was so hard to think straight, being so full of grief and disappointment . . . and feeling so strange from the whiskey. What had this man done to her? Was he just using her for his own fun tonight? Still, she thought maybe he was right that she needed to know all of it; and at the moment he was also right that there was no one else who could show her but him. He had been so good to her, protected her, helped her, defended her . . . "Ethan, I don't—"

Her words were cut off by his kiss, a deep, sweet, warm kiss that awakened an intense curiosity in her soul and made her return the kiss willingly. She remembered she had liked it when he parted her lips that first time he kissed her. This time she opened them willingly, and she felt Ethan laying her back onto the bedroll, yet she didn't really feel like she was there at all. It seemed they were floating gently, and where she would normally have demanded that he stop, she could not bring herself to utter a word.

"I think I love you, Ally Mills," he said softly, moving his lips to her neck. Slowly his hand moved to a breast, only this time she did not feel the horror she had felt the first time. He squeezed it gently, and through the thin cotton material of her dress and chemise, she could actually feel her nipple tingle. He kept moving his thumb over it, and fire seemed to sweep through her at his touch. "It's all right," he assured her, moving down to kiss her breast. The new touch made her gasp his name, and to her own astonishment, she lay still while he unbuttoned the front of her dress. He moved his hand inside, under her chemise. He touched her naked breast, gently fondling it while he found her lips again, kissing her savagely.

Allyson felt breathless, helpless. Never had she been this curious to know it all, to learn the secret of these womanly powers she was sure she would possess if she was fully awakened to a man. She breathed his name in deep sighs as he moved his lips to her breast then, tasting gently while he moved his hand down under her dress and up along her leg. Bad memories again flickered in her mind; but this time they were very dim, and she did not feel the compulsion to stop this man. There was a deeper need now, a terrible curiosity that had suddenly become more vivid.

She stared at the top of the tent, feeling as though she was lost in some magical dream from which she dared not awaken, not yet. She listened to the rain pelting against the tent and she felt lost in a world she'd never known, Ethan Temple's world of danger and wildness. Why couldn't she stop him? Had he somehow tricked her? Never had a man touched her like this without her feeling revulsion and fear. She tried to clear her mind, tried to determine if Ethan had just pulled off her bloomers, or if it was just her imagination. She could feel his hands, yet it was as though they were not touching her at all.

No! This was wrong! He was touching her in that secret place she had vowed no man would ever touch! A boy in the streets had tried that once when she was little, and it had frightened and shamed her. He would have done even more terrible things if Toby hadn't come along and beat on him. Now here she was letting this Indian man she had only known a few days do the same to her, only it was somehow different. He was touching her in a way that made her whisper his name, made her want to let him touch her more. His fingers worked in magical circles, while he smothered her mouth again in a hungry kiss, so gentle yet so intimate. Suddenly all the curiosity and wonder at being woman came to a rush of desire and need unlike anything she had ever known, and something new and powerful moved through her loins so that she felt muscles pulling and could not keep from groaning Ethan's name and arching up against his hand.

What had he done to her? And what did he think of her *letting* him do these things?

"Give it up, Ally. Marry me and let me take care of you." He was licking at her neck, moving on top of her. "We've both been fighting it, but we know it's the right thing to do."

He met her mouth again, his hands moving down to grasp her bottom. Something hard probed between her legs. No! Henry Bartel had shown her his ugly manpart once, had forced her to the floor in a utility closet and tried to do something horrible to her. She had hit him with a can of powdered soap and screamed bloody murder, had gotten him into a lot of trouble. It took a long time to get over that nightmare and the sick feeling it had left in her stomach. He had meant to stick that ugly thing into her, and she had decided then and there that no man would ever do that.

Yet here was Ethan, so handsome, so kind to her, so helpful and protective. He'd said he loved her, hadn't he? Did he really mean it, or was he just another Henry Bartel in different clothing, using a different approach to get himself into her? No! She wasn't ready for this! She didn't want to know yet. It was too frightening, too ugly. "Wait," she whimpered.

Ethan did not seem to hear. In the next moment she felt the terrifying pain, realized in that quick second what he had done. To this point the whiskey had dulled her senses, but it did not take away the reality of what had just happened to her. She felt a fire between her legs, felt the terror of Henry Bartel all over again. She pushed at Ethan, beginning to panic. What had she done? She had gone against every rule she had set for herself. He had poured his whiskey into her as a way of doing dirty things. Surely he was no different from Mr. Bartel. She began gasping in protest, beating at his face.

Ethan was taken by surprise. He had thought she was ready for this, wanted it. He had moved slowly and gently, had relaxed her first with whiskey, fondled her until she had reached a sweet climax. She had seemed so willing, but before he had a chance to find his own relief, she was fighting him as though she was being raped! He quickly lost his penetration, achieving only a partial climax before he found himself having to hold her down and keep a hand over her mouth before she let everyone nearby think she was being attacked. "Stop it!" he commanded. "What the hell is wrong with you?"

He ducked a fist, managing to get both her wrists into one powerful hand while keeping his full weight on her and his other hand clamped over her mouth. "Ally, it's all right. I didn't come in here to hurt you. Please don't do this."

She whimpered through her nose, and tears began to spill out of her eyes.

"Ally, I love you. Do you believe that?"

She shook her head, and he kept a firm hold on her.

"Why? All I've done is help you, protect you. Tonight I just wanted to make love to you, show you what it's like to be a woman. I thought we could overcome our differences, and that I could teach you that being with a man isn't always a bad thing. I haven't tricked you or tried to hurt you, Ally."

She squeezed her eyes shut and began crying harder. Ethan wished there was a way to kick himself for thinking she was ready for this, for taking advantage of her vulnerability. What could he have been thinking? He had let her drink whiskey. Now she would think he had only done it to break down her inhibitions. "Ally, please listen to me. You can't scream if I take my hand from your mouth, understand?" She just stared at him. "If you feel anything for me at all, don't scream. If men come and find me in here with you, me being Indian and all, they'll think the worst, and they're likely to string me up. At the least, they'd beat the hell out of me and I'd be hauled off to Fort Supply under arrest. Is that what you want?"

She stared at him for several silent seconds, then shook her head again. Ethan carefully removed his hand from her mouth, and she gasped, more tears coming. "Please get off of me," she whimpered.

Ethan let go of her hesitantly, keeping a close eye on her as he gradually moved away. He got to his knees then, turning around to adjust his longjohns and denim pants, which he had only opened at the buttons. He had not intended to do any of this when he came in here, but once he held her in his arms, the way she had relaxed against him . . . He meant only to get the painful part over with tonight, to move gradually with her. He figured if he had tried to get her completely out of her clothes and do even more intimate things, she would most certainly have gotten frightened and would have protested. He thought after tonight it could all be different between them, new and wonderful, but there she sat, shivering and sobbing.

"Please get out," she groaned. "I don't know . . . what happened to me. You tricked me . . . with the whiskey."

"Ally, I didn't trick you. I only wanted you to relax."

"You wanted the same thing all men want, and you'll never do that to me again! It hurts!"

"Of *course* it hurts. It usually does the first time, but most women don't cry about it. After a few times it begins to feel as good for the woman as the man. How in hell do you think women have five and six and eight children? They don't get pregnant by a kiss on the cheek. They get pregnant out of passion and love, out of allowing their husbands to—"

"I don't want to hear it!" She put her hands to her temples. "My head is spinning. You . . . you tricked me somehow. You're no different from the boys in the streets of New York . . . when I was little . . . and Henry Bartel and—"

Ethan grasped her arms. "I am *not* like them and you damn well know it! I just wanted to love you. What the hell is wrong with that?"

She studied his dark eyes. Where had her reasoning gone? He was Indian! She had let an Indian man touch her intimately, put himself into her body. Quickly she pulled her chemise and dress back over her breast, only then realizing it was still exposed. Oh, the shame of it! "Get out!" she sobbed. "You're the same! You're all the same!"

"Goddamn it, Ally, I *love* you! I want to marry you. I'm not trying to hurt you!"

She scooted away from him, pulling a blanket over herself. Deep inside a little part of her wanted to believe him, wanted to try again; but the memories were too ugly, and she was tired of being looked at as some helpless thing a man could use however he wanted. "I don't want this," she told him, her eyes wide, her body shaking. "Besides, you're . . . you're *Indian!* It isn't right."

Why had she said that? For some reason she suddenly wanted to hurt him, and since she couldn't do it physically, she would do it verbally; but the look in his dark eyes! At first it was hurt, then they showed a fierce pride. He said absolutely nothing. He simply turned away and pulled on his boots. A little voice deep inside told Allyson to apologize, but another voice told her to keep silent. She had found the best way to get rid of him, and so be it. She was not some sniveling, weak female who was going to be defeated by men like Nolan Ives; nor was someone like Ethan Temple going to talk her out of having something of her very own. She didn't need taking care of, and she didn't need some man sticking himself into her every night just to get his pleasure. He had brought the whiskey, used it to take advantage of her. Maybe it was a different approach than someone like Henry Bartel would use, but the result was the same. He deserved to be hurt, didn't he?

She watched him grab his slicker, gun, and hat. "Ethan—" He did not turn around or reply. He only strapped on his gun, then crouched through the entrance to the tent and disappeared into the rainy night.

Allyson slept fitfully, all kinds of visions parading through her head as the whiskey played games with her dreams. Sometimes Henry Bartel appeared, leering at her, touching her, making her want to scream. Then his face would become that of Nolan Ives. The man was laughing at her, his fat chin and jelly stomach jiggling, his eyes telling her she had better be afraid. Toby was in those dreams somewhere, calling for help. And then two Indian men appeared, one looking evil, a painted warrior who threatened to plant his tomahawk in her belly; the other was handsome, gentle, reaching out to comfort her. She wanted to go to him, but her feet seemed to be caught in clay. They would not move.

Throughout the night the dreams plagued her, interrupted only by fits of wakefulness, when she was sure she was not sleeping, yet she could not quite grasp her surroundings or get up. When she was awake she thought she heard voices, men talking close by, strange noises. She was subconsciously aware that it had stopped raining, then finally came more fully awake to realize it was morning.

She sat up, looking around the tent. Was last night real? Had Ethan really been here, tried to make love to her? She looked down to realize she still had a dress on, but all the buttons down the front were undone. "Dear God," she whispered. She carefully opened it to see her chemise untied at the front. Yes, Ethan Temple *had* been here. He really *had* touched her breast, tasted it. She looked to see her bloomers lying off to the side of her bedroll, and she put her head in her hands. What had she done?

She felt sick and her head ached, and right now she hated Ethan Temple for giving her the whiskey. One thing was sure, she was never drinking any of that stuff again! Why men liked it, she would never understand. She only knew that Ethan had used it to try to get his way with her, and she would never forgive him for it. Then again, she recalled that at first the things he did to her had felt more wonderful than she ever imagined such a thing could feel. He had told her he loved her, hadn't he? He'd said he'd marry her. Were the words just a ploy to get what he wanted? Maybe not. Now she remembered the hurt in his eyes when she called him an Indian, in a tone to imply that no white woman in her right mind would let an Indian man touch her. She remembered he had left without another word. Her remark had cut deep, but then he had hurt her, hadn't he? He had tried to do that ugly thing to her. He *had* done it! She still felt an aching sting in private places, and her mind raced with confusion over how right or wrong it had been to give herself to Ethan Temple.

She quickly changed and washed, frightened by the sight of blood on her inner thighs. What kind of terrible thing had that Indian done to her? Was it supposed to be like this? Was she injured? Would she die? She wished she knew one of the women around here well enough to ask if it was supposed to be this way, but even if she could ask, what would they think of her, drinking whiskey with an Indian, letting him get between her legs? She longed for another hot bath, but for now she would just have to wash herself. She pulled on clean bloomers, telling herself that she was glad she had hurt Ethan and chased him off. It served him right for injuring her like this.

She didn't need any man "taking care" of her, expecting recompense in the form of letting him have sex with her whenever he wanted. She had plans of her own, and she could do it alone. It had apparently stopped raining. Maybe she could salvage some of her bread dough, build a fire, and get some of her baking done today. She had to do something, anything, to stay busy and try to forget about last night. If Ethan came around, she would tell him exactly what she thought of him, and that she no longer needed him. He could go on back to Fort Supply or go see his father or whatever it was he needed to do. He had tricked her, used her, injured her. She no longer wanted to be his friend or anything else!

She rinsed her mouth and put on clean clothes, rolled up a blanket that showed more blood stains, wondering when she was going to find time to scrub her laundry. There was so much for an independent woman to do. She brushed her hair and tied it into a tail, then put a bib apron over her head and tied it at the back. She could see the sun filtering through the cracks in the tent opening, could hear the bustling sounds of a town awakening to another day. That was just what this was—another day—another beginning. Last night was behind her—forever.

She emerged from the tent to a warm spring morning. She breathed deeply of the fresh air, and she realized that she felt very different. Was it because she was a woman now? One thing was sure, she knew now how all men thought, what they all wanted. Now she understood the power a woman held. All a man needed was a hint of a promise that he could get between her legs, and he would do anything for her. She would learn how to use that power.

She turned then to notice there was another tent beside her own, a bigger one. A stovepipe was sticking through the top of it. Who had dared to put up a tent on her lot? She rushed over to it, charged inside. To her surprise, a cast iron stove sat in the center of the tent, not the new one she had wanted to buy the day before, but a good one, nonetheless. It was very warm inside, and she realized the stove was already lit. "What on earth?" She hurried to open a feed door beneath one of the ovens, to see red-hot coals glowing underneath. A coal scuttle sat nearby, loaded to the top with more coal. On it lay a note. She picked it up and unfolded the sheet of paper.

Ally, it read. *The stove is yours. Got it from another couple who was heading back to Missouri and didn't want the extra weight. If this is what it takes to make you happy, then I wish you all the best. By the time you read this, I'll be gone. I'm sorry if I frightened or hurt you. I only meant to love you. If I never see you again, I have to admit I'll never forget Ally Mills, and I hope you'll keep the good memories about this Indian and not the bad ones. You have too many bad memories already. Hold on to your dreams, Ally, and don't let Nolan Ives or anybody else stop you. Ethan.*

Allyson felt an odd sense of loss. This was what she had wanted, wasn't it? Why did she feel so sad and empty? She had hurt him so deeply, yet he had gone to all the trouble and expense of finding a stove for her. This must be the reason for the voices and noise she thought she heard last night. Her eyes teared as she studied the stove, part of her feeling joyous at having it, another part of her wanting to run out and find Ethan and beg his forgiveness for her cruel words; but she knew that he was probably already many miles away. After what she had done and said last night, she wouldn't blame him if he never came back. She remembered that look of fierce pride in his eyes when he left.

Now the tears began to slip down her cheeks, and she was filled with a new kind of grief. "Ethan," she whispered. She folded the letter and shoved it into a pocket of her dress, wiping angrily at her tears. He was gone, and that was the end of it. How strange it all felt, to have given herself intimately to a man who was now like a ghost to her.

Several short blasts from a train whistle nearby startled her, and she straightened, quickly wiping at her tears. This was no time for crying. She hurried back to her own tent to see about salvaging bread dough from the day before. She had a business to build, and all other things—grief, love, her own emotional state . . . and Ethan Temple . . . had to be put aside. There were more important matters at hand.

8

Allyson joined the crowd of thousands who were headed for the gathering on a hill east of the Santa Fe station house. Today was the first official town meeting, called by men who already considered themselves leaders of the new city of Guthrie. Decisions had to be made, since the estimated ten thousand settlers had spread out well beyond the allotted 320-acre town site. Boundaries had to be drawn, leaders had to be chosen, laws had to be made.

Because of her size, it was difficult for Allyson to see above the men, and she was one of few women present. Men who knew her and frequented her establishment helped walk her to the front of the crowd, where she saw that Nolan Ives was one of the men in charge of the meeting. She quickly shrank back enough to avoid his attention, and she worried what kind of rules he would devise that might help him get her property. She did not doubt his promise that he was not through trying to get hold of her land.

She was becoming more confident that that could never happen. She had been right about the power that could be gained from being a pretty woman in need of a man's help, especially a supposed widow. The progress she had made in the ten days she had been here was phenomenal. Once men began buying bread from her, and sampling her cooking, they began gathering around her like flies, almost stumbling over each other to help her in any way they could. Already a wooden building that would house her restaurant was nearly finished, most of the lumber donated, all of the labor free. A lot of the single men in town appreciated being able to enjoy "woman-cooked" food, and they were willing to do whatever it took to keep her in business.

On every street there were already other buildings, many of them finished, housing liveries, hotels, banks, lawyers' offices, supply stores, every kind of business imaginable. At an astounding rate, tents had been replaced by wooden structures, and Guthrie was a real town now. All that was left was to bring in law and order, decide on a sewer and water system, and settle some still-lingering arguments over ownership of town lots. She still worried that Nolan Ives might challenge her in that respect, but each day that he left her alone, she was more sure she was safe.

Besides that, she was making good money, which made her feel even more relaxed. Single men were willing to pay ridiculous prices for hot meals. Trains brought in fresh meat and produce, as well as blocks of ice. She had an ice box now, and was able to store more food and expand her menus. She had bought herself more "respectable" clothing, careful to keep her wardrobe in dark colors for the time being. After all, she was still a grieving widow. She wore her plainer dresses when she was working over a hot stove, but had more elegant dresses for occasions like today, hoping they made her appear a little older and more confident.

She pushed away the thought of the pretty blue dress with yellow flowers Ethan had bought her. It was still wrapped and untouched. She had not been able to look at it since he left. She forced back the pain it brought her to think about him, and she reminded herself she was doing just fine without him. She had even bought a second stove, and had hired an old man and a woman who had been recently widowed to help her with the work. The woman had lost her husband in the land rush when their wagon overturned and crushed him. They had sold everything back in Kansas, and she had no choice but to stay in Guthrie.

Overnight the little watering hole called Guthrie had turned into a city of ten thousand. The smell of fresh lumber filled the air. She had plans to build a rooming house around her restaurant, where travelers could get a room for a night, or citizens without a home could live for longer periods. With the money she was bringing in, and the constantly-growing business she gained from being near the railroad depot, in no time at all she should have enough to start expanding. If she wanted to build even sooner, a banker in town, Harvey Bloomfield, would probably loan her anything she wanted. Every time she came into the bank, he scrambled to please her.

It was amusing to think how easily she could use her feminine wiles to get what she needed, and she didn't even have to do those other ugly things to get it. She only had to let the men fantasize about doing them, while keeping her distance and an air of dignity. Being recently "widowed" helped keep the men at bay. She was glad none of them knew what she had let Ethan Temple do to her. She had not let herself think about it too much, part of her feeling ashamed, another part wondering if she had lost something precious in letting Ethan ride out of her life. He had awakened something in her that left her restless, left her feeling confused about her role as a woman, but she had convinced herself that Ethan's leaving was the best thing for both of them. The memory of Ethan Temple would eventually fade into the past.

Several men scrambled to find a crate for her to stand on

so she could see better, but the commotion, and the fact that she was as tall or taller than the others when she got on the crate, attracted Nolan Ives's attention, which she had been trying to avoid. Now that she had come to his attention, she decided to face the man squarely and show no signs of being at all intimidated. She was well aware he had already set up law offices in Guthrie, was building the biggest home around just outside of town, and was buying up all the town lots he could, offering the owners more money than they could resist.

You won't get my lots, Mr. Nolan Ives, she thought. *Not for any price!* She would never sell, for to her it was an insult to Toby. Besides, not only did her idea have the potential for great financial gain, but she took great pride in knowing she was succeeding all on her own, and she was barely seventeen! She remembered reading in a newspaper once back in New York about the Great American West being the land of opportunity. Now she knew what that meant. Her only regret was that Toby had had to die. It still hurt terribly to think of her brother or visit his grave.

She took a deep breath and gave her attention to what was taking place in front of her, as one of the men in charge shouted for everyone to quiet down, a difficult task with so many people gathered. Another man, introduced as Charles W. Constantine, an ex-mayor of Springfield, Ohio, climbed into a wagon and stood in its bed so he could be seen by the crowd. It was announced that he would preside over the meeting. A Reverend Robert Hill from Oregon would take notes and act as secretary.

Mr. Constantine announced that at least thirty states were represented in the crowd, but most were from the neighboring state of Kansas. A huge, roaring cheer went up from those from Kansas. People began shouting out the names of other states. Michigan! Indiana! Wisconsin! Texas! Mississippi! Georgia! Ohio! Constantine allowed them a few moments to out-shout each other, then commanded the crowd to try to quiet down so they could take care of matters at hand.

"Well, now you're in a new territory," the man yelled. "And once all these new settlements get organized, like Oklahoma City and Kingfisher, we can all come together and make this territory a new state, one of the last frontiers in America, and you're all a part of it!"

Again the crowd cheered. Allyson found herself cheering with them, caught up in the excitement of the day. Constantine reviewed decisions those in charge of the meeting had made, asking for "yes" or "no" votes from the crowd. Nolan Ives joined Constantine in the wagon then, helped up by two other men because of his obese condition. Once situated, he smoothed his silk suit and took a moment to look directly at Allyson.

"We are all aware that there are *some* among you who conveniently arrived here *before* noon on the twenty-second," he shouted. A round of "boo's" moved through the crowd, along with some name-calling. Allyson refused to cringe. She knew there were some who had their doubts about how she managed to claim two such choice town lots, but after her "husband" was killed before her eyes, and the respected scout, Ethan Temple, swore she had come there legally, no one but Ives had given her any trouble.

"They know who they are," Ives continued. "At first we called them Moonshiners; lately I've heard them called Sooners. We have proven some of those cases and tossed them out of Guthrie on their ears."

At that remark the crowd cheered, and it took a few moments again to quiet them down.

"Because original townsite plans the government drew up

favor the Sooners," Ives continued, "we have decided to extend Guthrie proper to the east for two blocks from the land office to a street we will call Division Street. The city will be expanded to the west by five blocks to Seventh Street, in the bend of Cottonwood Creek."

"Do we hear a vote of approval on this decision?" Charles Constantine asked.

An obvious majority approved by raising their fists and shouting "yes."

Ives announced that he was ready to make low-interest loans to anyone who needed to borrow money to expand their businesses, "but only those who can prove they are not Sooners," he added, again glancing at Allyson.

I don't need your dirty money, Allyson thought. Harvey Bloomfield would loan her anything she wanted, and he wouldn't ask her to prove a thing.

Charles Constantine announced it had already been decided that each town lot would be twenty-five feet wide by one-hundred-forty feet deep, streets eighty feet wide, alleys twenty feet. Nominations were taken to elect representatives who would select a corps of engineers to draw up a finalized plan to be approved by the Department of the Interior. Then came more nominations, to elect a full slate of city officials. Candidates would have to be able to prove they had entered the district legally, and the general public would vote on their favorites.

It was obvious the voting would last through the day and perhaps longer, so Allyson finally left to see to her business. Although she had closed her little restaurant for the day, there was much to do to get ready for tomorrow—more bread to bake, potatoes to peel. The work never ended, but it all belonged to her, and that made the back-breaking work easier.

She walked to her property, stood back, and studied the

new sign in front of the nearly-finished restaurant, which she had already decided would have checkered tablecloths and curtains to match. The sign read *Ally's Place*. It was all just like she had envisioned, and now that Guthrie was getting organized, it was bound to grow and thrive at an even faster rate. Those like herself, who were here at the beginning, could only profit from that. She just wished Toby were here to see what was happening and enjoy this with her.

"I'm sorry I have to lie about you being my husband, Toby," she whispered into the darkness. A sharp pain moved through her chest as the picture of her dead brother lying in her lap flashed through her mind. He had died so quickly, there had not even been time to say good-bye or tell him she loved him.

Another heavy pain gripped her. There was someone else to whom she had not had the chance to say good-bye . . . or express her love. *Was* it love she had sometimes felt for Ethan Temple? She supposed it was useless to wonder. He was gone. She had grown accustomed to finding out she couldn't trust anyone, and to losing things she loved. This new life, this business that she owned all on her own, this was something she was determined she would never lose, and she didn't have to worry about waking up some morning to find it gone.

"Hello, Pa," Ethan said as he walked into the bedroom where his father lay dying. He had been surprised to find out how sick the man had been. None of these white relatives of his had written to tell him. He was furious at the thought that his father could have died before he ever got to see him again. It was obvious why he had not been told. His paternal aunt, Claudia, and her husband, John Temple, his father's brother, did not want their "Indian" nephew coming to town and embarrassing them. That was clear enough from the cool greeting he got from his aunt and uncle when he arrived in Springfield.

His Aunt Claudia had become terribly flustered, even looked a little bit afraid when she first greeted him. She had made up excuses as to why there just wasn't room for him to sleep in the house—would he mind sleeping in the barn? If his father were not so ill, he would tell these people what he really thought of them. Apparently they thought he lived like the wilder Indians of old, figured sleeping in a barn would be just fine for him. Now every bone ached from the cold. Here it was December, and freezing cold at night, and he was relegated to a horse stall. He didn't mind camping out at night on the cold ground when his job called for it, but these were relatives. They could at least have offered to let him sleep on the floor in front of the wood stove.

His treatment had only made the memory of that night with Ally more painful for him, her words more biting. *You're Indian! It isn't right.* Maybe she was right after all, but after eight months away from her, he still could not stop thinking about her. And he had not stopped loving her, even though he sometimes wished he could give her a good shaking. If she would just have given him the chance, he could have shown her the pleasures of being a woman, the joys of love. Why did she have to be so damn stubborn? And why did she have to spout those words as though being Indian meant something horrible? He figured it was probably just fear lashing out, but the words stung, just the same.

To hell with her, he told himself. When was this battle over his feelings for her and the temptation to go back to Guthrie going to end? Maybe it would help being here with his father. God knew, the shape Lucas Temple was in, he was needed. He decided not to tell the man how the family had treated him. If Lucas were not so near death, he would get a hotel room in town, but the condition in which he had found the man made Ethan afraid to leave for more than a few minutes at a time. He stared down at a withered body that was slowly wasting away because of a disease the doctor called cancer. Lucas looked up at his son with no hint of recognition in his hollow eyes at first. Then he broke into a grin.

"You're . . . back," he muttered.

"Of course I'm back. Did you think after visiting you yesterday I was just going to leave? I'm here for as long as you need me."

Lucas reached out and Ethan took his hand. "You're a good son, Ethan. I should have stayed out there . . . with you; but you were so busy with . . . your army work. You wouldn't . . . have been able to take care of me."

"I would have found a way if you had just told me you were getting sick. I didn't know that's why you came back here, Pa."

The man watched him sadly. "I should have let myself die . . . the Indian way . . . just walked out into the wilderness with my blanket . . . and sat down and just waited for death to come. This is . . . no good here. I don't belong here anymore . . . but they're my people, just like the Cheyenne are yours."

Ethan squeezed his hand. "I'm half white, too, you know."

The old man managed a weak smile. "Only about ten per cent . . . in your heart." He stopped to cough, a deep, raspy, threatening cough that made Ethan feel sick inside. "You . . . do something for me . . . will you?"

"Whatever you want."

"You be sure to visit your relatives . . . up in the Dakotas . . . Sky Dancing Woman, Big Hands. They should know how you are . . . what has happened to me. I fear your grandmother . . . is also dying. Go and see her. Your mother would have liked that."

"I promise. I had planned on going anyway. I need to stay away from Oklahoma Territory for a while longer. Too many people, a lot more trouble. I spent the spring helping watch over the land rush when they opened more Indian lands south of the Cherokee Outlet, then spent the rest of the summer watching over the cattle trail along Deep Creek. I'm just glad I decided to come and see you when I did. I'm sorry I didn't come sooner. I didn't know you were so sick. Nobody told me."

The older man's eyes showed a spark of anger in spite of his health. "That brother of mine . . . he's so damned religious . . . if that's what you can call it. He thinks I'm a terrible sinner . . . for marrying your mother. Thinks our marriage . . . wasn't legitimate simply because I married an Indian woman. I should have known better than to come back here; but I . . . got a lot sicker after that . . . and I just never left. At least . . . John and Claudia have taken good care of me."

"Well, now *I'm* here. I'll take care of you myself, relieve Aunt Claudia."

"You don't have to stay, son. I know . . . how she's probably treating you. I know what she's like."

Ethan forced a smile. "I've known prejudice before, Pa. It's nothing new. It's just that I don't understand how people can behave like that and still call themselves Christians." Again he felt the dull ache in his heart at Allyson's cruel words.

Lucas took as deep a breath as he could, and it pained

Ethan to see his father this way. This man was once tall and broad and robust. Ethan got his build from his father, whose own ancestors had been German and English.

"Tell me . . . about the land rush, son. It must . . . have been something to see."

Ethan grinned, realizing how much his father would have loved to have been there. "It was really something," he answered. "You never heard such a rumble in your life as opening day. Right at twelve o'clock soldiers fired their guns and thousands of people who were gathered around the borders took off in every kind of wheeled contraption you can imagine, some just riding horses, some on foot, others coming in by rail. It was a real circus—fights, yelling, even gunplay." He thought about Toby and felt a pain in his chest. "Some even got killed fighting over who claimed which lots first. I'll probably never see anything like it again. That little watering hole called Guthrie turned into a city of about ten thousand people overnight. Can you believe it?"

In spite of his pain, Lucas grinned. "When it comes to my white relatives . . . I can believe anything. Mention free land, free anything . . . and they're stampeding like a herd of stallions after one mare."

Ethan sighed and let go of the man's hand, leaning back in the chair he had pulled up beside the bed. "Well, I guess in some respects you have to admire their determination. There was this one young couple, sister and brother, who passed themselves off as husband and wife because they figured being married would make it easier to claim their lots—even had to lie about their age." He went on to tell his father about Allyson and Toby Mills, wondering why he felt so compelled to talk about them, as though doing so would ease the fact that he deeply missed Ally. When he finished, his father frowned.

"Why do I get the feeling you . . . took a special liking to the woman?"

Ethan tried to shrug off the remark. "I did, but only because she's hardly more than a kid and had to continue on alone. I didn't have much choice but to leave. I've worried about her ever since."

"Ethan . . . Ethan," Lucas said chidingly. "You did not . . . have to leave. You are not obligated to the army. You could have . . . stayed there and got a job for a while just to keep an eye on her. I am thinking . . . maybe you left because you were beginning . . . to care a little too much for the woman. Right?"

Ethan rose and walked to look out a window. Two of his young cousins, Annabelle and Elizabeth, still lived at home and were feeding some chickens while his Uncle Tom mended a broken barn door. He knew part of the reason he was asked to sleep in the barn was because his aunt did not want him sleeping in the house with two pretty girls. She didn't have to say it; he just knew it inside. Just because he was Indian, she supposed he must surely be attracted to white girls, even his own cousins! "You know how it is, Pa. I'm half white, but I don't look much like it. It's not that she was especially prejudiced. We were good friends, nothing more. I just figured it wasn't worth pushing. Besides, she's still practically a kid."

"Your mother was fifteen when . . . I married her. We were happy."

"Well, it is also a case of a white man marrying an Indian woman. That's been pretty much accepted by most. An Indian man and a white woman is a different matter."

"You're half white and well educated. I . . . don't know if I would give up so easily. You need to settle, Ethan . . . have a family. I know my son, and I can tell you cared about this

Ally Mills. Maybe she cared about you . . . more than she let on. That life was all new to her . . . and she had just lost her brother. She was confused. Maybe if you went back now, she would be . . . better able to know what she wants. You at least . . . should go back to see how she is getting along. At least . . . put your mind at ease in that respect."

Ethan came back to sit down beside the bed. "Don't think I haven't thought about it, but she made it pretty clear that she didn't think it was right for a white woman to be with an Indian man." *I love her, Pa*, he thought.

Lucas studied his handsome son, sad at seeing him torn between two worlds. "How could any woman . . . Indian or white . . . not love you? You're a good man, Ethan. Don't let yourself . . . drift forever, son. Find yourself a good woman again . . . Indian or white . . . whatever."

Ethan rose and leaned over him. "Pa, don't be worrying about me. You know damn well I can take care of myself. Let's just concentrate on taking care of you."

Lucas's eyes teared. "There isn't much time to worry about that, son. I'm just so glad you're . . . here. I was afraid . . . I wouldn't see you again before I take my last breath." His eyes closed as weariness took over. Ethan stood holding his hand until it appeared the man had fallen asleep. He left him then to go back to the window. He watched Annabelle and Elizabeth and thought about Ally, who was nearly the same age as Annabelle. Allyson would be seventeen now. That meant that next spring she would be eighteen. Maybe by then she would be more ready to open up to the woman inside, but then maybe that woman wanted nothing to do with an Indian man. Or maybe she had already found some other man. Common sense told him just to stay away for good, but a keen desire to see her once more, to be sure she was all right and to see if maybe by some miracle she had changed her mind, told him he had to go back to Guthrie in spite of fearing he was a fool to do so. He had intended to talk his father into returning with him, but that would be impossible now. Lucas Temple was dying, and the only relatives Ethan would have left that he cared about were Indian. Since he was not totally a part of that life anymore either, he wondered just where he did belong now. An aching loneliness swept through him, and he glanced back at his dying father.

"Sleep well, Pa," he said softly.

9

Allyson lay listening to the ticking of her new mantel clock. It rested on her cherrywood library table, where an oil lamp cast its dim glow on the gold-edged face of the clock. She liked watching it. She took pleasure in the fact that she was slowly accumulating fine things. Right now it might only be a few possessions in one small room, but some day she would have a real house of her own. For now, this room near the kitchen was all she needed. She had put lovely lace curtains to the window, a woven Oriental rug on the floor, and her new dresses hung in an oak wardrobe. A little room off the bedroom contained a night table with a porcelain wash bowl and a chamber pot.

She could hardly believe how far she had come in just eleven months—she would be eighteen on her birthday in May, only two months away. She had three women working for her, helping her take care of a restaurant that seated thirty people, and two months ago an adjoining boarding house had been completed, thanks to a loan from Harvey Bloomfield. A good deal of free labor, she noted, had been provided by several single men who were hoping that Guthrie's lonely young widow would soon be looking for a new husband.

And wouldn't they love to marry a rich woman, she thought smugly. She had no interest in any of them, only in the continuing progress of her business. It had not been easy to keep going, after men like Nolan Ives and others in charge had imposed occupation taxes in order to bring water, sewer, and lighting systems to the town. Work had already begun on all three, but it was costing business owners anywhere from ten to seventy-five dollars a month! Her own tax was fifty dollars a month. Word was, Indian Territory would soon be officially called Oklahoma Territory, at which time saloons would be allowed to operate. The men of Guthrie couldn't stop talking about it, always complaining about the unavailability of good whiskey. Right now the only drink they could have was somethng called "hop-tea," which looked like beer but "tasted like slop," most said.

Allyson had never bothered tasting it. Since that night with Ethan, she wanted nothing to do with liquor. She had thought she could easily forget that night, once Ethan left for good, but the memory would not go away. Nor would this restless, vague need she had felt ever since, a feeling that something had been left unfinished. Sometimes she could see Ethan's face as clearly as if he were lying beside her, and the strange part was, sometimes she wished he *was* lying next to her. In spite of the pain he had brought her that night he left, she could also remember the sweet pleasure she felt at returning his kisses, the exciting, pleasurable surge of desire he had forced out of her when he touched her so magically in that private place. Sometimes she wanted to feel that way again, to understand what he had done to her. She could not imagine letting any of these other men touch her, or even kiss her, but it had been so easy with Ethan.

She turned over in bed, in an effort to shake away her thoughts. It was useless to think about a man who was never coming back and who had just used her anyway. Yes, she had hurt him, but he had hurt her, too. She just wished sometimes he would come back just to see how well she had done. She wished everyone she had ever known, especially everyone who had ever abused her, could see her now.

A wagon clattered past, and she thought how much quieter and more organized Guthrie was now. The streets had finally been cleared of gamblers who had squatted throughout the town and caused noise and disruption, pitching their tents right in the middle of the streets. That problem had been solved in two ways. A team of men had chained mules to two huge logs dragged up from Cottonwood Creek. The logs were as long as the streets were wide, and the men, well armed, had proceeded to drag the logs right down the streets of Guthrie, warning squatters that they had better clear out or the logs would smash right over their tents and gaming tables, and any people who might be inside. After that, huge fines were imposed on anyone who dared to reopen for business in the streets after they had been cleared. It had been Guthrie's way of handling a problem that the army would not help them with.

Guthrie had a full city council in charge now, and many laws had been passed to protect public morality and good order, laws that were strictly enforced. Allyson had breathed a tremendous sigh of relief when Nolan Ives had finally gone back to Chicago seven months ago, but she had seen him again today. He was back, and had reopened his law office. This time he had brought his wife with him. That was why she was having trouble sleeping. She still worried that Ives would drag her before the board of arbitration that adjudicated continued disputes over lot ownership. She knew Ives had those men in his pocket. If he wanted, he could open a case against her and drag her all the way to the federal court at Muskogee. He had the money to do it, but she didn't have extra to spend on getting her own attorney, nor the time to travel to Muskogee to plead her case.

She could only pray that Nolan Ives was finished with her. Before he left for Chicago, he had visited her twice, always with rough-looking men, asking that she sell her lots to him. Twice she had turned him down, in spite of the fact that he had offered her a large sum of money. For her it was not the money, but the principle of the thing, and now that she had built her boarding house and was paying her taxes like everyone else, she felt well established enough that even Ives could not give her any more trouble. He must have looked at every way possible to get her lots from her, but thanks to Ethan getting the papers signed and properly dated that first day, there was not much the man could do . . . unless he ever found out Toby was her brother, not her husband. That might be something he could use against her.

Her eyes finally began to droop, but she was suddenly awake again when she thought she heard someone fidgeting at the back door of the kitchen outside her room. She listened. Had she forgotten to bolt the door? She quickly rose and pulled on a robe, then took her pistol from under her pillow. She moved to the door to her room. "Who's out there?" she demanded, her heart pounding. She decided then and there she would trade the small derringer in for a bigger, more powerful six-gun, afraid the small pistol would not really stop a man. She screamed and jumped back when the door to her room suddenly burst open and a man loomed inside. By the light of her lantern, she recognized him as the gunman who had shot Toby nearly a year ago!

"Got a message for you," came his voice, "from Mr. Ives. He's back in town to stay. He's already bought up most of the lots around you. It's time to sell out, Mrs. Mills." The words were spoken in a threatening sneer.

Allyson stepped back, pointing the pistol at him. "I have told Mr. Ives before that *I* am *also* here to stay!" She had no idea how she had managed to find her voice. Her whole body tingled with fear.

The man glanced at the pistol and just grinned. "I ain't afraid of no stinkin' little pop gun, lady. And I ain't here to hurt you, at least not this time. Mr. Ives just wanted me to show you how easy it is to break in here in the middle of the night, says it ain't right for a little woman like yourself to be sleeping alone." His eyes moved over her. "Could be dangerous for a woman." He turned, then looked back at her. "You think about it. Take the money and run, before this place burns down around you some night or some man slips in here and takes over where your piss-ass coward of a husband left off."

"Get out of here!" Allyson seethed. "I might not be able to kill you with this gun, but it can do enough harm to bring you a lot of pain, especially if I put a bullet in your belly!"

She heard a low laugh. "You just remember you ain't got your big Indian buck around to protect you anymore. Why'd he leave anyway? If I was sharing your bed like he was, I'd stick around a while."

Allyson's eyes widened. "Ethan Temple never—"

"Save it, lady. Face the facts. You're little and weak and alone, and this ain't never gonna work. Sell out to Ives while he's still willing to pay you good money, before he finds out whatever the truth is about you and has you run out of town!" The man left, slamming the door to her room, then the outer door.

Allyson stood shivering yet sweating. She opened the bedroom door and peeked out, then hurried to the outer door and shoved the bolt lock closed, cursing herself for forgetting to do it earlier. She hurried back into her room, leaving the door open so she could see into the kitchen. She had thought Nolan Ives was finally going to leave her alone, but apparently she was wrong. Burn her out? Would he really do that? And would he really send a man or men here in the night to rape her?

Maybe she could hire men to guard her place at night. The trouble was, that would take money. Maybe she could offer free rooms to men who kept watch for her. It would mean less income, but it might be worth it. She was not giving up!

She moved to the bed, laying the pistol aside and putting her head in her hands. Why did Ives have to come back? Everything had been going so well, and he was the only fly in the ointment. The man had all the land and money it seemed right for a person to have. But some people just couldn't get enough, she figured. If she had truly taken her lots legally, she wouldn't be so worried. What would the man do next? Why couldn't he have stayed in Chicago?

She looked over at her pistol, trying to convince herself that Nolan Ives's tactics would not work. She was not going to be defeated by fear. She picked up the pistol and put it back under her pillow. She lay down again, thinking how nice it would be if Ethan were still around. He would know what to do about this. Ives knew she wouldn't complain to the law, because that might draw too much attention and create a new investigation of her ownership. That was the last thing she wanted.

She shivered, aching to sleep but knowing she would probably lie staring at the clock until dawn, and dawn would bring a new day's work. She decided she would post a "HELP WANTED" sign out front tomorrow. It wasn't fair that she should have to go to the expense of hiring someone to watch the place, but she figured she had no choice. Nolan Ives was still determined to get it.

* * *

Ethan tied Blackfoot and stood back to study Ally's Place, shaking his head at the perseverance and determination of the woman who owned it. So, Ally Mills had done exactly what she said she would do. It was hard to believe only a year had passed since he was last here. Guthrie was a full-fledged town, with organized streets and new buildings lining them and sporting every kind of business imaginable. Ally's Place was a fine-looking structure, and it was near a brand new train depot, an excellent location for travelers. Lace curtains decorated the windows, and beneath the establishment name on the sign were the words "ROOMS AND FOOD." He noticed another sign that read "HELP WANTED—DEPENDABLE MAN FOR NIGHT SECURITY." He couldn't help wondering what that was all about. Had Ally been robbed or threatened?

The building, freshly whitewashed, took up most of the two lots Ally had claimed, and pots of fresh flowers sat near the doorway. Ethan debated over whether or not to go inside. Did she still hate him for that last night? Too much had been left unsaid between them but the hurt had run too deep at first for him to stay. He had needed time away, and maybe it was the same for her. Fact was, maybe she had taken a husband.

He grinned at the thought. No, not Ally. She was married to her business. He threw down a cheroot and stepped on it in the dirt street. He removed his hat then, taking a deep breath before he went inside, wondering how she might look now. She was almost eighteen. Would she welcome him, or wish he had never come back? Most likely he was a fool to be here at all.

Because of the warm spring day, the door had been left open with only a screen door to go through. Ethan smelled bread baking and myriad other food smells, all wonderful.

He looked around at several tables covered with checkered cloths, most of them occupied. Business looked good. An older woman came out from a back room, carrying a tray of food. She looked a little surprised when she saw him, and Ethan felt the old hurt that would probably never go away. He figured she was wondering if Indians should be allowed in here. Fact was, most of the people seated were staring at him. What irked him most was that this whole territory used to belong to the Indians, and he glared right back at a couple of people who quickly turned away. The woman with the tray set it down on a nearby table and turned to him, smoothing her apron and looking nervous. "Is there something I can do for you?"

"Yes. I'm looking for Ally Mills. She around? I'm Ethan Temple."

The woman's eyes brightened. "Oh, Mr. Temple! Ally has mentioned you a time or two. You were the scout who helped her out when her husband was killed. She says you bought her her first cookstove."

Ethan nodded. "That's me." He wondered what else Ally had said. Did she mention he had loved her? Probably not. How could she tell anyone she had been at all intimate with an Indian? That night he left she had made it pretty clear she thought that was totally inappropriate. "Is she here?"

"Yes. I believe she's cleaning a room upstairs in the rooming house." She indicated some double doors to the left of the restaurant. "You just go through there, down the hall and up the stairs. You'll find her up there somewhere."

Ethan looked around the room again, noticing another woman come out with yet another tray. "Looks like Ally's business is really going great."

"Oh, yes, she's quite the businesswoman for such a young thing. She's hired two cooks and me, and another woman who helps her clean. People used to talk about how she would never make it, being so young and all, her husband getting killed before they could even get started, but she's got a lot of determination. This business is her whole life."

Ethan grinned wryly. "I'm sure it is. Thanks for your help." He turned and headed for the double doors, feeling watchful eyes as he left the room. He walked down a hall decorated with flowered wallpaper, counting five rooms on each side. He could hear voices here and there through the thin walls, and when he reached the last room before the stairway, a man came out carrying a covered bucket. Ethan suspected it held waste from a chamber pot. He had seen a horse-drawn night cart outside when he tied Blackfoot, and he had always thought driving one of those things and having to dump human waste had to be one of the worst jobs a man could have, but then he supposed someone had to do it. He nodded to the unsmiling man and headed up the stairs to a second floor, wondering where Ally had gotten the money so quickly to build this place. Apparently business had been good from the start, maybe thanks to that stove he'd bought her. Part of him had been so angry that night that he could have hit her, yet he'd felt like an ass at the same time. He'd wanted to make up for it somehow, hoped finding the stove when she woke up helped keep her opinion of him from being all bad. He could understand her reaction to his making love to her. She'd been awfully young, afraid of men, and he *did* give her that whiskey. But her remark about him being Indian, as though it was something terrible . . . that was hard to forgive and forget. So, why was he here? Why couldn't he just let sleeping dogs lie? What had drawn him back?

He knew damn well what it was. It was that long, thick hair the color of red-rock, those innocent blue eyes that made him want to possess her; it was the knowledge that underneath all that stubborn determination to be brave and totally independent, he sensed fear, and a need to be loved; and then there was the distinct feeling that there was still a woman inside that body who had not yet been fully awakened, even though he'd physically claimed her innocence. She had not totally given herself to him that night, not in heart and spirit, not in passion. Almost every night since then he had imagined how wonderful it would be if she'd give herself that way. Maybe she already had . . . but to someone else.

He moved down the upstairs hallway, saw an open doorway, heard a woman humming softly. He stopped then, approached more quietly, and peeked around the door to see a woman in a flowered print dress bent over putting clean sheets on a bed. He noticed the room was pleasant, with more flowered wallpaper and a little curtained-off area where there was probably a chamber pot and washbowl. Besides the bed, the room contained a nightstand with an oil lamp, a wardrobe, a small rug on the wood floor, and lace curtains at the window.

The woman straightened, her back to him. Her lustrous red hair was pulled back at the sides with combs—she was still slender, and maybe a little taller. Who else but Ally had that red hair? His voice caught in his throat, and he contemplated turning and leaving. A little voice somewhere deep inside told him he'd be better off, but his feet would not move. He stepped farther inside, swallowing before speaking. "Hello, Ally."

She quickly turned, with a look Ethan was sure was at first startled fear, as though she had been expecting someone to come after her. The look quickly changed to one of pleasant surprise. "Ethan!"

She was more beautiful than ever, a more mature look about her. Was it because she'd lost her virginity to him a year ago? Or was it just the independent success she had enjoyed not only as one of the few females in Guthrie who owned her own business, but one of the youngest? She came closer, looking as though she wanted to hug him, but holding back. "I never thought I'd see *you* again," she told him. She began to redden then, and dropped her gaze. "I mean . . ." She folded her arms and turned away. "What are you doing here? Where have you been?" She finally faced him again. "Why didn't you come back the next morning so I could thank you for the stove?" Her face was still red. "And I *do* thank you, Ethan. After what happened, I don't understand why you did that."

"I did it because contrary to what you believed, I really did care about you. I wasn't just trying to use you, Ally. I guess that's why I'm here, to make sure you understand that."

Allyson shivered a little as his dark eyes moved over her. This man knew intimate things about her, had put himself inside her. It made her feel almost as though she belonged to him, yet she didn't, nor did she even want to. He had caught her off guard, and the instant awakening of memories stirred a little wave of desire that surprised her. Why did he look more handsome than he did a year ago? There he stood, in tight denim pants and dusty, leather boots, a red shirt with sleeves rolled up to reveal muscled arms, dark skin. There were those disturbing dark eyes. His very presence filled the room. She thought she had gotten over the wondering and curiosity about what it might have been like to allow Ethan Temple to show her everything about being a woman, to lie naked beside him . . .

"I . . . when I saw the stove . . . I think I understood then," she answered. She smiled nervously, walking over to the window. "I'm so surprised, I don't know what to say, what to think." She put a hand to her hair, suddenly self-conscious of how she looked. She hadn't had a chance to put a little color on her pale cheeks or twist her hair up into a fancy do. Several people had left their rooms, and she would spend most of the day changing beds and doing laundry.

Ethan looked around the room. "Looks like that stove worked miracles."

Allyson smiled, glad the ice was broken, excitement and pride quickly filling her soul. "Isn't it wonderful? I'll bet you were surprised when you rode up and saw my building."

He smiled softly. "Not completely. I knew how determined you were. I just don't understand how you got that much money so fast. You even have hired help."

"Not just that, but I have to pay occupation taxes, fifty dollars a month." She held her chin proudly. "But I can afford it. Being so close to the train station, my restaurant is almost always busy, and most of my rooms are rented. A few people live here as a permanent residence, some just for a week or so, here on business. The rest are people who just need a room for the night—whatever. It all worked exactly like I thought it would." She took a deep breath and put out her arms, turning around. "Isn't it wonderful? I just wish Toby could see all this."

Ethan walked farther into the room. "Well, maybe he *does* see it, from up in heaven somewhere."

"I like to think that he does." She motioned to the nearby chair. "Sit down, Ethan."

He glanced at the pile of sheets on the floor. "You look pretty busy. Maybe I'd better come back."

Their eyes held, both of them needing to talk, to clear up old misunderstandings. "All right," she said. "You come back here this evening, and I'll give you the best meal you ever had, and then we'll talk." She grew sober. "We do need to talk, don't we?"

Ethan nodded. "Like I said. That's why I came back."

Why did she suddenly feel too warm? "Well, no matter how long you intend to stay, you *have* to stay at least one night. That means you'll need a room, and I won't let you stay anyplace but right here. The least I can do for that stove is give you a room for the night for free."

Why do you have to be so damn beautiful? he thought. "I'd like that." He looked around again. "This sure is a far cry from those two broken-down horses and that miserable tent, isn't it? You've done good, Ally, real good. I'm proud of you. Toby would be, too."

She folded her arms self-consciously again, wishing she could quit thinking about how it felt when he'd kissed her, touched her. She reminded herself of the one reason she never should have let him do either one of those things. He looked mostly Indian. She also reminded herself that this time maybe he had just come to see how successful she was and maybe get a share of it by trying to woo her again. Still, he didn't seem like a man who cared about those things. "Thank you." *This man was intimate with me, stole my virginity!* It felt so strange just to stand here talking to him like a long-lost friend, but then he was that, too, wasn't he? "I told you I could do it."

Ethan watched her, remembering this girl's ability to lie and put on a brave front. "Why the sign out front, asking for a dependable man for night security?" He caught the quick look of fear in her eyes.

"I'll explain tonight. Maybe . . . maybe you'd like to stay on a while, work for me?"

Ethan could not imagine anything more painful than having to be around her every day, having her come into his room to clean it, knowing she was nearby at night. He already knew that the quicker he got away from her again, the better; yet the word came out of his mouth as though someone else had put it there. "Maybe," he answered. "You okay? Did you get robbed or something?"

She smiled weakly. Here he was, the old, protective Ethan. "Nolan Ives is back in town and making sure I'm aware of it."

Ethan's face darkened. "Maybe I should pay him a little visit."

"No, not yet. We'll talk tonight." Allyson stepped closer, touching his arm, feeling a wave of desire when she did so. Suddenly it seemed he had not been gone at all. She wanted nothing to do with men, so why did this one give her these confusing feelings? Why had she let him do the one thing she never thought she'd let any man do? And why was she so glad to see him again, after the way he had hurt her, brought her pain and shame? She should hate him, and thought all this time that she did, at least a little. If only he hadn't gotten her that stove before he left. That was the kindest thing anyone had ever done for her.

"Come back tonight, around eight o'clock. I'll be closing up the restaurant then. I'll save us some food, and we can eat and talk alone. There are things I need to tell you, Ethan, and I know it's the same for you. I'm glad you came. I'm sorry . . . about what I said . . . that night . . ." She looked down then. "I didn't mean it . . . like it came out."

Ethan put a big hand over her own. "Don't worry about it. I'll be back at eight." He thought how he'd like nothing more than to grab her and kiss her and lay her back on that bare mattress behind her and make love to her all over again. "Don't work too hard."

She pulled her hand away. "I'm used to it. That's the only way to succeed here." She tossed her head. "Nobody in this town thought I could do this, but I'm still here, and look at this place! This is the most important thing in the world to me. It's all my own, and no one can take it away from me."

She was so sure. No, she hadn't changed much. "See you tonight then."

"Fine. If you want to put your horse up, there are stalls out back, or there's a livery just a little way up the street. You can bring your gear back here—give it to one of the women downstairs. They'll hold it until you come back tonight."

He wished he could read those blue eyes of hers, wished he knew if she had thought about him as often as he had about her. "Thanks." He gave her another smile before turning to leave. *Get on your horse and ride the hell out of here!* There was that little voice again. He agreed that was what he should do. He hurried down the stairs, through the hallway, through the restaurant, outside to Blackfoot. Yes, he'd leave right now. He'd seen her again, knew she was all right; also knew he wanted her again, and that was useless. To hell with tonight. He was leaving.

He headed Blackfoot on up the street, past a livery, halted, turned back, and took the horse to the man in charge. "Brush him down and feed him, will you? I'm not sure how long I'll be in town, but I'll be here at least tonight."

"Sure thing, Indian. Fifty cents a night."

Ethan ignored being addressed "Indian." He dug the money out of his pocket and handed it over. "I'll be back in the morning to exercise him. If I'm going to stay longer, I'll pay you then." He took his saddlebags and a small carpetbag down from Blackfoot, slung the saddlebags over his shoulder and headed back toward Ally's Place.

10

Allyson took one more look at herself in the mirror. She wanted to impress Ethan, to show him just how successful she really had become. He had already seen her restaurant and rooming house, and she had saved him a dinner of her best pork roast; but so far he had never seen her dressed as she was now, like a real lady, a grown-up woman who could afford fine clothes. She adjusted an ivory comb. It showed up beautifully in her red hair, which she had swept up into a cascade of waves that fell down her back. She wore just a touch of rouge at her cheeks and on her lips; and all that combined with a pair of little ruby earrings finished off her look. She pinned a small ruby brooch at the neck of her sheer batiste shirt; its high-necked, lace yoke made the pin look even prettier. There was also lace at the ends of the sleeves of the blouse, which she wore tucked into a black velvet skirt that accented her small waist.

She sat down on her bed to pull on a new pair of black leather shoes that had shiny patent leather toe-caps and high heels to make her seem taller. As she laced them, she remembered the day before the land rush, when Ethan had told her to go look for a new pair of shoes. That seemed like such a long time ago, yet here he was, back again as though returned from the dead. She hoped he would not misunderstand why she was making herself extra pretty this evening. It was not because she intended in any way to return to where they left off the night he left. She had not quite forgiven him for that, nor did she want any further romantic involvement. She simply wanted him to see how grown-up she was, a successful businesswoman, and she had done it all by herself.

She rose, checking in the mirror one more time, ignoring any lingering desires Ethan Temple had stirred in her. She must be strong tonight, strong and sure. She must ignore the womanly side of her that frightened her so, ignore the warm rush the sight of Ethan Temple brought to her blood. She must not give him even the slightest notion that this was anything but a thank-you for her stove, a pleasant renewal of an old friendship, and perhaps a business deal. No one could do a better job of guarding her business than Ethan. Trouble was, that would mean he would be around all the time, and she was not sure how either of them would react to that. She just hoped he could forget that last night together and real-ize it was only the whiskey that had made her so vulnera-ble—and admit his own guilt in giving her that whiskey in the first place. There were parts of that night that brought a pleasant ache to her insides, but when she remembered the last part, the pain, the humiliation . . .

She heard a knock at the outside door to the restaurant. She hurried out of her room, through the kitchen and to the door, peeking through the curtains to make sure it was Ethan. It was still just light enough to see his tall frame. She opened the door, struggling not to show her own pleasant surprise at how wonderful he looked. He was wearing dark blue cotton pants and a white French flannel shirt with thin blue stripes. She recognized the shirt as one of the latest in men's fashions. A deep blue silk tie graced his neck and he held a black felt hat. Indian or not, Allyson was sure no more handsome man walked the face of the earth. Why did he have to look like that? Combined with the knowledge of how strong and skilled and brave he was, and how kind he could be besides, it just made it more difficult for her to stick to her resolve that they could be nothing but friends.

"Ethan! You . . . you didn't have to get all fancied up."

He grinned, his dark eyes taking in her own elegant clothing and red lips. Now she wished she had just left herself plain. What must he think? "Well, look at *you*," he answered. "It's a good thing I *did* clean up." He took his hand from behind his back and produced a bouquet of flowers. "I figured if I expect you to forget and forgive the circumstances of my leaving here a year ago, I had better look and act like a gentleman." He sobered then, his eyes sincere. "I'm sorry, Ally. I took advantage of a very confused, upset young lady who was lonely and scared; but I want you to believe it was not for the reasons you think. I cared very much for you, but I didn't come back here to try to push you in that direction again. I only wanted to make sure you were all right, and I wanted to apologize."

Allyson took the flowers, surprised by the gesture. "I . . . I guess it was a little bit my fault, too. I accept your apology, as long as you . . ." She felt the flush coming to her cheeks. How often did he think about what he had done to her? Right or wrong, forgiven or not, it had happened, and it had left an odd connection between them, something that made it so difficult to look at him as just a friend now. "As long as you can put it out of your mind, and not think I'm . . ." She turned away with the flowers. ". . . a sinful woman."

Ethan struggled not to laugh aloud. Allyson Mills a sinful woman? Well, maybe she'd done some wrong things in her childhood, like steal, but she'd had her reasons. As far as being sinful in the way of men, she wouldn't even know how. He just wished he *could* put the whole thing out of his mind, but the way she looked tonight, filling out that lacy

blouse like a grown woman, the way she carried herself . . .
what man could forget how it had felt to be her first. How
many nights had he spent since then wondering what it
would have been like to strip her naked and touch and taste
and gaze upon her nakedness? No, he could not "put the
whole thing out of his mind," but if that was what she
wanted to think for now, he would let her think it.

"Ally, I've never once thought of you as having done anything wrong. It was all my fault. I took advantage. You
hardly knew what was happening to you. I understand how
you feel about the whole thing, and I've put it out of my
mind, I assure you."

Her back was still to him. "And I'm sorry, too, about calling you an Indian, as though it was something bad. I was just
angry. I wanted to hurt you."

"I know that."

Allyson left for a moment, coming back out of the
kitchen, carrying the flowers in a vase. She set them on a
table, still not meeting his eyes since their first remarks. "Sit
down, Ethan. You are now going to taste some of the finest
cooking in Guthrie." She looked at him then, suspecting
that was love she saw in those dark eyes. Damn him. Ignoring her own feelings was not going to be as easy as she
thought, but at least they had gotten over their initial un-
easiness, had gotten the apologies out of the way. She had to
be strong now, show him she was an independent woman
who needed no man. "I started out right away, just a few
hours after you left me that stove. I baked some bread, sold
it, and now look at me."

Ethan walked over to the table and pulled out a chair.
"You don't have to convince me, *Mrs.* Mills. Let me guess.
The single men of Guthrie, and probably a few married
ones, gladly lent you their time and labor to get this place
built."

Allyson put her hands on her hips, gazing into his eyes as he sat down. "Yes, they did. I have learned that a woman doesn't have to do anything questionable to get men to do her bidding. She simply has to *be* a woman, and if she is a lonely, grieving widow, young and helpless, it's all the more to her advantage."

Ethan laughed aloud, shaking his head. "It sure didn't take you long to figure that one out."

"I'm a smart woman, remember? You told me that yourself once."

His eyes moved over her again in that way he had of unnerving her. "I sure did, and I see I was right. Now, let me see if that cooking of yours is worth buying you that stove."

Allyson smiled, and Ethan saw a new womanliness in her that had not been there when he left. "I'll be right back with your food." She returned moments later with a large round tray containing a pot of coffee and two plates. She set the tray down and took one plate from it, heaped with pork roast, mashed potatoes and gravy, and corn. She then set a basket of hot rolls on the table with some butter, and poured him a cup of coffee. "When you are through with this, there is plenty of apple pie for desert," she said, setting her own plate down across from him. Hers contained only a little food.

"This looks great," he told her. "I'm not sure I'll have room for pie when I'm through, though."

She smiled, and Ethan realized he'd never seen her look so radiant, wasn't even sure he'd ever seen her smile those few days he had known her a year ago.

"I know how men eat," she commented. "You'll have room." She laid her napkin over her lap, and sitting directly across from him as she was, Ethan could not help noticing the full swell of her breasts beneath the lace of her silk shirt. He wondered, even after all she'd been through and what had happened between them, if she understood what her beauty did to a man. She already realized she could get men to do practically anything for her, but he'd bet she didn't realize how men probably fantasized about her, the ache she stirred in their loins. He realized that if he was going to save his own heart, he'd better leave Guthrie tomorrow.

"So, clarify a couple of things for me," he said. "I know you've made a whole lot of money here, but it couldn't have been enough to build this whole building and furnish it, plus pay hired help. Do you owe on it?"

Allyson sipped some coffee. "I got a loan from a Mr. Bloomfield. I think he hopes to marry me one day. He gives me the lowest interest of any other banker in town. It won't take me long to pay it off. After that, everything is profit, and it's all mine." She raised her chin. "Someday I'm going to contact the orphanage and tell them what I have accomplished." Her face fell then. "If only Toby could share all this with me."

Ethan swallowed some pork. "This is the best food I've had in a long time, and I'm not just saying that."

She smiled proudly. "Thank you kindly, Mr. Temple."

Ethan sipped his coffee. "You'd probably be better off never contacting the orphanage. They might turn around and somehow make trouble for you. I talked to a few people around town today, just inquiring about things. I hear the town council is pretty strict on enforcing rules about the Sooners, and you've got a prime piece of property here. If anybody in the right circle ever found out you weren't eighteen when you claimed this, let alone weren't even married, you could have a problem."

Allyson toyed with her potatoes. "I'm not so worried anymore. I'm well established, and I've made a lot of friends. You might be right, though, about the orphanage." She sighed. "I do appreciate what you did for me that day,

Ethan. I never could have done any of this if you hadn't been there."

He grinned. "I'm not so sure of that. You're a pretty determined woman." He swallowed more food, and Allyson got up to pour him a second cup of coffee from one of several fancy pewter pots used by the restaurant.

"Where have you been this past year?" she asked. She saw his smile fade, sensed he was troubled.

"Well, after I left here I went back to Fort Supply, reported in, went on to my usual duties of overseeing the trail drives through reservation lands around Deep Creek Trail. Then last November I headed for Illinois to find my pa in Springfield. I knew he'd gone there to visit his white relatives." He wiped his mouth with his napkin and took another swallow of coffee. "What I didn't know was that he was dying."

Allyson sat back down. "Oh, I'm sorry, Ethan."

He leaned back, meeting her eyes for a moment before looking away to hide the pain. "They call it cancer. It's a terrible way to die—a slow, painful death. I stayed there with him, helped my Aunt Claudia take care of him."

Allyson noted some bitterness when he referred to his aunt.

"I guess she appreciated the help," he added, "but she didn't appreciate my being there. She and her husband, my pa's brother, look at me as some kind of bastard. They never recognized me as their blood relation. Aunt Claudia didn't like having an 'Indian' around her daughters—made me sleep in the barn."

Allyson blushed, remembering her own harsh words the night he left. "That's terrible."

"Yeah, well, I tell myself I'm used to it, but a man can only take so much."

Allyson met his eyes, knew he was referring to their last

night together. "People don't always mean what they say, Ethan. And sometimes they react to things out of fear, or because they just don't understand."

He forced a grin, trying to seem unaffected. He picked up his fork again. "Hell, I know that." He sighed deeply. "At any rate, my pa lasted another four months. I just wish he could have been buried out here, could have come back once more. This is where he belonged, but by the time I got to him he was too sick to bother."

"You talked about him before. You were close." Allyson remembered what he'd told her about his mother, how he'd watched her die when so many Cheyenne were murdered at that place called Sand Creek. She had seen a lot of ugliness in her life, but so had he. "Didn't you say you had Indian relatives left?"

Ethan buttered a roll. "A couple of cousins and a Cheyenne aunt here in Oklahoma, an uncle, grandmother, and three more cousins up in North Dakota. I promised my pa I'd go and see them. I came here first to make sure you were doing all right."

"Oh." Allyson struggled to hide her disappointment. She had hoped he would stay on and work for her. "You're leaving soon then?"

Ethan watched her closely as he swallowed a piece of biscuit. He felt he knew this woman well enough to realize when she was hiding her fear. Everything was not as rosy as she made it out to be. There was still that HELP WANTED sign out front. "You need me to stay?" He noticed she had hardly touched her food. She smiled, but it was a nervous smile.

"Not if you have other plans. I only meant . . . well, I just thought we'd have a few more chances to talk again, but then I'm busy, and you have plans. After all, you did only come here to see if I was all right." She smiled again. "And as you can see, I am." She picked up the pewter pot and poured herself another cup of coffee. "I'm glad you did come by. I feel better clearing the air between us, knowing you're all right and being able to show you my place."

"Ally, I know how you can lie. Something is wrong. You mentioned earlier today that Nolan Ives was causing trouble again. You even said maybe I could work for you. You need someone to guard this place? What's been going on?"

She toyed with her cup as she spoke, wishing she *could* send him on his way. It would be easier on both of them. But who better to defend her against the power of Nolan Ives than Ethan?

She pursed her lips in thought, then finally told him. "Nolan Ives sent one of his men here last night. He broke in and . . . threatened me . . . let me know how easy it would be to burn me out or . . . get into my room in the middle of the night. He said I'd be wise to sell out to Mr. Ives. The message was very clear." She straightened, facing him squarely. "But I'm not budging, nor will I *ever* sell out to Nolan Ives. They'd have to kill me first!"

Ethan felt a deep anger at the thought of some man breaking in and bullying her, after all she'd been through, and considering her youth and vulnerability. It made him want to kill someone, and he knew what infuriated him most was the thought of some man forcing himself on her, taking what he knew damn well he now considered his, even though he could probably never actually possess her. He leaned back in his chair and folded his arms. "You've got your man. You don't need to pay me. All I need is food and a room to sleep in. I'll find part-time work during the day to pay general expenses and keep my horse at the livery."

Allyson wanted to hug him. "Just like that? What about going up north?"

"It can wait. What I'll do is keep watch for a few weeks,

and at the same time I'll interview a few men myself who can take over when I leave. I know better than you who'd be dependable and who can handle himself. You trust my judgment?"

"Of course."

"Then it's settled. That son-of-a-bitch Ives is not going to use his money and power to destroy what you've worked so hard for. I know what this place means to you, Ally."

Her eyes teared with gratitude. "It means everything to me, Ethan. I've always wanted to have something all my own. If it wasn't for Nolan Ives, I'd be the happiest woman in the world."

Ethan wondered if that was true. Didn't she realize there was still something unfulfilled in her life. Didn't she want a husband and family?

"I'll file a formal complaint with the law. They should know Nolan Ives has threatened you."

"It won't do much good. I have no doubt Mr. Ives has the law in his back pocket. He left for a while, went back to Chicago. I was hoping it was for good, even though he'd built a house here. He came back just a few weeks ago, and he's been buying up property all around me. He wants to choke me out, but I won't let him." She swallowed to keep back the tears. "I know men like you don't think much about material things, Ethan, but for me, this is everything. It's all I have, more than I've ever had in my life, and Toby died to help me get it. I can't give up, I just can't."

Ethan folded his napkin and put it on the table. "You won't have to. I'll make sure of it. You just show me which room is mine and I'll put my gear in it. I'll spend the rest of tonight keeping watch outside. I'll work at night and sleep mornings. Do we have a deal?" He put out his hand.

Allyson looked at the big, strong hand, remembered that

hand gently grasping at her breast, working magic in private places. She was almost afraid to touch it, but she reached out and clasped it. "We have a deal. Thank you, Ethan."

Ethan squeezed her hand lightly, rubbing the back of it with his thumb. He wondered why he always seemed to lose his good sense when he was around this woman. Hadn't he just told himself minutes ago that tomorrow he would leave for North Dakota? After all, he'd made that promise to his father, and he'd heard there was some kind of new trouble with the Sioux over a new religion.

He let go of her hand, telling himself this was just for a little while, just for the summer. Then he'd go north. He would not let this be anything more than a job, because trying to go any farther with Allyson Mills was like beating his head against a rock. He would set Nolan Ives and the law straight, find a good man to work for her, *then* leave. That shouldn't be so difficult.

Allyson was busy convincing herself of the same thing. For the moment she was just greatly relieved for Ethan Temple's mere presence. He would work for a while, find her a good man, straighten things out with Nolan Ives, and leave. That was all there was to it.

His touch left a tingle throughout her whole body, and for the moment she could not quite meet his eyes. She walked into the kitchen and returned with a large piece of warm apple pie, then smiled at the way he devoured it along with another cup of coffee.

"Well, God works in mysterious ways, Ethan. I prayed last night for help in knowing what to do about Mr. Ives, and today you showed up. Maybe now I can get a decent night's sleep."

He grinned. "Glad to oblige."

"You sure you aren't too tired to start tonight?"

"I'll be all right. We might as well show Ives right off that you're not folding."

They both rose, and she grasped his hands. "Thank you, Ethan."

Their eyes met, and Ethan was tempted to pull her close and taste that mouth again. "You get a good night's sleep," he told her. "You work hard—you need your rest."

She pulled away, turning toward the kitchen. "Come and get your gear. I'll show you to your room, then come back here and clean up. My room is right off the kitchen if you need me."

Ethan followed her, watching the gentle sway of her slender hips beneath the black velvet skirt, and flashes of how it had felt to be inside her stabbed at him. He got his gear, then followed her back through the double doors. She led him to a room at the end of the hall and took a key from a pocket of her skirt, unlocking the door. She turned then, handing him the key. The door swung open, and for an instant Ethan thought how nice it would be to pick her up and carry her to the bed. Would she fight him again?

Allyson felt a rush of desire mixed with fear. He towered over her, all strength, a man who had already claimed her, touched her in secret places. What was this she felt? What was this sudden urge to try that again, to know if something like that got more pleasurable as time went on? "I thought a room at the end of the hall would be quieter, since you have to sleep in the daytime. This room is away from the street, and as far as you can get from the kitchen and restaurant."

Ethan took the key, touching her fingers lightly. "It'll do fine."

Allyson suddenly felt an urge to run before she did something foolish. She ducked past him and headed back up the hall, turning at the double doors. "Thank you, Ethan. I'll see you sometime tomorrow. And please, be careful."

He grinned. "Always am."

She smiled, remembering other times he had defended her. "I know. It's just that I feel badly enough about Toby. I don't want another death on my hands because someone protected me."

He shrugged. "We all take our chances." He watched her disappear beyond the double doors, then picked up his gear and went into his room, throwing everything onto the bed. "You're a damn fool, Ethan Temple," he muttered. "A damn fool."

11

Ethan waited behind a stack of crates, sure he had seen someone move through the alley toward the back entrance to Ally's kitchen. He had been watching her place nights for almost two weeks with no trouble. Out of the several men he had helped Allyson interview for the job, two seemed well qualified, and he decided that if things were going to remain this quiet, he might as well have Allyson hire one or both of them and be on his way. There had been no problems so far, and seeing Allyson every day was taking its toll on his ability to resist the foolish desire to have her for himself. She had kept things cool and formal, "strictly friendship," she had said about their relationship; but he had read something more in her eyes, he was sure. That was what kept him here.

There! Someone darted close to the back entrance. He had long ago trained himself literally to see in the dark, having spent a good share of his life doing this kind of work, smelling out trouble, watching for people sneaking onto Indian lands. He moved on silent, moccasined feet from the shadows across the alleyway to a group of barrels near the back entrance. Someone was bent over near the back door, putting something down in front of it. He saw the flare of a match then, saw it being tossed toward the door. Whatever had been put in front of it burst into flames.

Ethan darted from behind the barrels just as the man

stepped back to observe his heinous crime. He rammed his six-gun into the man's back. "Put it out, quick!" he growled. "Or you're a dead man!"

"What the—"

"Hurry up!" Ethan jabbed with his gun, at the same time quickly yanking the man's own gun out of its holster and throwing it aside. The man hurriedly bent down and kicked away the hay he had piled at the back door. He stomped some of it out, and the rest continued to burn harmlessly in little scattered piles in the alley. Suddenly the man swung a foot around and landed it in Ethan's middle, sending him sprawling into the pile of empty barrels, which came crashing down around him. Ethan covered his head, felt the bruising blows to his back and arms. He quickly charged away from them, realizing the culprit was running down the alley.

Ethan was not letting him get away. He rammed his six-gun into its holster and took off after him, his youth and longer legs helping him reach his prey in moments. He leaped onto the man's back, knocking him to the ground, the man's face scraping through the gravel as he slid a couple of feet. Ethan jerked him up and yanked him around, swinging a big fist into his face. The man sprawled backward but got back up again, plowing into Ethan with his head down and shoving him against a building. Ethan gasped when his back hit the wall, but he managed to grasp the man by the shoulders, pushing him away and holding him at arm's length with one hand so he could use his other hand to slam his fist into the man's face. Again the culprit went sprawling, and this time got up more slowly. Before he could regain his senses, Ethan pulled him fully to his feet and slammed him against the wall of a building, ramming a powerful forearm against the man's throat and pinning him, pressing just tight enough to cut off most of his air and render him helpless. He pulled out his six-gun again and pressed its barrel against the man's temple.

"Now, let's get something straight," he growled. "I know who sent you! You tell Nolan Ives to leave Ally Mills and her place alone, or *he's* the one I'll be coming after, and this whole town will know what he tried to do! Everybody likes Mrs. Mills. They'd run Ives out of town on a rail if they knew he tried to burn her place down! I'll let it go this one time, but this is the last warning!"

Their eyes had adjusted to the dim lamplight in the alley, and Ethan recognized one of the men who had been with Ives a year ago, but not the one who had shot Toby. In turn, the man recognized Ethan. "What the . . . hell are you . . . doing back here . . . Indian?" the man managed to choke out. One of his eyes was turning black, and his lips were swollen and bleeding. One side of his face was scraped raw.

Ethan just grinned, blood trickling down his own face from a cut on his forehead. "The point is I *am* back, and every night I'll be prowling in the shadows around Ally's Place. If this happens again, you or whoever else comes around will be *dead!*"

"Ethan! Ethan, what's happened?" Ethan recognized Ally's voice. She was farther up the alley, looking for him. He stepped back, and the man he had chased down slumped to the ground. "Ethan!" Allyson spotted him and wrapped a robe tighter around herself as she ran toward him.

"Hey, what's going on down there?" a man called down from a window.

Ethan looked up, realizing it was the far end of Allyson's boarding house and the man roomed there. "It's all right," Ethan yelled up. "Just a little trouble with a thief. I took care of it. Go on back to sleep."

The man closed his window, and Ives's man got up and

ran off into the darkness, just as Allyson reached them. "What happened? I heard the barrels fall, and I saw some straw on fire in the alley! Ethan! You're bleeding!"

"I'm all right." He winced at the pain in his shoulders and one arm, knowing he was badly bruised from the barrels. His ribs were also sore. He'd been so intent on catching Ives's man that he hadn't noticed he was hurt until now.

"What happened?" Allyson put an arm around him as they walked back to the kitchen door.

"Three guesses. You saw some of the straw still on fire."

"Someone really tried to set fire to my building?" Allyson put a hand to her chest.

Ethan opened the back door, and they went inside. "I don't think he'll be back. I told him I know who sent him. Ives knows now that you're protected. He won't want to take the chance I'll catch the next man he sends and drag him out in public and make him tell who's behind all this. You're too well liked and Ives wouldn't want the publicity."

Allyson led him into her room and told him to sit down on the bed, then turned up the oil lamp on her nightstand. "Let me wash that cut," she said. She hurriedly grabbed a washcloth and towel from a drawer in her wardrobe, then went into her washroom and poured some water from a pitcher into a bowl, carrying it out and setting it on her nightstand.

"I could have taken this guy to the sheriff," Ethan was saying, wiping at some of the blood with his hand. "But I figured if we can end it right here, it's better for you. Trying to take someone like Ives to court wouldn't be easy, and it might stir up too much of an investigation into your own life again. It's best to let sleeping dogs lie if we can. Maybe Ives will think the same thing. Neither one of you wants the publicity, for different reasons."

Allyson wet the rag and wrung it out, then knelt in front of him and gently pressed it to the cut. "It's already scabbing over. All I can do is wash around it."

Ethan watched her, thinking how beautiful she was in the soft lamplight. For a moment they were both quiet as she gently washed blood from his face. Ethan noticed she was trembling, and he ached to hold her. Pain shot through his shoulders then, interrupting his tender thoughts.

Allyson saw him wince and catch his breath. "You'd better take off your jacket and shirt."

"I'm all right—just bruised. Wooden barrels are heavy, even when they're empty." He took the cloth from her and finished washing his face himself. "I'd better get back out there till dawn. I'll just have to wait till then to lie down and wallow in my pain." He smiled, but not convincingly.

"You should see a doctor, Ethan."

He laughed lightly and stood up, suddenly feeling uncomfortable sitting on her bed, having to look at her in that soft flannel robe, aching to touch the warm curves beneath it. "If I saw a doctor for every injury I've ever had, I'd be in his office at least once a week and I'd be broke trying to pay him. I don't need any damn doctor." He held the rag to his bruised right hand for a moment, then reached over and laid it in the bowl. He noticed then there was a little loose dirt on her sheets. "I'm afraid I got dirt on your bed. I should have brushed off better before I came inside."

Allyson looked over, a sudden memory stabbing at her—lying back in blankets, Ethan Temple hovering over her, taking her to a place she had never been before. But then there had been the sudden pain . . . "It's all right," she answered. She looked up at him, hoping he could not read her thoughts. "If all I get out of this is a little dirt on my bed, I'm lucky." She touched his arm. "What would I have done if you weren't there to stop him? I don't know what to say, Ethan."

"There's nothing *to* say. You hired me to do a job, and I'm doing it."

Her eyes teared. "What if he had killed you, or hurt you a lot worse?"

"You know I can take care of myself. And right now, he's hurting more than I am. You just go back to sleep knowing everything is fine."

Allyson could not resist the temptation to stand on her toes and kiss his cheek. "Thank you, Ethan." She watched his dark eyes, knew he wanted more than a kiss on the cheek. Everything had been very proper between them since he returned, and they had had plenty of chances to talk and share supper. They were friends now, and she wanted nothing more than that. But sometimes . . . when he was close to her this way . . . when she thought about all that he did for her . . . and remembered that night in the tent . . .

She turned away, nervously brushing the dirt from the bed. "Ives wouldn't be crazy enough to send anyone back again tonight, would he?"

Ethan rubbed his sore arm. "I don't think he'll send anyone back at all. Like I said, I gave his man a pretty stern message, and I doubt if Ives wants to look like the bad guy. He might try something through legal methods, but I doubt he'll stoop to something like this again. Fact is, I've found a couple of good men who could probably take my place. I'll keep watch myself for maybe another month, then I've got to go up to North Dakota. I can't stay here forever." *I can't be around you like this day after day, Ally, without wanting you.*

"I understand," she answered. *I don't really want you to go, Ethan, but I'm afraid of what will happen if you stay. I can't do that. I don't want a man in my life.* "Are you sure you're all right?"

He smiled rather bashfully. "No, but I'll know by tomorrow afternoon. These things always get worse before they get better. At least the bastard didn't shoot at me."

Her eyes widened, the child in her becoming curious. "Have you ever been shot?"

He opened and closed his right hand, working it against the pain. "The kind of work I do, I've been shot *at* several times, but so far I've only been hit once. I was handling some trouble between ranchers and Indians. One rancher apparently figured I was just one of the reservation Indians and took a pot-shot at me just because I was approaching to talk to him about coming too close to a reservation area. Luckily, some army troops were nearby and heard the shot. They came by and identified me." A look of terrible bitterness came into his eyes. "The cattlemen had me tied by the wrists to a saddlehorn, a bullet in my lower left side; I had nearly passed out. They were going to drag me through rocks and brush until I *was* dead."

Allyson stepped closer. "Why?"

His eyes moved over her with a look of terrible sorrow. "Because I was an Indian. That was all the excuse they needed."

Allyson thought about her own remark that first time he had left Guthrie, and she felt sick about it. "How can anyone be that cruel?" She knew immediately that he was also remembering what she had said.

"It happens. People form opinions without knowing all the facts. That's just the way life is, just like people judging you at first because you are young and a woman. They figured you'd never succeed, and I guess I was one of them at first." He sighed deeply. "Get some sleep."

Ethan turned and left, and Allyson walked to the back door, sliding the lock shut after he went out. She was sorry he had to go back out again, suspected he wanted nothing more than to be able to lie down and rest. His loyalty touched her heart, and she thought about his remark, realizing that she knew him so well that she hardly saw him as Indian anymore. She only saw Ethan Temple, the man, and that was what bothered her. Her arguments for not allowing herself to love him were becoming weaker, except for one. Loving a man meant being hurt and humiliated. It meant letting a man take his ugly physical pleasures, and that she could not tolerate.

"You hear what's goin' on up north on the Sioux reservations?" Hector Wells leaned against his saddle and took some chewing tobacco from a little leather pouch, shoving some into his mouth.

Ethan sat across a campfire from the man, smoking quietly. "I've seen a little bit about it in the papers in Guthrie, but no Indian in his right mind would believe words in a white man's newspaper. That's part of the reason I came out here to find you, to see if you knew more about it. I figured word would be all over the reservations down here, especially among the Cheyenne."

Hector chuckled. "Hey, Breed, I don't stick my nose in no Cheyenne affairs. You're all crazy."

Ethan smiled, keeping his cheroot between his teeth. "You nosy Cherokee know every damn thing that's happening with all the other tribes, just so you can stay ahead of things and blame all the bad stuff on us. You don't fool me."

Hector laughed louder. "The Cherokee are a smart people. You could take lessons." The man got to his feet. "I gotta go water a tree. I'll be right back."

Ethan was glad he had been able to track Hector down after trying to find him at Fort Supply. He had trained a new man for Allyson, then had to get out of Guthrie for a while just to get away from her. He'd told Allyson it was best to leave the new man on his own for a week or so, to see how he worked out. He figured he'd try to find out more about what was happening with his Sioux and Cheyenne relatives up north before he went there, so he'd have a better understanding of how he might be able to help them.

He was actually getting anxious to leave. He'd been in Guthrie for five weeks, and it was no longer possible to look at Allyson as just a friend. She had come into his room a few times while she thought he was sleeping, to collect his clothes and bring clean towels and such. She had been quiet as a mouse, but he'd known she was there just the same. And when she had stopped just to stare at him a couple of times, while he lay with his naked torso exposed from the waist up, it had taken all his willpower not to grab her and roll her into his bed, but that would only frighten her and make her hate him again, and he didn't want that. They were too different to actually spend their lives together, weren't they? If that was the case, then he simply had to leave again, and he did not want to part as enemies the way they did before. They had to part as friends so he would not feel that something was unfinished, or feel compelled to return again for some kind of apology.

"They call it the Ghost Dance religion," Hector spoke up, interrupting Ethan's thoughts to explain what was happening with the Sioux. He had returned to take his place near the campfire. "I heard about it from a Cheyenne who just came down here not long ago. He's married to a Sioux woman. They left to live here on the Cheyenne reservation because he is afraid there will be big trouble over this new religion. The whites don't like it."

Ethan watched the flickering flames of the campfire, wondering when it was all going to stop—the broken promises, the taking of Indian lands . . . the hope most of his Indian relatives still held that it would all change and somehow one day they would get all their land back. That was never going to happen. He sat up a little straighter, poking at the fire. Coals popped, and a few red sparks rose into the dark night. He had found Hector camped along the North Canadian River, near the northern edge of the Cherokee Outlet. The man had been hunting for meat for the army.

Ethan puffed at the cheroot, grinning at the satisfied look on Hector's face. "It makes you feel real important to know something about my people that I don't know, doesn't it, Hec?"

Hector smiled. "If you quit hanging around those white people in Guthrie, you'd know what was really happening," he teased. "But anyway, it's more a Sioux problem than Cheyenne. I know you have a grandmother and a couple of cousins living up there with the Hunkpapa because they married into the Sioux; I guess there ain't a lot of difference between the Sioux and the Cheyenne, is there?"

"Not a whole lot, except that the Sioux have a little more of their own original land left."

"Maybe not for long. This Cheyenne I talked to, he says the government is after that Sioux land, and you know what that means. His name is George Red Fox. Anyway, this new religion is coming right at a time when the Sioux are refusing to sell any more land, and it has made them even more determined. George Red Fox, he says it all started with a Sioux called Kicking Bear. He heard a voice tell him to go far to the west to the land of the Fish Eaters—that's what they call the Paiutes, you know."

Ethan grinned, realizing that Hector just loved to think he knew more than anyone else. "I know."

"Well, the Fish Eaters, they told Kicking Bear that Christ had returned to earth. To prove it, they took him to a place called Walker Lake, in that place called Nevada. Kicking Bear claimed that when they went to this place, the Christ appeared, only he was not a white man. He looked Indian. He taught them a special dance called the Dance of the Ghosts. It is a form of worship, and through this dance, the Christ said that the People can bring back all their dead relatives and they will live again. The Christ told Kicking Bear and the Fish Eaters that the more they dance, the more hope there is of this happening. The earth will someday soon be covered with new soil, which will bury all the white men. The new land will be covered with green grass and buffalo, trees and clean water and wild horses. While the earth is being renewed, those who dance the Ghost Dance will be raised up into the air and held there until it is all done, then set back down to live among their relatives who have been brought back to life. Kicking Bear and his friends, they hurried to catch a train back to the reservation. He says the Christ flew above them, teaching them the proper songs for the Ghost Dance and telling them to teach the People this new faith and telling them of this wonderful resurrection that is to take place."

Ethan threw what was left of his cheroot into the fire. "They believe this?"

Hector nodded. "George Red Fox says a lot of Indians, from Nevada all the way back to the Dakotas, are dancing this dance, taking turns so the singing and dancing goes on almost constantly. Yes, they believe it very much. A Paiute Messiah called Wovoka was the first to teach about this new religion, and after Kicking Bear traveled out there and saw the Christ for himself, he knew it was true. Perhaps he fasted and what he saw was a personal vision, but he believes it very strongly, and so do the others. They have made sacred garments for themselves called Ghost Shirts. They are painted with magic symbols, and they believe that when they wear these shirts, no harm can come to them. That is the dangerous part. They think soldiers' bullets cannot penetrate the shirts. Even Sitting Bull thinks this religion could be a good thing. He has had Kicking Bear teach the Ghost Dance to his people. The dancing has spread like a prairie fire, and everywhere in the hills of the Dakotas, George Red Fox says one can hear the singing and drumming, all through the night. It has made the white people very nervous. They think the Indians are gathering and preparing to make war. That Indian agent, White Hair McLaughlin, he is trying to put a stop to it. The whites do not seem to understand that this new religion is based on Christ. George Red Bear says part of the teaching is that the Indians are not to harm anyone. They are not to fight, but the soldiers and whites, they think the Indians are going to make war. George Red Fox says there will be much trouble over it. He decided to leave. He is married to a Sioux woman, but because he is Cheyenne, he can come here to live. He is afraid of the trouble that is coming up there."

Ethan sighed deeply, leaning back against his bedroll. "He's probably right. I don't like the sound of it. Rumors of Indians getting ready for war make white people too damn nervous, and we both know what that can lead to. The Indians don't even have to have guns to give the whites an excuse to murder, pretending self-defense."

Hector just grunted. He knew Ethan had bad memories about Sand Creek. His own people had had their share of suffering at the hands of whites convinced that Indians and whites could not coexist peacefully. For his own people, memories of the Trail of Tears was what brought the pain. "You better get up there and see your kin before something bad happens," he finally spoke up. "Maybe you can make them come down here where they'd be safer."

Ethan rubbed at his eyes. "I'll try. I have to go back to Guthrie first for a few days, then I'll head on up north."

Hector poked at the fire again. "What's in Guthrie that you gotta go back? Ain't nothin' in that noisy white settlement for a man like you."

Ethan continued to stare at the campfire. "Just a little business to settle. I had a job—need to collect a few expenses."

"I'm sorry about your pa dyin' and all that. I just don't know why you didn't come straight back here afterward, or go on up north. Why Guthrie?"

Ethan pulled a blanket around his shoulders. "Jesus, I *said* you Cherokee were nosy. You're sure proving it."

Hector turned his head and spit tobacco juice out into the grass. "And you Cheyenne ain't no good at coverin' up. Seems to me I remember last year you talkin' about havin' to watch over some pretty young girl—when we was talkin' that day I came to get you just before the land rush. I remember seein' her then. She wouldn't be the reason you came back to Guthrie, would she? Fact is, maybe she's the reason you left for so long in the first place."

"Yeah? Maybe you should just mind your own business."

Hector eyed him closely. "She's white."

Ethan scowled at him, adjusting a rolled blanket under his head and turning over so his back was to the man. "So what?"

"Stay away from it, Ethan."

Ethan closed his eyes, but all he could see was Allyson's face. "Easier said than done. There's more to it than you know, but I'm not stupid enough to think it can really go anywhere. Once I leave this time, it's for good."

Hector chuckled softly. "Sure. You been inside her yet?"

Ethan sighed in mock disgust. "You dirty-minded old bastard, go to sleep!"

There was nothing but silence for the next several minutes. Finally Ethan could hear Hector putting more wood on the fire, then make a few grunting sounds as he settled into his bedroll. "So, you love her, huh?"

Ethan rolled his eyes, but he had to admit it felt good to tell someone. "Yeah, I love her, but she's made it real clear she doesn't want a man in her life, let alone an Indian."

"You're half white and fine lookin'. She wants you, all right. She just don't know it yet. You gotta be patient with them white women. They don't know how to show affection like Indian women do. Comes natural to Indian women. Them white women, they gotta work at it."

Ethan grinned to himself. "I don't think in this case it's worth being patient. I'm better off just getting the hell out." He heard a low chuckle.

"Oh, you'll leave, all right. But you'll go back. Somethin' about gettin' the scent of a certain woman, a man can't hardly stay away."

"Thanks for telling me what you know about what's happening up north, Hec, but stay out of my personal affairs, would you? You're getting too old to get punched in the mouth."

Hector laughed out loud. "I ain't afraid of no punch from no weak Cheyenne. Now, us Cherokee men, we know how to handle women."

"Yeah? How come you don't have one sleeping in your bedroll tonight then? How come three wives have left you?"

"Oh, I was just too much man. I wore them out."

This time it was Ethan's turn to laugh. It helped alleviate the worry he felt over the new religion sweeping among the Sioux in the north. He could see nothing but disaster resulting, especially from the belief that the ghost shirts could protect his people against soldiers' bullets. Still, he was almost glad for the diversion. He had all the more reason now to go see his grandmother, to leave Guthrie and Allyson Mills. This time he really, really was not going to come back.

Allyson studied the lovely hat she had spotted in the window of Jacobsen's Millinery. She stepped inside and walked over to the window, looking at it even more closely, taking it from its stand. "I'd like to try this on, Mrs. Jacobsen," she told the owner. "And maybe this—"

Her words caught in her throat when she saw a man who had stopped near the window to light a cigar. He took a couple of puffs and looked up the street, glancing into the window for a moment, but did not notice her. Allyson, however, could not help noticing him. She stepped back, her heart pounding, afraid he would see her.

"Mrs. Mills? What's wrong? You look pale," Mrs. Jacobsen said gently.

Allyson looked at the woman, struggling to keep her composure. "I . . . I do feel a little ill, but I think I'll be all right. I'd like to take this hat in front of the mirror in your dressing room, if you don't mind."

"Certainly."

Allyson followed the woman into the small room at the back of the store, where she was out of sight. "I'll just be a moment. I'd like to try it on alone."

Mrs. Jacobsen smiled. "Do you need a glass of water or anything?"

"No. I'm fine."

"Well, that lovely green hat will look beautiful on that red hair, Mrs. Mills. You be sure to come out and show it to me when you have it the way you want."

"Thank you."

The woman left, and Allyson wilted into the chair in front

of a dressing table. She looked into the mirror at a freckled face and blue eyes and red hair. She had not changed all that much over the past year, except for the way she dressed and carried herself. Henry Bartel would recognize her in a minute, and with a business like hers and her name splattered all over the front of the building, how long could it be before he came there for a meal and figured out who the owner was—or ran into her in the street?

She breathed deeply to quell her growing panic, suddenly wishing Ethan would get back but not sure what difference it would make. Henry Bartel! What was he doing here in Guthrie? Was it just by chance, or had he tracked her here? Either way, there would be hell to pay if he found her.

12

Allyson wiped her hands on her apron and hurried through the restaurant and down the hallway toward Ethan's room, leaving the kitchen help to continue with the evening rush. She had something more important to attend to, and she was not taking the time to wash and change first. Ethan was not the type of man who cared if a woman looked a little frazzled or had flour dust on her face. If she was going to convince him she loved him and wanted to marry him, she had to start right away. It was the only way she could think of to hang on to her business, and one thing she was sure of about Ethan was that wealth meant little to him. He was the only man she could trust not to try to take over her business—he knew what it meant to her.

Why had Henry Bartel come to Guthrie, of all places? *Just for the excitement, he says, and to get away from the noise and filth of the big city,* Jack Carter had told her. She had spotted Henry again after leaving the millinery shop two days ago and had followed him, being careful not to let him see her. He had gone into the newspaper office, and after nearly an hour had finally left. Allyson had gone inside then to ask Jack, the newspaper owner, who it was who had just been there.

Oh, that's a new teacher come to town! Carter had answered, very pleased that Mr. Henry Bartel, a former teacher and attendant at a New York orphanage, had come to Guthrie to inquire about starting a new school. *Mr. Bartel will be a fine addition to our community!* he had added. *I am going to put an article in the paper about him, letting people know the man intends to start a school. He'll be using the church for a while at first, until we can get a real school built. I'm sure there will be a town meeting about it.*

So, Henry Bartel had come to Guthrie to stay! It was the last thing Allyson had wanted to hear. If he hadn't seen the crowds at Arkansas City and gotten caught up in the excitement of the land rush when he came out here on that orphan train, he probably never would have left the orphanage . . . or had he already been out here for months, searching for Toby and Allyson Mills, two runaways who had stolen money from him? Maybe that was what had brought him back. Then maybe he had given up the search and decided to settle in Guthrie. There could be another reason for his presence. Maybe he had gotten in trouble again at the orphanage and was kicked out. It made her sick that such an evil man would be teaching children. Maybe she should say something, but she feared that no one would believe her word against his. She could lose everything.

Whatever the reason for Bartel's being in Guthrie, he was bound to discover her any day now. She was too well-known for him *not* to find her. He might even come to her restaurant to eat!

She hoped she had bought herself a little time when she told Jack she had only inquired about him because she thought she knew Bartel. She had assured the newspaper owner that she was mistaken, and asked that he please not mention it to Mr. Bartel, as the man might get the wrong idea about her inquiry and it could look improper. All the way back from the newspaper office she had felt almost faint from nervousness that anyplace she turned, she could run into Henry Bartel. She had not left the restaurant since then, and for the past two nights she had thought about her options. What could she do about the man? Not only had she stolen from him, but he knew her real age, knew she had never been married to Toby. If Nolan Ives ever got wind of that, she would be in trouble, unless . . .

She knocked on the door to Ethan's room, taking a deep breath for courage. She wouldn't *really* be lying, would she? After all, she *had* missed him, and she *did* have special feelings for him. She just had not planned on acting on those feelings. She shivered at the thought of what bringing a man into her life meant sexually, but it was a small sacrifice, wasn't it? And who better than Ethan?

The door opened, and Ethan stood there in denim pants and a blue calico shirt that was still unbuttoned, revealing a muscled chest and stomach. He looked surprised to see her. Allyson could not help glancing at his bare skin and remembered their last night together, and for a brief moment she wavered. She met his dark gaze then, and saw the curiosity there.

"Ethan. I . . . I just heard you were back. I came right away. I . . ." She smiled rather wistfully, reminding herself that it would not be so easy to fool Ethan Temple by flirting like she did with other men. He knew her too well, and what made it all the more awkward was the fact that this man had already been intimate with her. "I missed you . . . more than I thought I would."

Ethan frowned, his defenses already alert. Something was different about her, but he wasn't quite sure yet just what it was. He had only been back for a few minutes, planning to change and have a talk with the new man he had hired to watch the place at night. He figured if things were going fine, he would leave in a day or two for the Sioux reservation.

"You missed me, did you?" he answered. "Well, that's a surprise. Something wrong? Did you have a run-in with Ives or something?"

"Oh, no! Nothing like that." She couldn't tell him the truth. She couldn't beg this man to marry her just to save her business. He would be insulted. He had to believe it was what she really wanted. "I just . . ." She feigned embarrassment. "Ethan, I feel like a fool, after all the things I've said in the past . . . about us . . . about me . . . how I don't want a man in my life." She folded her arms, looking down at the floor. "I just got to thinking while you were gone, about you leaving soon for good and all that. I mean, I know it's important for you to go up north, and I'd never stop you, but . . ." She raised her eyes to meet his, in all sincerity. "Ethan, I'd like you to come back after that. I've thought about it a lot while you've been gone, and I decided that as soon as you were back here I was going to tell you the truth and get it off my chest. I tried to ignore it because I'm afraid to depend on anyone else, afraid of men when it comes to—well, you already know. But you're different. I've grown to trust you, even depend on you. And I . . . I have to tell you . . . I love you." She turned away, pushing a piece of hair behind her ear. "There, I've said it." She started to walk away.

Ethan came after her, took her arm and pulled her into his room, closing the door. He grasped her arms. "What the hell is this all about?"

Allyson met his eyes, her own filling with tears. She hoped he would believe the tears were because she loved him and didn't want him to go away. Truth was, they were tears of fear—fear of Henry Bartel and what he could do to her—fear of losing all she had worked for. She needed a husband, and quick. Considering what a husband would expect of her, Ethan was the only man she could turn to, the only one she could bear to have in her bed. After all, he had already staked his claim, hadn't he?

Earlier in the day she had checked with the land office, and the agent told her that if she married again, her land and business would by law belong to her husband. As far as she was concerned, that meant that no matter what was discovered about her, once she had a husband, no one could take away her land or her business. If that man was Ethan, he would never take it from her or make her sell it. They could just keep on working here together as they had been for the past several weeks. The worst she would have to do is pay Henry Bartel his three hundred dollars, and everything would be fine.

"It's about me being a fool, trying to convince myself I can do this all alone," she answered. "I've proven what I set out to prove, Ethan. That doesn't mean I have to live alone the rest of my life. I know you have special feelings for me. You've tried to hide it, but you wouldn't have come back here if that wasn't true. We've both been fighting those feelings. It just took a few days away from you for me to realize that I don't want you to leave again—not for good, anyway. I don't care if you go see your relatives in the north." She flung her arms around him, resting her face against his bare chest. "Just promise me you'll come back."

Ethan hesitantly moved his own arms to embrace her, his mind racing with confusion. He knew Allyson Mills could be a clever liar, but why on earth would she lie about something like this? It made no sense. "Ally, why don't you tell me what's really wrong?"

She raised her face to meet Ethan's gaze, tears on her cheeks. This was something Ethan Temple could not help her with in the usual way. Guns and fists would not change what Henry Bartel knew. There was only one way he could help, but he would never marry her if he thought it was for anything but love. "Can't a woman change her mind? Surely you've known all along I've been fighting my true feelings, Ethan. I was just afraid; but after all these weeks, I'm not afraid any more. Your being gone the last few days just opened my eyes to what I really wanted." She pulled away, pretending to be embarrassed at having embraced him. "Maybe I've taken too much for granted. I . . . you told me last year . . . that night . . . you said you loved me. I figured, maybe you still do. In fact I, I *hope* you still do. After what we did, I was frightened." She turned and looked at the floor again. "I insulted you because of that fear. I wanted the pain to go away—wanted *you* to go away, so I said something cruel. But I always regretted it, and ever since then . . . I've always felt like . . . like I belonged to you . . . because of what happened between us."

It all seemed too good to be true, yet she seemed so sincere. All these months Ethan had dreamed about her, ached for her, imagined she would say something like this. He could think of no good reason whatsoever that she would be saying these things except that she must truly love him after all. What had seemed impossible when he left a few days ago was now his for the taking.

"Ally, I don't know what to say." He touched her shoulder, and she turned to embrace him again. Ethan kissed her hair. He already knew he loved her, wanted to settle, take a wife. A wife. Was she saying she was ready to *marry* him? "Ally, I can't just say I love you and then keep working here without—"

"You don't need to say it, Ethan." She looked up at him. "I'm ready for whatever you want. Just don't ask me to give up my business. You know how much it means to me. There are other women in town who help their husbands and still manage to take care of children. You *do* want children, don't you, Ethan? Surely you don't want to just wander the rest of your life."

He searched her eyes, trying to determine if this was some kind of trick, but his heart would not let him see anything but love. "You saying you want to get married?"

She reached up and touched his face. "Whatever it takes to keep you here with me, to make you always come back to me. I'm afraid when you're gone. It feels so good to let you hold me, to feel your strength, your—" Her words went unfinished. Ethan met her lips in a hot kiss that almost made Allyson forget the real reason she was going to marry this man. His warm lips parted her mouth, bringing back memories of how pleasant and exciting it had been to let him do this once before. She told herself she could manage the pain, could overcome the bad memories. She had only to lie in this man's bed and let him have his pleasure, and she and her business would be safe. That was not such a terrible price to pay. After all, Ethan did have a way of stirring strange desires in her.

He left her mouth, picking her up so her feet left the floor, then kissed her neck. "Tonight. Let's get married tonight then," he told her. "Out here in this country people have done stranger things. I've known widowed women to marry complete strangers just to have a man to take care of them and their children. You and I, we already know each other . . ." He kissed her eyes. "And I've already been inside you, woman. I want that again, Ally. I want you in my bed tonight."

The words stirred a passion in her that surprised even Ally. She turned her face to meet his lips again, thinking how crazy all this was, but probably not to someone like Ethan. He was wild and determined, knew what he wanted.

He was not a man to fuss with any proper formalities. He simply took what he wanted. This had all worked out even better than she had planned. Yes, do it quickly, before Ethan discovered the truth, before Henry Bartel came over here and found her. Do it quickly, before her friends found out, before there was time for the newspaper to pick up the story and print an article that the widow Mills was marrying again. Henry Bartel might see the announcement and could spoil things before Ethan was legally her husband and the owner of her property.

"Yes," she whispered between kisses. "I'll marry you tonight. There is no reason to wait, is there? We already know each other so well."

Their lips met again in another hungry kiss, and Allyson realized that she liked it more than she thought she would. She certainly could not ask for a more handsome, more able man, nor one who would be kinder or more gentle, yet would always protect her.

Ethan laughed, swung her around, then picked her up full in his arms and carried her to his bed. He threw her on it, moved on top of her.

"No!" she protested with a smile. "I want it to be legal this time, Ethan. Let me go and clean up and change, and then we'll go find the preacher. I know where he lives."

Eager anticipation and gentle love shone in Ethan's dark eyes. "Don't take too long."

"I'll close up early." She realized then that her hand was touching Ethan's chest. She rubbed at it lightly, beginning to understand even more fully how easily a man could be manipulated. A little voice told her it was dangerous to try to fool someone like Ethan Temple, but once they were married, what difference would it make? A few tears, the right touches, and he would forgive anything. After all, he loved her. He would do anything for her. She would just have to get used to having to lie in his bed. Maybe she would even learn to enjoy it. After all, this much had been quite pleasant. "I have a ruby ring that was my mother's," she told him, "the only thing I have that belonged to her. I found it one day and hid it so my father couldn't sell it to buy whiskey." All the while she talked, he kissed her eyes, her cheeks, her lips, her neck. She had to admit that his virility, his bravery, and the way he touched her made her feel safe, loved. Something about his rather wild nature, the dark, dangerous look about him, excited her. "We can use it for a wedding ring until you can buy me a real one."

Ethan grinned. He had not felt this happy since his wedding night with Violet. Whatever had compelled Allyson Mills to change her mind and realize she loved him was just fine with him. He had dreamed about this for over a year.

"Meet me back here at eight-thirty and we'll go find the preacher, get him out of bed if we have to," he said.

Allyson returned the smile. She looked so happy, felt so safe. It all seemed too good to be true, but here she was in his arms, returning his kisses, wanting to marry him. He had not had to fill her with whiskey first. This was the real Allyson, and she wanted him to be her husband, wanted to share his bed tonight.

He got up, pulling her to her feet. She grasped his hands then and squeezed them. "I love you, Ethan." She turned and hurried out, and Ethan watched her disappear down the hallway. He closed the door again, leaning against it, breathing deeply. Hector would probably tell him he was crazy to marry a white woman, and maybe he was. A little voice warned him that all this time Allyson Mills had thought it was improper for a white woman to marry an Indian. What had changed her mind? He supposed she simply looked at him differently now because she knew him so well. They were good friends, and she had apparently gotten over the problem of his heritage. He was, after all, just a man, a man who loved her very much. He couldn't see one thing wrong about it.

Stay away from it, Ethan. Hector's words nudged at him, but the thought of waking up tomorrow morning with Allyson's naked body lying beside him, that red hair spread out on his pillow, destroyed all his doubts, all his ability to reason. She had always had that affect on him, but it didn't matter now. She loved him. Before the night was over, Allyson Mills was going to be Mrs. Ethan Temple.

Henry Bartel fixed his hat as he looked into the mirror in the entranceway of the rooming house. He had considered trying another one called Ally's Place when he first got off the train in Guthrie, but he knew such a new town probably didn't have a school, which meant the church would have to be used in the beginning. He had therefore deliberately sought out a rooming house near the only church in town so he would not have so far to walk to and from classes. Ally's Place was several blocks away.

He thought the name was interesting. It made him think of Allyson Mills. "Ally" was what her brother had called her. He had given up wondering what ever happened to those two. He could only hope they had fallen into a terrible fate, something fitting for two little thieves who had stolen church money. He had often dreamed about finding them, but by the time he had finished delivering all the children from the orphan train, he had taken ill with a very bad cough that turned into pneumonia, and the others who had come with him had hurried him back to New York. He had been bedded down in the train's caboose near the heating stove. It had been a miserable trip all the way around, but he figured he could make up for it in some respect if he could ever get his hands around Ally Mills's pretty little throat.

The doctor in New York had told him he had to get away from the "bad air" of the city, and when his term of service at the orphanage was over, he had decided to come back out to this great, arid West to see if his health might improve. Besides, it felt good to get away from all those runny-nosed brats. He would be putting up with more brats out here when he started the school, but he was a good disciplinarian. He'd make them toe the line. At least these children would have families. He was tired of wild, unruly children who had known only street life or were so distraught over losing their parents that they were not like normal children at all. To hell with all of them. Better times were at hand. He liked it here in Guthrie. The air was better, and a man had opportunity out here.

"Going out, Mr. Bartel?" asked Chloris Deacon, the owner of the rooming house.

"Just for a little stroll. It's a nice night."

Mrs. Deacon smiled, and Henry turned toward the door, then looked back at the woman, wondering inwardly if there might be a way to get into her bed. She was about his own age and was widowed last year when her husband was killed when his wagon overturned. Over meals, the woman had not failed to tell him all about her ordeal, how she had risen above her sorrow and used the savings her husband had brought with them to start her own rooming house.

"Tell me, Mrs. Deacon, I've been so busy these first three days that I never thought to ask. Who runs that other boarding house? The one near the railroad depot? I used to know someone named Ally."

"Oh, she's the sweetest thing, so tiny and pretty. Her name is Allyson Mills, and she's just a young thing. It's such a tragedy, you know. Her young husband—I believe his name was Toby—was shot and killed the first day of the land rush over a squabble about whether or not they had claimed their lots illegally." She noticed Henry grow pale. "Mr. Bartel? Are you all right?"

Ally Mills! It couldn't be! Henry struggled with his emotions, quickly deciding he must not alarm this woman. Maybe she was a good friend of Ally's. Maybe she would tell her he was in town, and he didn't want that—not if this Ally Mills was who he thought she might be. He'd like nothing better than to surprise her! "Yes. Yes, I'm fine," he murmured, taking a handkerchief from his pocket and pressing it to his forehead. "It's just an after-affect of the pneumonia," he lied. "Sometimes I just suddenly break out in a sweat." He turned away. "You say the woman was married? Toby Mills was her husband?"

"Yes, sir. So young they were, much too young to be married, but out here a person can expect to see anything."

I'll just bet, Henry thought. "Well, that doesn't sound like the Ally I knew. What does she look like?"

"Oh, just a small thing, like I said. I'm not sure of her age, but she has to be over eighteen because that was the age you had to be to claim a lot. A very lovely young woman, she is, pretty blue eyes, beautiful red hair. There are a lot of men in town who would like to snag that one. She's quite a little businesswoman. Started out just baking bread for people, now has a restaurant and a rooming house! Of course, it's been easy for her to find men willing to provide free labor, which certainly helps."

The last words were spoken with a hint of bitter sarcasm, but Henry hardly heard the woman. All he heard was blue eyes and red hair, a "husband" named Toby. It was *her!* Allyson Mills! All this time he had wanted to find her, and now she had fallen right into his lap! It was all he could do to keep from jumping with joy. The little bitch! "Well, that's not the woman I knew," he said, tipping his hat to Mrs. Deacon. "You keep this door locked now. I'll be back within the hour."

"Yes, sir. Have a pleasant walk, Mr. Bartel. Oh, and if you're thinking of going over to Ally's Place to eat or something, I wouldn't. She closes around eight every night, and it's now eight-thirty. The restaurant does have very good food, I'm told. Perhaps you could go there for breakfast and have a look at Mrs. Mills to make sure she isn't the person you knew."

"Thank you for the advice, Mrs. Deacon."

Bartel left, his thin lips pressing into a wicked smile. So, Allyson Mills was right here in Guthrie! How could he not have thought of that in the first place? After all, she and Toby had run off the train into the middle of the crowd waiting at Arkansas City to join in the land rush. With the money they had stolen from him, they could have bought the supplies they needed to get started. Allyson was an intelligent, resourceful girl, and had apparently decided to start her own business. Too bad it had cost poor Toby his life, but then at least he was rid of one of them. Now there was just Allyson, with no brother to defend her.

Husband and wife! He laughed out loud at the thought of it. They must have thought making people think they were married would help them seem older, maybe give them an edge in claiming their lots. Whatever the reason, it had apparently worked. "But not for long," he muttered. Allyson Mills was a little thief, an orphan, not married, and certainly not eighteen when she claimed those lots. Her claim was illegal! What better way to repay her for what she had done than to destroy her business. The little witch probably thought she had been very clever, must be revelling in her success; but if he had anything to do with it, that success was going to be short-lived!

He knew now where he would walk. Mrs. Deacon had said Ally's Place was closed by now, and people were probably sleeping peacefully in their rooms. Fine. He didn't want to give Allyson Mills any warning anyway. She was going to get a surprise visit in the morning. Just the look on her face would tell the authorities all they needed to know. He headed for the land office, which was kept open all through the night because of continued claims and disputes. This one would be a humdinger, and "sweet" little Allyson Mills would be found out for what she really was! She'd learn quick enough how fast people would turn away when they know they've been lied to, when they find out she had come out here a homeless orphan, that she was a common thief, and that Toby Mills had not been her husband at all! He licked his lips, almost able to taste revenge.

13

Ethan opened the door at one end of the boarding house near to the rented rooms. At night the double doors at the other end were kept locked so the restaurant and Allyson's room were inaccessible to boarders. The hallway was quiet, except for the sound of someone coughing across the hall from Ethan's room. He frowned, moving an arm around Allyson and leading her to his room. "This just doesn't seem right," he grumbled. "We should go someplace special tonight."

"In Guthrie? There *is* noplace special."

"There's a couple of hotels."

"I know, Ethan, but we decided on this so quickly I didn't have time to plan. I've got to be here in the morning to open up as usual. When I can make better arrangements, I'll take a few days off and we can go anyplace you want." Allyson hugged him, trembling on the inside at what would be expected of her now. She had made vows to love, honor, and obey. Loving and honoring a man like Ethan would not be difficult, but obeying, that was something else. To her the word meant being forced to cower under someone's rule, like at the orphanage, to obey men like Henry Bartel or suffer the consequences.

She loved Ethan for his friendship and support, and she was sure she could eventually learn to love him the way a wife was supposed to love a husband, although she wasn't sure just how that was supposed to feel. She respected his bravery and skills, but a tiny voice nudged at her a little over the fact that she had married a man who was half Indian. She had grown up knowing hardly a thing about Indians and imagining them as a strange people, wild and un-Christian, whom no white woman would consider becoming involved with intimately, unless she was captured and forced. Now here she was willingly married to one!

Ethan led her into his room, and she felt herself breaking into a cold sweat. She reminded herself she had done nothing wrong in the eyes of God, except, perhaps, not telling Ethan the whole truth about why she had married him. She meant to keep her wedding vows, even meant to allow Ethan his "husbandly rights" before this night was over. She would play the dutiful wife, as long as it meant keeping all that she had worked so hard for. "I should go down to my room and get a change of clothes and a nightgown," she said softly.

Ethan sighed, grasping her arms and looking around the room. "These damn walls are paper thin. This is a crummy way to start a marriage. I'd like it to be nicer for you than some man's tiny little room in a boarding house."

She smiled at him. "Ethan, we just discussed that. We made a quick decision and this is how it will have to be for the moment." She rested her head against his chest. "At least we're married." She gave him a squeeze. "What would it be like if we were married the Indian way?"

Ethan rubbed his hands over her slender back, thinking how small she was, realizing how much he must have hurt her that first time. She no doubt remembered that, was probably afraid of what was to come. "Oh, there would be a ceremony not totally unlike a Christian one. Then the bride and groom go riding off alone to a tipi already put up for them far from the village so they have privacy. They spend about a week there, making love, getting to know each other intimately. That's the way I wish it could be for us."

She pulled away. "We'll find some time to do something like that," she promised. She reached into the handbag that hung by a cord on her arm and took out a key. "I'll go and get some of my things and be right back."

Ethan leaned down and kissed her lightly. "Just be assured I'm not going to force anything on you tonight, Ally. We have all the time in the world for that, and I know you have some bad memories that make it difficult. The last thing I want is for you to be afraid of me."

Ally felt the blood rushing to her face. She turned toward the door. "Things were different that first time. I mean, I was scared to death, and I was still in shock over Toby, plus I really hardly knew you . . . and, of course, I had drunk that whiskey. Now you're my husband, and I feel much closer to you." She turned to look up at him with wide blue eyes. "I want our marriage officially consummated tonight, Ethan. You have that right, and I want to learn *not* to be afraid. You're the only man I know who can teach me without my hating his touch." She turned away again. "I like it when you touch me."

She hurried out the door then, hoping he believed her. Well, it *was* true, but she wasn't all that sure she wanted it to happen again this quickly. Still, just in case Bartel should come bursting into her restaurant tomorrow, she wanted to be sure her marriage was totally, positively legal so in case Ethan got angry over her real reason for marrying him, he couldn't back out and have it annulled.

Ethan watched the door close, then turned away and removed his boots, throwing them into a corner. He began unbuttoning his shirt, still wondering if he'd been rational in what he had just done. None of it seemed real, and he could just hear Hector Wells teasing him about the "white man" part of him being weak in lusting after a woman. Maybe he was. Something didn't seem quite right about all of this, yet he'd gone ahead and gotten married, ignoring all warnings, leaving all questions unanswered. He didn't want to question anything. He loved Ally Mills Temple with every bone in his body. The only thing that bothered him was that she seemed in such a hurry, and deep inside he could not help wondering if there was some other reason.

He pulled his shirt out and took it off, then unbuckled his belt and yanked it out of the pant loops. The only other thing that ate at him was the minister's reaction to Ally marrying an Indian. *Are you sure about this, Mrs. Mills?* the man had asked, looking somewhat embarrassed as he looked Ethan over with obvious disapproval. *Mr. Temple is half Indian,* he had said bluntly, as though Ethan was not even there. *Mr. Temple is just a man, Reverend,* Ally had replied, *a very good man who loves me and whom I love in return. Besides, he is half white.* Ethan had been proud of the first part of her answer, but the last statement left him wondering whether he should take it as just a statement of fact or an insult. Did she mean she was acknowledging and marrying only the white half of Ethan Temple, as though it was a disgrace to marry the Indian but all right to marry the white?

He turned and threw back the bedcovers, hoping the damn bed wouldn't squeak too much. He shook off the minister's insult. He was used to such remarks, and he decided Ally didn't mean to insult him by her own remark. He had to quit doubting her and enjoy the fact that she was now his wife. Once she learned to enjoy the sexual part of marriage, the woman in her would be happy and fulfilled, especially once she had a couple of babies. Ally was just young and feisty, needed to mellow a little. She'd be a damn good wife overall.

He took a rawhide tie from his hair and shook it loose, wishing he could take Ally to a tipi far away from everyone like he'd done with Violet. That had been a beautiful night for them both, Violet passionate and willing in spite of the pain. He told himself to remember that Ally was not Violet. He actually laughed lightly at the comparison. No two women could be more different in looks, background, and personality. Just then Allyson came back inside and set down a carpetbag. Ethan walked over and swept her up into his arms, kicking the door shut and whirling her around before carrying her over to the bed and plopping her onto it. He moved on top of her, catching her mouth, which was slightly open with surprise, keeping it open with a hot kiss and running his tongue into her mouth suggestively.

Allyson wasn't sure what to think or do. Part of her was suddenly on fire, curiosity again ripping through her in sudden desires that were new—yet the old fears were still there. Ethan left her mouth then and kissed her eyes.

"Don't worry," he told her. "I'm just happy, Mrs. Temple. You get your gown on and get into bed. I won't even look when you change if you don't want me to. I promise just to hold you against me tonight. Nothing else will happen unless you want it to."

Allyson studied his dark eyes, feeling like a witch for using him. Still, that was only part of it. She really did mean to be a true wife to him. It was just that she was still learning to love him, whereas Ethan Temple already seemed to love her as passionately and devotedly as any man could. "All right," she agreed. "I'll go in the washroom and change, and you get into bed."

Ethan grinned and kissed her once more. "I love you,

Ally." He let her up, and she took her carpetbag into the washroom and closed the curtain. Ethan stripped and turned down the oil lamp, then climbed under the covers to wait. After several minutes he heard her voice and sensed a tremor in the words.

"Promise to be gentle and go slowly, Ethan," she said, her voice high-pitched, almost like a frightened little girl.

"I told you I wouldn't force you or hurt you, Ally."

She opened the curtain then, and Ethan's smile faded into surprise and a look of near-worship. She stood there stark naked. He'd already been inside this woman, but this was the first time he'd looked upon her total nakedness. It was a beautiful sight to behold, her breasts full and high, their pink nipples erect and begging to be tasted. The patch of hair between her slender thighs was as red as the hair on her head. He'd never seen anything like it. Her skin glowed like an angel, and that was what she looked like standing there. He could see her trembling.

"I said I wanted this to be a complete marriage," she told him. "I meant it."

Ethan sat up. He could see she was having trouble making her legs move. He threw off the covers, and her eyes widened as she looked him over. "It's all right, Ally. Everything will be all right."

Ally studied his body. Suddenly he seemed bigger than ever, and when she saw that part of him that would invade her tonight, she understood why it had hurt the first time, was terrified of how it would feel again. He couldn't possibly fit that whole thing inside of her, could he?

Now he was picking her up, laying her in the bed, moving in beside her. She told herself she must do this, and no more handsome specimen could be found in Guthrie, maybe not in all of Oklahoma. And he loved her. She couldn't ask for much more. She closed her eyes, obeying his every gentle command . . . *breathe deeply, relax, let me make it nice for you, Ally. I love you so.*

This was not so bad. She actually wanted to return his kisses, to touch his muscled arms. She felt no fear or desire to stop him when he gently fondled her breasts, massaging, toying with her nipples, making her groan for more. His hand moved downward, his kisses still smothering her and erasing all inhibitions as he traced his fingers to that magical place only Ethan Temple had ever touched.

How did he know that touching her this way brought an unexpected wantonness to her soul? His kisses were hot and inviting, his tongue invading her mouth while his fingers moved inside of her with teasing little thrusts that made her whimper. Then he was toying with that magical spot between her legs that made her feel on fire; then back inside of her again, keeping up the glorious, suggestive thrusts until she felt crazy with the need for more. She had not expected it to be this easy, this wonderful, this natural, and she wasn't even drunk!

His lips moved down over her neck, and he gently took one of her nipples into his mouth, softly licking, pulling at it, his fingers still working a magic that made her willingly open herself to him. He lingered at her breasts, whispering words to her about how beautiful she was, how ripe and delicious, even saying things in the Cheyenne tongue that she did not understand, yet the words excited her. He moved down farther, licking at her belly, working his tongue down to her most private place. She grasped his hair and protested. She was not ready for this much brazen openness. Not yet. He made no objection. He moved back over her belly, licking his way back over both breasts, her neck, back to her mouth.

She felt a wonderful explosion deep inside then that made her push up and press herself against his fingers. He moved a finger back inside her again, feeling deep, making her want more, something bigger, something that would fill the incredible need she suddenly felt. He smothered her with kisses then as he moved on top of her.

She stiffened, but she opened herself to him. In the next moment she gasped as he quickly entered her with a hard thrust. This time there was very little pain, and to her surprise, she welcomed it. He was whispering and moaning her name, ramming into her with a rhythm that made her feel wild with desire. Her breath came in gasps, and she gripped his strong arms, wondering what had happened to the inexperienced Ally Mills she had been only minutes ago.

It was just like that first night. He had touched some magic button in her that made her change into a wanton woman. Was it the Indian in him, some wild, aboriginal witchcraft? Did Indians of old do this to captive white women to make them surrender? Or was it something else? Could it be that it was this wonderful only because she loved him more than she thought she did? Or maybe she was just releasing her own wickedness, allowing herself to experience being with a man simply because it felt good.

But it wasn't supposed to feel good, and she wasn't supposed to care this much, not yet. It was supposed to be ugly, something done only out of duty. She was supposed to be doing this only as a way of consummating the marriage so everything would be legal. She did not love Ethan Temple like a wife should, did she? That was supposed to come later.

She felt something pulse inside of her, and Ethan gasped her name, his broad, dark shoulders hovering over her, his whole body trembling. She knew instinctively he had reached his own climactic moment. It was now official. The marriage was consummated. They could just quit and go to sleep now, couldn't they? So why in God's name did she want to do it again? He stayed inside of her, and she felt that mysterious part of man that had always frightened her growing larger again, pushing deep, making her arch against him in a need to take all of him inside of her.

"Stay right there," Ethan whispered, nibbling at her lips. "I'm not through with you yet, woman."

Allyson gladly obeyed.

Nolan Ives hoisted his hefty body out of his huge, leather office chair to greet the three men who entered his office. One of them was Cy Jacobs, the land agent who was in charge of the five-member board of arbitration that decided cases regarding lot ownership. Cy was a short, slender man, totally bald except for a thick ring of hair that circled around the back of his head from ear to ear. He sported a mustache and spectacles and enjoyed the authority he held. He was also easy to bribe, and had helped Nolan swindle several people out of their land; from the look on his face, he had news of another deal he knew would please Ives.

One of the two other men was a stranger to Nolan, the thinnest man he'd ever seen, with piercing eyes ablaze with something that looked like anger and revenge. Walking in behind Cy and the stranger was the new town sheriff, for what he was worth. Harper Seymour was a potbellied, age-ing man who could handle a few town drunks but not much more than that. When things got really serious, a U. S. Marshal had to be called in.

"Well, gentlemen, to what do I owe this visit?" Nolan asked, shaking hands with all three of them. He grunted as he sat back down in his chair.

"I've got some good news for you, Nolan," Cy answered with a smug grin. "Looks like you can get those two prime lots away from Allyson Mills without even having to pay for them."

"What?" Nolan's puffy eyes lit up, and he grasped the arms of his chair.

Cy chuckled. "This man with me is a Mr. Henry Bartel, former overseer at an orphanage back in New York City. He came out here a couple of days ago to live, decided he'd open a school in Guthrie. He's a teacher."

"So? Get to it, Cy!"

"I became familiar with this country over a year ago when I accompanied a train full of orphans here to be adopted into various homes, mostly farmers," Henry spoke up, holding his thin nose slightly in the air. He simply glowed with arrogance. "When we reached Arkansas City, two of the most trouble-making orphans decided to bolt and run. I never found them. When they ran, the girl stole three hundred dollars off of me. She was a little thief who gained her experience at picking pockets in the streets of New York City. Since arriving here, I have learned what happened to those two, and I intend to have the girl arrested. When I told the sheriff here who it was, he told me we should get the land agent in on this, and also you. He said you had an interest."

"Me?" Nolan looked from Henry to Cy, then began to grin. "Allyson Mills is the runaway thief?"

Cy grinned. "The same. Mr. Bartel here says the boy with her was her brother, *not* her husband! And she was only sixteen at the time, which means she was not of a legal age to claim that land, let alone the fact that she filed falsely as Mrs. Toby Mills and is a thief. I have a feeling the land agent who was here before me was bribed to let her keep her claim. She might have a lot of friends in this town, but when they find out how she's been lying to all of them, she won't get any support. We're on our way over there right now to arrest the little bitch and inform her that her claim is no longer valid. I thought you might like to accompany us."

Nolan chuckled deep inside so that his big belly shook. "Well, well. So the poor, grieving widow isn't a widow at all! She's nothing but a thief off the streets of New York City, using peoples' sympathy to get what she wants. I'll be damned." He grasped the arms of his chair to help push himself to his feet again. "Thanks for coming to get me, Cy. I wouldn't miss this for anything." He walked around his desk to a hat rack, took his silk hat, and put it on.

"I don't like arrestin' a woman, Nolan," the sheriff grumbled. "Especially a pretty little thing like Mrs.—I mean Miss Mills. We don't even know her side of the story."

Nolan sniffed. "I don't give a damn if you arrest her or not as far as what she stole from Mr. Bartel. That's between her and him. All I care about is the fact that she filed for that land under false pretenses, which means she's going to lose it. Cy knows how much I want those lots. That little bitch has fought me every step of the way, figuring she had me outwitted. I just want to see the look on her face when she finds out I've finally won. Let's go!"

The four men headed out, the heavy-set Nolan Ives walking with unusual briskness for his size, his eyes glowing with sweet victory.

Ethan leaned back in his chair, rubbing his stomach. He had just finished eating a royal breakfast, cooked and served by his new wife, who was now serving breakfast to other boarders. He watched her, taking deep satisfaction in her beauty, in knowing she was Mrs. Ethan Temple . . . in remembering a kind of passion he had not known in a very long time. Allyson Temple was awakening to her womanhood, discovering the joy of sharing her bed with a man.

They had not slept much last night, but she'd still gotten up at the crack of dawn to start baking biscuits and cooking sausages. It irritated him a little that she couldn't take time away from her business on her first day of being married, but he fully understood what all of this meant to her, and he supposed he'd better see about finding a job in town for himself. Ally was not about to give up any of this, but there really wasn't a lot for him to do here. Ally had her own routine, and he was just in the way; but not at night. At night the beautiful woman he watched serving another table belonged only to Ethan Temple. He could hardly wait for the day to end again, hoped maybe someday he could persuade her to give up the business or at least let others run it so they could have a farm or ranch someplace out of town where it was quiet, and where they could be alone more often in a nice place to raise kids.

Life was going to be damn good. He just had to be patient and not push her too fast on anything. She was young and determined and impetuous, but full of energy and love and an eagerness to please. He wondered now when he would be able to make himself leave. He'd made that promise to his father, and he really was concerned about what was happening in the North; but he hated leaving her now. It was impossible, for the time being, to think about sleeping without her beside him; and now that she was his wife, how could he leave her here alone?

He loved her today even more than he did last night, and yet he couldn't quite rid himself of his doubts about why she had married him so suddenly. He hated himself for still thinking she could have some reason other than just plain loving him, and he scolded himself for his lack of confidence in her. He rose from the table to take his cup to the kitchen to get more coffee when the screen door to the restaurant swung open and four men loomed inside, one of them barely able to squeeze himself through the doorway. It was Nolan Ives.

Ethan slowly set down his coffee cup. He noticed Allyson straighten and stare at the men, then begin to pale. Ethan looked back at them—Ives, Cy Jacobs, and Guthrie's excuse for a sheriff, Harper Seymour. He did not recognize the fourth man, but he watched them as all four approached Ally with a look of determined authority.

Ethan moved closer, ready to defend his wife against whatever these men had come here for. Others in the room watched the confrontation in bewilderment.

"Miss Mills, I'm here to arrest you for stealing three hundred dollars from Mr. Henry Bartel," the sheriff announced.

14

Patrons in Ally's establishment gasped and whispered among themselves at the sheriff's announcement. The lovely young Widow Mills being arrested for stealing money? One of those present, a reporter for the local Guthrie newspaper, whipped out a small tablet and began taking notes.

At first Allyson said nothing. She only folded her arms and glared back defiantly at all four men who had invaded her restaurant and interrupted her customers' breakfast. In that one brief moment of silence, Ethan got the distinct impression that Allyson was not at all surprised by the intrusion. She seemed ready for it. He quickly moved to her side, putting a hand to her waist.

"What is this all about, Sheriff Seymour?"

"That's what I'm askin' Miss Mills here."

"Her name is Mrs. Temple. We were married last night."

"Married!" Nolan Ives looked at Cy Jacobs, both of them in shock. One woman whispered something to another, and Ethan did not miss the word "Indian." The newspaper reporter was writing fast.

The sheriff nodded toward the thin, ugly man with him. "Do you recognize this man?" he asked Allyson, breaking the stunned silence.

Ethan's hand tightened around Allyson's waist, as he realized now who the stranger had to be. Some of the help came out from the kitchen to gawk.

"Yes," Ally answered, her eyes beginning to fill. The dreaded moment had come, sooner than she thought. "I recognize him," she said with a strong bitterness. She glared boldly at Bartel. "He is Henry Bartel, and he is a dirty old man who liked to fondle young girls at the orphanage where he worked in New York City! I lived in that orphanage for four years! I know him, all right."

Bartel reddened deeply. "Dear God," a woman behind them exclaimed, waving a handkerchief in front of her face as though she was about to faint.

Ethan felt his own anger rising. He had heard enough about Henry Bartel to know he hated the man. Now, somehow, he had found Allyson, something she had always dreaded; yet she seemed to expect the visit. "I think you'd better get this man out of here, Sheriff," he spoke up, "before I do something to him that will land *me* in jail! What's the idea—"

"It's all right," Ally interrupted. "I can pay Mr. Bartel back, right now," she told the sheriff. "All I have to do is go to the bank. If he wants to add on interest, I'll pay that, too. Just please get him out of my establishment."

"Don't you get all arrogant with me, you thieving little slut!" Bartel barked.

At those words, Ethan lunged at the man, grabbing him by the lapels and slamming him backward onto a table. "I've heard a lot about you, you sonofabitch! Did you tell the sheriff here *why* Ally ran away from you? Did you tell him what you do to little girls?"

"She's lying!" Bartel growled.

"She's my *wife*, so watch what you say about her!"

Ethan heard a click and moved his head just enough to see the sheriff was holding his six-gun on him. A few people got up from their tables and backed away. "Let the man go,

Mr. Temple. I know your job is to protect Miss Mills here, but right now she's under arrest, and there isn't anything you can do about it."

Ethan straightened, pulling Bartel up with him. He gave the man a shove before letting go, his mind racing in confusion. Everything had happened so suddenly, he couldn't think straight. He only knew he had to defend Ally. "I told you, her name is Mrs. Ethan Temple, not Miss Mills," he told the sheriff.

The reporter wrote frantically. *The widow Allyson Mills has married the half-breed Indian scout, Ethan Temple, who had been working for her as a guard . . . Allyson Mills, accused of being a thief by a man who runs an orphanage in New York City, admits her guilt!* The words conjured up all kinds of images. And what was this about Ally Mills Temple stealing money? It seemed an incredible accusation against a young woman the town had grown to love.

"Like my wife told you," Ethan continued, "she can pay Mr. Bartel the money."

"The money belongs to the orphanage, not to Mr. Bartel," Ally spoke up.

"It was *my* money!" Bartel protested. "And you lifted it from me, you little pickpocket!"

Allyson kept her eyes on the sheriff. "If you choose to believe the money belongs to Mr. Bartel, there is nothing I can do about it after all this time, but you might want to wire the Holy Mary Catholic Orphanage in New York City and ask them about it. Either way, I'll pay the money, but I want you to know that at the time I took it I was desperate and had no choice. I always intended to pay it back, but for the moment I just wanted to get as far away from Henry Bartel as I could." She let her tears show, hoping they would soften the sheriff. "Please don't arrest me, Sheriff Seymour. I fully admit what I did. I don't know what kind of lies Mr. Bartel told you about how it all happened, but I was desperate. We were being shipped out West by train and placed in the homes of strangers, people we didn't know. We weren't sure how they would treat us. And Mr. Bartel—he's a cruel, wicked man. I was afraid of him. I just wanted to get off that train."

"It isn't the money that's important, and you know it," Nolan Ives spoke up. "Those tears aren't from regret over what you did. They're from the fact that you know you're going to *lose* this place, Miss Mills, or Mrs. Temple, whatever you call yourself. You know that if Mr. Bartel here found you and has gone to the sheriff, then he must have told us *everything* about you by now, like the fact that you weren't married when you claimed these lots. The man with you then was your *brother*, not your husband! You lied about the facts, and claimed these lots illegally!"

Now it all came together for Ethan. Nolan Ives had already gotten wind of the truth about Allyson's age and circumstances when she claimed her land. He felt like punching the sheriff. The man must have run to Ives right away, and had probably been paid by the fat bastard to let him know anything he might find out about Allyson that could be used against her.

One of the women who'd come out from the kitchen drew in her breath in surprise when she heard Ives's remark about Toby being Allyson's brother and not her husband. Ethan realized a lot of people were going to be angry with Allyson about this. They had held a lot of sympathy for the "poor young Widow Mills" when Ally first struggled to get her business started. Allyson had played on those feelings, using them to get people to help her. No one liked being made a fool of. He could feel Allyson trembling.

"We also know that not only were you and Toby Mills brother and sister, rather than husband and wife, but you were also only sixteen and seventeen at the time those lots were claimed," Ives continued. "*Both* of you were *under* the legal age of eighteen." Ives slipped his thumbs into his vest pockets. "You took these lots under false pretenses, Mrs. Temple, and that means your claim is not valid and this land and everything on it is up for grabs." He stepped a little closer, his bloated face pink with victory. "There isn't even any sense in taking this before the review board, because it's all cut and dried, thanks to Mr. Bartel here. As of now, this place is *mine,* lady, so start packing!"

Whispers moved through the others present, and Ethan stepped closer to Ives. "You back away, Ives, or you'll tangle with me again!"

Allyson folded her arms defiantly. "Yes, and Mr. Temple is my *husband* now, not just an employee. That means that this place belongs to *him,* not to me." She looked at Cy Jacobs. "Isn't that right, Mr. Jacobs? You told me that if I married, my lots and my business would belong to my husband, and no one could take them away from me."

Nolan Ives turned angry eyes to Jacobs, who fumbled for words. "Well, I . . . I didn't know you meant to go and *get* married practically the same day!" Jacobs answered angrily.

Ethan listened in surprise, his defensive attitude suddenly beginning to change. Ally had already talked to Cy Jacobs about marrying? When? Why? Had she already known Henry Bartel was in town? Here he had just been thinking how some of Ally's friends would be angry for being used by her, but he was starting to wonder if he had been the biggest fool of all. Something was beginning to make sense now, something he didn't *want* to make sense.

"Well, I *am* married now, and Mr. Temple is most certainly of a legal age," Allyson told Jacobs. "You can't just take this place away from me so easily now, Mr. Jacobs. My husband and I will contest this all the way to the federal court at Muskogee if we have to."

Ives's face was a dark red from rage. "What the hell is this all about, Jacobs?" he demanded. "When did this woman come and talk to you about getting married!"

Jacobs looked from Allyson to Ethan. "Just a couple of days ago." He put his hands on his hips. "What kind of a mock marriage is this, anyway?" he demanded of Ethan.

Ethan suddenly wondered that himself. He was caught unprepared, torn between the duty of defending his wife and a growing anger at the woman himself. She had done it again! She had lied and cheated to keep her land and business, only this time she had used *him* to do it. He felt like a total fool, and discovering all this in front of a roomful of people only made him angrier. "Maybe you should ask my *wife* that," he said.

The words were spoken calmly, but Allyson caught the note of rage behind them. She looked up at Ethan with tear-filled eyes, and even through the blur she could see his face was even darker, his near-black eyes on fire. "Ethan, I—"

"Save it for later." He looked at Cy Jacobs. "The point is this place is apparently mine now. We'll pay off Henry Bartel and that will be the end of it."

"No, it won't," Jacobs answered, suddenly looking victorious.

Nolan Ives took hope in that look. People in the background stood staring and listening, many shocked at the things they were hearing about Allyson Mills. She had lied and cheated, stolen money, then married a half-breed just to hang on to her property! How could she sleep with an Indian? Was her business *that* important to her? Was there no end to the woman's deceit? Many of them had had pity for the poor young widow, but now they knew she was no widow at all, never had been.

"Tell me, Mr. Temple, what tribe of Indians are you related to?"

Allyson felt a growing alarm.

"Cheyenne," Ethan answered.

"And are you registered on the Cheyenne reservation as being legally entitled to government allotments and entitled to live free on the reservation if you would so choose?"

Ethan bristled. "I am."

Jacobs glanced at Ives and grinned, then looked at Allyson. "You married the wrong man, Mrs. Temple. Your husband is officially an Indian, not a white man, which means he cannot own this land. This land was purchased *from* the Indians by the government, for sale to white settlers only. Indians can't claim it, and your husband here is registered as a Cheyenne."

Allyson shook her head. "No, that can't be. He's . . . he's also half white. That has to count for *some*thing!"

Of all the insults Ethan had had to endure over the years, nothing hurt more than that remark. He had ignored that little voice that had told him there had to be a reason for Allyson Mills to suddenly want to get married. Now he knew what it was. Disappointment and anger raged in his blood.

"If he's registered as an Indian, there's no changing it after the fact," Jacobs was telling Allyson, both of them talking as though Ethan wasn't even there. "A half-breed has to choose, lady, one or the other. Ethan Temple chose to officially be Indian."

Allyson stiffened, struggling to find some kind of legality to her claim. "You never mentioned Indians couldn't own anything. I—" She turned and looked helplessly at Ethan.

"And *you* never told me you were officially registered as an *Indian* under federal law!"

The words stung. He had actually let himself believe this woman loved him for himself, that she had come to overlook the fact that he was Indian, had married him out of honest love and desire. *Stay away from it, Ethan.* He could hear Hector's words so clearly. *You goddamn fool,* he told himself. He was so stunned that for the moment he could find no words to answer her.

Allyson immediately realized how her remark must have sounded. She had seen Ethan Temple angry before, but there was something in his dark eyes now that went beyond that. "Oh, Ethan, I didn't mean that the way it sounded," she said quickly, but she knew it was too late. Her heart pounded with panic. If she lost Ethan's support, she was doomed. Her business! Everything she had worked for!

"Your claim that Ethan Temple owns what you have here is invalid," Jacobs spoke up, his whole body puffed up with arrogance.

Allyson looked back at him, more tears coming. "You can't—"

"Besides that, the fact remains you claimed these lots under false pretenses," Jacobs interrupted, "and you obviously arranged a quick marriage because you thought that would save you; but you don't have a leg to stand on." The man took some papers from the inside pocket of his suit coat. "You are being officially evicted, Mrs. Temple. You have three days to gather your personal belongings and find other accommodations. This land now belongs to Nolan Ives. I'll have the sheriff here give you twenty-four hours to bring three hundred dollars to his office to give to Mr. Bartel, or you will not only be kicked off this property, but sent directly to jail. Perhaps we can even arrange for you to be extradited to New York City." The man grasped Allyson's hand and shoved the papers into it. "Three days."

"You . . . you can't do this," Allyson told him, shivering with horror. She couldn't lose all this! She had worked too hard! She had risked her life! Toby had *died* for it! "This isn't fair. I've worked myself nearly to death to build this. I was a settler, too. I had a right—"

"You were underage!" Ives roared. "You lied and cheated, and don't think I have ever believed for one minute that you and your brother weren't Sooners! You not only lied about everything, but you sneaked through the lines that night and were here before anyone else! Your Indian buck here might have stood up for you that day, but I knew the *truth!* And now *he* knows the truth about why you married him! I can tell by the look on his face he didn't realize what was going on. You've lied to one too many people, Mrs. Temple! Just be sure you pay back that money and get yourself out of here in three days, or you'll be in *jail,* husband or no husband!"

Ives turned his hefty body and stormed out, followed by Jacobs and the sheriff. Henry Bartel stepped closer to a shaking, pale Allyson. "You get me that money quick, Missy!"

Ethan pictured the man touching a young Allyson, scaring and humiliating her. He felt rage at how Ally herself had lied about why she married him, and that rage found expression through his fist, which crashed into Henry Bartel's thin, fragile face. The punch caused a cracking sound, and people gasped at the sickening blow. One woman screamed and ran back into the kitchen. Bartel went flying halfway across the room, knocking over two tables on the way. He landed face-down and covered his face with his hands, screaming that Ethan had broken his nose. Blood began dripping through his fingers.

Sheriff Seymour hurried back inside, his gun drawn. "That's enough, Temple! Touch the man again and *you'll* go to jail, too!"

"He deserved it," Ethan fumed. "And the mood I'm in right now, I wouldn't go pulling a gun on me, Seymour! Just go on and get the hell out of here, and take that bastard with you!" He grabbed Allyson's arm; she could feel his strength, knew he wanted to hurt her, too. "My *wife* and I have some things to discuss!" He dragged Allyson through the double doors toward his room, while witnesses gasped and mumbled and the reporter flew out of the building to get to the newspaper office.

"Three days!" the sheriff called out to Ethan.

"Fine!" Ethan fumed, more to himself than anyone else. He squeezed Allyson's arm harder as he forced her into his room. "I don't have much to pack. *I* can be gone in *less* than three days!" He slammed the door shut. "And I *will* leave, as soon as I get the *truth* out of *you!*"

Allyson rubbed at her sore arm and turned away. She heard Ethan groan, heard him moving around behind her, opening a drawer. A few clothes landed on the bed . . . the same bed where they had done such wonderful things the night before. None of this had turned out like she had planned, and right now she didn't know which was worse . . . losing her restaurant and boarding house . . . or losing Ethan Temple. It was obvious she was not going to hang on to either one. She had always thought her business was the most important thing, but after last night . . .

"It isn't like you think, Ethan. Please don't leave."

"It's *exactly* like I'm thinking!" He grabbed up his saddlebags from a corner and began cramming things into them. "I can't believe I was so goddamn *stupid!* Something kept trying to tell me there had to be a reason you suddenly wanted to marry me when I got back, but I didn't want to believe it. I wanted to believe it was *real*, that you loved me and wanted me for me, not because I was a man who might help you hang on to your property!" He strapped on his six-gun. "It must have been real disappointing when you found out my being Indian ruined it all. Something tells me you *never* would have married me if you had known that. That remark you made that first night a year ago about me being Indian should have warned me. I should have realized then that attitudes like that don't change overnight." He straightened, looking dangerous and furious. "I'm sorry my being half white doesn't *count* for something, Mrs. Temple!"

Allyson swallowed, not sure whether even to touch him. Ethan was a big man, and she had seen him angry before. It was very intimidating to have that anger directed at her. "Ethan, you know how much this place means to me." The tears of desperation came then. "But I didn't marry you just for that, I swear."

He leaned closer, and she wondered if he might hit her. "And I'm tired of your goddamn lies!" He brushed past her, almost knocking her down. He grabbed up a carpetbag and began throwing more clothes into that.

"Ethan . . . what are you doing? Where are you going?"

"Up north, which I *should* have done in the first place. I should never have come back here to see about you."

"But . . . what am I going to do? I . . . I need you."

He snickered bitterly. "You don't need me, Ally, certainly not now that you know my Indian blood has spoiled your plans." He straightened, glaring at her. "You don't need anybody but yourself. You used to say that all the time, remember?" He walked to the wardrobe and took out more clothes. "You'll manage. You always do, don't you? You'll find a way to lie or cheat or steal or use someone to get whatever it is in life you're looking for." He turned to stuff more things into the carpetbag, then faced her, a terrible hurt in his dark eyes. "How about last night, Ally? Was *that* a lie, too? Was it all just an act, pretending to be the good and loving wife? My God, you practically *prostituted* yourself just to keep this place! I might as well have been with a whore last night!"

"Don't say that!" she screamed. "It wasn't like that at all, Ethan! You must know that." The tears came harder then. "And . . . and I made it legal. There was nothing wrong with it."

Ethan closed his eyes and breathed deeply for self-control. Oh, how he wanted to hit her, but he could never lay a hand on her and he knew it. The worst part was he loved her as much as ever, but right now his anger and humiliation far outweighed any feelings he had for her. He watched her, wishing he could feel sorry for her, but he only felt a cold bitterness, even though she stood there looking so small and helpless.

There is nothing small and helpless about her! that voice inside reminded him. "Ally, maybe it was legal on paper; but what about in your heart? I was making love to you because I truly *did* love you. You were just consummating a marriage because you thought it meant you could keep your property."

"No! I mean . . . it was like that at first . . . but after, I realized I really *do* love you, Ethan."

He shook his head. "A man has his pride, Ally. That's something you don't understand yet. It runs a lot deeper than you think. You say I used you that night a year ago, but I didn't. I loved and wanted you, and I would have stayed if you hadn't made it very clear how you felt about me being Indian. When I came back here I didn't give much thought to there being anything like that between us again, for the same reason. Then suddenly you went soft on me, made me believe you *had* fallen in love with me, made me believe you didn't see me as Indian anymore but just as a man."

"But I *do* see you that way, Ethan," she sniffled.

"No, you don't. Jacobs was right. You *did* marry the wrong man. You married a man who won't be used, and you *used* me, Ally, in a lot worse way than what I did that night I made you drink a little whiskey. My intentions have always been the same, but yours haven't." He walked into the washroom, coming back out with a couple of towels and his razor. He threw them into the carpetbag. "You know something? You're stuck with an Indian husband now. Isn't that ironic? I'll bet you could just crawl under a rug."

"Don't say that!" She met his eyes. "Please, Ethan. It isn't like that at all. Don't go away! I'm *not* ashamed of your Indian blood. I love you!"

He smiled bitterly. "You don't know how you feel about anything, and my leaving is the only thing that is going to make you think about what you've done. Don't expect me to turn around and make this all easy for you, because I'm not going to. Right now, I *need* to go away, to sort out how *I* feel about *you*."

Her slender shoulders shook in a sob. "But . . . don't you love me any more, Ethan?"

His eyes moved over her, and pain filled him at the memory of their night together. God, how he wanted her that way again, but it was all spoiled now. If he stayed with her right now he'd hurt her somehow. It just wouldn't be the same. "I honestly don't know, Ally." He sighed deeply. "I would have stood up for you all the way out there if you had just been truthful about the whole thing. You could have told me you knew Henry Bartel was in town. You could have told me what you feared would happen. Maybe I could have found a way to do something about it without you having to lie your way into being my wife. Maybe in time we could have done all this the *right* way, for the right *reasons*." He walked to his chair and picked up his hat. He moved to grab his rifle from a corner of the room, then threw his saddlebags over his shoulder.

"Ethan, please, *please* don't go! They're going to take it away! They're going to take it all away, and I worked so hard for it! If you leave me, too, what will I do? Where will I go? How long should I wait for you? Please come back. You *will* come back, won't you?"

Damn her. He wanted to be able to hurt her without it bothering him. "I'll come back, but I don't know when. You've got money. Pay Bartel off and find yourself a job. You'll manage. You're a strong, determined woman, who will do anything to get what she wants. You'll get by." He picked up his carpetbag and headed toward the door.

"Ethan, wait! We have to talk about this! I'm your *wife!*"

Ethan studied the lustrous red hair, the pretty blue dress with yellow flowers, the one he had bought her a year ago. How could he have been so happy just a few minutes ago and so miserable now? "It's just a piece of paper, honey, one that didn't do you any damn good after all. Save your tears. They won't work with me. You just think about things while I'm away and decide whether or not you want to stay married to an Indian for the rest of your life. If not, I guess you'll just have to be a divorced woman."

Her body jerked in a sob. "But . . . how long will you be gone? Will you at least write, let me know you're all right, when you're coming back? Ethan, you're my *husband!*"

His dark eyes drilled into her. "That's right, and until I decide what to do about that, you remember that you *have* a husband! Don't be prostituting yourself with some other man just to get something you need!"

The words cut deep. "Oh, Ethan, you know better," she said, turning away. "You know it in your heart."

She began crying harder, and for a moment, Ethan was tempted to go to her, hold her, try to forgive her; but stubborn pride reminded him she had blatantly used him and was probably doing it again right now, thinking those tears would touch his heart. He felt as though someone had just rammed a fist into his gut. He turned away without another word and left.

Allyson heard the door at the end of the hallway slam closed. The tears came harder then. She walked to his bed, crawled onto it. His scent lingered there, the smell of man and leather. When she got her idea to marry him and allow him his husbandly privileges to make it legal, she had not considered the fact that she might really fall totally in love with him; that she might discover she enjoyed being naked in his arms, letting him be intimate with her, feeling him inside of her. She had truly been happy this morning when she woke up to his kisses and once again opened herself to him willingly before getting up to start the day. She had thought how wonderful it was going to be in his arms every night.

Now all she had was the memory of one night. There might never be any others. She had intended to talk to him tonight, to get it all out in the open, tell him she had fallen in love with him after all. She figured if she could tell him in the right way, he would forgive her. But now this had happened. She wished she could shoot Nolan Ives and Henry Bartel and Cy Jacobs.

No. She wished she could shoot herself. She deserved this. She should have known her tears wouldn't work on a man like Ethan, should have realized he wasn't a man to be used so easily.

Never had she hurt so deeply, not since Toby died. Right

now she felt like Ethan had died, too. She grasped a pillow and pressed it against her, aching to have him beside her, but he was gone. Maybe he would write and tell her he was never coming back. Maybe she would never see Ethan Temple again. She never dreamed before last night that such a thought would bring such wrenching sorrow.

15

"She is young, Running Wolf. Youth takes patience."

Ethan sat near a campfire with his Cheyenne grandmother, Sky Dancing Woman, who always referred to him by his Cheyenne name, Running Wolf. A black kettle filled with potatoes and rabbit meat hung simmering over the flames, and every once in a while his grandmother would get up and stir it. In the distance Ethan could hear the constant drumming and singing of the Sioux, as the tribe rotated its members in taking turns at keeping up the unending Ghost Dance ritual. They believed that if they kept up the dancing, their dream of a returning Messiah who would bring back their dead would be realized even sooner. Ethan's uncle, Big Hands, and his three cousins and their wives were all involved in the dancing.

All the way here, through the various Sioux reservations, Ethan had seen and heard the same thing—special dances, special songs, special "protective" Ghost shirts, as well as the constant vigilance of nervous soldiers who tried to assure even more nervous white settlers that the Sioux were not planning to make war. It was a volatile situation, and Ethan was glad he had come. He had decided to volunteer his services as a scout, interpreter, and general go-between for the army, hoping to use what expertise he had in these situations to help avoid unnecessary misunderstandings and conflict; but he could not avoid a feeling of dread about the whole situation. Whites were demanding action, wanting the army to put a stop to the new Indian religion that was making the Sioux feel stronger again.

Ethan was glad for the diversion. It kept his mind off of something he would rather not think about—more to the point, a red-haired woman he ached to hold again, to touch, taste, enjoy again. He had needed to tell someone, to sort out his feelings. His grandmother had always been easy to talk to—still was, even though he was a grown man now. For her sake alone he was glad he had come. She was more frail than he had ever seen her, and he knew deep inside that once he left her again, she would die before he ever got to come back, *if* he came back. Maybe it was time to make a final choice. If he did go back to Allyson, he would have to live for once and for all the white man's way in the white man's world.

"I have the patience, Grandmother," he told the old woman. He sat shirtless, his hair brushed out long over his shoulders. It was hot, like it usually was in the Dakotas in July. He supposed few places had such extremes of cold in winter and hot in summer as this land did, but it was beautiful country. He just wished he could have seen it when the buffalo ran so thick a man could walk on their backs. His grandmother loved to tell that story. "If what she did was just a mistake of youth, I could put up with it," he continued, speaking in English. His grandmother had learned to speak the white man's tongue from missionaries, convinced it was the wise thing to do. "But what she did was deliberate and heartless. I won't be used that way. She made a fool of me. I can hardly believe I was stupid enough to believe she really loved me for who I am."

The old woman smiled, showing no teeth. "You should

be easy for any woman to love," she answered. "You are pleasing to the eye, my grandson, strong and handsome."

Ethan grinned bashfully. "White women don't see me that way."

"Oh, I think you are wrong." She shook a bony finger at him. "You look in the mirror, but you do not really see yourself, Running Wolf. Just today, when you took me to the reservation supply post, I saw a white woman watching you. She was the wife of one of the soldiers, but that woman, she could not stop staring at you. I know it is because you are so fine-looking. You turn women's heads, Indian and white."

Ethan chuckled. "You're just prejudiced because I'm your grandson." He reached over and took a pouch of tobacco and a cigarette paper from his gear. "Even so, I should never have considered marrying a white woman: I should have stayed on the reservation and looked for another Indian woman." He began rolling a cigarette.

"Maybe. But sometimes a woman gets in your blood, and there is nothing you can do about it. I am thinking maybe this red-headed woman you call Ally is deeply regretting what she did. I am thinking that once she slept with you, even if she only married you for her own gain, she woke up feeling different. A good woman cannot lay with just any man without having feelings for him. Surely you could tell when you were with her that way if she truly wanted you or was just pretending."

Ethan thought about their wedding night, the glorious ecstasy, Ally's surprising, unbridled passion. Once she had gotten over her fears and ugly memories, she had turned out to be more woman than he had expected.

"It's hard to say, Grandmother. You had to know her. She's quite the little actor, a clever liar. Whether she was serious about that or not, it doesn't erase the rest of it."

His wounded pride made it impossible to think she had been sincere. Little Miss Ally Mills had not wanted a husband at all. She had only wanted to hang on to that damn, precious business of hers, and she was determined and enterprising enough that she would probably find some other way to be independently wealthy, with or without him. She had been taking care of herself against all kinds of opposition since she was ten years old. If she could survive in New York City, she could certainly survive in a place like Guthrie, Oklahoma. He was not going to crawl back to her this soon. It served her right to wait and wonder. The only way she would ever know if she really wanted him was to be away from him for a while.

"I'll write her," he told his grandmother. "She'll know where I am. If she's really sorry, really wants to be married, really loves me, she'll write back and tell me so, ask me to come back. I'm not going back there on my own. She'll have to ask me. I've done enough crawling, made a big enough fool of myself."

"Hmmm. And what if she is as stubborn and proud as you? Then she might never ask."

"Then that will be the end of it. I'll go back in six months or so and tell her she can have a divorce." He took a deep drag on the cigarette. "You didn't see her face, Grandmother, when they told her I was no use to her because I was registered as an Indian. I can't forget that look, not ever. I knew right then how I'd been used."

The old woman reached over and patted his arm. "There must have been something lovely and good in her, Running Wolf, or you would not have lost your heart to her. Maybe in time, when she is more of a woman in mind and heart and not just in body, she will understand the value of the man she married."

Ethan took hold of her hand. "Maybe. Right now I'm just as concerned about what's going on here. We shouldn't be discussing my problems. I'm a big boy, Grandmother. I'll figure out how to settle them. Right now it's you I'm worried about, and what's happening up here."

Her brown eyes suddenly grew troubled. "You mean the new religion."

Ethan nodded.

Her eyes were moist. "You are right to worry, as *I* am worried. The new religion makes our people happy, makes them dance and sing; but the soldiers, they are always telling us we must stop. They say the white people think it is a bad thing, that we are preparing for war. But it is not like that, Running Wolf. The new religion tells us we must harm no one, that we need never go to war again. We only need to dance the right dances and sing the right songs, and the Messiah will come and save us, bring back our loved ones, make the land rich and full of buffalo as it once was."

Ethan studied her old, wise eyes and the thousands of wrinkles in her aged face. "Do *you* believe this?"

"I believe it is a nice dream, and that is all we have left, Running Wolf . . . just dreams. We tell stories of the old days and pretend it can be that way again, but deep down inside, most of us know it cannot be. Ever since the day Long-Hair Custer was killed, so many summers ago, nothing has been the same, and it never will be."

Ethan's heart ached for the pain in her eyes. It had been thirteen years since Custer and his men were killed, and life had been hell for the Sioux and Northern Cheyenne ever since. Now they were reduced to reservation life, and it was destroying their spirit. There was a time when the Sioux and Cheyenne lived and migrated freely throughout the Great Plains, from Canada to Kansas, from the Mississippi to the

Rockies. Those days were long over, but those who danced in the distance believed life could be that way again.

He thought about Ally again, how intent she had been on "owning" something, claiming it, working herself nearly to death to make it succeed. That was the nature of the white man, totally different from the Indian way of life. Now the white man "owned" all the land that once belonged to the Sioux and Cheyenne. They would never give it up or give it back. The part of him that was white understood that, but he also understood the free spirit of his Indian relatives, understood their theory that no man could own land. It belonged to everyone. It was an age-old difference that would probably never be settled satisfactorily, and the two vastly different beliefs clashed within his mind and heart, leaving him torn between two worlds.

It had always been easy for him to lean toward his Indian blood, and he had been so happy when he married Violet. Now there was another woman in his life, a white woman, different from any female he had ever known, in spirit, in looks and in the world from which she came. How could he ever have thought it could work between them? She knew the white world in ways he had never experienced; his Indian world was just as foreign to her as New York City and orphanages and surviving in gang-run alleys was to him.

"Maybe you can help your uncle understand that the new religion will only bring us trouble," his grandmother was saying.

Ethan rose and walked a few feet away from her, telling himself that for the time being he had to stop thinking about Ally. He was determined to stay away long enough to make her either want him desperately or give him up. For now his concern had to be these relatives. He had promised his dying father he would do this. He stuck the cigarette between his lips and watched the dancing in the distance. A few soldiers assigned to patrol the reservation sat on horseback watching.

"I can try, Grandmother," he answered. "But this is the happiest I have seen the Sioux and Cheyenne in a long time. If nothing else, this new religion is good for the heart and spirit. They have needed something like this, something that gives them hope for the future, something to keep them from drinking themselves to death or putting guns to their heads. There had been too much hopelessness. Pa told me once that the saddest thing on earth is a proud warrior whose spirit has been broken."

"It will lead to tragedy, Running Wolf. I feel it in my old bones. I do not want to be alive when it happens."

Ethan looked down at her. She seemed so small sitting there, her hair white, her shoulder bones protruding through her worn deerskin dress. She was the picture of a people and a way of life that was fading into the past and would never be again. He knew in that moment that once whatever was to happen here was settled, he would truly have to choose; and by then there would be no choice left for a man like him. He would have to return to the white man's world. Whether or not Ally would share that world with him was yet to be seen, but the fact remained that she was still legally his wife. He had been gone a good six weeks. Maybe it was time to write and let her know how to get hold of him, if she even wanted to. Maybe she had already filed for a divorce on her own. Most white women would rather die than be branded a divorced woman, but Ally wasn't like most women. If divorce was to her advantage in getting something else she wanted, she would do it. When Ally Mills Temple wanted something, she went after it with every ounce of passion in her. Trouble was, she had made love with that same kind of passion, and he could not get her out of his blood, much as he was sure he should. He had to face the fact that she had never really wanted to marry him, and that was something he could not live with or forgive.

Yes, he would write her—send off a letter tomorrow. He would give written consent for a divorce. She could use that to make things legal on her end and get it over with. In fact, much as she deserved to be known as a divorced woman, he would make it even easier on her by giving her a statement swearing the marriage had never been consummated. That way she could get an annulment and never have to say she had been married at all.

He threw down his cigarette and put it out with his foot. Why did he care about making it easy for her? Why did he still care about her reputation or allowing her to save face? *For God's sake, you're still trying to find ways to protect her,* he thought. He knew why. He still loved her.

Allyson scrubbed another sheet, stopping for a moment to wipe sweat from her brow. She looked at her tiny hands, the skin red and cracked from doing so much wash and battering her knuckles against the ripples of the scrub board. She wanted to cry at her predicament, but refused. Life was not always going to be this way. She would find a way out of this.

The people of Guthrie had not been very kind to her after the newspaper splashed her story all over its front page. Now she was branded a liar, a cheat, a thief, God knew what else. Since her husband had left, she knew people also thought her nothing short of a whore for marrying him just to try to keep her property, let alone the fact that she had married an Indian, which she knew many of them thought was totally beneath any white woman. Even so, she suspected most felt more sympathy for Ethan than for her. She had lost friends, and finding work had not been easy. No one wanted the "tainted woman" of Guthrie working for them. Wives did not want their husbands to hire her, and no one seemed to think she deserved a second chance.

She had finally found work at Guthrie's little hotel, but was not allowed to mingle with the general public. She was relegated to the laundry room, scrubbing sheets and towels and hanging them out to dry. It was a back-breaking project, day in and day out. The first few days her arms ached so badly that she suffered terrible pain trying to keep up, but eventually her muscles adapted.

She began scrubbing again, her mind whirling with ideas about how she could rise above this. She still had some money left in Mr. Bloomfield's bank. More and more she was realizing she had to get out of Guthrie, start over someplace new. She had done it once, she could do it again. She had stayed here only because she thought Ethan might come back; but the letter she had received nearly a month ago had dashed that hope. Every time she thought of it, the tears welled up again, but she fought them. If that was the way he wanted to be, then fine. Every morning since then she had awakened determined to go to a lawyer and end the marriage, but every day she found an excuse not to go.

Why didn't she just get it over with? Ethan had actually been kind enough to send her a statement swearing he had not consummated the marriage. She didn't even have to be divorced. She could just erase the marriage if she wanted. So why couldn't she go through with it?

She scrubbed harder, angry with herself. Because she loved him, that's why. She didn't *want* to end the marriage. She knew deep down inside that Ethan didn't want that either, but his letter had made a lot of sense. They were too different. It could never have worked anyway. She was young. She should get on with life, find a white man to marry. He was probably right, but she had not given up hope he would still come back, that his love for her would rise above the pride and hurt feelings. She thought about him every night, longed to have his arms around her again, to let him bring out the woman in her in that exotic way he had of making her feel wanton and passionate, making her want to please him in thrilling, intimate ways. She ached for the wonderful feeling of being safe and protected, loved and desired.

She blinked back tears and shoved the sheet into the hot water, turning away and wiping her hands on her apron. Who was she kidding? Ethan was not coming back. His letter had rung with finality. *We both know it's best to end the marriage. We live in two different worlds, Ally, and you want things I can't give you.* She couldn't keep waiting, and she couldn't keep working here. She would be an old lady before her time. Fact was, she couldn't even stay in Guthrie. She had to go someplace where no one knew her, where she could have friends again and start over. She'd had a taste of independence and having something of her own. She wanted that again. If she was going to live out the rest of her life without a husband, she would make it just fine on her own. She already knew she could do that. She also knew there would be no other man in her life. Ethan had been the only one she could give herself to that way. Besides, she still didn't quite understand men and that damn pride and their blustery, demanding ways. She wanted nothing more to do with the male species. Ethan was the only one who had come close to what she wanted in a man, but he was out of her life. All the others seemed to just lust after her body, or were cruel bullies like Nolan Ives.

Yes, that was the answer. She would leave Guthrie. She would start over, and she didn't need a man to help her do it. It hurt to think of leaving Toby's grave behind, but it also hurt to see that building of hers now owned by Nolan Ives. The sign reading Ally's Place, had been ripped down, replaced by one that simply read Guthrie Hotel and Diner. She had worked so hard to build it, remembered the early weeks of baking bread and pies in a black, iron stove inside a hot tent . . . the stove Ethan had bought for her, even after she had hurt him so deeply.

I'll be here for quite some time, Ally. There is a lot of trouble here for my Cheyenne relatives, and I've taken another job as an army scout. I want to stay until I see what is going to happen. My grandmother might need my protection. You can get a divorce or an annulment, whichever you choose. I have enclosed statements giving my permission either way. I'll probably be here until at least next spring, so I am giving you your freedom, something you never really wanted to give up anyway.

She sniffed back tears. What was done was done. Maybe Cy Jacobs had just made it up about Ethan not being able to own land, but it wouldn't make any difference. Ethan had been too badly hurt to care about staying around and fighting. Now he was gone and so was her business. It seemed she was always losing those she loved most, but she knew part of it was her own fault. There was no repairing the damage she had done.

One thing was sure—if she was going to rise above all that had happened and start over, she had to get out of Guthrie. More and more, throughout the morning, an idea had been forming in her head, planted there last night when she sat in the hotel lobby reading a newspaper. She had overheard two men talking about a place called Denver. *That's the place to go if you're wanting to start a new business,* one of them told the other. *There's been a new gold strike at Cripple Creek, you know. Denver is on a boom again, growing like crazy. They say a man can go there and make a fortune. Those miners will pay outrageous prices for the simplest necessities.*

The words were music to her ears. Denver. Allyson had taken note of everything the man had said. A person could get there easily now by train. Just hop on the Santa Fe north to its east/west route in Kansas, and ride it into Colorado to the Denver & Rio Grande, which traveled straight north into Denver. She had enough money to do that. Once there, she could work for someone else for a while until she figured all the possibilities and what the best business would be for her to try. The risk of traveling alone to someplace new was certainly worth getting away from what she was doing now, and especially worth getting away from staring eyes and whispers. People could be so cruel. If only they understood her reasons, knew what she had been through with Henry Bartel back in New York and what life had been like as an orphan in the streets.

She walked back to her scrub board, wishing it wasn't such a hot day. The August heat had been miserable. The man she'd heard talking had said it was cooler in the mountains, and he had described country that sounded beautiful. She'd never seen mountains. As long as she had come this far, she might as well keep going. Things certainly couldn't be any worse in Denver than they were here.

She would wait one more month to see if maybe Ethan would change his mind, then she would leave. She had considered writing him, begging him to come back, but she didn't want him that way. He had to come back of his own accord. Much as she loved him, she couldn't bring herself to crawl for any man. Ethan Temple was not going to turn Allyson Mills into a whining beggar who thought she couldn't manage without a man to help her!

"Get to work, Mrs. Temple!" Allyson was roused from her daydreaming by Jed Parsons, the owner of the hotel. "Hilda is bringing down more sheets."

Allyson nodded and reached into the hot water to grasp a sheet and begin scrubbing again. Her skin stung from being rubbed so raw, but she scrubbed harder in her frustration and determination. She hated being treated like common help! Allyson Mills, who once owned a restaurant and rooming house of her own at only seventeen! How dare people treat her this way! She wanted it all back, and she would find a way to do it! She was not going to take orders and work like a little slave for someone else. That's how life had been at the orphanage. She had gotten away from that kind of living, and she would do it again.

She was not going to put up with this miserable life and these rude people just because she thought she should wait for Ethan Temple. He had made it very clear he wanted her to divorce him or get the marriage annulled, whichever way she thought best. Fine! Tomorrow. She would see about it tomorrow. Then she would leave Guthrie and all its bad memories behind her. She had no chance here. Denver sounded like as good a place as any. Besides, Ethan would probably never follow her there. It was best that he stayed out of her life for good.

Suddenly she had to stop scrubbing. There it came again, that sudden wave of frustrated desire at the thought of Ethan, the quick little pull at her heart at the realization that deep down inside she loved him with every bone in her body. She breathed deeply, then picked up the sheet and stuck it into the wringer and began turning the handle to feed it through. She had to stop this, had to stop hoping and pretending. She had to start thinking only of Ally Mills Temple. Later today she would go to the train station and find out what it would cost to get to Denver.

16

Ethan poured himself some coffee, then set the pot back down on the wood-burning stove. He had the stove stoked as hot as he could get it, and it was still cold in the cabin. He set the cup on a table and pulled on his deerskin jacket, dreading going out. From what he had already seen out a window, it looked as though a blizzard was in the making. Winters in the Dakotas could be violent and bitter.

He sensed the soft thumping then of a horse approaching through the snow outside and walked back to the window to see a soldier ride up and dismount. It was Lieutenant Jack O'Toole, and he looked worried. The tension on all the Sioux reservations had grown to almost painful proportions, and Ethan knew something was bound to blow sooner or later.

He hurried over to the door and opened it before the lieutenant could even knock. A biting December wind blew in with the man, who nodded a greeting to Ethan and immediately walked over to the stove. He removed his gloves and began rubbing his hands over its top. "My God, it's cold out there!" he exclaimed.

Ethan closed the door and took another sip of coffee. "Bitch of a day to have to be out."

The lieutenant did not answer right away, and Ethan sensed something was very wrong. He had come to know O'Toole well on several scouting expeditions as well as having acted as interpreter for him on several occasions. O'Toole was usually talkative and joking, but when he glanced at Ethan just now, Ethan saw an odd sadness in his eyes. "What's up?" he asked.

O'Toole sighed deeply. "Things are getting way out of hand, Ethan. You're right. It's a bitch of a day to be outside, but Colonel Anderson told me to come and get you. We're all headed down to the Cheyenne River reservation—might need you to do some interpreting. Big Foot's following is building, and they've fled the reservation and gone into hiding to keep practicing the Ghost Dance. They're no real threat, of course, mostly women and children, but you know how outsiders look at any Indians who leave the reservation. They figure they're on the warpath."

Ethan frowned, taking another swallow. "Why can't people just let them worship as they please? Nobody stops the *whites* from practicing whatever religion they want."

O'Toole shivered and turned his back to warm it near the stove. "You know how it is. The Indians get stirred up like that, the whites think they're out for war. Agent McLaughlin and General Miles both believe it and are determined to put a stop to it."

Ethan sneered in disgust. "Miles hasn't even been out here to see what's really going on. He hasn't tried to understand that this is all the hope and joy the Sioux have. As far as McLaughlin, he's worthless. The man shouldn't be out here at all, but then I can't think of any *other* Indian agents who are worth a damn either." He walked back to the window to see the snow was falling harder. "My pa was one of the few who did the job right, and they ended up firing him."

Lieutenant O'Toole took off his hat and ran a hand through his thick blond hair, almost afraid to tell Ethan the worst of the news. He liked the man, had worked with him often over the past few months, had seen him grieve deeply when his grandmother died two months ago. He knew Ethan had once had a white wife somewhere in Oklahoma, but didn't talk much about her, and O'Toole wasn't sure of the whole story. For over six months Ethan had talked about maybe going back to Guthrie to see the woman once more but that it probably wouldn't do much good. It was obvious he was still in love with her, but the marriage was apparently over, and increasing problems on the reservations had kept Ethan here.

"We're supposed to go find Big Foot and get him back onto the reservation," O'Toole said aloud, "but that's not the real reason I'm here, Ethan. I've got some real bad news."

Ethan turned from the window. "Spill it."

"Sitting Bull. He's been killed—shot—by his own Indian police, just south of here. We were on patrol on the northern border. A sergeant just rode up here to tell us."

Ethan felt his whole body tingle with dread and sorrow. "My God," he muttered. "This means big trouble."

"It sure does, and I blame General Miles. He figured Sitting Bull was the instigator in all this Ghost Dance mess and ordered him arrested. He figured it would be easier if Indian police did it instead of soldiers, but I guess there was some kind of misunderstanding between the police and those close to Sitting Bull. They're pretty sure the first bullet that hit him was by accident in a scuffle between the police and those trying to stop them. Then I guess the police thought Sitting Bull was going to order them killed or something, I don't know. One of them shot him in the head. The Hunkpapas are terrified now. Hundreds have fled, and I don't doubt your uncle and cousins are among them. A lot of them are headed to Pine Ridge, probably figure Red Cloud can protect them. Others have run to find Big Foot. Those are the ones who have to be brought in, since they fled the reservation completely. It's one big, damn mess, and with Sitting Bull killed, things are getting hot and soldiers are scared. You know what that can lead to."

Ethan rubbed at his eyes and turned away. "Yeah. Nervous trigger fingers." He sighed deeply. "The worst part is, the Sioux really believe if they remain peaceful, a Savior will come and end all of this. But no white man would believe the Indians won't retaliate for Sitting Bull's death. They'll take any little movement as a threat, and somebody will shoot first and ask questions later."

"How fast can you be ready to ride out with me?"

Ethan felt a great need to mourn, yet the reason for his sorrow was something abstract, something he couldn't even name. "Where's your camp?"

"Only a couple of miles to the southwest, down by Fox Creek. The colonel wants to head down to the Cheyenne River reservation right away and start hunting for Big Foot."

"Give me an hour. I'll meet you at your camp. I'd like to stop on our way and see if my uncle or cousins are still on the reservation. Like you said, they're probably already gone, but I have to know."

"Sure thing." The lieutenant put his gloves back on. "I'm sorry about Sitting Bull. I really am."

The man left, and Ethan began packing his gear. Sitting Bull dead. Such a great and famous leader. He'd even traveled with Buffalo Bill Cody and starred in his Wild West shows. Killed by his own Indian police. It was all so ironic and unnecessary, the result of the government coming in and turning Indian against Indian. They knew that was the best way to break them, and they had done their job well.

What a goddamn mess! He slammed things around, angry with everyone—the government, Indian agents, soldiers, Indian police, himself. And Ally. If not for her, he wouldn't even be up here involved in this tragedy. Annulled. She'd had the marriage annulled. He'd gotten the papers three months ago, along with a letter of apology for how she had hurt him, a thank-you for allowing the annulment.

I really did learn to love you, Ethan, but we both know it was all wrong. Don't bother trying to find me in Guthrie, if you should ever come back here. I am going to Denver.

Denver. What the hell did she think she was going to do in Denver? He could understand why she would leave Guthrie, but Denver was a lot bigger, and she was still so young. Still, if any woman her age could fend for herself, it was Ally. God only knew what trick she had up her sleeve next. He told himself there was no sense worrying about her anymore. She obviously wanted to end the marriage as much as he did, or at least he'd thought he did until he got the letter saying it was really over. He reminded himself she had never really loved him in the right way, for the right reasons, so why should he continue to think about her and worry about her . . . and long for her? It was done with. *Everything* was done with—his marriage, Old Grandmother dead, disaster ahead for his Cheyenne relatives, the rest of the Indians relegated to a pittance of land. Where did that leave him? He didn't seem to belong *any*where.

He rolled up his blankets and piled everything onto the table. He'd have to saddle Blackfoot before he could pack anything onto him. He pulled on his thickest, knee-high winter moccasins, feeling a need to weep for what was happening to the Sioux and Cheyenne, but there was no time for that. He was glad Old Grandmother had died before she knew about this. It would have broken her heart. He had at

* * *

Ethan breathed deeply to keep himself from vomiting. Back at the Episcopal mission he had already found two of his cousins, Red Crow, only seventeen, and Standing Eagle, a twenty-five-year-old man with two little sons. Both were badly wounded but would live. Now he had the grim task of helping dig the dead, frozen bodies of other Sioux and Cheyenne from the deep snow so their bodies could be counted and identified. The sight of so many dead, all left behind in a blizzard by the soldiers, was almost more than any man could take. They lay frozen into the positions in which they died. Looking almost ominous, old Big Foot was in a half-sitting position, his arms bent, his hands seeming to beckon others to join him in death, probably a much more peaceful place than that he had known in his last days on earth.

Ethan kept his back turned, quickly wiped his tears, and fought a desire to kill . . . just kill anyone . . . out of grief and anger. There was no reason for any of this. He and Lieutenant O'Toole and the others had come upon the "battle" scene only moments after it was finished. There was still confusion over what had happened. The soldiers claimed an Indian named Black Coyote started it all by refusing to give up his weapon. Standing Eagle told Ethan it wasn't that way at all. He said Big Foot was already near death from pneumonia when the soldiers found and surrounded their camp. His coughing was so bad that the old man had been spitting up blood. Even so, the soldiers had demanded he come outside with the others and surrender all weapons.

Everyone had obeyed, according to Standing Eagle. *But that was not enough*, his cousin explained, in tears himself as he told the story. *The soldiers went into the tipis and carried out everything, all our supplies, throwing them into a pile. Then they told us we had to all remove our blankets and coats, even though we were freezing, so they could search us. That is when they found Black Coyote's rifle, but he had not given it up because it was new and he was proud of it. He did not understand what was happening because he cannot hear. The soldiers spun him around, got him all confused. A gun went off. I do not even know if it was Black Coyote's gun. I only heard the sound, and right away the soldiers who surrounded us began shooting us. We had no weapons, no defense. We could only run, but they kept shooting, even at the women and children. It was a terrible thing.*

Ethan could not control mental flashes of another terrible massacre, images of his mother lying stripped and bloody. It was like Sand Creek all over again. The few survivors who were found were brought back to the reservation, but the soldiers were cared for first, while men casually tried to figure out what do with the wounded Indians. If not for the mission opening its doors, he wondered if they ever would have gotten help.

He turned back to watch two men dig another frozen body out of the snow to carry it to a wagon, tossing it in as though it were an old log. A blizzard during and after the massacre had hindered rescues, and only those obviously still alive were taken away at first. How many of these they found now had been alive then? How many had just lain and bled to death or froze to death? They had been here for four days, silent, lying in the whispering snows like stone guardians of a land they could not keep.

This had been no battle. It had been a slaughter, just like he was afraid would happen. Most of the soldiers who had been killed or wounded were hit by their own bullets in the crossfire. The Indians had already given up their weapons. It was all so stupid and unnecessary.

A tear froze on his cheek as he walked over to help lift another body. The soldiers who worked with him said nothing; now that it was over, he knew some of them felt as badly about this as he did. Still, many would tell their grandchildren about being a part of the "last Indian war." His head ached with the thought of what the papers would make of this. Again the soldiers would be made out to be the brave ones who had sacrificed their lives to finally put an end to the "Sioux uprising." No one would tell the truth. He just wished he had gotten to Big Foot sooner. Maybe he could have done something to prevent this.

What was his goal now? He had none. Thank God his father and mother and grandmother were gone and had not lived to see this. Now his uncle, Big Hands, and his other cousin, Red Crow's and Standing Eagle's nineteen-year-old brother, Crazy Fox, might also be dead. He had come here to help at the pleading of his other two cousins, who wanted to know if their father and brother were among the dead. If Ethan could find them, he intended to keep the bodies separate for their own family burial rather than let them be thrown into a mass grave as the others would be. After all, Big Hands was his mother's brother and Crazy Fox was her nephew.

PEACE ON EARTH, GOOD WILL TO MEN. That was what a sign that hung in the Episcopal mission had read the night he helped bring in wounded Indian men, women, and children four days after Christmas. It was all so ironic. The Savior the Sioux thought would come and renew the land and bring back their dead had not come. Instead, many more had died. He'd been told that just before the shooting started, a medicine man named Yellow Bird had begun to dance the Ghost Dance, singing to the others not to be afraid. Their ghost shirts would protect them from soldiers' bullets, he said. Now they lay with holes ripped through those shirts.

He breathed deeply to control his own anger and grief and

searched for two more hours, a search that led several hundred yards in many directions away from the initial site of the slaughter. Wounded Indians had crawled away, trying to find warmth and safety, only to freeze to death in a ravine or behind a bush. It was late afternoon when he finally found his uncle, Big Hands. Crazy Fox lay beside his father. They had apparently clung to each other for safety and warmth and had died that way. He trembled as he had to use his shovel to pry the bodies loose from the ground.

"We'll take them," a soldier told him, preparing to tie a rope around Big Hands to drag him to a wagon.

"Don't touch him," Ethan answered.

The soldier backed away at the look on Ethan's face.

"Let him be, Sergeant." Ethan recognized Lieutenant O'Toole's voice. "They're relatives."

"I've got orders. If he's looking for trouble—"

"You don't want to mess with this man right now, Sergeant. Go on and help the others. Ethan will take care of these two."

The sergeant glared rather defiantly at Ethan before turning away and walking off. Ethan watched him, wanting to kill.

"Watch yourself, Ethan. You look Indian, and some of these men are still nervous and trigger-happy."

Ethan looked at the lieutenant, his eyes smouldering. "The mood I'm in, I don't much give a damn. At least I'd be able to take a few down with me."

The lieutenant sighed. "Let it go, Ethan. Take your relatives and have your burial. More killing and you losing your life isn't going to change any of this or make it go away. You know that."

Ethan looked down at his uncle and cousin. "Yeah, I know." He turned away to get Blackfoot, bringing the horse back to where the bodies lay. He had devised a type of sled out of wood and branches and had tied it to the horse so he would have something to carry the bodies on. To his surprise, the lieutenant offered to help him load them and tie them on. Ethan thanked him and started to mount up to take the bodies back to reservation headquarters. The lieutenant touched his arm.

"You need to get away from here, Ethan. It's done with now, and there isn't anything else you can do. The way you were raised, you can't just stay here on a reservation the rest of your life. Do yourself a favor and get the hell out of here. Go on back to Oklahoma or wherever."

Ethan turned away. "To tell you the truth, Lieutenant, a man like me doesn't quite know *where* he belongs. I don't know just what I'll do now."

"What about that wife you told me about once?"

The words brought a dull ache to Ethan's heart. "She wasn't so sure she wanted to be married to an Indian. She had the marriage annulled."

"I'm sorry. You're a good man, Ethan. Don't let this bring you down. You're smart and skilled, and although you probably don't want to hear it right now, you remember that you *are* half white. Too many of your Indian friends and relatives are falling into alcohol and hopelessness. Don't let that happen to you."

Ethan looked over at a freight wagon pulling away, loaded with frozen bodies. "I'm not sure what I'm going to do." He looked back at the lieutenant with tear-filled eyes. "It hurts, Lieutenant. It cuts deep, like someone wrenching a knife in your gut."

O'Toole put a hand on his shoulder. "I know." He gave the shoulder a squeeze and left, and Ethan turned and mounted up on Blackfoot.

"Let's go, boy." He urged the horse into a slow walk, heading toward reservation headquarters, dragging his homemade sled and its silent, frozen cargo. He wondered if Ally had heard about what had happened here, and if she cared.

17

March, 1891 . . .

Allyson ducked her head against a winter storm that pushed its way out of the mountains and was dumping deep snow on Denver. She could not let the weather stop her. She would see Attorney Calvin Gibson today and pester him again to find out about her investment. The man was not going to put her off any longer, and if he thought he intimidated her just because he was someone of experience and authority and she was a young woman of no particular importance in Denver, he would find out different!

She wore her finest winter dress, a lovely green velvet with a fitted bodice decorated with little white ivory buttons that led up to the high, lace-trimmed neck. She wore a darker green velvet hat with a brim that kept snow off her hair, and a matching deep green cape and gloves. She knew enough about men to know they seemed to pay more attention to a well-attired woman who stood her ground, and she was going to be both today. She had been trying to get Gibson to find out about her investment in prospecting at Cripple Creek, but the man was always "too busy." He had promised to look into it a week ago, and still she had not heard from him. She had almost no money left, since Mrs. Reed had gone and sold the rooming house and moved back to Illinois. Because she had grubstaked a prospector just before that, Allyson did not have the money to buy the rooming house from the woman. She had put every cent into

the hopes of finding gold, and now she worried that the prospector she had financed nearly three months ago, a fifty-five-year-old widower named John Sebastian, might have simply run off with her money. If Attorney Gibson could not find out what had happened with the man, she would go to Cripple Creek herself!

It was Gibson who, through a newspaper advertisement, had arranged the meeting between prospectors who needed money and supplies, and those who wished to grubstake them in return for a share of the profits if they struck gold. Allyson had been the only woman to show up at the meeting, and the men had laughed at her until she slapped her money on the table right along with the rest of them. She decided that since Gibson had set up the meeting and had received a fee from both the prospectors and the investors, it was his responsibility to follow up on the results, although Gibson did not agree. He felt he had done his part in simply bringing prospectors and investors together, but she was working too many hours to be able to go to Cripple Creek and find the information she needed. Gibson was a man who had connections. It couldn't possibly be too much trouble for him to inquire about Mr. Sebastian and find out if he had filed a claim. She was not going to be swindled out of her hard-earned money.

She walked down a cold hallway to the door with glass in it that had ATTORNEY CALVIN GIBSON painted on it. She had been here before, and Gibson had always had an excuse as to why he had not been able to get any information. As far as she was concerned, he was just being lazy and stubborn.

Sebastian had seemed so trustworthy. He even had letters from other investors for whom he had found gold. He was experienced at prospecting, one of those men who simply enjoyed the hunt but, as he had explained, never kept his

claim once he found gold. She had been told she would be informed the moment the man found any kind of vein and would be given first option to buy him out completely, since she had financed the expedition in the first place. At the least, she was to get half the profits if Sebastian sold the claim to someone else. In the meantime, she had continued working for the new owner of the boarding house, as well as taking a second job in a laundry until late into the night. She had saved more money faithfully—probably not enough to buy a claim, but it was always possible. It was at least enough to get to Cripple Creek if she had to. She was going to make sure Sebastian did not sell the claim behind her back and take off with all the profits.

She took a deep breath and walked into Gibson's secretary's office, determined she would not leave until she got the information.

"May I help you?" The secretary, a stout, gray-haired woman, looked up at Allyson from her desk.

"You know why I am here, Mrs. Lang." Allyson stood stiff and stern, refusing to let the older and very daunting woman make her leave again. "There is certain information I need from Mr. Gibson, and I intend to get it."

The woman stiffened and rose. "You need an appointment. I have told you that before."

"And Mr. Gibson never has any information for me when I come! Maybe if I begin pestering him daily, he'll find out what I need to know just to get *rid* of me!" Allyson gave the woman a sneering smile and marched right past her and into Gibson's office.

"Wait a minute!" Mrs. Lang moved toward her, but Allyson already had the door open and was parading inside. Gibson looked up at her with a scowl as his secretary followed Allyson into the room. "I tried to stop her, Mr. Gibson—"

"It's all right, Evelyn. Close the door."

Allyson turned and gave the woman a look of victory, and Mrs. Lang glared back, her huge breasts heaving beneath her lacy blouse as she sighed deeply in disgust. She left, and Allyson turned her gaze back to Gibson, a small-built man with thinning brown hair and bad teeth. The man leaned back in his chair, looking Allyson over as though she stood there naked.

"I figured you'd be back sometime this week."

"Well, you figured right. And I will be back here every single day from here on until you get me the information I need." Allyson held the man's gaze squarely. She had grown used to being looked at the way Gibson looked at her now, well knew what most men were thinking when they stripped a woman with their eyes. The little bastard! There was only one man she had never minded looking at her like that, but she had lost him, and it was no one's fault but her own.

"Sit down, Miss Mills," Gibson said.

Allyson kept her chin high as she moved to a chair across from his desk, thinking how Gibson's small, round spectacles made him look like a little owl. He was not much of a specimen, not like Ethan Temple . . .

The thought made her blink and look away. Why was it Ethan came to mind at the oddest moments? And every time it happened, it brought a quick little pain to her chest and made her take a deep breath.

"I *do* have some news for you at last, Miss Mills," Gibson was telling her. He leaned back in his chair. "Fact is, I was going to send for you."

Allyson removed her gloves. "Well, it's about time! What have you found out?"

"You aren't going to like it."

Allyson felt a hint of panic. All her money! "Has John Sebastian gone and sold a claim without telling me?"

Gibson leaned forward then, actually showing some concern. "Quite the contrary. The man did find gold and staked a claim, but now he's dead."

Allyson's look of haughty determination faded. "Dead! When? How?" Her mind began spinning with the possibilities. Did that mean she owned a gold mine outright?

"That's the interesting part. My connections up at Cripple Creek tell me that he was found at his diggings—shot in the head. Someone obviously killed him deliberately."

Allyson untied her cape. "*Deliberately!* Murder?"

Gibson rose then, walking to a table where he kept a decanter of whiskey. He poured himself a small shot. "Would you like a drink, Miss Mills?"

Whiskey. It brought back another memory. "No, thank you. I don't drink."

The man poured his drink and looked over at her. He raised the small glass, then gulped down the whiskey. "You're such an innocent, Miss Mills. My suggestion is that you get out of this mess right now. Out of all the bigger mine owners, you can probably find one who'll buy your claim, even though, I'm told, it's proving to be pretty worthless so far."

"So, I *do* have a legal claim!"

Gibson shrugged, coming over and sitting on the edge of his desk. "You do. Sebastian had found some placer gold in a creek that ran through the claim. That usually means there's more in the mountain above the creek, but he apparently didn't find any. My connections have sent me a map and all the information. What he found is hardly enough to live on, mind you, but it's a legitimate claim. The problem is, why was Sebastian murdered? It could have been a grudge thing, maybe over a card game or something. But it also could have been someone who wants that claim, for whatever reason. Like I said, it's not worth a whole hell of a lot. At any rate, if someone *is* after it, that means there is big trouble up there, Miss Mills, the kind of trouble a young lady like you doesn't want to get involved in."

Allyson looked down at her gloves, twisting them in her hands, trying to think. How she hated being told she couldn't do something, especially when someone thought that just because she was young and a woman . . . She looked up into Gibson's spectacles, seeing the haughty humor in his brown eyes. He thought she could be easily frightened and would give it all up right now! "And I suppose *you* would handle the sale of my claim to whoever might want it, for a percentage of the profits, of course?"

The man smiled. "Of course."

Allyson rose. "No, thank you. I grubstaked Mr. Sebastian, and now he's dead. That means I legally own a mining claim."

"What good will it do you if you can't mine it? With Sebastian murdered, no one else is going to have the guts to go in there and keep digging."

Allyson walked past the man to a window, looking out at the mountains that lined Denver's western horizon. "Then I'll mine it myself."

Gibson let out a sneering grunt. "You can't go up there. What do you know about mining? Besides that, you're a pretty, young, single woman. How long do you think you would survive in a place full of thousands of men who haven't seen anything better-looking than their horses'—"

Allyson met his eyes, refusing to look shocked or afraid. "I can learn, Mr. Gibson. You might be surprised at how easily I adapt to situations, and how hard I can work. I don't doubt that in my nineteen years I've worked harder than you have in your whole life, and you must be almost three times my age." The man reddened a little in anger and insult. Allyson took delight at the look on his face. "As far as being afraid of all those men, I think most men recognize a proper lady when they see one. Those who don't will just have to answer to my pistol. In fact, I'll buy myself a rifle or a shotgun before I go. And I don't think too many men will be willing to kill a *woman*, do you? Besides, whoever killed Mr. Sebastian wouldn't dare kill me, too. It would be taking too great a risk, stir up too much trouble. Whoever it is probably thinks he can just take over the claim or easily buy out whoever backed Sebastian." She walked back to stand in front of Gibson. "He figured wrong. It's pretty obvious why Sebastian was killed. That claim must be worth more than we think. Why should I sell it for a pittance when I might make a fortune from it?"

Gibson got up from his desk and faced her. "You're crazy. A woman can't go up there alone and dig for gold. It's damn hard work, and obviously too dangerous."

Allyson smiled. This was a challenge, like the day she decided to run off that orphan train and join the land rush. "*This* woman can do it, Mr. Gibson."

"You're only nineteen years old, and you don't know the first thing about prospecting! You don't even know how to find the claim! On top of that, it's still *winter* up there! Everything is buried in snow!"

Allyson decided not to tell the man that she wouldn't *really* be nineteen until May. After all, it was only two months away. She picked up her cape and threw it around her shoulders. "I am perfectly aware of the season, Mr. Gibson, and I have been here long enough to have heard all the stories about snow in the Rockies. But that doesn't stop the mining from continuing, does it?" She smiled, feeling a new excitement growing in her soul. "Like I said, I can learn everything I need to know. You told me you have maps. I'll simply hire a guide to take me up there."

"You can't be serious!"

"Please give me the maps, Mr. Gibson. You've done your job. The rest is up to me."

He scowled, walking around behind his desk and opening a drawer. "Use your head and sell out. You can get a good price, I'm sure."

"Oh, I don't doubt that. Someone will give me a few hundred dollars, claiming the site is worthless, then turn around and mine it and make millions. I prefer the millions in my own pocket." Allyson reached out and took the maps from him, suspecting Gibson had pulled things like this before. He could be a silent partner with whoever bought these supposedly worthless claims, then share in the fortune once they were properly mined. "I would like a signed paper from you, Mr. Gibson, stating you have no further interest in me or my claim. I don't want you to come running and claiming I owe you something when you find out I've struck it rich."

Gibson reddened with anger at her haughtiness. "I am not part of some kind of scam here, Miss Mills!"

"Aren't you? You seemed awfully sure that I would sell out right away. For all I know, Mr. Sebastian isn't dead at all. Maybe he found a good vein and you paid him off to leave it and go on to other digs, thinking I would in turn sell out. Then you and whatever mine developer with whom you've made a deal can take over the claim."

The man's eyes did seem sincere then as he leaned closer. "I'm telling you, Miss Mills, that John Sebastian was murdered. I don't know why, and I have nothing to do with anything going on up there."

"Then write that all down on a piece of paper and sign off any rights you might think you have to the claim. I want to be sure it is all mine, free and clear. I also want a letter from you that I can give to the claims office up at Cripple Creek, proving I grubstaked Mr. Sebastian and am the rightful owner."

Gibson sighed in resignation, turning to his desk and sitting down. He took out a piece of paper and dipped his fountain pen into an inkwell. "Fine. It's your funeral," he grumbled. "I predict that within a few days you'll either be dead or wishing you *were*. If the work or the weather don't get to you, whoever wants that claim will . . . or maybe something *worse* than death will happen at the hands of men who simply like the way you look. Either way, you'll never survive."

The man began writing, and Allyson swallowed back her own secret terror. She walked back to a window to wait while Gibson wrote. She reminded herself that she had faced danger before and had survived. She would simply use her womanly charms, make the men feel sorry for her. For any man who had other thoughts about her, she would have a shotgun ready. As far as the work, she wasn't afraid of that. The claim John Sebastian had staked must have great potential, or someone would never have had the man killed, if that was what had really happened. Maybe it *was* just an argument over cards or something, just some enemy of Sebastian's who carried out a grudge. That would have nothing to do with her. There could be all kinds of reasons for the man's death.

The fact remained she had a gold claim! Things were not going well for her here in Denver, so what did she have to lose? She was going to Cripple Creek! If the gold claim didn't work out, maybe she could find some other work up there to get rich. After all, she'd heard plenty about those wild mining towns, how men would pay a fortune just to get a shirt laundered. She wondered why she hadn't thought to go there before now.

"Here's your damn paper," Gibson told her after several minutes of writing. He held it out. "I think you're crazy. Whatever happens to you up there, you deserve it."

Allyson took the paper and read it. "Is your secretary a notary? I want this witnessed."

Gibson rolled his eyes. "Yes, she can notarize it. We'll do it on your way out, and for my part, I hope I never see you again. I feel obligated, though, to urge you once more not to go up there. Sell the claim, Miss Mills."

Allyson picked up her gloves and began pulling them on. "That claim is all I have in the world, Mr. Gibson, and I have no one to answer to but myself, so I guess it doesn't matter much what happens to me." She picked up her handbag.

"Miss Mills, if I may be so bold, you're a beautiful young woman who could have any man in Denver at the drop of a handkerchief. There are a lot of single, wealthy men who I am sure would be glad to have you for a wife. Why are you doing this?"

Allyson met his eyes, realizing he looked at her like all other men—as a poor, helpless woman who couldn't get by without a man; or, like Henry Bartel, as a poor, helpless woman to be *used* by any man who wished to take advantage. "Contrary to your notions, Mr. Gibson, not all women need a man to be successful and survive. If I am going to become a wealthy woman, I will not do it on the coat strings of some man who treats me like a paper doll and supports me as though I were some helpless creature incapable of earning my own way. I have survived a father's abuse and the lowest forms of human life in the alleys of New York City. I have survived abuse by a bastard of a man who ran the orphanage where I spent four years, made my way through the land rush in Oklahoma and built my own restaurant and rooming house there. By hideous fate I lost it all, but I did not let it get me down! I came to Denver to try another route, and now perhaps I have found it. I am going to Cripple Creek and I will learn how to mine my claim. If God is with me this time, I will make my fortune. I won't need to hang on some man's arm and be *Mrs.* So-and-So to do it!" She turned and walked to the door, waited for a surprised Gibson to come into his secretary's office with her. "You might like to know that I *have* been married once, Mr. Gibson, but I discovered I didn't need him after all."

She tossed her head and opened the door, walking to Mrs. Lang's desk. Gibson followed her, asking his secretary to witness the papers he had just written up. "She's going up to Cripple Creek to mine the claim herself," he told Mrs. Lang.

The hefty woman gasped. "You can't be serious!"

"I most certainly am," Allyson answered, becoming more determined every time someone told her it couldn't be done.

Mrs. Lang shook her head and scowled, signing the papers. "You are behaving like a foolish child," she said, handing Ally the papers. "God be with you, Miss Mills."

Allyson kept her look of confidence. She thanked both of them and walked out, heading back down the hallway, needing to get away quickly to hide her tears and her inner terror. Could she really do this? Maybe it *would* be a lot easier just to sell her claim, but then her lips puckered in anger at the thought. Calvin Gibson and the big mine owners who would like to buy her out, they were all just like Nolan Ives, figuring they could take advantage of a young woman whom they thought had no experience and could easily be fooled and frightened.

Not this time! This claim was something no one could take from her. It was hers legitimately, no lies, no strings. If she handled things right, using her eyes and womanly charms to win over the friendship and support of the men around her, no man would dare give her trouble.

You can do this, Ally Mills, she told herself. The first thing she had to do was find someone to guide her up to her claim. It would take every cent she had left to outfit herself and have enough left to take a train to Colorado Springs, but so be it. If the mine didn't work out, she could still sell the claim later on and get into some other kind of business. There were fortunes to be made at Cripple Creek!

She hailed a public carriage and asked to be taken back to the rooming house. There was so much to do. Cripple Creek was up in the mountains near Pike's Peak, nearly sixty miles south of Denver. The first thing she had to do was go to Colorado Springs and find a guide, then find out what she would need to take with her. The basic mining tools she'd already paid for should still be up at the claim.

The carriage was an open one, and she bent her head a little and pulled her cape tighter around herself against the cold air, wondering just how cold it really did get in the mountains. Thank goodness spring was just around the corner. Maybe by next winter she would have found a rich vein and could start having it professionally mined. She could build herself a fancy home at Cripple Creek and sit in its warmth while men dug more gold out of her fabulous mine.

Her thoughts were interrupted when the carriage passed two men wearing buckskin clothing. She stared at them, her heart taking a little leap, as it always did at the thought that Ethan might come and find her; but neither man was Ethan.

She thought how he would have made the perfect guide, would have protected and helped her. Was he even still alive? She didn't dare think of it. Men like Ethan simply did not die. They were invincible, weren't they? Besides, if he was dead, he could never, never come back to her, and deep inside she liked to carry the hope that he would.

She took a map from her handbag and opened it, studying the little red "x" that showed where her claim was supposed to be. Maybe she really was crazy to do this, but she had no one to answer to but herself, no one who cared about her. That was what hurt the most. Since Toby died there had been only one person who would have really loved her and protected her, and she had let him go. Why should she care anymore about what was wise or crazy, safe or dangerous? Oh, there was one way she was sure to make a fortune at a place like Cripple Creek, but she would rather be shot up at the mine than to sleep with men for money. She could not think of anything more horrible than strange men touching her, using her body. Only one man had been able to break down the barriers. Only one man had made her want to be a woman, had left a burning desire still lingering deep in her soul.

The carriage pulled up in front of the boarding house, and she paid the driver and stepped out. She would begin packing right away, then see about getting a ticket on the Denver & Rio Grande south to Colorado Springs. She was going to mine her claim, and anyone who wanted to try to stop her be damned!

18

Ethan gazed out the window of the Atchison, Topeka & Santa Fe Railroad car carrying him toward Pueblo, Colorado. He had no idea why he was doing this, no real plan for what he should do next. He only knew that Allyson was no longer in Guthrie. People told him she'd gone to Denver, just like she'd said she was going to do in that letter she wrote him so many months ago. For some reason, when he discovered she really was gone, it had hit him with painful reality just how much he missed her, even though he knew it was probably best this way.

Did she know about what had happened up at Wounded Knee? Did she wonder about him, think about him as often as he thought of her? He was headed west now, with no particular ideas in mind other than to get away from the hell and misery left for the Sioux in the Dakotas and the painful memories in Oklahoma. He would find work elsewhere. Part of him considered trying to find Allyson in Denver, but what would be the use? It would just reopen old wounds when he saw her again and then had to let her go.

No. He'd get off in Pueblo, unload Blackfoot and his gear, and head on farther west, just pick up jobs here and there until he knew what the hell he wanted to do; or he could stay on this train, take the Denver & Rio Grande north to Cheyenne, then ride the Union Pacific west to San Francisco. He didn't think, though, that he could stand being on

a train that long. He was already tired of this one, and he had only been on it since catching it north out of Guthrie and up into Kansas. He didn't like being cooped up in a rattling, swaying car with a bunch of strangers who gawked at him because he looked Indian, nor did he like the smell of the smoke that drifted into the cars through their open windows from the engine's smoke stack. If it wasn't such a hot day, the windows wouldn't have to be open, and right now he wished he was out riding on Blackfoot, breathing fresher air.

He never would have taken a train at all if he were not so anxious to get out of Guthrie. Once there, seeing Ally's rooming house, remembering that first day he saw her, remembering their wedding night in one of those rooms, it brought back a flood of memories that were still more difficult to deal with than he thought they would be. Nothing was the same now. He couldn't just go back to his old job scouting for the army. In fact, the army wasn't needed in quite the same way as it once had been in Indian Territory. Everything was becoming more settled; civil law was taking over and after what had happened at Wounded Knee and the realization of how much land had been lost to the Indians in Oklahoma, combined with memories of Ally, it was simply too difficult to stay there and try to get back to his old life. There *was* no old life. Even old Hec was gone. He had died while Ethan was in the Dakotas. Most thought it was a heart attack. He'd gone to sleep and simply never woke up again. The loss of his old friend had hit hard, and it seemed everything he had cared about was gone . . . his grand-mother, his father, his friend, Violet, the sweet freedom of his people . . . and Ally.

His thoughts strayed to the present when he noticed four men riding hard alongside the train. It began to slow down, but Pueblo was still several miles away. They were literally

in the middle of nowhere, which meant that if the train was slowing, there was some kind of barrier on the tracks. The approaching riders immediately triggered an alarm. Train robbery had become a rather rampant pastime for outlaws— he had once helped the army track down one gang of train robbers who had hidden out in Indian Territory. In practically every town where the train stopped there were posters of men wanted for train robbery, like Oliver Curtis Perry and the James Gang. A national detective agency, called Pinkerton's, had taken over where the law and the army could not keep up with such outlaws, and many had been apprehended; but the problem still existed, and Ethan's sixth sense told him it was happening again right now.

Quickly he removed his gunbelt, casually looking around to see that no one noticed. He hid it under a coat he'd laid on the seat next to him, taking a quick inventory of how many people were in his particular train car. Several had gotten off at Dodge City, a few at Bent's Fort. There were about twenty left on his car, only two of them women. One man in particular had the appearance of being quite wealthy, decked out in a silk suit and hat, a gold watch chain hanging from the pocket of his paisley satin vest. He was an older but handsome man, gray at the temples of his slicked, black hair, and his dark eyes held a kind of arrogance, as though he was accustomed to giving orders. The man sitting beside him seemed to be someone he knew well, and from watching them earlier, Ethan got the distinct impression the other man was some kind of bodyguard. As far as Ethan could tell, he was the only man on the train besides himself who was armed.

The train came to a full stop, and people began to mumble with concern. There were only two passenger cars on this particular train, plus a mail car. Ethan had barely fin-

ished taking inventory when a large man barged through the door at the back of the car, waving a gun. "Nobody move!" he ordered.

One woman screamed and ducked down, and everyone else just stared in fear. A shot rang out somewhere, and Ethan could hear a lot of shouting down by the mail car. "Let's have it, folks," the robber ordered. "Money, watches, jewelry, anything of value."

The intruder stood perhaps six-foot-six, sported a grizzly beard and long hair, and had the appearance of a man who cared about as much for human life as he did a rabbit's. Ethan had seen his kind before. He turned away, keeping still as the man moved through the car collecting valuables in a gunny sack. "Everybody cooperate, and we'll be outta here in no time, soon as they get the safe open in the mail car. Ain't any of you got nothin' valuable enough to die for, so just be smart and hand it all over. Let's see your wallet, mister," he ordered a man at the back of the car.

"No!" the passenger protested. "I worked too hard for this money!"

Ethan heard the click of a gun hammer being cocked. "You willin' to *die* for it? I don't know you for shit, mister, and if I have to blow your head off to get that wallet, I'll do it!"

One of the women whimpered.

"You bastard," the passenger mumbled.

Ethan turned just slightly, enough to see the man drop a fat wallet into the gunny sack. It was then the robber pistol-whipped the man, who let out a grunt as the blow opened a bloody gash in his head. He slumped over in his seat. "I don't like to be called names," the robber grumbled. He turned his dark gaze to the others. "You folks either cooperate or die, it's that simple. I got plenty out there to back me up, so whip out those valuables, take off them rings and watches and throw them in this bag! I ain't a patient man!"

He moved up the aisle toward Ethan. Terrified passengers dumped their possessions into the bag. Ethan noticed the wealthy-looking man appeared to be furious. His dark eyes glittered with rage. He was obviously not someone accustomed to being ordered to give up his valuables. He glanced at the man beside him, and Ethan saw the second man reaching into his suit coat. By then the robber had reached their seats. "Well, now, looks like I've hit the mother lode. Pretty fancy watch there, mister. Let's have it."

More gunshots were being fired somewhere outside. It seemed to Ethan they came from the mail car. Someone in the second passenger car screamed. "Hurry it up, George!" a rider outside their own car hollered.

"I'm comin'," the robber yelled out. His huge physique seemed to fill the entire car with terror. The well-dressed passenger wearing the gold watch was obviously seething inside but he held his tongue as he removed the watch from his vest pocket.

"What you got under that coat, mister?" the man called George asked the rich man's traveling companion. "A gun, maybe?"

Ethan could see the wealthy man's companion had apparently been thinking about pulling a gun, but had changed his mind. His face grew beet-red, and without a blink of regret or hint of warning, the robber fired his pistol, opening a hole in the man's chest. There came more screams from the women, and the wealthy man's eyes widened in horror. He dropped his watch into the bag, then pulled out a wallet and dropped it in also. His dark eyes drilled into the robber, a look that spelled murder.

George quickly moved on up the aisle then. Terrified passengers couldn't get their valuables out quickly enough after seeing the man shoot a passenger point-blank. Ethan waited, sitting near the front of the train car. There were only the two women and one man in front of him. George approached, pointed his six-gun at Ethan's head. Ethan just glared at him. "Do I look like a man who has a lot of valuables?"

George looked him over. "You *look* like a goddamn Indian, but that don't mean you ain't got money. Anybody that rides a train has *some* money. Let's have it!"

Ethan obliged, pulling out a pouch attached by a rawhide cord to a belt loop on his pants, then tucked inside. He untied the cord and held it out. "Not much."

"It'll do, Indian." George eyed him a moment, then ordered him to give up the knife at his belt and throw it out the window. Ethan obeyed, realizing the man thought the knife was his only handy weapon. He waited then, watching the robber turn away and give his attention to the two women. "Maybe I ought to take one of you with me as part of my catch," he threatened.

"Please don't hurt us," the younger one whimpered. "I have a husband and children."

George snickered. "Well, your man ain't here, but *I* am!"

Ethan reached for his Colt .45, carefully and quietly drawing it from under the coat.

"Stand up, lady," George ordered. "I want to get a look at my loot."

Before the woman could rise, Ethan's gun was cocked and shoved into the robber's back. "Mister, you might be big, but a bullet from this .45 in my hand will sever your spine just as easily as any other man's. Now drop your weapon, or I'll open up a hole in you so big I can reach through and grab that gun myself!"

The robber temporarily froze. "You crazy, mister? I got a lot of friends out there."

"Makes no difference to me. I'm an Indian, remember? I've got nobody who gives a damn about me, so I can take the chance. Now, let go of that six-gun!"

"I'll kill one of these women first. You want that?"

Without another word, Ethan pulled the trigger, and George's body lurched forward, an ugly, bloody hole in his spine. Both women screamed in horror and ducked into their seats, and others gasped. "My God!" one man exclaimed.

Ethan quickly bent down and grabbed the gunny sack from the robber, then turned to eye the others and make sure another robber had not boarded their car.

"What's going on in there, George?" someone outside shouted.

Ethan ran down the aisle, shoving the loot into the hands of the wealthy man. "See that everybody gets their things back," he ordered. "Everybody stay down!" he said a little louder, moving to an empty seat and looking out the window. Without hesitation he fired at the rider who had been calling to George. The man held a sack similar to George's. His horse reared as the man and his bounty fell. Ethan quickly exited his own car and charged into the second passenger car. People screamed, thinking he was another robber. He spotted no one with weapons, figuring the man outside on the horse had already robbed this car. "Stay low!" he ordered, as he ran through that car to the mail car.

"Hal's been shot!" one of the robbers was shouting. The voice came from the mail car.

Ethan pressed his back against the end of the car, away from the window in the door.

"Let's get out of here!" someone else exclaimed.

Three men exited the mail car. "George! Where are you?" one of them shouted.

"Right here," Ethan answered. He crouched and took aim, catching the three thieves off guard. He shot one down before the other two could react, but then they opened fire on Ethan. Bullets zipped past him, one taking a chunk of wood out of the corner of the mail car. A piece of it skimmed across Ethan's left cheek, cutting it deeply. Ethan wasn't sure if it was the wood or a bullet, but there was no time to wonder. He scrambled to the top of the car, firing back. He hit one of the two men. He had been holding an even bigger sack of bounty than either George or the other man who had robbed the passengers. Ethan figured it was mail.

The fourth man took off at a gallop. Ethan fired at him again, but he was too far away to hit with a six-gun and Ethan's rifle was with his gear stashed in the cattle car. He stayed low, then noticed two more men riding off from near the train's engine, where Ethan figured they must have been holding the engineers hostage while the robbery was taking place. He waited a moment, then decided that must be all of them.

"Come on out!" he called to the men inside the mail car. "Whatever they stole is still here." He stood up and ran along the top of the car and down a narrow ladder and around to the side door. "Everybody all right in here?"

"Ted here is hurt, but he'll be okay," a man answered.

Ethan looked inside and saw two men, one lying on the floor holding a bleeding leg. "I got three of the robbers," he told them. "The other three rode off. I think everything they took is still here."

"Jesus, mister, you took a chance! You all right? Your face is bleeding pretty good."

"I'm all right."

The man quickly handed Ethan a handkerchief. "Here. Use this."

Ethan took it and thanked the man. "I expect the robbers set up some kind of barrier up ahead. We'll have to get a few passengers together to help break it up so we can get your wounded man to Pueblo. There's one dead passenger in my train car, and one dead outlaw."

"Go get the engineers. They'll help—oh, here's one of them. Frank! This man saved the day—shot three of them—saved all the loot! How do you like that?"

The one called Frank looked very shaken. "I'll be damned." He walked closer to Ethan, putting out his hand. "Thanks, mister. You just might be up for an award from Pinkerton's. I heard one of them robbers say their boss was Jimmy Clairborne. He's wanted all over Kansas for train robbery. I'm almost sure Pinkerton's has money on his head. You'll get some for sure just for saving the loot, but if one of them dead men is Clairborne, you'll be even richer!"

Ethan held the handkerchief to the cut on his cheek, his gun still in his right hand. "Pardon me if I don't shake your hand," he answered. "My hands are a little full right now."

"No problem." The engineer looked at the two dead bodies sprawled outside. "Why'd you do it? You could have got yourself killed."

Ethan shrugged. "I don't like being ordered around, that's all. When one of them threatened one of the women, I knew I had to do something. Besides, I'm an army scout. I've gone up against men with guns before."

"Well, you're apparently right good with that gun. Who the hell are you, Indian?"

"Name's Ethan Temple." Ethan winced at the pain in his cheek, suspecting the wood chip had bruised his cheekbone.

"Well, thank God you were along. You be sure to check at the Pinkerton office in Colorado Springs, if you're headed that way, and see if you've got some reward money coming. We'll take these bodies with us and see if we can identify them."

Ethan hadn't even considered a reward and wasn't even sure why he had risked his neck for a bunch of people he didn't know. It just irked him to see someone bullying innocent people and threatening women, and he didn't like any man taking what belonged to him. Considering he had nothing better to do, he figured he might as well check in at Colorado Springs. He could use the money, if there was any due him. "Can we get underway real soon? If not, I'll just unload my horse and ride the rest of the way."

"Oh, I think we can get going within an hour," the engineer answered. "They disconnected some rails, but they're lying by the side of the track. I have men who can get them back in place. I don't think that bunch of no-goods actually damaged the track itself."

Ethan dabbed at his face wound once more, realized the bleeding had slowed. "I'm going back to my own car to see about getting my money back. I need a smoke."

"You deserve one," the engineer answered with a grin. "Go have a rest. We'll clean up the bodies and have the train back on track within an hour."

Ethan nodded and left, returning to his own passenger car, where people greeted him with exclamations of gratitude for getting back their valuables. Two of the men were dragging out the hefty body of the robber called George, and the well-dressed man with the gold watch was directing two other men to lay his friend's body in the mail car and cover it. "I'll see he gets a decent burial when I reach Colorado Springs," he said, a look of disgust on his face. Ethan guessed the wealthy man had expected his friend or body-guard or whatever he was should have done more to help. He pushed his way past the man, answering questions about what had happened to his face, who was dead, when the train would get underway again.

He got to his seat and reached for his gunbelt, buckling it back on and tying the holster cord around his thigh. He sat down and took a cheroot from his jacket, lit it, and took a deep drag.

"We're so grateful, sir."

Ethan looked up at the younger woman with whom the outlaw had threatened to ride off.

"I hope you're all right," she said.

Ethan kept the cheroot between his lips as he lightly touched his cheek. "It's just a flesh wound. Does it look bad?"

The woman leaned a little closer, blushing, apparently embarrassed to be talking to a stranger. "It's a long cut and looks a little deep, but it's scabbing over."

Ethan had to look away from her blue eyes. Her very presence reminded him of Allyson, and he remembered the day he had stood up for her against Nolan Ives. Who was protecting her now? Was she all right?

"Can we do anything for you?" the woman asked.

"I'm fine." He finally looked at her again. "You might as well sit down. It's going to be about an hour."

One of the engineers climbed aboard then, announcing the problem with the track and asking everyone to be patient. He announced that one of those shot was believed to be the outlaw Jimmy Clairborne, declared Ethan their hero for the day, and said if he was right, Ethan might get a reward. Ethan did not really appreciate the attention, but suffered through more compliments and thank-yous. He picked up his gun and checked the chamber. Five bullets had been spent. He reached into his gunbelt and began re-loading. He was putting in the last bullet when someone came over and sat down in the seat facing him.

"That was a hell of a job you did, mister. What's your name?"

Ethan looked up to see the man with the gold watch smiling at him. He figured the man who had been with him must not have meant much to him, since he didn't look very upset. "Ethan Temple."

The man nodded. "My name is Roy Holliday. Ever hear of the Golden Holliday mine, up at Cripple Creek?"

Ethan whirled the gun chamber, then shoved the weapon into its holster. He puffed on the cheroot, then took it from his lips, blowing out smoke. "I'm not familiar with that part of the country. I'm from Indian Territory."

Holliday's eyes moved over him. "Half-breed?"

Ethan studied him a moment, wondering what the man was after. He nodded. "Part Cheyenne. I've worked as an army scout for quite a few years."

"Any family?"

Ethan frowned. "What's it to you?"

The man grinned more. "I might have a job for you. You certainly took care of those outlaws with no trouble. I like a man who shoots first and asks questions later. That's what the guard with me should have done. Now he's dead."

Ethan looked the man over, guessing him to be perhaps fifty. "Out here that's how a man survives." He puffed on the cheroot again. "To answer your question, no, I don't have a family. And I do need a job. What would I have to do, play bodyguard?"

Holliday laughed lightly, showing white, even teeth. "No, I have other men for that job." There was something in his dark eyes Ethan didn't fully trust.

"As you have probably figured out," Holliday continued,

"I am a very wealthy man, which is why I usually take a guard along with me when I'm traveling. I'm on my way back from visiting a sister in Topeka, plus I had business in Chicago, so I've been gone a couple of months. I actually live in Colorado Springs, but I don't have a family of my own. That big house of mine seems pretty empty, so I spend most of my time up at my offices up at Cripple Creek. Actually, I own several gold and silver mines in the Rockies besides Cripple Creek—some up at Leadville, Central City, Pike's Peak. At any rate, back to your question about the job. We're starting to have a little trouble at the mines, mostly at Cripple Creek. I need good men like you to keep the miners in line."

"What kind of trouble?"

Holliday shrugged. "Threats of strikes mostly. Problems over wages. Some of the miners are forming unions and making demands that are costly to the mine owners. We might have to ship in some strikebreakers from other parts of the country if the miners do walk off the job. That would mean big problems. I need men who can keep things under control, men who can guard gold shipments, that sort of thing. You want the work?"

Ethan studied the man a moment. He already didn't like him, but what difference did that make? He needed the work, and he sure as hell didn't have anything better to do at the moment. "What does it pay?"

"Five dollars a day."

Ethan's eyebrows arched. It took two weeks to make that much working for the army. "A day?"

Holliday grinned again, apparently pleased to have impressed the Indian. Ethan decided to let him revel in his own ego. "A day. It could be dangerous."

Ethan put the cheroot back between his lips. "Doesn't

make much difference." He held the man's eyes squarely. "I have to go to Colorado Springs anyway to see if I've got that reward money coming. I'm headed noplace particular, so I'll try it out for a while, but I'm not one to go bullying innocent men, Mr. Holliday."

"You wouldn't be bullying them. You'd just be keeping them in line, for their own good. I don't want any of them to get hurt. But don't go thinking they're all innocent. They have a job to do, and I'll not stand for laziness or troublemakers. Your job is to root out the ones stirring up problems and make sure my operations run smoothly. I'll assign you to the Golden Holiday. Do we have a deal?"

Ethan leaned forward, resting his elbows on his knees. "Where would I sleep?"

"There are all kinds of log cabins and mine shacks up there. I'll set you up. I'll also have someone show you the ropes as far as mining, how the mills operate, that kind of thing. You'll learn it all in no time."

Ethan took another deep drag. "You don't know anything about me."

Holliday removed his silk suit jacket, revealing a ruffled white shirt. He began rolling up the sleeves. "I know all I need to know, just from watching you. But if you want to give me the name of your former commander, I'll wire him and see what he has to say. Where were you stationed?"

"Fort Supply—Indian Territory. I watched over cattle drives through Indian land and helped keep people in line during the land rush of '89. I've spent the last few months up in the Dakotas—did some scouting up there, too, mostly out of the Standing Rock Reservation. I'll write down some names for you."

"Fine. After you've seen about your reward at Colorado Springs, leave word at my office at the Holliday Hotel in

Colorado Springs where you can be reached. I'll ride up to Cripple Creek with you—you can meet the other men."

Ethan leaned back. "They might not like an Indian being in charge."

"They do whatever I tell them to do," Holliday replied, a threatening look in his dark eyes. "They know better than to cross me. A word of advice to you, too."

Ethan nodded. "I don't cross a man, Mr. Holliday. I say what I think right up front. I don't like being used—if I think that's happening, I'll quit, no matter what the pay."

Holliday grinned. "That's the way I like to hear a man talk." He put out his hand. "We'll talk more after we hook up in Colorado Springs."

Ethan shook his hand, which was unusually cold for such a hot day. "Fine." Holliday rose and returned to his seat. Ethan couldn't help wondering if he had any feelings at all for the man who had been sitting right beside him and was shot point-blank. It was as though he considered him just another loss, perhaps like losing some stock in a mine. Fact was, maybe losing stock would upset him more. He figured Holliday was not a man to have very deep feelings about anything except his mines and the money they made him; but then that was not his problem. At least he'd found a job, and it paid damn good. He'd never been to a mining town like Cripple Creek. It might be an interesting diversion. He needed something like that, something to keep him busy, keep him on his toes and keep from thinking about what had happened to the Sioux and Cheyenne . . . all his losses . . . Allyson. If he knew his geography, Cripple Creek was a good sixty miles from Denver. There was little, if any, chance he would run into her in a place like that.

19

Allyson awoke to the feel of something running over her legs. She gasped and sat straight up, grabbing a six-gun that lay on a crate beside her cot. Her first thought was that someone had broken into the cabin and was touching her, but when she came fully awake she realized a rat had scurried across her bed. By the dim light of a lamp she'd left lit, she saw the hideous animal disappear through a hole under the door jamb.

She shivered at the sight, wondering if she would ever get used to it. She hated rats, but up here in this rickety cabin, there was little that could be done about them except to keep food in safe containers.

Mountain rats, her guide had called them. *Everybody up here has problems with them. Just keep your traps set*. The man had been very nonchalant about it, as though the rats were no more unusual than a pine tree. For a full day after first arriving two months ago, she had used the rats for target practice, learning to shoot her new Colt .38 Frontier pistol by sitting quietly and waiting for a rat to appear. The deserted cabin had been full of them at first, and it had been difficult not to change her mind and catch a wagon or mule-train out of Cripple Creek back to Colorado Springs. Only the thought of gold kept her here, along with a determination to prove to herself and to men like Calvin Gibson that she could do this.

She had managed to get to Cripple Creek by leading her own two mules, purchased at Colorado Springs and heavily laden, behind a wagon train of supplies being brought up for the miners. It was a long journey, fraught with dangers, not just from grizzlies and such, but, at least at first, from the men who drove the wagons. None of them believed she would survive the trip up, walking the whole way, but she proved them wrong, and by the time they reached Cripple Creek they had a new respect for her. She had made sure they all knew she had a gun and would use it if any of them got any "funny ideas." She had made her own campfires and cooked her own food, and by the time they reached Cripple Creek she had even cooked meals for the rest of them.

Cripple Creek was a wild town, full of men hungry for a pretty woman. It disgusted her to realize what was on all their minds. Her only salvation had been the men of the supply train, who quickly set other men straight as they moved through town, letting them know that Miss Allyson Mills was a respectable woman who had come there to work a claim and not for the reason most of the other women were there. Painted women, some in fancy dresses, others looking more pitiful, stood in front of saloons and hung out of the windows above them. Allyson was happy to learn that most of the men there and up here at the mines were almost in awe of a proper lady, and many had practically gotten into fist fights trying to be first in line to offer their services as guides. However, since she didn't know any of them, she had chosen one of the men from the supply train who had already offered to see her up to her claim. His name was Stan Bailey, a bearded old man familiar with these mountains but who had himself given up digging for gold and preferred taking other odd jobs. Stan had brought her up here, and on their way out of town, men had laughed, some placing bets on whether or not she would stick it out or give up; several wished her good luck. She'd been told there were a few other gold-seeking women scattered through the mountains, "but none as young and perty as you!"

She sighed and rubbed at her eyes, then got up from her cot, which had apparently been hand-built by John Sebastian. She walked to the door, making sure it was bolted, then looked down at the hole underneath the door jamb. She would have to find a way to plug it. That would help with the rat problem, which had improved greatly since she had begun keeping traps set. The traps and a few supplies were found still intact in the crudely-built pine cabin. Sebastian, who someone had buried out beside the cabin, had managed that much, and whoever had killed him had not disturbed anything in the cabin. But rats had taken over, and it had taken a good week to get them under reasonable control. Now that the weather was warming, the problem was not quite as bad, since the rats were not so anxious to look for warmth.

Apparently it was not claim-jumpers who had killed Sebastian. No one had disturbed the site, and no one had tried to claim ownership. She had checked with the land office before coming up, and her name was shown as the owner of the claim, since she had grubstaked Sebastian. Everything seemed to be in order, and she had decided she didn't have to worry about someone trying to do to her what had been done to Sebastian. Whoever killed him must have just had a personal grudge. It was the only explanation. The claim was all her own now, and she had all summer to work it. She hoped that before the worst of winter returned next season, she could find her own "bonanza," as these miners called a major strike, and be able to afford to hire professionals to mine it properly. As much snow as there still was in these mountains, and as lonely as she felt already, she was not sure she could manage a whole winter buried up here. Besides that, she would have to hire someone to cut and stack enough wood to last her for months, which she really could not afford to do—and there was no doubt the rats would be a hundred times worse. There was also the problem of buying winter feed for her two mules, which she didn't want to give up. She needed them when she went down into town for supplies, if she could even find her way. She had not been back to Cripple Creek since old Stan had brought her up here, and she was beginning to run low on food. She did not look forward to making the trip alone through bear country, but she supposed she would just have to. She just hoped she could remember the right trail.

The trip up here had been a full day's journey from Cripple Creek, all of it on a steep, winding trail. She had never seen quite such beautiful country, full of little waterfalls from spring melt in even higher elevations, giant boulders everywhere, looking slick and smooth where they lay in stream beds. Stan Bailey had told her that a lot of the streams would be gone by summer, once most of the heavier snow at the mountain peaks had melted. They had waded through more snow themselves to get here, the rich smell of wet pine in the air. Now spring flowers bloomed everywhere, peeking up through melting snow in rainbow colors.

In spite of the dangers of animals and the elements in this rugged land, she had found a kind of peace here, but her first view of the cabin in which she was expected to live had brought her great disappointment. She wasn't sure she could bear such a crude shack, but Stan had assured her it was actually better than some others. *The man here before you did an okay job buildin' it*, he'd told her. It was made of roughly-hewn pine boards, and air could easily get through the cracks. A potbellied, wood-burning stove was left inside, and there had even been a supply of wood on the sagging porch. She had left her prettier dresses packed in boxes; she certainly would not need them up here. In fact, with her hat on, and if she kept her hair twisted into a knot under it, a person would hardly know she was a woman. She wore a man's pants and shirts, clothes that would have fit a young boy. She could find no men's sizes small enough to fit. The weather was still quite cold even though it was May, and when she was outside she wore a heavy woolen jacket that hid her breasts.

After showing her how to pan for gold in the little creek that ran past the cabin, as well as explaining how to use the sluice left behind by Sebastian, Stan, who was anxious to get back to cards, women, and whiskey in Cripple Creek, had finally left her on her own. He had promised to inform neighboring miners of her presence and warn them to show her some respect. He had also promised to return and check on her.

It had only taken a couple of days after he left for the horrible loneliness to set in. Never had she felt so totally abandoned, not even in the streets of New York City. At least then she had had Toby.

Now there was no one. She didn't have enough money to hire a man to help her full-time, and she could not imagine trusting any of them, no matter how polite they might be at first, to live up here with her and help her work without eventually expecting something more than money in return. Besides, it would look bad to have some stranger living up here with her. No, she had been determined to do this all on her own, and she would. Faithfully, every day for long, long hours, she worked with the sluice, rocking it, learning how to pick out the gold specks and drop them into a jar of water.

Stan had taught her that true gold, because of its weight, would sink to the bottom, no matter how small and thin the speck was. She was becoming more adept at fishing through the drag in the sluice, finding not just gold, but a few garnets and even some silver. She had learned that what was left besides the dirt was called *gangue*, worthless minerals that could be tossed aside.

It was slow, tedious, sometimes back-breaking work, and for the first couple of weeks she was so sore it was agony to move her arms. Still, she was used to hard work, and after a while the pain went away. Her guess was that she was probably retrieving around five dollars worth of gold a day out of the stream bed that ran down the side of the mountain behind her cabin and flowed alongside it. *That could mean there's a bonanza farther up*, Stan had explained. *You ought to start diggin' into the mountain behind the cabin. Could be that's where the gold is comin' from, but you need a man to help you.*

She could not afford that. She had tried wielding a pick herself, chopping into an area that John Sebastian had apparently already started exploring, but it was slow, almost impossible work for a woman. She had decided that maybe if she could glean enough gold and silver and garnets out of the stream bed instead, she could sell what she found and afford to get better tools, maybe even afford to stay in Cripple Creek and hire more professional miners to dig into the mountain. There were none up here to help—all the men were too involved in their own prospecting.

The closest prospector to her site was an old man nearly a mile away, and a mile up in these mountains was like ten miles on flatter land. She was truly on her own. Stan had explained that one of the biggest mine-owners in Colorado, Roy Holliday, owned two mines in the mountain behind her cabin, but on the other side of it. Every day she could hear muffled explosions in those mines, sometimes feeling the ground shake. It had been frightening at first, but she had gotten used to it.

She tried to imagine how rich Roy Holliday must be. She had never met him, but she remembered seeing a hotel and several other businesses in Cripple Creek with his name on them. That was how rich she wanted to be someday, and she had every reason to believe it could happen to her just as well as to someone like Roy Holliday. Surely he had started out just like this, but then some men involved in the big mining had already been rich and had simply used their money to buy up prospectors' claims so they could be professionally mined. She didn't want to have to sell out that way. She wanted it all to be hers. She even daydreamed sometimes about going back to Guthrie a very rich woman, wearing the latest fashions, arriving in a fancy carriage pulled by beautiful horses. She would find Nolan Ives and wave stacks of hundred-dollar bills under his nose. It was a wonderful dream, but it was clouded by the little voice that told her all that money could not bring the happiness she had known for one night in the arms of Ethan Temple. Money could not embrace her, love her, make her feel on fire with the need to have a man filling her, tasting her, bringing her physical ecstasy.

Where was Ethan now? She walked over to lay her .38 back on the crate beside the cot, then put a little more wood in the stove. She climbed back into bed, fully dressed, except for her boots. She didn't trust the men in these mountains enough to sleep in just a flannel gown. No one had given her trouble, but a woman always had to be ready. She pulled the covers over herself, thinking how much more pleasant it would be in this lonely bed if Ethan were sleeping beside her, how much safer she would feel, how much better she could sleep knowing he was there.

Was he even alive? She had been so sure that with time

she could forget him, stop wondering and worrying about him, stop feeling so guilty about the way she had hurt him. Time had not helped much after all. It had been a year since their one night of marriage. She did not doubt there was more he could have taught her about being a woman, and part of her ached to learn it all; but only one man could have taught her, and she would never see him again. Even if he *tried* to find her after all this time, which was unlikely, he certainly would never trace her all the way up into the mountains above Cripple Creek.

She jumped slightly then when she heard another muffled rumble. This one made her flimsy shanty shake enough to spill some little particles of dirt caught in the roofing boards. The dust landed on her face, and she quickly sat up and blinked, brushing it off. "Damn," she mumbled. Here she was hacking away as best she could at a project she was beginning to think might be hopeless, and men at the Golden Holliday were blowing out tons of gold in one swoop. It irritated her that it was rich men like Holliday who made the most money in mining. It took money to make money, and she was determined to have it both ways.

Ethan approached the Holliday Hotel, went inside, and asked the clerk where he might find Roy Holliday himself.

"His office is on the second floor," the man answered, pointing to a stairway. "Go to the door at the end of a hallway. His name is on the glass."

Ethan thanked the man and headed up the stairs. He had ridden Blackfoot and a pack horse up here from Colorado Springs. He would have come up sooner with Holliday, but he'd had to wait a whole week in Colorado Springs for the money he had coming from Pinkerton's. There had indeed been a price on the head of Jimmy Clairborne, who had turned out to be one of the men Ethan had shot and killed the day of the train robbery. Now he had a full thousand dollars stashed in a bank at Colorado Springs, more money than he ever dreamed he'd have in his life, certainly too much to carry on his person into a wild town like Cripple Creek.

What he would ever do with all that money, he wasn't sure. Right now he didn't even need it, so he would let it sit and collect interest. With what Holliday had promised to pay him, he'd get by just fine. He walked to the door at the end of the hall on the second-floor hallway, where he saw Holliday's name. He heard voices inside and knocked on the door. "Come in." Ethan recognized Holliday's voice. He went inside, noticing another man there—a big, burly man with a beard, who eyed Ethan suspiciously when he entered the room.

"Mr. Holliday," Ethan spoke up. "I finally made it."

"Well, Ethan, come on in! Did you get your money?"

"Yes, sir, one thousand dollars. I left it in a bank at Colorado Springs."

"Good idea." Holliday nodded to the second man. "Wayne, this is Ethan Temple, the man I told you about who put a stop to that train robbery." He looked back at Ethan. "Ethan, this is Wayne Trapp, my right-hand man."

Ethan looked at the man a second time, nodding, knowing he should like him, but feeling an instant animosity. Trapp nodded in reply, but his blue eyes, set in a pudgy, whiskered face, told Ethan he didn't like him one bit. Was it because he was Indian? Maybe it was because Trapp felt his own job might be threatened.

"I hear tell you shot up a couple of wanted men, saving the boss's gold watch and his money," the man said. He stood up from his chair, and Ethan suspected it was to reveal his size. He stood as tall as Ethan, but was built like a grizzly bear, with a huge chest and shoulders. Ethan figured he was more fat than muscle, considering the size of his belly. He put out his hand, squeezing Ethan's in a childish attempt to show his strength. "The boss says he's hired you to work up at the mines."

"I'm going to give it a try. I've got nothing else going right now."

Trapp looked him over. "Yeah, well, a breed don't often get far in life, does he?"

Their eyes met challengingly, and Ethan let go of the man's hand.

"Now, Wayne, I told you I don't want prejudice to get in the way here. Ethan's damn good with his gun, and he's a former army scout. I owe him for what he did on that train, and I don't want you making trouble." Holliday laughed, a rather forced laugh that seemed more threatening than jolly. Ethan figured he was hinting to Wayne Trapp that he had better mind himself or suffer the consequences, whatever that meant. The man came around from behind his desk and shook Ethan's hand. "Wayne here isn't real fond of Indians. His mother was killed by Cheyenne when he was a little boy."

Ethan shook Holiday's hand, then turned his attention back to Trapp. "Well, we have something in common then. My Cheyenne mother was raped and murdered by white men at Sand Creek when I was three years old."

The remark seemed to set Trapp back a little. "Well, the boss says we have to work together, so I reckon that's what we'll have to do. Just don't try steppin' on my toes or takin' over my job, Indian."

Ethan mused to himself about what a childish brute this man appeared to be. Was this the kind of men "the boss" liked to have working for him, men who catered to his every command, obeyed him like trained dogs? If so, Ethan knew he wouldn't last long. He turned his attention back to Holliday. "Just exactly what *will* I be doing?"

"Have a seat, Ethan," Holliday answered, going back behind his desk. "I'm glad you finally made it here. I've been wondering if and when you'd show up. Would you like a cigar?" He opened a silver box on his desk. "The finest—from Cuba. Every man enjoys a good smoke."

"Don't mind if I do," Ethan answered.

Holliday watched him take the cigar, along with a match from a little silver cup on his desk. He had no doubt Ethan Temple would make a damn good guard up at the mines, but he suspected he wouldn't be able to lead him around by the nose like he could Wayne Trapp and a lot of the others. This big half-breed in buckskins was not a man impressed by wealth. He did a job because it was a job, no matter who it was for, and he had an air of independence and pride about him that told Holliday he probably could not be bought. No, he wouldn't use this one for any underhanded dealings. That was for men like Trapp. He let Ethan take a couple of puffs watching the pleasure on his face at the taste of the smoke. "What did I tell you?"

Ethan sat down, his long legs sprawling from the small wooden French chair. "You were right. It's a good smoke."

Holliday grinned. "Welcome to Cripple Creek, Ethan. I'll let you rest a couple of days if you like. Then Wayne will take you up to the Golden Holliday, show you where you can sleep, and take you around the mine. Actually there is a Golden Holliday Number One and a Number Two. You'll work at Number One. That's the biggest and employs the most men. We keep men working there around the clock, taking out both gold and silver. Number One is where we've had the most grumbling over wages, that sort of thing. The men are trying to organize a union, so anytime you see them gathered in bunches, break it up. Same goes for whenever you see them fighting among themselves. I have a few Chinese working up there, and sometimes there's trouble over that. They don't like Chinese, but the Orientals are damn good workers and work for less pay, so I keep them on. Once in a while I'll also need you to guard the purified gold shipments sent from the mills up at the mine down here to Cripple Creek. From here to Colorado Springs and on to the Denver mint, they're guarded by professionals, former marshals, and some Pinkerton men. You'd make a good lawman or Pinkerton man yourself."

Ethan shrugged, taking the cigar from his mouth and rolling it between his fingers. "Working for you will be fine for now."

Holliday kept his grin, but Ethan knew it was false. The man was good at acting friendly, but he was probably a bastard at heart. All that money, and he didn't even have a family. He'd already heard that a lot of people didn't like Roy Holliday, and that he conducted business in a sometimes ruthless manner. His money and power made him almost untouchable, but Ethan figured how the man lived his life made no difference to him, as long as he didn't ask him to do something underhanded. What he expected Ethan to do sounded simple enough.

"Well, I'm glad to give you the job, Ethan. You can leave with Wayne here in two days—he's going up with a couple of other men. They can teach you the ropes. In the meantime, pick any room you want here at the hotel. You'll sleep here until you leave. God knows the ride up is a bitch, camping out in the cold mountains and all."

"That won't bother me. I've slept under the stars at least

half the nights in my life." Ethan rose. "Thanks for the offer of the room."

"Sure thing." Holliday also rose. "If you're in need of some good whiskey and clean whores, try mine—the Holliday House, just up the street. The women there will wear you out enough in one night that you won't have need of another one for a long time. It won't matter that you're Indian. All you have to do is tell them you work for me."

Ethan wondered if the sly, inadvertent insults would ever stop. "Thanks for the tip." Yes, he could use a shot of whiskey, and he hadn't been with a woman since that night with Ally. Maybe he would take the man up on his offer. It was just that ever since Ally, he figured no other woman could satisfy him like that, not even one who knew all the ways to please a man. With Ally it had been more than physical, or at least that was what he had thought at the time. It still hurt to realize she had just lain there and let him have his way with her because she needed to consummate her marriage and make it legal. "Where do I meet up with Wayne and the others?"

"Day after tomorrow," Trapp spoke up. "Right here, six A.M. It's a good day's ride up to the mine."

Ethan nodded. "I'll be here." He turned and left, thinking how he liked this country. It was wild and rugged and beautiful. He wouldn't mind this work at all. It would keep him busy, and that was important. He didn't want time to think about Wounded Knee . . . or Ally.

Trapp watched Ethan leave, then turned to Holliday. "You didn't tell me he *looked* so Indian."

Holliday eyed the man closely. "Treat him right, Wayne, no funny business. He's a good man. I want him put in charge of the northern section of the mine."

"But that's where I usually—"

"I said the northern section! You'll take over the southern half. Joe Carson is quitting. He's worried they'll find out he had a hand in that murder. He wants to get out of here and head for California."

Wayne knew better than to argue. Ethan Temple would be holding as important a place in the rank as he did. Since Ethan was new, it didn't seem fair. "Whatever you say," he answered, always afraid to argue with Holliday. "It just grates me that murdering John Sebastian didn't do us any good. That stupid woman who grubstaked his claim is still up there workin' it herself. Word is she's just a slip of a thing—young, too."

Holliday stuck his cigar back in his mouth and walked back around his desk to sit down. "She's still working that claim by herself?"

"Sure is."

Holliday puffed thoughtfully on the cigar. He had deliberately arranged the murder of Sebastian to take place while he was out of town, which would help divert attention away from himself. To his delight, he had discovered after getting back that most people were of the opinion that Sebastian had been killed by someone carrying a grudge.

"It's a good thing you've left the woman alone," he told Trapp. "Harming her so soon would just stir up people's curiosity again, maybe even anger. Up here, if an honest, innocent woman gets killed, the other prospectors and miners might get real angry and demand an investigation." He met Trapp's eyes. "What's she like? A proper lady?"

Trapp grinned in a kind of sneer. "Appears that way. Not even married. Her name is Allyson Mills, and she's only about nineteen. She carries a rifle and a pistol, and word is she'll use them on any man who gets the wrong idea. She's determined to mine her claim herself—don't seem interested in sellin' it."

Holliday frowned. "I figured once Sebastian was out of the way, whoever this woman was, she would contact the land office and offer to sell. Fact is, I was going to look her up and make an offer after I got back. Maybe I still will. She must be getting pretty lonely and afraid and disgusted about now, ready to give up."

Trapp shrugged. "You can go on up and give it a try, but so far she ain't give up. We can scare the hell out of her if you want."

"No. Just scaring her would leave her alive to tell the story, and people might figure out what we're up to. We can't kill her either. I'll have to try some other route. She must not have found that hole farther up in the mountain above her cabin that Sebastian blew out of there. When I heard about the value of the gold samples he brought out, I knew I had to have that claim. That vein is worth a fortune. I just hope you and the others hid it good enough that the woman won't find it. I'll go up there, maybe tomorrow, and make her a good offer. She'll probably be happy as hell to see another human face—and ready to leave that rat-infested little shanty."

Trapp nodded. "I hope you get your hands on it. Anything you want me to do, just let me know."

Holliday laid his cigar in an ashtray, frowning. "There is one other thing I can try if she won't sell."

"What's that?" Trapp's mind was running wild with desire to scare the woman off. There was one sure way to do it. Once she was raped, she wouldn't have any fight left in her.

"I'll hire a geologist. Considering the location of her mine, there is a damn good possibility that the vein Sebastian found stems from my own mine behind it. If the apex of that vein comes from my mine, that claim is legally mine anyway. She wouldn't have a leg to stand on. I'll look into it. In the meantime, leave her alone." He rose from his chair again. "And don't mention her to Ethan Temple. The man risked his neck on that train to protect a couple of women, so he probably wouldn't like the idea of our threatening some poor young thing up there trying to mine her own claim. Leave him out of it, and tell the others to do the same. For the time being, that claim and John Sebastian's murder will not be talked about, nor will—" He paused. "What the hell is her name, anyway? I forgot."

"Allyson Mills."

"Yes. Allyson Mills. Keep the name to yourself, especially around Temple. And stay away from her claim. I'll find some other way to run her out."

Trapp nodded and left as Holiday walked to a window to gaze at what he called Holliday Mountain. If he had his way, he would eventually buy every claim up there. His father had been cheated out of a fortune by his partner, leaving him penniless. He had committed suicide, and ever since then, Holliday had determined to earn back a fortune of his own. He had never let anyone get in his way, had given no thought to family or anything else, only to someday being even wealthier than his father had once been. He had found that wealth at Virginia City and had run his father's former partner out of business in San Francisco, reducing the man to ruin. That had been a pleasant task indeed. He'd had his victory, but by then it wasn't enough. Now his only goal in life was to get richer.

The local assayer in Cripple Creek was paid well to let him know of any unusually valuable claims. John Sebastian's had been one of them. Now it belonged to Miss Mills, and if it was as valuable as the assayer claimed it was, all the other claims up there could be just as rich. He wanted them all. Apparently practically all of Eagle Mountain was running with gold, and he wasn't about to let anyone else lay claim to any of it, especially not some slip of a woman like Allyson Mills.

20

Allyson raised the pick, grunting as she landed it into the diggings John Sebastian had started before he died. Why he chopped away in this spot, she couldn't be sure. There was nothing here but hard, worthless rock, but maybe the man knew what he was doing. One day a week she spent the whole day doing this, just on the chance that she would come upon something important. From the nearby creek she had panned and collected enough little specks and nuggets of gold in her water jars that she was sure she must have three or four hundred dollars worth, but that was a pittance compared to what a person could make from a vein of gold.

Stan had pointed out the extent of her site, thirty feet wide, running along the creek in front and up along where it trickled out of the mountain on which her little cabin was perched. According to the map, she owned a hundred feet into the mountain and another thirty feet across once she got inside, then back out to the creek bed again. She also owned a good two hundred yards straight up the mountain behind her cabin. The problem was cutting into all that rock. She had no idea how to use explosives, nor could she afford to hire someone who did. She could only hack away at the hard rock herself, and in two months she had only cut about four feet inward. Somewhere back in there was the source of the flowing water, and, in turn, very likely the source of the gold she had found in the creek bed.

She had tried chopping at the stone around the small hole in the mountain from which the water ran, but it was pure granite, and her pick hardly made a dent. The first time she had swung at it, the pick had landed so hard that she thought the vibration through the handle might have broken her hand. She'd had to let go and rub her hands for several minutes before she could try the pick again. Now she was hacking away at somewhat softer rock underneath the water's source, figuring to tunnel her way to it, which must have been what John Sebastian was trying to do. It was back-breaking work, and after a day of it she could barely move the next morning.

At least it was warmer today, and most of the snow around the cabin had melted. Now it was mid-afternoon, and she didn't even need a jacket. Swinging the pick had worked up a sweat, making it seem even warmer than it really was. Every once in a while she would stop and let a spring breeze that swept down from higher elevations cool her perspiring body until she had the energy to start over again.

She had decided that within a week or two, if Stan did not return with more supplies, she would have to make the trip into Cripple Creek to get what she needed. She would take what gold she had already found and have it weighed and get whatever it was worth, then put that money into a bank, after keeping out enough for more supplies. If she couldn't get rich the quick way, she would do it the hard way, day by day, panning, using the sluice, swinging the pick. She had no particular need to hurry, other than wanting to live in town again and get away from this awful loneliness.

Something rustled in the underbrush nearby, and at first she thought someone was spying on her. She quickly threw down the pick and grabbed up her rifle, but by then two little bear cubs emerged from the bushes, heading for some berries growing beside the cabin. She relaxed a little, slowly moving back, surprised that they did not seem frightened by her presence. She smiled at the sight of their furry little bodies and their boldness as they ambled right past her to the bush. Cautiously she walked a little closer, enjoying the company of anything alive, wishing they could talk. One of them growled at her, but only playfully. A moment later she heard her mules beginning to squeal as though terribly frightened. She hurried around the front of the cabin and to the other side where they were tied, but before she could reach them, she was greeted by a huge grizzly. It rose up on its hind legs at the sight of her and growled, the claws on its front paws extended threateningly.

Allyson gasped and for a moment just stood there frozen. Then she remembered Stan's warning—*Anytime you see bear cubs, get away fast. You can be sure the mother is around close, and in the spring, there ain't nothin' more ornery than a mother bear out of hibernation, especially a grizzly.*

She had no doubt this one was a grizzly, mainly from its size. Stan had said they were the biggest breed of bear there was. Its fierce roar turned her blood cold, and as it walked toward her as though to attack, she did not even think to fire her rifle. Instead, she dropped it and ran. She could feel the bear close on her heels, knowing she would never outrun the animal if she had to go far; luckily, she only had to run around to the front of the cabin and get inside. She could barely get her breath for the fear that surged through her, and she tripped as she stepped up onto the rickety porch, falling to her knees.

The bear roared right behind her, and she screamed when she felt it swipe at her leg. She was instantly on her feet again, running through the door and slamming it shut, bolting it. Just as quickly she hurriedly closed the wooden shutters over the one front window, then ran to the only other window and closed that one also. Her breath came in frightened gasps, as the bear was already growling and scratching at the door. She prayed the flimsy cabin could withstand the animal's rage and wouldn't fall down around her from the great weight of the animal pushing at the door.

"Ethan," she whimpered, wondering why his name sprang so easily to her lips. He'd know what to do—he could probably bring the bear down with one shot. It was then she remembered she had dropped her rifle outside. All she had was her .38 pistol, and she doubted that a bullet from that would stop such a big grizzly, unless she was lucky enough to shoot it between the eyes. Considering its size, she could never even reach high enough to hit it there.

She cowered in a corner, closing her eyes and praying for the bear to go away. Finally the growling and scratching stopped, but she could still hear both the mother and cubs grunting and wrestling outside, just under a side window, where the berry bush grew. She could do nothing but wait—and hope that the bigger grizzly would not harm her mules, which continued to bray wildly. Her heart pounded so hard that her chest hurt, and for the moment she wondered why she was here at all. She probably had enough money to go back to Denver, or at least to Cripple Creek, and start a little business of her own again, but that didn't seem like enough now. For all she knew a bonanza lay waiting for her inside this mountain, and she was going to find it.

After several long minutes it was quiet again. She cautiously made her way to the side window and very slowly opened one wooden shutter. She saw no bears. She breathed a little easier, deciding just to stay inside and wait a while to make sure they were gone. It was then she felt the sting at the back of her leg, and looked down to see the grizzly's claws had torn through her denim pants and into her skin. She had heard that pure alcohol or whiskey sometimes helped a wound heal better and kept infection from setting in. She hurried to her first-aid supply and took out a bottle of alcohol. She doused a rag with it and pulled the pant leg up to her knee, then reached behind her leg to wash the cuts. She screamed from the terrible sting, dancing around the cabin to ward off the pain. When it finally subsided, she wrapped her leg with gauze, hoping there would be no infection. She knew that people sometimes died from such things, and she was certainly not ready for that!

Suddenly she could not control her tears. The thought of needing help, maybe even dying, made her realize how alone she was, how dangerous this place was for someone like her. This was the most despair she had felt since she had arrived. The grizzly had shown her how vulnerable she was. In just one more second, the animal would have had its claws into her back and would surely have flung her around like a rag doll, sinking its claws and teeth into her throat. She could have been killed in a horrible way, or at least terribly mutilated and scarred.

Weariness from swinging the pick most of the day settled in with her loneliness and a kind of shock from the bear attack to create a depression she could no longer fight. Sometimes it seemed everything was against her. She had tried so hard back in Guthrie, and had lost. Now it seemed her gold mine was another fruitless venture. She didn't have the money to mine it correctly, or the strength to do it properly on her own. She had never been more lonely, and the grizzly had shown her how easily she could get hurt or die up here without anyone ever knowing.

Her tears came in a torrent, a mixture of terror and loneliness. It hit her harder than ever that she missed Ethan much more than she ever thought she could after such a long time. She had thought she had stopped loving him, but at moments like this, all she could think about was how wonderful it would be if he were here helping her, protecting her. She hated admitting she needed those things, but right now it was the truth and there was no getting around it.

"Oh, Ethan," she wept into her pillow. "Ethan."

The processing mill was the noisiest place Ethan had ever been. At the upper level were giant crushers that broke the ore into small pieces, and from there it was sent to a second level and put in water. Half-ton stamps smashed the ore even more, into a gravelly liquid that was passed through screens, then, according to Wayne Trapp, dropped into what was called vanners. The vanners were wide belts that mechanically shook the ore, winnowing out lead and part of the silver. What was left contained all the gold and more silver. It went into amalgamating pans and was cooked for eight hours with mercury and chemicals, then put into settling tanks. Huge boilers produced the steam to run the equipment, and the noise inside was a lot for a man to take eight to twelve hours a day.

Ethan was beginning to sympathize with the miners as far as wages were concerned. Any man who did what they had to do, risking their lives deep in the bowels of the earth day after day, or working in noisy mills like this one, deserved good pay. Men like Roy Holliday were making a fortune off the back-breaking work of men for whom he cared nothing about.

He'd been down in the Golden Holliday Number One long enough to know he could never bear going down there every day. It was hot and smelly and terribly dangerous, and in most of the shafts he had not even been able to stand up straight. It was not difficult to understand how easily men could get disgruntled doing that kind of work, and he had been glad to get out of there. He was accustomed to fresh air and the open skies, not to living like a mole.

He exited the mill, where everything seemed to be in order as far as the workers were concerned. His ears rang from the noise, and he longed to ride farther into the mountains just for the quiet. He mounted Blackfoot and headed up the mountain to the trestle that supported the tracks along which cars full of ore were pushed into the mill by men from the mine. The mill itself sat into the side of a mountain, which had been hacked into tiers to accommodate the various levels of the mill. The Indian in him felt sick at the way these mountains were being cut up. He could almost feel the pain of Mother Earth, screaming to be left alone.

This job went against his grain more than he had thought it would, but for now he figured he'd stay. He had noplace else to go, and he was earning good money. He had decided that after a year or so he would take that money and his reward money and maybe go to Wyoming, or even eastern Colorado, and build himself a ranch. That was the kind of thing he'd really like, something of his own where he could work out in the open air, work with horses, live on wide-open land. He didn't really believe a man could "own" land, but he had to accept the fact that that was how it was done now, thanks to white settlement out here. He couldn't live like an Indian anymore, and if he wanted a ranch, he'd have to buy the land.

He had always had his doubts that the land agent in Guthrie was telling the truth when he said Ethan couldn't be the owner of Ally's lots because he was a registered Cheyenne.

If not for the hurt of realizing why Ally had married him, he might have stayed and fought the decision, considering the fact that he was half white. But knowing Ally had used him had taken the fight out of him. He saw no reason now why he couldn't own land in Wyoming if he had the cash money to pay for it.

He headed toward the mine entrance, nodding to a supervisor standing near the elevator shafts that hauled men and ore in and out of the mines far below. In the distance the noise of the stamping mill was joined by the roar of motors in the shaft house, where steel cables on huge cylinders were used to raise and lower the elevators. The entire mining operation had been fascinating to learn about, but Ethan already knew he didn't want to be around it for too long at a time. There was great tension among the miners over the dangers of their job, their wages, and against the Chinese.

In the ten days he had been on the job, Ethan had seen what a firm hold Roy Holliday had on his workers. If a man didn't give his all, he was promptly fired and replaced. Ethan suspected it was Holliday's way of keeping the help rotated so they didn't have much of a chance to get to know each other too well, which could lead to forming labor groups. Even so, Ethan did not doubt that some of them had found ways to meet after hours. Their work called for aching labor in eight- to ten-hour shifts down in hot tunnels that dripped constantly with water. There was always danger of cave-ins, deadly fumes, and accidents from explosives, and none of the men felt they were being paid enough for the risks they took to make men like Roy Holliday richer. Ethan tended to agree with them, but he had a job to do, and he would do it.

There came a whirring sound then, and Ethan knew that the cable operator in the shaft house was hauling up a load of men. More were waiting nearby to ride back down on a new shift. The supervisor at the elevator waited and watched. The two-thousand-foot journey from the bowels of the mine to the surface took several minutes.

"Another stinkin' day of work and another million for Roy Holliday," one of the waiting workers grumbled. "Hey, Indian, how much does Mr. Gold Britches pay you? We don't need no Indian babysittin' us, you know."

Ethan just glanced at the man. It was a worker named Trevor Gale. Wayne Trapp had told Ethan that Gale was one of their biggest troublemakers, not one just to complain about wages, but about everything else. Holliday was on the verge of firing the man, and if he were not better than the other regular miners, he would have by now, but Trevor was one of the best at the use of explosives. Not every man could place a charge of dynamite perfectly the way Trevor could. Trouble was, he was a big Irish loudmouth who considered everyone whose skin was not lily-white beneath him. Two of his brothers also worked for the Golden Holliday mines, and both were nearly as troublesome as Trevor. Ethan did not answer the Irishman, figuring trouble could be better avoided if he ignored the man.

"Look at the Indian," Trevor told the others. "New man. I wonder why Holliday hired him. He don't seem to have much in the way of guts, and who the hell is going to take orders from a red man? That's almost as bad as taking orders from a goddamn Chinaman."

Several of the other men laughed, and the supervisor standing near the shaft glanced their way. "Shut your mouth, Trevor, or you can find work at some other mine."

Ethan rode Blackfoot near the shaft, then dismounted and tied the animal. He noticed most of the other men backed off a little, even though Trevor kept making crude remarks about Indians and Chinamen, moving himself closer to two Chinese men standing in line. "Looks like he's been drinking," Ethan told the shaft supervisor. "I don't think he should be down there working with dynamite today."

The supervisor, Ed Humble, scowled. "The bastard needs to be fired. He knows he's valuable. That's why he gets away with so much."

Ethan moved closer to the man, keeping his voice low. "If he ends up blowing up half the mine and costing Holliday men's lives and lost time in having to re-dig, he won't seem so valuable then. I say we don't let him go down today."

Humble sighed. He didn't like taking orders from a new man, let alone an Indian, but in this situation he figured Ethan was probably right. "You figure to be the one to pull him out of line?"

Ethan smiled sarcastically. "Unless you want to do it."

"No, thanks. He's twice as big as I am."

"Is there somebody else who can handle the dynamite?"

"Stu Cowans can. He's second man with explosives."

Ethan nodded, then took off his leather hat and hung it over his saddlehorn. He turned and walked toward the waiting men. He wore his six-gun on his hip, and a big hunting knife on a belt at his waist. He stood as tall as Trevor Gale, both men built roughly the same. "Let's go, Trevor. You're not going down today."

Trevor had been insulting the Chinese, making them cower. He turned at Ethan's words, his blue eyes changing from contempt to deep anger. His face reddened, making his black hair seem even blacker. "What's that, Indian?"

"You heard me. You've been drinking. You're not going down today."

The Chinese men stared in fright, and most of the others

backed away even more. Normally they would stand up for another miner, but today they had to agree that Trevor Gale had no business down in the mine handling dynamite.

Trevor removed his hardhat and set down his bucket of tools. "I'll go wherever I damn well please, Indian! You haven't been around here long enough to be giving orders to me or anybody else! I don't know why in hell Holliday hired a damn Indian to do his dirty work, but I'm not taking orders from any Breed!"

Ethan stepped forward. "You'll take orders from *this* one! Pick up your things and get on back home."

Trevor backed up a little, but he just grinned. "I'm not going anyplace, Indian." Without warning, he reached over and grabbed one of the Chinese men by his long pigtail, yanking the man in front of him and pulling out a knife of his own. "Either I go down, or I cut off the Chinaman's tail. You know how important a Chinaman's pigtail is to him, Indian? Probably about as important as your own long hair. Pagan, that's what it is! But you think it has something to do with your manhood."

He held the knife against the Chinaman's tail, and the little Chinese covered his face. "No! No!" he protested. "You no cut off hair! I die of shame!"

Trevor glared at Ethan. "If I cut this off, there will be trouble from the rest of the Chinese, and then *all* the miners will be going at it, and it will be all your fault, Indian. You're a new man. You want that on your shoulders?"

"Let him go," Ethan demanded. He could feel the Chinaman's pain, knew that the long hair was important to him. He felt sorry for the Chinese and the way they were treated by the others. He well knew the pain of being different.

Two cages full of miners changing shifts finally reached

the top of the shaft. Ed Humble signalled the cable operator in the shaft house to hold up, and he left the gates that released the men locked. "Just stay there a minute," he told them, deciding it would be dangerous to release even more miners.

"Hey, what's goin' on?" one of them demanded. "Let us out of here."

"I'm walking this Chinaman to the cages and we're getting on, Indian," Trevor warned Ethan. He started forcing the trembling, weeping Chinaman toward the cages. Ethan knew he had to do something quickly, before the miners being held up in the cages broke loose and made even more trouble. All it took was for a couple more men to join Trevor's side, and a riot would take place.

"What's wrong, Trevor? You *afraid* of me?" Ethan goaded. "Is that why you're hiding behind the Chinaman? You can cut his tail off if you want, but it won't stop me from keeping you from going down today!"

Trevor hesitated, his face reddening more at being called afraid. The men in the cages were growing louder and more restless, and one of those in line waiting to go down called out to Trevor. "Let the Chinaman go, Trev. The Indian's right. You've been drinkin'. It's best you don't go down today."

Trevor literally flung the poor Chinaman out of the way, yanking his pigtail to the left and tossing his body with it. He moved closer to Ethan then, waving his pocket knife. "No Breed accuses me of being a coward!" he sneered. "And no Breed gives me orders! If I don't work today, I don't get *paid!* You're not keeping me from that, Indian!"

"You should have thought of that before you had something to drink. You know the rules, Gale."

"I'm going down, and you can't stop me!" Gale started to

back himself into line. Ethan headed for him, and Gale jabbed at Ethan with the knife. Ethan grabbed his wrist and pushed the knife hand away, while with his right arm he took hold of the Irishman around the neck and yanked him around and to the ground.

The crowd of miners looking on broke into a roar of hooting and howling, all of them enjoying the fight. Gale kept trying to stab at Ethan, who grasped his wrist with both hands, banging it against the ground. Trevor used his free hand to punch at Ethan's face, then managed to rear up and haul Ethan over onto his back. He kept his knee in Ethan's stomach, and all the while Ethan kept hold of the man's right wrist, managing to grab hold of the knife hand itself and bend it backward. The tip of the knife cut into Ethan's left forearm, but he held on until Trevor cried out with pain and dropped the knife.

Then Ethan slammed a big fist into the Irishman's face, sending him sprawling. Ethan got to his knees, grabbed the man by the shirt front, and yanked him up with him as he got to his feet. He landed a fist into Trevor's middle, then another blow to his face. The man went sprawling and seemed to be unconscious. Ethan turned to pick up the pocket knife, but before he could stand up straight again, Trevor landed into him, and both men rolled in the gravel, punching and wrestling. Trevor tried to get Ethan's gun from its holster, but in a split second Ethan had the man on his back and had his own knife out, its seven-inch blade posing a much greater threat than Trevor's pocket knife had. Ethan pressed the blade against Trevor's face, the tip of it just under his eye.

"Don't you know better than to get into a knife fight with an *Indian?*" he sneered. "You get up and go home, Gale. Stop this right now, or I'll pop your eyeball right out of your head!"

The crowd around them quieted. Trevor's eyes were wide, and he looked down toward the knife blade, which made his eyes cross when he did so. "You Indian bastard! If I get up and leave, that doesn't mean it's over between us!"

"Fine! But it's over for today! You're not going down there and risking the lives of all the other men just because you're *drunk!*"

Trevor breathed deeply, his face filthy and covered with sweat. "You bastard!"

"I've been called every name in the book, Gale. I'm used to it." Ethan got up, jerking Trevor up with him, keeping the knife pointed toward the man's throat. "Get going!"

Trevor stood there panting, blood trickling down his cheek from where Ethan had nicked his skin. His embarrassment was evident. Trevor Gale took pride in being one of the few men who never lost a game of wrist-wrestling or a fistfight. He backed away, pointing a finger at Ethan. "Me and my brothers, we'll get you for this!"

Ethan shoved his knife back into its sheath. "I'm shaking in my boots," he answered.

Trevor looked around at the others, some of whom were laughing at him now. Even the little Chinaman was laughing. The Irishman turned and walked away, and Ethan worried about what all this could lead to. Trevor had been humiliated today, and even though these men had laughed at him and enjoyed the fight, Trevor Gale was also looked up to by many of them as a leader. If he decided to stir up more trouble over this, he might find men to back him, especially among those who had not seen the fight and did not know the real reason for it. He wasn't sure what Roy Holliday would think of what had just taken place, but he felt he'd done the right thing.

He turned and picked up Trevor's knife, noticing his arm was bleeding. He walked over to his horse to get some gauze out of his gear, and he heard a mixture of compliments and insults from the miners.

"No more trouble now," Ed Humble told those in the cages. He released them, and they walked past Ethan rather sullenly, none of them quite sure of the cause of the fight. The new shift began boarding the elevator cages, one of the men telling Ethan he'd done the right thing.

"Piss on the Indian," one of the others grumbled. "He's one of Holliday's puppets. Trevor wasn't all that drunk. The Indian probably had orders to stir up trouble and make Trevor look bad so Holliday would have an excuse to fire him. Everybody knows he's the best, drunk or sober."

"Just get on board and get to work," Humble told them. Once the elevator was fully loaded, he signalled the cable operator, and the grumbling, arguing men disappeared into the mountain's depths. "You did all right, Ethan," Ed Humble told him. "It was the right thing. I'm just glad it was you and not me. I don't think I could have handled him. I watched him beat the hell out of Wayne Trapp once in a bar fight, and you know how big Wayne is."

Ethan finished wrapping the cut, saying nothing. Roy Holliday was due up here tomorrow—something about going higher up in the mountains to talk to some of the individual prospectors. Ethan figured the man was trying to buy up more claims. Whatever Roy's reason for coming, he'd explain to him what had happened here today. He'd either be pleased or fire him, or maybe just fire Trevor Gale. Right now he didn't care. One thing was damn sure—he'd earned his five dollars today and then some. He brushed dirt from his clothes and hair, hoping there wouldn't be bigger trouble over this. He closed Trevor's knife and shoved it into his pants pocket. "I'll give him back his knife tomorrow, if he's still employed and sober," he told Humble.

"That arm all right?"

"It will be." Ethan remounted Blackfoot. "I'll be back when the shift is ready to come back up." He rode off, heading his horse up a trail past the processing mill, up and beyond all the noise, until he reached a quieter place where he could look down at the mine shafts and the mill, Cripple Creek nestled in the mountain another half-mile below.

A shadow moved over the trees then, and he looked up to see an eagle floating quietly above him. The quietness of his surroundings, the smell of pine, the soft hum of wind through the needled trees made him wonder what the hell he was doing here.

The ranch. He had to think about starting again somewhere, away from the miserable hopelessness of the reservations in the Dakotas and Oklahoma; away from places like Guthrie, where painful memories faced him; away from wild, noisy mining towns like Cripple Creek. Just a few more weeks at five dollars a day and he'd have plenty to get started. The only trouble was, no matter where he went or what he did, he would always be haunted by what might have happened to Allyson Mills. Time had not healed anything. In fact, it seemed that the passage of time had only made things worse. Guilt had set in—maybe he should have stayed. What if she needed him? No matter what her deceptions, she had, after all, been his wife. He had let his damn pride get in the way. Maybe they could have worked things out somehow.

The ground shook with an explosion deep beneath the earth. He turned Blackfoot and headed back to continue his routine ride around the perimeter of the Golden Holliday Number One. In a couple more hours a load of gold gleaned from the mill would be ready for shipment to Cripple Creek. This time he was to accompany that shipment all the way to

Colorado Springs, a job he welcomed. It would get him away from the noise and lawlessness, the dirt and overbearing crush in this uncivilized, often ruthless, gold town. Maybe he would pay another visit to Lynn Brady, the pretty, young, red-haired prostitute he'd found at the Holliday House. She had reminded him of Ally.

21

Roy Holliday followed Wayne Trapp up the steep trail that led around the back side of what he considered Holliday Mountain. He would not ordinarily go up into these remote places to visit prospectors, but he'd been told that Allyson Mills was quite the stubborn woman. Maybe impressing her with his fine black horse and his obviously expensive clothing would have an impact and make her see how miserably inept she was at mining her claim. He had worn deep-blue worsted trousers with narrow-gauge black stripes and a white silk waistcoat with deep blue embroidery trim, over which he wore a black cashmere morning coat. The high-buttoned waistcoat was set off at the neck with a black bow tie.

Men in these mountains didn't usually dress this way. He had brought along more rugged, warmer clothes, as any wise man did who ventured into places like this, just in case the elements or an accident compelled him to stay longer than the one day. He and Wayne had left almost before dawn, with the intention of reaching Allyson Mills's claim by two o'clock. Once there, he intended to talk the foolish young girl into selling out to him, after which he would come back down to Cripple Creek the same day. If it got too dark to travel before they reached the town, he had enough clothes along to change and make camp for the night.

He used to do more of this, in the early years, but now he

had other men who did such things for him. He remembered the first days of struggle—a number of men had had to die for him to get what he wanted. Through murder and bribery and, finally, simple financial power, he had managed to amass a fortune in gold claims without anyone being able to point one finger his way. He had far outdone the fortune his father once enjoyed, and destroying the man who had brought his father to ruin had been a satisfying experience indeed.

Now there was this woman—that was certainly a new challenge. He just couldn't quite bring himself to have a woman killed, and he hoped she would make this whole matter easy for him. If not, before he caused her any harm, it was still possible that her vein stemmed from his own mine. In that case, there would be no argument. Her claim would belong to Holliday Enterprises and she would have to leave whether she liked it or not.

"How much farther?" he called out to Trapp.

"Maybe an hour."

Holliday shivered slightly in his morning coat. No matter how warm it got farther below, it seemed it was never quite warm enough in these higher elevations. He found it amazing that any woman, especially a young, pretty one, would dare to come up here alone and try to work a claim. She must be quite something.

Trapp came to a level area and stopped his horse to rest it. "We'll have to get off and walk the horses for a ways," he told Holliday. "The climb is even steeper from here up. They can't be carryin' our weight."

Holliday almost laughed. Wayne Trapp weighed a good hundred pounds more than he did. "Whatever you say. It's been a long time since I've been up in parts like this myself. I haven't even been to the mine since I got back from my trip. It's been close to three months."

Trapp dismounted with a grunt. "I expect you'd be best to stay away a little longer, till things cool down a bit again. Ever since that thing between the Indian and Trevor Gale a few days ago, there's been a lot of grumblin' goin' on. Trevor is the one startin' it all, sayin' now Roy Holliday's men are startin' to beat up on the miners for nothin'."

"I wouldn't call being drunk and handling explosives down in a mine *nothing*, Wayne."

Trapp turned to face Holliday with a look of one who knew all there was to know. Holliday knew he liked thinking he was his right-hand man. It always amazed him that people like Wayne Trapp had no idea they were being manipulated. But Ethan Temple, there was a man who couldn't be fooled that way.

"Trevor Gale can handle explosives just fine no matter what shape he's in. I've seen him go down there when he could hardly walk straight," Trapp said. "Your biggest concern, you've said, is avoidin' trouble, and the Indian spells trouble. The way Ed Humble says it, there probably wouldn't have been a problem at all if Ethan Temple hadn't been there. Gale started the whole thing because he didn't like no Indian watchin' over him. I tried to tell you, Mr. Holliday, men don't like takin' orders from no Indian. You ought to get rid of him."

Holliday pulled a thin cigar from inside his morning coat, grinning. "You'd like that, wouldn't you? Face it, Wayne, you just don't like the man and you resent me for hiring him." Holliday could read the jealousy in Wayne Trapp's eyes, but the man just shrugged.

"Who you hire and fire ain't my business."

"You're exactly right," Holliday answered, a hint of a threat in the words. He lit his cigar and puffed on it a moment, watching the worry in Trapp's eyes. He enjoyed the way some men could be so easily impressed and so easily threatened. "If my memory serves me right, Trevor Gale beat the hell out of you once, didn't he?"

Trapp's face began to redden, and he scowled. "He jumped me from the back, just wanting to make trouble in the saloon. The drunken bastard had made a bet he could knock the hell out of a Holliday man."

Holliday chuckled. "Well, he proved that, didn't he?"

Trapp's lips pressed together in an effort to control his anger.

Finally Holliday took out another cigar and handed it over. "Have a smoke, Wayne, and don't get yourself all worked up."

Wayne took the cigar with a mumbled thank-you.

"I know there have been a lot of times when I should have fired Trevor Gale. Fact is, I have. I've sent men to his house, and his brothers', too, with dismissal papers for all three. Word is they're getting too organized, especially since that thing with Ethan. Union men with a grudge who know how to use dynamite are not the best kind to have around. Let them all find work at some other mine."

Wayne scowled, still holding the unlit cigar. "How come you waited all this time and just now fired them?"

"I just told you why. They're starting to make too much trouble."

"Then you ought to fire the Indian, too. If not for him, none of it would have happened, and you wouldn't have lost your best explosives expert. All he did was make it more evident that you're willing to use force against your own men."

Holliday puffed on his cigar. "Wayne, face it. Ethan Temple did exactly what he should have done, something *you* never would have or could have done. He put Trevor Gale in his place, and in spite of one of my men using force against a worker, the others understand that he did it to protect them. Letting Trevor go down in that mine in the shape he was in would only have shown them that I don't give a damn about their safety. I've been keeping my eyes and ears open, and there aren't that many now who are so ready to follow Trevor's union movement. Thanks to the Indian, they have a new respect for the men who work for me." He took a deep breath of fresh air. "Hell, maybe I should give him *your* job. The man has more tact and more guts. The others see an honesty in him, and they like that."

Holliday watched Wayne's face literally pale. "Mr. Holliday, I gave up botherin' with a family, gave up ever doin' anything else with my life in order to always be available for you, to be your right-hand man. You thinkin' of replacin' me with an *Indian*, a man you've only known a few weeks?"

You didn't give up a damn thing for me, you big buffoon, Holliday thought. *You work for me because it makes you feel important. It's the best job you'll ever have in your whole stupid life*. He chuckled aloud and shook his head. "I wouldn't replace you, Wayne. For one thing, you know too much; and for another, Ethan Temple is too honest to be right-hand man to someone like me. I just like to watch you get your back up now and then." He stuck the cigar back into his mouth and smiled as relief flooded Trapp's puffy face. "I'm just saying the Indian is a good man. He helped me out more than he realizes. I think maybe I'll keep him around. Maybe I'll put him in charge of troubleshooting, and have the other men report to him whenever they suspect something is getting out of hand and let him take care of it. He has an honest, direct way of doing it that the men respect. Maybe he can eliminate the resentment, I don't know. It's just something to think about."

Wayne lit his cigar, then turned and took hold of his horse's reins, starting up the even-steeper trail. "How are you gonna avoid resentment when you're talkin' about makin' the miners take orders from an Indian?" God, he hated Ethan Temple, hated *all* Indians, but Temple in particular. If that sonofabitchin' redskin thought he was going to take his place as Roy Holliday's favorite, he had better think again. Trouble was, how could he get rid of Temple without Holliday knowing? The man liked Ethan, and that presented a problem.

"I don't think his being Indian will make much difference after a time. Besides, he dresses like a white man and he speaks well. And just the fact that he took down Trevor Gale has won him some respect. Nobody has ever put Trevor in his place before."

Trevor Gale. Wayne thought about how much the man must hate Ethan. Maybe his dirty work could be done through Trevor and his brothers. He made no reply to Holliday's remark about no one ever putting the Irishman in his place before. He considered it a personal insult, but he was not about to argue with Roy Holliday. He felt like he was walking on dangerous ground now, as though his days were numbered as long as Ethan Temple was around. He had to find a way to get rid of him.

"Hey, boss, maybe this Allyson Mills has died or somethin'," he spoke up, wanting to change the subject.

"We probably won't be that lucky."

"There's a lot of things we could do to break her will," Wayne answered. "I'd sure enjoy it."

Holliday smiled, following with his own horse. "I'm not into abusing women, Wayne, at least not that way. If I'm lucky, it won't matter anyway. It will take a while yet, but I've got a geologist working on the location of that vein. I just hope she hasn't found it herself yet." He stopped, now able to see the sorry-looking shack much higher up on the mountain. "If the woman is still panning for gold and just collecting a few dollars a day, it should be easy to convince her it's not worth the hardships and loneliness she must be suffering up here. Those things and the elements should be enough to break her. The smell of big money to sell out will make her give up even quicker. You'll see."

They moved back into the trees again, and thunder rolled somewhere on the other side of the mountain. A storm was coming. Had the woman experienced a fierce mountain storm yet? They could be very frightening and violent, even to a man. He grinned to himself. If summer storms didn't discourage the little bitch, just wait until her first winter up here. That would really do it. Prospecting a remote claim the slow way couldn't be a much more lonely, discouraging job, and being practically buried alive in these mountains in winter could do things to a person's mind. If the woman wouldn't sell out now, she'd sure as hell be ready by next spring.

Allyson looked up at the dark clouds rapidly billowing over the top of the mountain. A bolt of lightning suddenly ripped out, and at the same time she heard a loud snapping sound. Not far away the top of a pine tree came crashing down, landing in the creek. Instantly Allyson grabbed up her rifle and ran for the cabin, leaving a good amount of gravel in the sluice. Before she made it all the way up the steep bank from the creek to the rickety cabin porch, huge drops of rain were already pelting the ground. A great burst of thunder made her jump, and just before she reached the porch she thought she saw another movement. Her first thought was that it was bushes blowing in the wind, but when she glanced to her left, she saw two men on horses.

For a moment she froze, clinging tightly to her rifle. How long had they been sitting there watching, or had they just now noticed her? Up here no one could be trusted, that was sure. Since old Stan left, no one had been here, and one of the two men watching her looked mean. He was big as a bear, and she didn't like the look in his eyes.

She finally found her legs and hurried inside, closing and bolting the door. She thought she heard someone yell "Miss Mills!" before the door closed. She opened one shutter and cocked her rifle, pointing it out the window. A moment later the two men were in front of the cabin, and the rain was beginning to pour harder. They quickly tied their mounts and moved onto the porch to get out of the rain. Neither of them could miss the sight of the rifle barrel sticking out her one and only front window. The burly man held back, but the other one, an older man who was handsome for his age and well dressed, approached her.

"Miss Mills, we mean you no harm. Can we please come inside out of the rain?"

"No, sir," she answered. "Speak your piece and leave." Deep inside she had to admit that it felt good to hear another human voice, but she was not about to let two strange men into her cabin. The fancy-dressed man smiled, but his dark eyes did not show the warmth that normally went with a grin.

"My name is Roy Holliday. Perhaps you've heard of me?"

Roy Holliday! He owned half the mountain! "I've heard of you. What do you want?"

"Well, if you've heard of me, you know I own the two biggest mines on this mountain, which means I am a reputable man. I assure you I've not come here to do you harm. I'd like to talk to you about buying your claim. Please let us in. The rain is coming down harder."

Allyson watched his eyes. She had been insulted and used by men enough to know when they thought they were pulling the wool over some ignorant young woman's eyes. She didn't trust this Roy Holliday. So what if he *did* own a mountain of gold? Besides, the man with him gave her the shivers. "You're already out of the rain standing right there on the porch," she told the man. "You've said what you want, so you can just leave as soon as it stops."

Holliday laughed as though it was a big joke. "I haven't even told you what I would pay for your claim. Don't you even want to *talk* about it? My goodness, woman, you're living under dangerous and miserable conditions up here, and I happen to know there isn't enough gold on this side to shake a stick at. Won't you let me come in and tell you about my offer?"

Allyson kept the rifle leveled. "No. I'm not ready to sell." She glanced at the bigger man, who stepped a little closer. "You keep back, mister, or I'll blow a hole in all that blubber on your belly! There's no one who'd blame me, being up here alone like I am."

The big man scowled and started to speak, but Holliday put his hand up to keep him quiet. The rain came down in a torrent, and the horses whinnied and shuddered, one of them trying to get its head up under the porch. Roy Holliday came a little closer, leaning on a porch post only a few feet from the window. He scrutinized her closely, then put on another pleasant, but, Allyson guessed, forced smile.

"Miss Mills, you're just as beautiful as all the men in town told me you were. And how old are you? Eighteen? Nineteen? Why would a lovely, proper lady like you bury herself up here grubbing for a few dollars worth of gold a day? Don't you realize that in no time the work and the elements will quickly destroy your youth and beauty? And don't you realize the dangers? Wild animals, woman-hungry men—" Another bolt of lightning ripped overhead, followed by a tremendous roar of thunder that even made the big man with Holliday jump. He moved closer to the front of the cabin as the wind caused the rain to blow in on them. "Let alone the elements," Holliday spoke up louder, ducking closer. He came so close to the window that Allyson had to back away a little so he could not grab the barrel of her rifle.

"Come through that window and you're dead," she warned. "I don't care *how* rich and important you are."

Holliday put up his hands. "All right. Like I said, I'm not here to hurt you. I have even brought up a few supplies in case you're running low."

Allyson had to admit that was good news. She'd been hoping old Stan would show up soon, figuring if he didn't come within another week, she'd have to make that trip down to Cripple Creek. If not for the lingering terror from the grizzly attack and her fear that the big bear was still out there somewhere, she might have already gone. For two days after the attack she had not even gone out of the cabin. She had simply drowned herself in tears, groveling in misery, fighting that part of her that wanted to give up. She had just gotten back some strength and courage, and now here was a man offering to buy her claim. She could take his money and get out, back to civilization, to hotels and theaters and bath houses and nice dresses, and maybe make enough on the sale to start her own business again.

"What kind of supplies?"

"Oh, just general things, food mostly, a couple of blankets, coffee, things like that."

Allyson frowned. "Why?"

Holliday grinned again. "Because I knew you were up here alone and as far as anyone knew, you haven't been back to town since you got here. You're a woman alone, for heaven's sake. I was worried you'd had a bad time of it. Maybe you were hurt, or didn't know your way back down— anything could happen. Don't look a gift horse in the mouth, Miss Mills. I don't expect any money for the supplies. I'm just trying to offer a kind gesture."

More thunder rolled, and Allyson considered letting the man inside, but then she figured it had been his choice to come up here. She hadn't asked him, nor had she requested the supplies.

"Men like you don't just make kind gestures to strangers," she answered. "You aren't worried about me, Mr. Holliday. You're just trying to bribe me."

Holliday's smile faded. He studied what he could see of her through the open window. She was a wisp of a woman, so insignificant that the only thing that stood out through the filmy upper glass was her bright red hair. She was more stubborn and cautious than he had expected, and he didn't cotton to having anyone hold a gun on him.

"Think what you want, Miss Mills. Suffice it to say I've come here with supplies that I intend to leave, and to make you an offer for your claim. If you have one ounce of common sense in that pretty head of yours, you'll sell this worthless piece of ground and get yourself back to civilization, marry some man, and settle down and have babies like women are supposed to do."

Allyson bristled. "I hate to tell you, Mr. Holliday, but I'm not like other women." The rain began to lighten up a little as the swift-moving storm made its way to more distant places.

Holliday folded his arms in front of him. "I never would have guessed."

Allyson moved a little closer to the window but kept the

rifle hoisted. "Why would you want to buy my claim if it's as worthless as you say it is?"

The man's dark eyes narrowed. "I didn't say it was worthless, Miss Mills. The point is, you will never be able to glean enough gold or silver to afford to mine it properly. I have the money and equipment to do it right. My hunch is it will never produce all that much, probably just enough to make a small profit. As long as I own so much of this mountain already, I'd like to buy up the rest, that's all. I guarantee that whatever I pay you will be a lot more than you will ever dig out of here on your own."

Allyson put on an air of arrogance. "Well, I think it's a little strange that the man I sent up here to prospect was mysteriously murdered. Now here you come wanting to buy my claim. Will *I* end up murdered, too, if I don't sell?"

The rain suddenly subsided to a light drizzle, and thunder rumbled farther in the distance again. "Miss Mills, do you really think a man in my position, with all my money, would stoop to jumping worthless claims for a few extra bucks?"

Allyson gave him a sneering smile. "Maybe. I'm no fool, Mr. Holliday. There's a reason you want this claim, and I intend to mine it myself for a while longer and see if maybe I can discover what the reason is. If I work hard enough, and I guarantee I am *not* afraid of work, I might be able to save up enough gold to afford to bring in somebody to help me dig into the side of the mountain and find out where the gold in that creek is coming from. At the least, I have to give it a try. I haven't been here long enough to know for sure what's here."

Holliday lowered his arms, and the big man with him loomed into the sight of the window. "Damn it, woman, you can't keep digging up here all alone," Holliday insisted.

Suddenly the wooden door to the shack burst open as the log she used as a bolt splintered. Allyson screamed and jumped back, as the big man loomed in the doorway. "Get out!" she warned, raising the rifle to a firing position. "Get out or I'll kill you!"

Trapp just grinned. "A lot of things can happen to a woman alone," he threatened. "A lot of men know you're up here, and there ain't many women pretty as you down in Cripple Creek. You'll have to barricade yourself better than this, lady, if you want to keep them out." He chuckled, his fat face creasing around his ugly blue eyes. " 'Course, then, there's bears, bobcats, wolves, rats . . . let's see. Oh, and dead cold winters when you can't hardly keep a hot enough fire to keep yourself from turnin' blue. You'll need lots of firewood. You gonna chop it yourself?" He rubbed at his grizzly beard. "Accidents can happen. You could get hurt or get sick, and there won't be nobody here to help you. A lot of men have died up here all alone, missy, and they were a lot stronger and knew more about what they were doin' than you do. You'd best give some thought to Mr. Holiday's offer."

Allyson struggled not to shake visibly. It angered her to be threatened this way, and without another thought, she lowered the rifle and fired it into the floor right in front of the big man's feet.

"Goddamn, sonofabitch!!" Wayne yelled in surprise, jumping back.

Allyson cocked the rifle and fired again. "Are you a good dancer, mister?" Again, she fired a shot into the floor. Wayne reached for his own pistol, but Allyson raised the repeater, quickly cocking it to slip yet another shell into the chamber. "Don't do it! I may not be the best shot, but at this range a *two*-year-old couldn't miss!"

"Get the hell out of there, Wayne," Holliday ordered. "That was uncalled-for."

The big man backed away, glaring at Allyson, his

thoughts easy to read. Allyson kept the rifle raised, and Holliday himself stepped into the doorway, surveying the damage. He met Allyson's gaze. "Wayne will fix this door for you before we leave. I'm sorry for his rudeness. He gets a little carried away at times."

"Is that so?" Allyson's blue eyes blazed like fire. "You came up here posing as quite the gentleman, Mr. Holliday. I can see now you are certainly far from that. No gentleman travels in the company of a fat bully like that one out there! Just get off my claim, and take your supplies with you. I'll not be bribed *or* threatened! And I won't be fooled into thinking this claim is worthless. You've just shown me it must have a value far higher than I imagined! How you can know that, I'm not sure, but you do, and you want it for yourself. I've gone up against men like you before. You're all alike!" She stepped a little closer, and she could see that Holliday was a little worried she just might pull the trigger. "This is my claim, mister, and whatever it takes to mine it right, I'll do it myself! I'm not selling out cheap and watching someone else make a fortune. I want my *own* fortune, and I'll earn it myself, not by wearing some rich man's wedding ring! Now get moving, and don't come back, or the next time I'm in Cripple Creek I'll tell the whole town how Roy Holliday came up here and tried to threaten a helpless woman and tried to steal her claim. I don't think you want the men at Cripple Creek to hear a story like that, do you?"

Holliday glowered at her, and Wayne Trapp stood outside on the porch looking ready to kill. "Have it your way, you little bitch," Holliday told her. "You won't survive the winter up here, and when they find you dead of cold or starvation next spring, I'll take over your claim without having to dish out a penny! You're going to lead a very hard, lonely life up here, lady, one that will quickly age you well beyond your years; and all for a few hundred dollars in bits of gold and silver! *I* was ready to offer you three *thousand* dollars, but to hell with it! It will be worth whatever small profit I might have made just to come up here next spring and find your thawing body rotting away up here in this flimsy cabin! You're thinking and behaving like a *child,* Miss Mills, but then you *are* just a child, a very *stupid* child with big dreams that will never come true!"

The man turned and left, and Allyson walked closer to the broken door, watching both men mount their horses, Holliday cursing about a wet saddle. He whirled the beautiful black gelding in a circle, then faced Ally. "Stay alert, Miss Mills. These mountains can be very dangerous!" He turned his horse and left, and the big man called Wayne glared at her a moment longer.

"*Real* dangerous," he added with a sudden grin. He rode off behind Holliday, leading the pack horse carrying the precious supplies Allyson could have had for the asking.

Allyson breathed deeply to keep from wilting into a puddle of tears. Would they come back, or perhaps send other men? *Was* she a fool? Three thousand dollars! Just think of the things she could do with that much money. It was a tempting offer indeed, but to take it would be giving in to Roy Holliday's brutal threats. Oh, how she hated giving up on anything, or giving in to men like Holliday! She could never enjoy that three thousand dollars knowing she'd given up her pride and courage to get it.

She walked off the porch and pointed her rifle into the air, firing it twice more to startle the men's horses. She heard one of them curse and a horse whinny. "Get out and stay out!" she screamed. She stood there until they disappeared, and for several minutes after that. The storm had moved on, leaving in its wake a sudden, strange silence. Water dripped from pine trees, and the pungent smell filled the air, heavy and warm. There was not even a breeze, which only accented the stark loneliness.

Allyson walked back onto the porch and stared at the broken door, wondering how she was going to fix it before night fell.

You're going to lead a very hard, lonely life up here, lady . . . these mountains can be dangerous . . . Trouble was, he was right, and she hated it when someone was right, especially someone like Roy Holliday. She wondered how Ethan would have handled this. It sure would be nice to have him here right now. Surviving on her own was getting harder every day, and for one brief moment she considered running out and calling for Holliday to come back, telling him she'd sell the claim and asking him to take her back to Cripple Creek and civilization; but her fierce pride prevailed. Besides, she didn't trust the big man with him.

She walked inside and picked up a box of shells, then turned away and headed back down to the creek, keeping her rifle ready. She decided that for tonight she would just nail the door shut and find a way to bolt the shutters. If she had to, she'd just open the shutters and window and use that to go in and out for the time being. Maybe old Stan would show up soon, and he could fix the door for her.

She reached the sluice and set her rifle against a tree, putting the box of shells on the ground beside it. She wished Holliday had not mentioned the supplies. She sure could have used them, especially the coffee. She hadn't had a good cup of coffee in a week now. Through tear-filled eyes she picked up her shovel, dug into the creek bed, and dumped the soil into the sluice. She began rocking the sluice, washing the soil back and forth so that any gold would fall into the riffles at the bottom, but for the moment she couldn't really see what she was doing.

She stopped and reached into the cold water, splashing some onto her face. This was no time for tears—there was work to be done. Besides, she had to be alert in case Roy Holliday or his fat bully returned.

22

Allyson breathed easier when Cripple Creek came into sight. Up at her claim she could see the town below through certain openings in the trees, but actually reaching it took a lot longer than it would appear to, looking at it from above. She had started out at dawn and now it was late afternoon.

She figured she would probably never know what had happened to old Stan. For all she knew he had gone on to some other town. Her supplies were dangerously low, and she'd had no choice but to make this trip with her two mules and empty gunny sacks to haul food and other necessities back up the mountain. Besides, it was time to find out how much gold she had and turn it in for cash, which she would leave in a bank in Cripple Creek. She didn't feel comfortable being up on that mountain alone with several pounds of gold dust and particles, let alone a few dollars worth of garnets.

It was good to see people. Right now she didn't care that her greeters would be mostly prostitutes and rude, rugged miners. Just the sight of other human life would be a comfort, as long as she didn't run into Roy Holliday or the big, fat man called Wayne. It had been nearly two weeks since they had invaded her little domain on the mountain, and she hadn't had a good night's sleep since. She reasoned that life could be a lot easier if she just sold her claim while she was here and never bothered going back, but Roy Holliday was just like Henry Bartel and Nolan Ives. She would not let him defeat her. Besides, she was sure there must be a valuable vein somewhere on her claim, and Holliday knew it. That had to be why he was so anxious to get it from her. The thought of the millions that could be hers was all she needed to keep going.

She reached the outskirts of town and looked up at the mountain down which she had just come, feeling a certain pride of accomplishment. She had actually found her way, braving the dangers of bears and woman-hungry men who might be lurking in the heavy forest of pine and aspen that had surrounded her most of the way. It had actually been a rather pleasant trip, with summer flowers beginning to bloom everywhere. Everything around her had been a splendor of colors splashed against the bright green of the aspen leaves, the darker green pine, the brown bed of old pine needles on the forest floor, the white trunks and branches of the aspen rising into a brilliant blue sky, and all around a backdrop of purple mountains that still carried white snows on their peaks.

She removed her woolen jacket. It had been cold up at her claim when she left that morning, but even though Cripple Creek was itself in a high elevation, it was warm enough not to need a jacket. She thought how much more pleasant it must be by now down in Denver, pleasant June warmth, the luxury of bricked streets and theaters, restaurants and fancy hotels. She could sell out and go back there and live like a real lady, wearing her pretty dresses again.

She flung her jacket over one of the mules. No. She would not give up yet. She had all summer to look for the vein she was sure existed. Maybe if she didn't find her bonanza by winter, then she would sell out, but not yet. She continued into town, which bustled with activity. At first she was barely noticed. She had deliberately wrapped her breasts tightly so they would hardly show under her shirt, and her hair was twisted into a knot on top of her head, then covered with a hat. She wanted no attention. When she first left Cripple Creek, men had crowded around her, and it had worried her that so many knew she would be up at her claim alone. Apparently most of these men had enough respect for a proper lady that they had decided to leave her alone, but it was still best to draw as little attention as possible. She well knew most men could not be trusted, and Roy Holliday surely had a lot of men working for him in this town. She did not want any trouble from any of them, especially the big one who had broken the door to her cabin.

She made her way past the Holliday Hotel, looking hardly any different from any other prospector who might come down out of the mountains. She glanced at a horse that looked familiar, a buckskin-colored gelding with four black feet. Ethan had a horse like that, but then it certainly was not the only horse in the world with that coloring. Seeing it brought a little wave of remembrance, a little jolt of hope it could belong to Ethan. It made her wonder what she was going to do with her personal life from here on. Whether she hit it rich at her claim, or sold it and went back to Denver, the fact remained she was still alone, and she could not imagine feeling as comfortable with or being loved by any man who could compare to Ethan Temple in looks and skill and bravery. She had thrown away the best man she would ever know, and she did not doubt that he all but hated her. Maybe she was doomed to be an old maid all her life. If that was the case, she would rather be a rich one than a poor one; but sometimes she thought how she might not mind being poor if Ethan was back in her life.

She moved on past the hotel toward the assayer's office.

* * *

"There's another big gold shipment going to Colorado Springs next week," Roy Holliday told Ethan. "Ever since I fired Trevor Gale, he's been stirring up trouble, and because of the friends he has among the miners, he knows when every shipment goes out. The man knows explosives, and I wouldn't put it past him to try to blow up my freight wagons and turn my gold into dust and scatter it from here to Denver."

Ethan stood leaning against a wall. He lit a cheroot. "You want me to oversee the next shipment like I did the last?"

Wayne Trapp sat at the side of the room glaring at Ethan, still hating the idea that Holliday had so much confidence in and admiration for the Indian. Ever since Ethan had come into the picture, Wayne suspected he had somehow lost some of his importance in Roy Holliday's eyes. If he wasn't careful, or if he didn't find some way to get rid of Ethan Temple, someday he was going to be out of a job altogether.

Holliday leaned back in his leather chair. "No," he answered Ethan. "Just leading the gold train won't ensure it won't be blown up. I'd like you to start scouting the whole trail a couple of days before the shipment. That's what you're best at, right?"

"Scouting?" Ethan shrugged, keeping the cheroot between his teeth. "It's all I've ever done."

Holliday put his hands behind his head and his feet up on his desk. "Then I want to utilize your best talent. Indians have a way of smelling things out, hearing better, seeing better. Hell, you've done the same thing for the army for years, so why not for me? If Trevor is going to try anything, he'll most likely plant explosives somewhere along the way beforehand, setting it up so he can wait till the wagons come along, then push a plunger and blow everything sky high. I want you to start early and ride that whole trail down to Colorado Springs, keeping your eyes open for anything suspicious, any sign of any digging being done in the road, that kind of thing. Head back up then, looking for the same thing, maybe up along the cliffs above. Trevor could set some explosives there and set off a deadly avalanche of boulders. He might not try anything at all, but I want to be ready. Then when the wagon train sets out, I want you to ride ahead of it, again keeping your eyes open for anything suspicious."

"I think if Trevor tries anything at all, boss, it will be up at the mines," Wayne put in. "One well-placed explosion could close down a mine for days, maybe weeks."

Holliday took his feet down from the desk and leaned forward to take a cigar from the silver box on his desk. "I'm well aware of that. That's why I've got good men up there keeping an eye on things, and keeping Trevor Gale and his brothers well away from the mines. The last I heard they were trying to get work at the Silver Lady up on Calico Mountain, but other mine owners have heard what troublemakers they are. Nobody will hire them, which is going to make them even angrier at me." He glanced at Ethan. "You did the right thing, Ethan, not letting Trevor go down that day, but it's costing me time and men just to keep an eye on Trevor and his damn drunken brothers. It's not your fault, just a fact of life. The extra cost is still nothing compared to what it would be to have one of my mines blown to bits and most of the men with it. I'd rather spend the money on precautions."

"When do I head out to start scouting?" Ethan asked.

Holliday looked at Wayne. "Shipment goes out next Tuesday, six days from now," Trapp told him, taking pride in being one of the few who knew just when the gold would be hauled to Colorado Springs.

Holliday thought a moment. "Get started tomorrow," he told Ethan. "That will give you time to ride all the way to Colorado Springs and back again before the gold train pulls out. Can you do it?"

Ethan removed his hat and wiped at his forehead with his shirtsleeve. This was the warmest day he could remember in a long time. "You're the boss, and I sure as hell don't have anything better to do."

"You'll be well paid," Holliday told him. "I'll—"

"Hey, it's her!" The shouted words in the street below interrupted their conversaton. "Hall told me she's at the as-sayer's office—brought in some gold!" The words floated up through an open window of Roy Holliday's second-story office. Ethan noticed Holliday and Wayne Trapp look at each other as though they knew something he didn't. Trapp walked to the open window through which the words had come and looked into the street below.

"Somethin's up. A couple of men are runnin' up the street like there's somethin' to see." He turned to look at Holliday. "You think she could have made it to town by herself?"

Holliday glanced at Ethan as though he wasn't sure Ethan should be hearing what was being said. He looked back at Wayne. "A person gets short enough on supplies, he or she has no choice. Go on out there and see what's going on. It might not even be who we think it is."

Wayne chuckled. "Who else would the men around here make a fuss over? He headed for the door, then hesitated before opening it. "What if it *is* her?"

Holliday grinned slyly. "Just let her know you're around and we haven't forgotten she's up there, but don't make a big scene in front of the miners. Go easy and just make your presence known. Maybe she's here to sell out."

Wayne grinned in return and headed out. Ethan watched

Holliday, wondering what the fuss was about. "Something going on I should know about?"

Holliday rose and walked to the window himself, watching Wayne head up the street. "Not really. Just some woman mining a claim all by herself. The men in town think she's some kind of brave saint, but all she is is a near-child—a foolish, dreaming child at that. She thinks she can make a fortune off her claim, but it's practically worthless. She's up there risking her life for nothing, when she could be living in comfort down in Denver with some wealthy man giving her everything she could want. Hell, she's pretty enough to have any man she desires. Why she chooses to stay up there and risk death is beyond me. She's a stubborn little thing." He turned away from the window. "I tried to buy her out a week or so ago, but she chased me and Wayne off her claim with a rifle. Can you believe that?"

Ethan's heart ached at the words. It sounded so much like something Allyson would do. "I knew a woman like that once," he answered rather absently, staring down at the cheroot he had just taken out of his mouth. "I was even married to her for a little while."

"Married? I never even thought to ask if you'd ever been married."

Ethan continued to watch smoke curl up from his thin cigar. "Had a Cheyenne wife a few years back. She died. Then I met Ally. Turns out she only married me to keep title to some property she had back in Guthrie. When she found out being married to an Indian didn't help her any, that was the end of the marriage. It lasted all of one night." He shook his head and put the cheroot back to his lips. "That was one hell of a night, though."

Holliday chuckled. "That's kind of a coincidence, you calling her Ally. The woman up at that claim—her name is

Allyson. Allyson Mills. She wouldn't by any chance be—"
The man watched Ethan literally pale. Ethan took the cheroot from his mouth and walked past Holliday's desk to look out the window, then turned to look at Holliday with eyes literally on fire with excitement.

"Red hair? Young?"

Holliday's smile faded. "Yes," he answered, "but you don't think—"

"My God!" Ethan exclaimed. He dropped the cheroot into an ashtray and strode on long legs to the door, charging out and down a stairway without a word of explanation.

"Jesus," Holliday mumbled. Was it the same woman? What the hell would Ethan Temple think or do if he found out she had been threatened by himself and Wayne? "And Wayne's stupid enough to give her more trouble, which is the last thing I need happening in front of the miners," he muttered aloud. He got up and hurried out himself—he could already see a crowd gathered around the assayer's office up the street.

Allyson carefully replaced the lid on the small jar that held all the precious gold flakes and nuggets she had managed to glean from the creek at her claim. The assayer, Lloyd Hunt, had told her the gold, a little over a pound of it, valued roughly two hundred and fifty dollars—not much for the dangers and hard work of the past three months. She could make that much in two months back in Guthrie when she had the restaurant, and at least there she was safe and could enjoy the company of other people and the convenience of living in town.

"I'll make out a slip declaring its value," Hunt told her as he wrote something on a piece of paper. "You can take it to the bank and exchange the gold for money." He handed her the paper and looked up at her over spectacles perched on the end of his nose. "That's pretty raw stuff, Miss Mills. From what I can determine, the nuggets contain strictly gold, no silver, but extracting that gold in its purest form takes work, so you aren't getting the full value of the nuggets. Pure gold is always worth more."

"I understand."

Hunt frowned, his freckled, bald head shining in a shaft of late-afternoon sunlight. "Miss Mills, considering the fact that those nuggets aren't pure gold, you really have no bonanza up there. I hate to see someone so young and pretty waste her best years slaving away at something that is really not worth that kind of work. You really ought to give up on that claim. Sell it to someone who can afford to get inside that mountain and mine it right. At the rate you're going, you'll never have enough money to do that."

Allyson took the paper and shoved it into her pants pocket. "I suppose men like Roy Holliday pay people like you to say that." She watched the man's face and head redden slightly, and she knew she was right. "You think I'm dumb just because I'm young and a woman, but I've been around, Mr. Hunt. I have also met Mr. Holliday and his fat companion, and not by choice. You'd better not be lying about the value of my gold."

Hunt just shook his head. "I'll admit some of the bigger miners like to know what's being found up there, but I don't lie about the value of what is brought in to me, Miss Mills, and what you're digging out of that creek up there is hardly worth the effort." The man studied Allyson's tired but pretty eyes. Her sunburned face sported a few freckles, and he suspected her figure under her too-big denim pants and loose shirt was much nicer than she was allowing anyone to see. She was a delicate wisp of a woman, damn brave, he thought. He was tempted to tell her the truth about her claim, that if she just went up higher on that mountain, she'd find another digging—this one left by John Sebastian. The gold from that digging had been worth a fortune, almost pure nuggets, but Holliday paid him well to keep quiet about it. He personally didn't want to think that Roy Holliday could have had anything to do with John Sebastian's death. He didn't like being involved in murder, and he couldn't bring himself to believe that a refined, wealthy man like Holliday would stoop to such tactics just to get his hands on another mine. He already had all the money any man could ever want.

"I happen to believe that somewhere up there I'll hit the big one," Allyson replied. She slipped her jar into a leather bag to guard it against breaking. "I'm not giving up yet, Mr. Hunt. You can tell that to Roy Holliday." She headed for the door, then hesitated when she saw a small crowd gathered outside. "Damn," she whispered.

"A young lady pretty as you and up there mining a claim all by herself is going to attract attention in a town like Cripple Creek, Miss Mills," Hunt said. "That's just the way it is."

Allyson took a deep breath, moving the jar into her left arm and resting her right hand on the butt of the six-gun strapped to her hip. Behind her, Lloyd Hunt almost laughed out loud at the sight. Allyson opened the door, and a couple of dozen men stepped a little closer, staring.

"How'd you do, Miss Mills?" one old man asked her. "You find that bonanza yet?"

Allyson realized they were all rooting for her, and it gave her the courage and determination to go back to her claim. Suddenly it didn't matter so much that all her hard work had only brought her two hundred and fifty dollars, part of which she would have to use for supplies. "Not yet," she told them. "But I'm not giving up."

"That's the spirit, ma'am," another told her.

"That's stupidity," came another voice. Allyson recognized the low, gravelly sound even before she turned around to see Wayne Trapp standing behind her. He grinned through brown teeth. "How much did you get, Miss Mills? A hundred dollars? Maybe two hundred?" He spit tobacco juice at her feet. "Ain't much for riskin' your life—" His eyes moved over her hungrily. "And your personal reputation up there every day. You could have a damn good life, lady, if you just sold that claim. You ain't never gonna make no money off it."

Allyson held her chin high, so concentrated on Trapp that she did not notice another man looking at her from around the corner of the building. Ethan had come on foot, leading Blackfoot by the reins and taking a back street to the assayer's office, wanting to be sure who the commotion was about before making his presence known. He watched the slender young woman with a big leather bag under one arm, overwhelmed with a mixture of joy and disbelief. He didn't have to see her face to know it was Ally. Just the sight of that small frame, the sound of her voice, the way she was standing up to Wayne Trapp, all told him what he needed to know. How in the world had she ended up here at Cripple Creek? How long had she been here without his knowing it, and how did Wayne Trapp know her?

"How much I made and whether or not I choose to keep mining my claim is none of your business, Mr. Trapp," she answered boldly.

Ethan grinned, almost wanting to cry, hating her . . . loving her. Ally! Should he even bother to see her? Did she hate him for leaving her and never coming back? One thing was certain, the way she stood up to Trapp, she had not changed one bit. Some of the other men were shouting their support for her answer.

"You just remember, little lady, how easy it is to break into that flimsy little cabin you've got up there at your claim."

Ethan could not see them from where he stood around the corner of the building, but he knew Trapp had spoken those words. What did he mean by that? Had he already paid Allyson a visit? What the hell had he done? It seemed incredible that Ally would actually dare to stay up on the mountain alone to mine her claim, but then this was Allyson Mills. A man shouldn't be surprised by anything she did.

"Maybe you would like all these men to know what a brute you are," Allyson retorted.

Ethan peeked around the corner of the building to see Allyson turn away from Trapp and face the crowd. "Mr. Trapp and his fancy boss, Roy—"

"Well, well, Miss Mills!" Roy Holliday interrupted, moving through the crowd and to the steps of the assayer's office. "I see you finally made it back down to Cripple Creek. How did you do? Did you get much gold out of that claim?" The man smiled affably, putting on a grand show for the men who were watching. "We've all been rooting for you."

Allyson stepped closer to the edge of the boardwalk in front of the building, and Ethan noticed the gun on her hip. He grinned at the sight.

"Is that so?" she answered Holliday. "You didn't seem to be rooting for me when you and your friend paid me a visit a week ago and broke my door down."

The miners mumbled among each other, and Ethan's anger began to build at her words. Roy Holliday had been bullying Ally. Why? To get her claim? What the hell did Roy Holliday care about one woman's claim? The man had millions.

"Now, Miss Mills, you know that was an accident. Wayne just doesn't know his own strength. I've apologized for that." He turned to the crowd. "We're all rooting for the little lady, aren't we, boys?"

They put up their fists and cheered and nodded, and Ethan could see Holliday was trying to smooth over an embarrassing situation. What had really happened up there? He had never really liked Roy Holliday, but he didn't think the man was capable of stooping low enough to harass a woman. The fact that it was Ally made him even angrier. It seemed that all her life she'd been bullied around by some man.

"What your man did was no accident!" Allyson insisted to Holliday. *That's it, Ally girl*, Ethan thought. *Use their sympathy. Get the miners on your side and Holliday can't do a thing to you.* She was at it again, using the woman in her to gain help and sympathy. She was facing the miners now, Roy Holliday standing in front of them on the steps. "Mr. Holliday and his paid thug here came to visit me at my claim," she told the miners. "They threatened me and tried to force me into selling out. Mr. Trapp even broke down my door, but I made him dance a pretty dance with my rifle, and he promptly left!"

All the men laughed, and Trapp's face began to turn red. "You lyin' little bitch!" he growled. Before Holliday could stop him, he grabbed for Allyson, who tried to draw her six-gun. Trapp grasped her right wrist so she could not grab the gun, and in the struggle she dropped the leather bag. Everyone could hear the crashing sound.

"Let her go, you damn fool!" Holliday told Wayne. "We don't treat women this way, and you know it!"

The tension in the crowd was heavy.

"She was gonna shoot me," Wayne protested.

"And she'd have every right!" Holliday retorted. He reached down to help Allyson to her feet, but she yanked her arm back, glaring hatefully at him. "Don't you touch me." She could not hold back the tears then, realizing the jar full of gold had broken. It would be a mess trying to sort out glass from gold flakes inside the leather bag. The bank would not take it the way it was. She had been so careful, had taken hours gleaning the little flakes from her many jars of water and getting everything into one bigger jar.

She wiped her tears with the back of her hand and knelt down to pick up the leather bag, when someone else stepped up onto the boardwalk. At first she saw only leather boots and denim pants. "That was a damn stupid thing to do, Trapp," came a voice. It sounded very familiar.

"It was an accident," Trapp protested.

"Like the door to her cabin?"

Ethan? No, it couldn't be! Allyson looked up, hardly able to see his face at first because of her tears, but he was certainly tall like Ethan.

"You plan to do something about it, Indian?"

Indian! Allyson sniffed, started to rise. "Stay put," Ethan gently commanded. Allyson obeyed.

"Ethan," she whimpered. "How—"

He walked past her. "I suggest you get down on your knees and apologize to Miss Mills, and then I suggest you go into the assayer's office with her and help her sort out her gold from the glass. We all know what was in that leather bag. With the jar broken, it will take hours to get it all separated."

"Look, Ethan, Wayne's done a stupid thing, I'll agree," Holliday spoke up. "I don't want any trouble. I'll help sort the gold."

Ethan kept his eyes on Trapp. "Stay out of this, Holliday. I am no longer under your employ."

Employ? Ethan worked for Roy Holliday? Allyson stared up at him in disbelief, scooting against the wall near the door.

"I ain't apologizin' to no back-talkin', gun-totin' shrimp of a woman who's crazy enough to try to mine gold all on her own," Wayne answered Ethan, straightening and giving Ethan a belligerent stare. "Anybody comes to this country to mine for gold has to accept all the dangers and risks that comes with it, man or woman. If she can't handle herself, she ought to sell out and get the hell out of Cripple Creek!"

Ethan removed his leather hat and threw it down near Ally. "It's real easy to bully a small woman who weighs a good hundred and sixty or seventy pounds less than you, isn't it, Trapp? How about picking on somebody closer to your own size. Think *you* can handle *that?*"

Trapp threw down his own hat, and some of the men pulled an embarrassed and enraged Roy Holliday out of the way, shouting at Ethan to "take Wayne Trapp down a notch or two." Ethan suspected a lot of them would like to do the honors, but the man was so big, none of them had cared to try.

"I can handle *you* any day of the week, you goddamn Indian," Trapp answered. "You come in here tryin' to get my job. We'll show Roy Holliday here and now who the better man really is."

"Wayne, I don't want—" Holliday's words were interrupted when Ethan suddenly landed a big, hard fist into Wayne's soft middle. Wayne's body jerked back slightly, and he let out a loud grunt, his eyes bulging with surprise. Before he could react, Ethan repeated the blow, a hard, fierce slam to the man's soft belly, then twice more, until the man doubled over. In spite of his size, Ethan jerked him to his feet as though he weighed nothing, and while Trapp grasped at his gut with his hands, Ethan rammed his fist into the man's face, sending him sprawling over a railing and into a watering trough just below it. He landed with a huge splash, and immediately the sides to the trough broke away, spilling out what was left of the water. Wayne rolled off of it and landed groaning on the ground.

A cheer went up from the crowd, and Ethan picked up Wayne's hat and walked down the two short steps to the trough. He placed the hat on Wayne's head. "You've got to stop so much eating and drinking, Trapp. That big belly of yours is getting much too soft. Being big doesn't help you if it's mostly fat."

The men all laughed, and Ethan turned to face Roy Holliday. "I'll be back later for whatever pay you owe me."

"Ethan, let's talk about this. You're too good a man for me to lose."

"I never have liked you, Holliday, but I thought I could work for you, until today. I don't work for a man who bullies a woman, especially when that woman used to be my wife."

The word *wife* was mumbled and passed through the crowd of men. "She was married to the *Indian?*" someone exclaimed.

Ethan left Holliday and went back up onto the boardwalk. He reached down and took hold of Allyson's arm. "Let's go. We've got some talking to do."

"Ethan, how did you end up here?" Allyson sniffed and wiped at her eyes again.

"How about telling me how *you* got here?" He took the leather bag from her. "Come on, let's get away from town first." He helped her up, and to his surprise, she flung her arms around him and hugged him tightly.

"I can't believe it's you," she wept.

He wanted to still be angry with her, to yell at her for being dumb enough to come to a place like Cripple Creek alone and risk her person and her life trying to mine a claim; wanted to hate her for how she had hurt him; but all he could do was give her a gentle squeeze and kiss her hair. "Come on. Blackfoot is right around the corner." He led her to his horse—the men stared as he lifted her up onto it. He handed her the leather pouch, then mounted up behind her. They headed out of town.

23

"I looked for you in Guthrie," Ethan said as he led Blackfoot up a mountain pathway that led out of town. "I hoped maybe you'd still be there. Everybody thought you'd gone to Denver, just like you said in your letter. I was going to look for you there, but then I figured maybe you didn't want to be found. It was pretty obvious when you sent me those papers to sign that you didn't want anything more to do with me."

Allyson rubbed her eyes, her head aching from the strain of her trip and the unexpected events of the last hour. "I thought *you* wouldn't want anything more to do with *me*. That's why I tried to make it easy for you." There came the unwanted tears again. It felt so good to run into someone she knew, someone she could trust, even though he might hate her now. She knew Ethan Temple. Even if he hated her, he would help her if she needed it.

He halted Blackfoot, dismounted and lifted her down, taking the leather bag and tying it over his saddlehorn. "We'll sort through this later." He removed her hat and studied the familiar red hair and her sunburned face. She seemed just a little taller, and as pretty as he remembered. Had he really bedded this wisp of a woman, and had she really been as passionate and loving as he remembered? Was that all an act, or was it real at the time?

Their eyes met and held, and behind it all was something

else. Ethan didn't want to believe it could be love. Surely she had never loved him, and he'd be a fool to think he still loved her. He turned away, fishing through his gear for a smoke. "All right, let's have your story. What are you doing here in Cripple Creek?"

Allyson struggled with her emotions. Ethan Temple was even more handsome than she had remembered him. She had been so sure she had gotten over him, but to see him again, to ride on Blackfoot nestled close to him, to see how he had stood up for her again . . . it all came flooding back, all the womanly desires he had stirred in her, all the agony of knowing she had hurt him, lost him. He was probably still lost to her. She was not going to make a fool of herself by making the first move now. She had to wait and see just what *he* was feeling, what he intended to do now that he had found her again.

She sighed and sat down on a flat rock. "I left Guthrie because there were too many memories there, most of them bad. Besides, people weren't very nice to me after everything that happened."

Ethan snickered, inwardly struggling to pretend he didn't care about her anymore. "I wonder why. All you did was lie to everybody there, use people to help you get ahead, play on their sympathies. I can't imagine why they would be upset about that."

She rested her elbows on her knees and put her head in her hands. "Ethan, please don't. I know how much I hurt people, especially you. If people just understood my reasons . . ."

He lit the cigar and took several puffs. "I understand them, maybe better than you do. The trouble with you is you don't know what's really good for you, what's really important in life, and it isn't money." He walked a few feet away from her. "So, you went to Denver. Why? Just for the hell of it?"

"I guess." Allyson stared at a little wildflower blowing in a soft mountain breeze. "It was a growing city, busy, exciting. I figured with what little money I had left after all my debts, I could start over there. I never got one cent from Nolan Ives for all I had put into improving those lots. I needed a way to make back my money. At first I worked for a rooming house and did laundry, whatever I could do to get ahead." She pulled the ribbon and pins from her hair and let it fall. "The trouble is, it's expensive to build something of your own in Denver. I needed a way to get rich quicker, so I took what savings I had and grubstaked a prospector. His name was John Sebastian. He came up here and filed a claim. The next thing I knew, the man who helped connect me with Mr. Sebastian checked on how he was doing and found out he'd been murdered up at the claim."

"Murdered?" Ethan turned around then, somewhat stunned by the transformation. The boyish-looking Allyson Mills had suddenly become a beautiful woman. Her red hair spilled over her shoulders fetchingly, and he remembered seeing that hair cascading around milky-white shoulders and breasts, partially hiding the pink fruits of those breasts so he had to push the hair away to find them. *Damn her*, he thought. If he wasn't careful he'd fall all over again, and she'd find a way to use him for this new venture. "He's sure it was murder?"

Allyson shrugged. "The man was shot in the head. Most figured it was somebody who had a grudge against him, since no one tried to file on his claim. Now I'm beginning to wonder." Allyson met his eyes. "Roy Holliday and that fat man you beat up today came to visit me about a week ago. They threatened me with bodily harm and something worse than death if I didn't sell out to Holliday. The fat one broke down my door, but I shot at him and made him get out of my cabin. They both finally left, but I haven't had a decent night's sleep since. Now I'm wondering if Mr. Holliday had something to do with John Sebastian's death. He might have known the man's backer was a woman, and figured a woman would never come up here and take over; but I proved him wrong. As anxious as he was to get hold of my claim, I can't help thinking it must be richer than I know. He knows something about it that I don't. I'm sure of it."

Ethan turned and gazed at the surrounding mountains. "You really went up there and worked your own claim?"

Allyson rubbed at her forehead again. "I couldn't afford to hire someone to help me. I've learned a lot. An old guide named Stan took me up and showed me the basics of panning and using a sluice. The gold in that leather bag is worth about two hundred fifty dollars—not much for three months of hard labor and living in constant fear. I was even chased by a grizzly. His claws left scars on the back of my right leg, and there are still claw marks on my door, which is now nailed shut because I don't know how to fix it. I go in and out of a window." She tossed her hair behind her shoulders. "I ran low on supplies, so I figured I'd bring in what gold I had and see what it was worth, put the money in a bank, get started on a savings. I'll have a fine time now getting it sorted out of all that broken glass."

Ethan stuck the cigar between his teeth and walked back to where she sat. He sat down in the grass near the rock. "Holliday actually came up there and threatened you?"

"Yes." Allyson met his eyes. "He's a cruel, vicious man, Ethan. What are you doing, working for someone like that? You aren't that way."

He took the cigar from his mouth and looked back out at

the mountains. "He's never asked me to do anything like that. My job has been to keep trouble from erupting among the miners. A lot of them are thinking about striking over wages and hours. I've also been spending time guarding gold shipments to Colorado Springs. I've never really liked Holliday, but he paid damn good, and as long as he didn't ask me to do something dishonest, I figured I could work for him. I knew he was a bastard in a lot of ways, but I never figured he was one to bully a woman."

Allyson studied the long, dark hair that hung from under his leather hat, the broad shoulders. A shiver moved through her at the memory of their wedding night. He had awakened something beautiful on the inside, leaving her aching to feel that way again. Part of her wanted that back, wanted to be in those strong arms again, to feel his mouth exploring her own, tasting her breasts, feel those strong fingers touching her in ways that made her feel on fire. He would probably never again want her that way. "How did you meet Holliday?" she asked.

Ethan puffed on the cigar once more. "I didn't know what to do with myself after Guthrie. I couldn't go back to living on the reservation any more. It's all changed now. Most of the Indian land in Oklahoma has been lost to whites. Up north it's even worse for the Sioux and Northern Cheyenne."

"I read about Wounded Knee. I worried you might have been there, been hurt. I didn't know how to find out. In fact, I was *afraid* to find out, so I never asked."

Ethan wondered if that meant she still cared about him. He thought about how she had hugged him when he first found her today, but then that was probably gratitude for his help. "I was there," he answered. "But I didn't get there until right after it happened." He sighed deeply. "There were bodies everywhere, mostly women and children. It was horrible. A snowstorm hit right afterward, and they couldn't get to the bodies right away. Some were still alive but froze to death waiting for help that never came. Some crawled off into bushes and creeks, trying to get away. Mothers were found hovering over their babies trying to keep them warm. It wasn't until four days after the massacre that the weather cleared enough so we could go pick up bodies. They were all frozen in grotesque poses, some looking like they were reaching out for help." His voice broke, and he puffed quietly on the cigar for a moment.

"I'm sorry, Ethan. What happened to your relatives?"

He sniffed and took a deep breath. "My grandmother had died a few weeks before that, and I'm glad of it. She never lived to see what happened. My uncle and a cousin were killed in the massacre and a couple more cousins were wounded. They'll be all right." He shook his head. "I just couldn't stay there after that. There's nothing left. Their spirits are broken. They'd been practicing a new religion, thought a Savior was going to come and rescue them and bring back all their dead relatives and the buffalo. They know now that will never happen. The old ways are gone . . . just gone."

Ethan got up, clearing his throat. "At any rate I came back to Guthrie, visited what's left of my relatives on the Cheyenne reservation near there, found out a good friend of mine from my army scouting days had died, and decided I had to leave there, too. Like you, the area held too many memories. I just headed west for the hell of it, part of me thinking maybe I could find you, but not sure that I should. Roy Holliday happened to be on the same train and it was robbed. I managed to stop the robbery, saved a lot of people's jewelry and money, and shot up some of the outlaws. Holliday liked the way I handled it and offered me a job on the spot as a troubleshooter at his mines up here. I sure as hell didn't have anything better to do, and I wanted to get some money saved so I could maybe go to Wyoming and build a ranch there. A man has to settle sometime in his life."

Yes, he does, Allyson thought. Was he thinking of looking for another woman, taking a wife so he could settle and have children? She never thought she would want those things for herself, but the thought of having them with Ethan . . . *Stop it!* she told herself. Ethan Temple surely wanted nothing more to do with her, and she had her gold mine to think about. She thought about his remark that she didn't know what was really important in life, and that it wasn't money. Didn't he understand that for someone like herself, money was the only way she could have power, her only protection?

She looked up to catch him watching her, seeing the hurt in his eyes. "I'm sorry, Ethan. I never got a chance to tell you calmly, and I didn't realize until you were gone how much I—" She looked away. "Cared for you. It wasn't all just to save the business. I mean, it's not as though I didn't have any feelings for you at all."

He grinned with sarcasm and shook his head. "You just don't get it, do you? Maybe it's because you're just too young to understand a man's pride." He walked closer to her. "Whether you had a little feeling for me, or a lot, the fact remains you wanted to hurry up and get married because you thought having a husband would save you. It didn't work, and when I saw the look on your face when Cy Jacobs told you you'd married the wrong man because I was Indian, I knew what you were thinking, Ally, and it didn't feel good. I'm just a man, Ally—Indian, white, it makes no difference. No respectable man wants to be used and made a fool of."

"I know." She closed her eyes. "I can never make up for that. I don't even know why you allowed me to get an annulment instead of labeling me a divorced woman. I don't blame you for leaving and not coming back, either, but now that you *are* here, maybe . . . maybe you could come back up to my claim with me. I can trust you, and I'm tired of being up there all alone." She met his eyes again. "I'm scared, Ethan."

Well, that's a start, he thought. At least she was admitting she was afraid, something she didn't like doing.

"I can't pay you, but up there a person doesn't need much. I'll pay for all the supplies. I heard you tell Holliday you were through working for him, so you're a free man now."

Ethan decided not to mention he'd gotten a thousand-dollar reward for killing a notorious train robber. If there was to be anything at all between them again, it had to be real, not because she wanted to get her hands on his money. Why he even thought there *could* be something between them again, he wasn't sure, except that if he went up to her claim with her, he already knew he couldn't be around her without wanting her again. What was this she did to him? He had no control over his emotions, even after all these months apart and thinking he was done with her. He put the cigar back in his mouth and walked past her to stand on a ledge from which he could see most of Cripple Creek.

"Do you realize what you're asking? After what we've had between us, it's too hard just to be casual friends again, Ally. I don't think I could do that, and after all the hurt, I can't let things get serious again. Besides, I don't even trust you anymore."

Allyson stiffened. He'd wanted the remark to hurt, and it did. "Ethan, I said I was sorry, and I meant it. All these months I've worried and wondered about you, realized I felt more for you than I realized."

"But the most important thing to you right now is that gold, isn't it? You're still aiming to get rich, determined to go back up there and keep digging. You'd just be using me again, Ally. You need a man to help and protect you, and along comes good ole Ethan Temple, right? What if I asked you to give it all up, to start over with me someplace new, to settle down and help me run a ranch? Would you give up that gold mine?"

She got up and folded her arms stubbornly. "Ethan, that's not fair. The fact remains I *do* have a gold claim, and if Roy Holliday wants it, then it must be worth something. I have to keep working it and try to find out what's really there. If *you* owned it, you'd do the same thing."

He shook his head. "Gold and riches don't mean that much to me. I just want some peace in my life and a good woman at my side. I thought I had that, but it only lasted about twenty-four hours."

Allyson reddened and looked away. "I can never make up for that. I can only tell you with all sincerity that I thank God I found you again, that you're all right. I can only hope you will believe me when I tell you that after . . . after you made me your wife, my feelings changed. I truly *wanted* to be your wife in every way. It didn't matter anymore that you might help me keep my property. All that mattered was that Ethan Temple was my husband and I . . . I thought I loved him. Now there are too many hard feelings to talk about love, but we could at least spend some time together, learn to be friends again. We owe that to each other. I want to salvage something from all the hurt, Ethan. There must be a reason God helped us find each other again."

Ethan dearly wanted to believe her, but he was cautious.

Allyson Mills was a determined, headstrong woman who could lie as easily as she breathed. She wanted to find her bonanza, and she needed a man to help her do it. It irritated him that it meant so much to her, yet the memory of her tears when Wayne Trapp broke her treasured jar of gold tore at his heart. There was something pitiful about her in spite of her stubbornness and feisty ways. "I don't know," he answered. "I have to think about it. Besides, what would all the men in this place think, you up there alone with a man? In their eyes it will be even worse because I'm Indian."

"Let them think what they want. I've never cared about those things." She tossed her head. "We could always say we're still married—that we never got a divorce or an annulment." Allyson came closer, her beautiful blue eyes pleading. "Please, Ethan. It would give us time to talk, to make up for all the hurt. God must mean for you to help me, or he wouldn't have brought you to Cripple Creek. If I strike it rich, I'll share it with you, fifty-fifty. I'll put it in writing if you want."

He watched her sadly. "I don't need anything in writing. I don't even *want* half. If I go up there with you, it will be to help an old friend, not because I expect a share of the proceeds. That's the difference between us, Ally. I do things because I feel certain people deserve to be helped, and because I want to do it. I don't use people to help me get what *I* want."

She studied his handsome face, wondering herself how she could work with him day after day without falling into his arms and his bed again. "Is that what you think I'm doing?"

"What else am I *supposed* to think? You've done it before. Now here we are, reunited for only a couple of hours, and you want me to go up there with you and help you chop out the side of a mountain so you can be a rich woman. Once you find your fortune, I don't imagine you'll want anything more to do with an Indian man. You were obviously embarrassed to be married to one once you found out I couldn't help you keep your property."

"It wasn't that way, Ethan." She studied the way his dark hair blew fetchingly around his handsome face. "I wasn't ashamed or embarrassed that you were Indian. I was just disappointed that your being Indian meant I would lose everything after all. I couldn't help my first reaction to knowing that. I had worked so hard for all of it, hardly sleeping, always afraid of Nolan Ives finding a way to take it all away. When he finally did, it just hurt so much. The disappointment you saw wasn't because you were Indian. It was just that I was losing everything. You took it more personally than it was meant. I . . . I loved you, Ethan. I never realized how much until you walked out."

He waved her off and turned away. "I don't want to talk about love. Not now."

"Fine, but the fact remains we were married. We . . . we made love, and there was . . . *is* . . . something special between us that will never go away now. We need to find out how we really feel." She touched his arm. "You can't tell me, Ethan, that you aren't glad you found me, that you haven't worried and wondered about me, that no matter how angry you were you could just stop loving me that easily."

Ethan sighed, turning slightly to look into the blue eyes he had dreamed about almost every night for over a year. "I don't want to talk about love, Ally. Too much has happened. I've seen the results of misunderstandings between white and Indian. You and I come from such different worlds, and we both want something different out of life. I should have known better than to marry you in the first place." His gaze traveled over her in that way he had of setting fire to her loins. "But what's past is past. I'll say it once. I did love you, but I've lost those special feelings. It doesn't mean I don't care about you or that I won't help you. I just need some time to think about it."

Allyson felt like crying. She realized that convincing him how sorry she was about what she had done—that she had never regretted anything more in her life and that she had realized she really did love him—was going to be almost impossible. She looked down and turned away. "Maybe you coming up to my claim isn't such a good idea after all. I just thought—" She shrugged, deciding to show him it didn't matter. "I've needed someone to come and help me dig into the mountain, someone with some strength. I just can't afford to pay someone, and there isn't one man in this town I would trust to stay up there with me. I didn't mean for it to sound like I was just using you again." She faced him, holding her chin high. "It's a legitimate offer. Fifty-fifty if I strike it rich. You do what you think is best. I'll stay in a hotel tonight—not Mr. Holliday's, of course. I'll buy what supplies I need this afternoon and head back first light. You can come or not."

Ethan grinned. "You never change, do you?"

"I'm sorry if that disappoints you."

Ethan walked over and picked up the reins to Blackfoot. "Get on. I'll take you back to your mules and help you and the assayer sort through the mess in that leather sack. You go on to the bank and get your supplies, whatever you have to do. I have some things to straighten out with Holliday."

"Fine," she said nonchalantly. She walked to the horse and took her hat from the saddlehorn, plopping it on her head.

"You'd better twist that hair back up under the hat. I don't think you understand how fetching a woman looks to a man when her hair is falling all over her shoulders."

She glanced at him, then walked to the rock to pick up the ribbon. She quickly tied her hair, then began repinning it, wondering just how "fetching" she looked to Ethan Temple right now. She put her hat back on over her upswept hair, then managed to mount up on Blackfoot by herself. Ethan came over and took hold of the reins, leading the animal back toward town.

"Aren't you getting up here with me?"

Ethan looked back at her, his eyes moving over her again. "Right now I'll think more clearly with you up there and me down here."

Allyson felt her cheeks flushing red. Was he saying it still excited him to be close to her? She was not going to admit it yet, but deep inside she knew she still loved the man. Seeing him again, how he looked, how he handled himself, even the smell of him . . . it all brought back the memory of that one night of passion, and the realization that she had loved Ethan Temple even before she realized it herself. But he'd been hurt, and she had to be careful, tread lightly, or she would lose him forever. Finding him had been the most wonderful thing that had happened to her in a long time, and she was not letting him slip away again.

"Are you coming back with me then?" she asked. Ethan did not reply right away. He just kept walking, puffing on the little cigar. Allyson frowned in annoyance. "Ethan, you wouldn't really, really let me go back alone, would you?"

He stopped walking, turning to look up at her. "For God's sake, woman, you must know what we're both looking at here." He looked angry. "We were *married* once. We've been *lovers.*" He looked away. "If you can call what happened love. At least it was on my part."

"Ethan, it was on my part, too. I wish you would believe that. I didn't expect it, but that's how it turned out."

He sighed deeply. "All right, here's how it is." He looked up at her again, saw her cheeks looked rosier and realized he had flustered her by mentioning their intimacy. He took the cigar from his mouth. "I tried real hard to forget you, but now that I've found you again, I feel a certain responsibility. I always did feel a little guilty for walking out like I did, but you didn't seem to want me back anyway. No matter what has happened between us, I still care enough about you that I can't let you go back up there alone, and I know that right now that's what you're determined to do. You're not about to listen to any common sense I might try to hand you because you're as stubborn and pig-headed as you ever were! For the next few months I want an understanding between us."

Allyson pursed her lips. "What kind of understanding?"

"Honesty, for one thing. Are you capable of that?"

"Well, I . . . I—"

"I won't be used again, Ally. I'll go back up with you because I'd worry too much about you if I don't. I can't guarantee I won't want you the way any man would want a woman after being alone with her for weeks. If that happens and you're not ready to truly commit yourself to me, then I'll have to leave. But you'd by-God better not take me to your bed with words of love just to keep me up there to help you! It's going to be real or not at all. I don't even want to *talk* about love for a while, but if we *do* find out we still love each other, then I want it understood and agreed-to right now that we give it one year at the most."

"Give what one year?"

He rolled his eyes in exasperation. "The *mine*. If it doesn't pay out after one year, we sell the claim, take the money, and go live like normal people. I want a ranch of my own, Ally, and I'll need a woman to help me with it, to give me children. There was a time when I thought you were that woman, but now I'm not so sure. After some time together, we'll both know, but I want that chance."

"If we strike it rich, you'll have that chance," she answered. "Either way you can have half of whatever we get out of there, and you still should have enough to get started with."

"Fine. If we find out we don't love each other and don't belong together, I go my way and you go yours, and that will be the end of it."

Their eyes met, both knowing that now that they'd found each other again, it would be next to impossible just to drift apart once more and forget. "All right," she answered. "No pretending. You are officially hired, and we split the profits fifty-fifty. We get one year together to find out how we really feel. Then we either go our separate ways, or we go build that ranch in Wyoming."

"No matter what happens with the mine. If we hit a bonanza, we hire others to mine it right and we still get that ranch. I'm not staying up here forever, Ally. We can always settle in the valley near Colorado Springs. If we don't hit it big, but we want to stay together, we sell the claim. I want that understood."

"Fine. A year should be plenty of time."

Ethan wondered what it was about her that made him lose his mind this way. He was probably walking right back into trouble. "Yeah, plenty of time for a lot of things," he answered. "I mean it, Ally, about being honest."

"I won't lie to you, Ethan, about anything, ever again, but

please don't lie to me either. You have every right to try to hurt me, and you've been working for Roy Holliday. You wouldn't just pretend to be quitting, would you? You could act as a spy for him, agree to go back with me just to see if I hit it big, maybe try to talk me into selling, using old feelings to sway me."

Ethan snickered. "You know me better than that. I'm not a man to work both sides of the fence. Besides, nobody sways you when you set your mind to something." He turned away and started walking again, sticking the cigar back between his lips, grumbling.

"What?" Allyson asked.

"I said you make me crazy," he spoke up louder. "What I should do is give you a good kick in the ass and say good luck and let you go back up there alone."

She smiled. "You're exactly right."

He stopped again. "What if I put it the other way?" he asked. "What if I gave you the choice—go back up or sell out right now and come with me to the valley?"

Her smile faded. "Well, I . . . I couldn't—"

"Just what I thought," he said, turning away to start walking again. "At least you're being honest about it. That's a start."

She was going to say she couldn't let him out of her life again, but she decided not to tell him . . . not right now. She had a claim to mine, and at least now she had help. Maybe it was best he thought that was all she wanted. "Thank you, Ethan," she said softly. "You have no idea how grateful I am, especially after the way I hurt you. I know you have every right to stay out of my affairs."

"Well, I'm right back in them again, fool that I am. I don't know why we keep getting thrown together."

She smiled again. "Maybe it's just a curse."

He looked back up at her, this time with a handsome smile that stirred deep desires and sent a wave of remembrance surging through her. "That's one way to look at it," he answered.

He continued walking then, and Allyson felt warm and happy and excited. She'd found Ethan Temple! It was like a miracle. She had Ethan *and* her mine! Everything was going to be wonderful now! Thank God she had come to town when she did. Now she didn't have to go back up there alone.

"You're a stupid damn fool!" Roy Holliday roared at Wayne Trapp. It had been three hours since his run-in with Ethan, but although he had changed into dry clothes, Trapp was still nursing a broken, swollen nose and still feeling the hideous ache in his gut from Ethan's vicious punches. "I told you to go easy on the woman, and what do you do? You *bully* her, right in front of the miners, and in front of Ethan Temple, who used to be *married* to her, for God's sake!"

"How was I to know that?" Trapp argued.

"It wouldn't matter if you did or didn't, if you had handled the situation the way I *told* you!" Holliday shouted back. "Now everybody out there thinks I go around bullying people out of their claims!" He lowered his voice for a moment, leaning close to Trapp. "For God's sake, they might even start wondering about why John Sebastian was shot—that maybe *I* had something to do with it!"

"You told me to go and see what was happening."

"That's right—just go and see, not threaten the woman in front of everybody! Now the miners are all behind her, and she damn well knows it! She'll use that, don't you understand? On top of that I'll probably lose one of my best men!

Now that he knows she's up there and she's been threatened, Ethan Temple will probably go back with her to watch over her. There won't be one damn thing I can do to talk her into selling! Temple will probably find the damn vein and that will be the end of it, unless the apex of that vein stems from my mine. The geologist I hired still isn't sure." Holliday began pacing while he fumed.

Wayne winced as he shifted in his chair. "I'll make up for it some way, Mr. Holliday."

Holliday turned and glared at him. "You've gotten fat and careless this past year, Wayne. I won't tolerate much more of it. As far as Ethan Temple and that woman are concerned, we have to wait and see what he's going to do; but if he goes back up there with her, I don't want you doing *any*thing, not for a while. All fingers would point to us. All we can do is hope they don't find the real vein and that they give up after one good, harsh winter up there. If not, maybe we can make a move in the spring. We have to be very careful, whatever we do." He turned and walked to a window. "Damn! I almost had her! Can you believe the irony of it? Ethan Temple was once *married* to that she-devil! A fine pair they make. I wonder what the whole story is behind that one."

"Ain't many proper white women who'd marry an Indian. Maybe we were wrong thinkin' of her as a lady. You should have let me have at her when we were up there. That would have broke her down good, and apparently I wouldn't have been soilin' anything special. She's already been had, by an *Indian*, no less."

"Maybe we can use that to keep the miners from siding with her too heavily, especially if Temple goes up there with her. It won't look very good."

Wayne started to grin, but it hurt his face too much. "It sure won't."

Someone knocked on the door. Holliday looked at Wayne. "If it's Temple, keep your mouth shut and stay in that chair. Come in!" he called out.

The door opened, and Ethan stepped inside. He stiffened when he spotted Wayne Trapp sitting there, and his dark eyes glittered with pleasure at the sight of the man's battered face. The look Trapp gave back told him the man would like to see him dead, but he stayed in the chair and said nothing. Ethan moved his gaze to Roy Holliday. "I'll be taking my back pay now. You owe me a hundred and fifty dollars for the past thirty days."

Holliday sighed with disgust. "Ethan, let's talk about this."

"There's nothing to discuss. I heard what you did up at Ally's claim. I don't do business with men like that." He looked at Wayne again. "I should have killed you."

Wayne started to rise. "You red-skinned sonofabitch! When I'm better—"

"Wayne!" Holliday snapped the name. "Sit down and shut up! You've caused enough trouble today. Any more and I'll fire you! You're damn lucky I haven't already." The man fished some money from his desk drawer while Wayne settled back into his chair, still glowering at Ethan.

"You and I ain't finished with each other," Wayne grumbled.

Ethan stepped closer. "Any time you want more, look me up."

"And where will that be?" Holliday asked. "You getting back together with your wife?"

"She's not my wife anymore." Ethan stepped up to the desk and took the money Holliday handed to him. "I'm not sure what I'm going to do. I just know I can't work for you any longer. I might go up to Ally's claim with her, now that I know she's been threatened. She may not be my wife, but I still care about her. She's determined to find her bonanza, and I can tell you that trying to discourage her from her dreams is like trying to smash a rock with a stick. It can't be done."

Holliday sighed with a scowl. "Ethan, no matter what she has told you, it wasn't as terrible as you think. I went up there with a damn good offer of three thousand dollars. I was doing it out of concern for her safety. A woman alone just shouldn't be up there fighting the elements and wild animals, let alone the thousands of woman-hungry men. It's just too dangerous. I thought I was doing her a favor. She could live very well on three thousand dollars, and start her own business someplace more civilized, like Colorado Springs or Denver. If you really care about her, you'll try to talk her into selling. You know damn well I'm right in saying she shouldn't be up there, and you know how hard it is to properly mine a claim without men and the right equipment. I assure you that claim will never yield enough for her to go to this much trouble to try to hang on to it. You tell her my offer still stands." He came around from behind his desk and put out his hand. "You have my word that whether you stay with her or let her go back up alone, she won't be bothered by me or Wayne or any of my men. I made an offer and she rejected it. That's the end of it."

Ethan shoved the money into his pants pocket. "Why is it I don't believe you, Holliday?" He did not take the man's hand. Holliday finally dropped it, his dark eyes beginning to smoulder with rage. Ethan realized he was seeing the real Roy Holliday. Maybe he *was* a killer. Maybe he had John Sebastian murdered, then figured the woman who had grubstaked him would sell out with no argument. He hadn't figured on running across a woman like Allyson Mills, and the thought of Ally going up against men like Holliday and Wayne Trapp brought back all of Ethan's old feelings of protection. "I hope this *is* the end of it," he warned. "You don't want to have to answer to me if something happens to Allyson Mills, I assure you. I'm grateful for the original job offer. You've paid me well. I think you understand why I'm quitting."

Holliday snickered. "I understand. Go on with you then. You're a good man, Temple. You could have gone far with me. I was already thinking of promoting you, but you've made your decision, so don't come crawling back later on wanting your good-paying job back."

Ethan glanced at Wayne Trapp again. The man gave him an arrogant stare, as though to tell him he was crazy to give up a job with Roy Holliday. "If working for you means ending up like this fat bully, then no, thanks. I'm glad I'm getting out now."

"You goddamn Indian!" Wayne retorted, again starting to rise. Ethan just turned and walked to the door, stopping to look at both of them.

"Stay away from Ally and her claim, or the next time neither one of you will live to tell about it," he warned.

He turned and left, and Holliday glared at Wayne Trapp. "Get out of my sight for a while." He turned away and went back to his desk.

Wayne got up with a deep sigh, hating Ethan Temple more than any man he'd ever known. He'd been humiliated today, in front of a couple of dozen miners, let alone in front of that bitch of a woman. He would not forget this, and somehow he would make Ethan pay! He *and* the woman would pay!

24

"I'm afraid you'll be eating mostly beans and flapjacks," Allyson told Ethan. They were nearing the site of her claim, both weary from a full day of constant climbing.

"That's better than army food," Ethan answered. "All woman-cooked? Or do we share that job, too?"

Allyson looked back at him. He had purchased two extra mules and a wealth of mining supplies—two extra pickaxes, shovels, hatchets, buckets, pans, even more food. She had not expected him to do so much, and she felt undeserving. "You'll be doing the heaviest work, hacking into this damn mountain. I'll do the cooking. I've been cooking mostly over a campfire outside. I guess in the winter all I'll have to cook on is the top of my heating stove."

"Either way, I've cooked for myself for years. You don't have to do it all."

"I don't mind. After all, I learned plenty when I had my restaurant back in Guthrie." Guthrie. Everything that had happened there seemed so unreal now. Poor Toby had been dead two years already. He would have so loved this adventure. What a long way she had come from the streets of New York City, digging into the side of a mountain with a half-Indian man as her companion! That man knew every inch of her body, had invaded it, claimed it. Did he still feel as though she belonged to him? Deep inside, she felt that way herself, but she had to remember what was really important, and that was her gold claim. She didn't even know if Ethan could ever again love her the way he had in the beginning. She had to be careful not to begin to care too much. He might leave her again, next time for good.

The cabin finally came into sight. "Here we are," she told Ethan. She ducked under some pine trees, then splashed through the creek and into a clearing that led up to the sorry-looking cabin. "The finest rooming house on this side of the mountain," she joked. "The only trouble is, we have to go in through the window."

Ethan looked around the site and spotted the area where she had been chopping into rock to the left side of the cabin. He was amazed she had made what little progress she had. It was gruesome enough work for a man, but for a woman as small as Ally, it was nearly impossible. He smiled at the thought of her picking away at it with her thin arms, and he knew that was what he still loved about her, that stubborn determination to make her own way, no matter how hard she had to work at it.

The cabin itself was a miserable-looking shack, and he could not imagine that she actually thought she could survive up here through the winter. Where did she think she was going to get wood? Chop and haul it all herself? There was only a tiny pile left on the cabin porch. As he drew closer he noticed the claw marks on the front door made by the grizzly. Wayne Trapp had broken down that same door, which was now nailed shut because she didn't know how to fix it. He found her courage incredible for one so young and small, but then her spirit made up for her build. In spite of how angry she made him at times, and no matter how she had hurt him, he would never stop admiring her strength and bravery. He could just picture her shooting at Wayne Trapp. The bastard! If he'd touched a hair on Allyson

Mills's head . . . He wished now that Trapp had drawn his gun. He'd like nothing more than to kill the man.

"I'll give you the grand tour," she was saying. She tied her lead mule to a porch post. "This is my lovely home. Come inside and have a look." She stepped up onto the porch and walked to a window, ducking through it. Ethan tied his horse and mules and followed, finding it more difficult to climb in through the window because he was so much bigger.

"First thing I'm doing is fixing the damn door," he complained. "I bought some new hinges before I left." He got inside and straightened up. Allyson stood near a potbellied, wood-burning stove.

"You like it?" she asked with a grin.

Ethan looked around the shabby cabin. He could see light between the boards, which meant it would be miserably cold in winter. The plank floors had a sway to them, and there was a puddle in one corner, apparently left from the roof leaking during a rain. A homemade cot sat in another corner, and just when he glanced at it he noticed a small rat run from under it and out through a hole between two wall boards.

"I've gotten way past them scaring me," Allyson explained. "After a while you get so lonely up here, you don't even mind the rodents and wild animals."

Ethan sighed, shaking his head. "It's worse than I expected."

"I told you it was pretty bad."

Ethan met her blue eyes. "You've really been up here alone for three months in this rat-infested, leaking place?"

Allyson shrugged. "It's better than no shelter at all, wouldn't you say?"

Ethan laughed lightly. "A damn tent would be better."

"Maybe. But in a tent I would be more open to a bear attack. No, thanks. I'll take hard walls, primitive and poorly-built as they may be. I don't need a grizzly or a wolf trying to rip apart my tent while I'm in it."

"Good point." Their eyes held, each of them wondering if the other was thinking the same thing. What about tonight? Where would Ethan sleep? Ethan turned away then and walked over to inspect the door. Allyson thought how his big frame seemed to fill the cabin, how wonderful it was going to be to have him here, someone to talk to, someone to turn to in times of danger. Nothing could stop her now that Ethan was here! It struck her then that she was happiest when Ethan was around. There was at least one person in the world who cared about her. Maybe he didn't love her anymore, but he cared.

"I'll have this thing fixed before nightfall," he told her. "I'll go get a crowbar to pry it off. Maybe in a couple of weeks I'll go back to town and get some tar paper to cover the outside of the walls and the roof—help against drafts and leaks. We can pack some straw around the edges where the walls meet the floor. That will help keep out drafts. I brought some poison along to set out for rats."

Allyson breathed a deep sigh of relief. "Oh, Ethan, it's so good to have someone here who can make this place a little more livable."

He turned, feeling a warmth rush through him at her closeness. She had removed her hat, and strands of red hair spilled around her face. He quickly moved away from her. "Well, it's too late to do any digging tonight, and I'm too damn tired, but I can go ahead with the door." He ducked back through the window. "Soon as I get the door off, you can start unloading these mules. They need a rest."

Allyson climbed out after him. "There's a single privy

over in those trees." She pointed to a cluster of scrubby pine beside the cabin. "I'm afraid the only way to wash is to carry in a bucket of creek water. It's clear and clean. I can only hand wash. I don't have a tub up here, and a woman alone can't very well go bathing in the creek for all to see. Besides, the creek water is too cold."

Ethan tried to ignore the deep urgings the picture brought to mind, Allyson naked in the creek, her red hair falling around milky-white shoulders and full, firm breasts. "Maybe I can manage a tin tub the next time I go to town. It would be a bitch getting it up here, but in winter it would be nice to have." He already knew he'd never make it through a whole winter up here without crawling into Allyson's bed. Fact was, she must be wanting a man by now. Could they do something like that just out of friendship? A man could, but a woman? Of course, Ally was no ordinary woman. Still, he didn't want it to be like that between them. "I'll just spread out a bedroll on the floor tonight for sleeping," he told her. "When the nights are warm, I might even sleep outside."

Allyson began unloading supplies. "Well, inside the rats will crawl over you; outside it might be something worse."

Ethan laughed. "I've slept under the stars most nights of my life. Don't forget I'm half Indian." His smile faded. How could she forget that?

Allyson did not reply, afraid whatever she said might be taken wrong. She continued putting away supplies while Ethan repaired the door. She built a fire outside to make supper and began slicing some potatoes into a pan of bacon fat. She had not been this happy since one night in Guthrie, over a year ago. How often did Ethan think about that night? She looked over at the cabin, where he was opening and closing the door. The sun was settling behind the mountain, casting them into a dark shadow. It would be dark soon, and somewhere on the other side thunder rolled.

Ethan tended to his horse and the mules, carried his gear into the cabin, then came out to sit with her near the fire and eat. For a few minutes neither of them spoke. Somewhere in the distance wolves began their howling.

"That used to frighten me," Allyson spoke up. "I've even had wolves come sniffing around my door." She met Ethan's eyes. "I really think you'd be safer always sleeping inside," she told him. "Up here it's so dangerous."

He grinned. "Ally, I've lived with the animals and the elements all my life, but for tonight I'm taking you up on your offer, since I think it's going to rain before morning." He wondered how much safer it really was inside. Out here a man could lose his life, but in there, he could lose his heart, and he wasn't sure right now which was worse. His heart had been sorely wounded one too many times.

Allyson suddenly could not keep a few tears from spilling. "I'm so glad you're here, Ethan," she said quietly. "I really mean that, and not just because I need your help." She quickly wiped at her eyes. "It's just good to find you, to know you're all right and that . . . that somebody cares."

He set down his plate and watched the fire for a moment. "I feel the same way. After losing so much in Oklahoma, my grandmother dying, seeing what I saw at Wounded Knee, I was feeling pretty lost myself."

"I was part of the hurt. I wish you would believe me when I tell you how sorry I am, and that . . ." She swallowed, unable to go on.

"I know," he said gently. "I believe you, Ally."

She smiled through tears and set her own half-finished food down. She had lost her appetite. "I'll clean up here. You make sure the animals are secure for the night. We'd better turn in. I'd like to get an early start." She finally met his eyes. "Do you know how to pan for gold, what to look for when you pick away at those rocks over there?"

He smiled. "I've learned plenty since coming up here to work for Holliday. I know what to do."

Their eyes held, and she nodded. "Good. I won't have to show you everything."

"Quite the accomplished miner, are you?" he teased.

Allyson breathed deeply and held her chin proudly. "I don't mind saying so." She looked around at the cabin, down to the creek. "It isn't much, Ethan, but it's all mine. I guess you know what that means to me."

He laughed lightly. "Oh, yes, I think I do."

She smiled almost bashfully. "You can do me another favor and clean my guns sometime over the next few days. I'm sure they need it, and I don't know how." She got up and began scraping her potatoes back into the frypan, where they would keep warm all night and could be eaten in the morning. She placed a heavy cover over the pan to keep out animals who might be brave enough to try to snatch the food off the fire. She felt Ethan close to her then. He took her six-gun from its holster on her hip. "Might as well start tonight," he told her.

Allyson felt a shiver at his closeness. He left her to check on the mules and Blackfoot, then went inside. By the time she finished cleaning up she went inside to see Ethan had the gun taken apart and spread out on the crude wooden table inside the cabin. His dark hair was undone and hanging over his broad shoulders. Allyson thought how he looked even more handsome by the light of the oil lamp: not only handsome, but dangerous and provocative, his dark eyes watching her as she moved to the cot. She sat down on it and pulled off her boots, feeling suddenly too warm.

"I'll wash up in the morning. I usually sleep in all my clothes. I've gotten used to it. I was always afraid someone might come along in the night, and I figured I'd better always be ready and dressed." Why was she explaining all of this? So he would understand why she didn't change into a nightgown? She could, now that Ethan was here to protect her through the night; but suddenly she felt awkward and embarrassed. Here was a man she had slept with, a man who had done things to her some women might consider sinful, and now she was afraid to undress in front of him.

"I won't look if you want to get into a nightgown. Might feel good to sleep comfortably for once."

She smiled nervously. "It's all right. I'm fine this way. Maybe after a while . . . well, you know . . ."

He smiled with a hint of sarcasm. "Do whatever makes you feel most comfortable. I didn't come up here to jump into your bed the first night. Fact is, I didn't come up here to jump into your bed at all. I thought we had that understood."

Why was she suddenly disappointed? "Yes, we did." She drew back the blankets. "Well, I'm pretty tired. Good night, Ethan. I hope the rats don't disturb you too much."

"We'll get along just fine."

Allyson crawled into bed, noticing he had already returned to cleaning her gun. He studied the parts intently under the lamplight, seeming not to be the least bit disturbed by the fact that they were in the same room together and she was in bed. She had thought maybe he still desired her like he used to, part of her wanting him to desire her, actually hoping maybe he would try something. He had left an unsatisfied, aching need deep inside her, and his brawny presence in the room, the memory of what it was like to be bedded by Ethan Temple, had made her crave that ecstasy again. Apparently, Ethan had no interest. Maybe he never would again. She turned over to face the wall so he would not see her tears.

Ethan began putting the six-gun back together, pleased she had been smart enough to buy herself a good Colt .38. He glanced over at the cot, studying the red hair spread out on the pillow. Never had he ached so badly to climb into bed with a woman, not even on their wedding night. This was different. Now she was forbidden fruit, dangerous. Getting into bed with her meant falling in love all over again, because for him, with Allyson Mills, it couldn't be any other way. He was not ready to make that mistake again.

The weather turned hot, even in the mountains, and Ethan was sure he had never worked so hard in his life. What was really needed was explosives, but he wasn't sure he knew enough about dynamite to try using it. He could bring half the mountain down on them both, or at the least destroy their only shelter. Day in and day out he clawed away at the side of the mountain, while Allyson worked the sluice at the creek.

Being constantly near her had not been easy, and Ethan worked extra hard just so he would keep himself too weary to care much about sex or his feelings for Allyson. Still, after a few weeks of back-breaking labor, his muscles were not only building, but becoming accustomed to the work, so that each new day was not quite as tiring as the last. As he adapted, so did his energy, so that after six weeks of work, he wasn't nearly so tired at the end of the day.

He made a trip back to Cripple Creek for more supplies and had brought back the tin bathtub for Allyson, wondering at his stupidity. He knew damn good and well that the thought of her slipping bare naked into that tub was going to drive him insane, and it had. She had used the tub last night, while he cooked their supper outside. He could hear the water splashing, hear her singing, envision the perfect lines of her supple body. He remembered everything about her, the smell of her, the taste of her, the feel of a taut nipple at his lips.

He had seen desire in her eyes many times, but his biggest problem was allowing himself to trust her. If she would let him come to her bed, would it only be to keep him satisfied so he didn't change his mind about staying and helping her? Surely she knew he was a man of his word. He had promised her a full year, and he meant to keep that promise; but to do it strictly on the basis of friendship was already becoming difficult.

He remembered how she had looked last night when she came to supper, wearing a flannel gown, her hair still wet, combed back from her delicate face. It was the most feminine he had seen her since coming up here, and he could still smell the lingering scent of lilacs.

"Damn!" he cursed under his breath as he took another swing at some rock that was softer than that he had dug through the last few weeks. A few more chunks fell, but he saw nothing interesting. He would sift through it later. He stopped to wipe his face with a bandana, then took a drink from a jug of water sitting nearby. He had dug his way roughly four more feet into the mountain, adding to what John Sebastian had already dug. He was about eight feet in totally, and he wondered if he shouldn't start putting in some kind of supports. He dropped the pickax and walked out of the man-made cave to go to the cabin and get a hatchet. "I'm going to cut and strip a few pines for support posts," he yelled to Allyson.

Allyson waved to him, watching him after he turned away. The hard work was putting even more muscle on his hard, lean body, and whenever Ethan wasn't looking she found herself staring at him, wondering if a more perfect specimen of man existed anyplace on earth. She could not help wondering how he must feel about her by now, if he really still didn't want her, or if he was just being stubborn. He had been every bit the gentleman, making no moves toward her at all. Was it because he really had no desire for her, or was he just being proud and stubborn? Maybe he was afraid . . . afraid, like she was. She didn't want to hurt that way again, and it was obvious Ethan didn't either. Both of them had suffered great losses already.

Ethan removed his shirt as he walked away with the hatchet in his hand. She studied his narrow hips and rippling muscles, his brown skin shining in the ray of sunlight that hit his shoulders before he disappeared around a bend in the trail that led away from the cabin. He could look so dark and menacing, but when he smiled, when those eyes twinkled with humor, he was most handsome of all. Still, those moments were rare, and she knew he often thought about his relatives in the North, wondering if he should be with them. Would he leave her after all? And if she threw herself at him to get him into her bed in order to make him stay, would he think she was trying to trick him again?

Of course he would. He would think she was prostituting herself again. He would never believe she wanted him just for himself, that she feared losing Ethan Temple more than she feared losing her claim: but for now she could not give up that claim. She was sure they were close to hitting the big one, and inviting Ethan Temple to her bed just might scare him off. She couldn't let that happen. She needed him.

For the next two hours Ethan chopped away at medium-sized pine trees, hacking off all the branches and dragging the poles to the cave, laying them in a pile. Finally, covered with sweat, he came over near her and walked into the cold creek water, then sat right down in it and lay back, splashing water over his chest and face and letting out a wild war whoop from relief.

"I'll cut some more poles in a couple of days," he told her. "We're also going to need firewood, and lots of it. I won't be able to dig every day, Ally, with all the cutting I've got to do."

Allyson threw another shovel full of dirt from the creek's bottom into the sluice and began rocking it, every day hoping that pure golden nuggets would fall through the rocker into the cleats beneath it, but the only thing she caught were tiny particles of gold that had to be put into the jars of water so they would separate from worthless gangue. "You're on your own schedule, and you've worked pretty hard these last few weeks. You dig when you want, and cut wood when you want. I need both."

I need both. Ethan wondered at the remark. *She needs her big Indian buck to do the hard work. That's all I'm here for,* he told himself. He wanted to believe that. It made staying away from her easier. Didn't she realize how hard she was making it for him when she wore her blouse half unbuttoned because of the heat? Didn't she know he could easily see the outline of her breasts beneath that blouse? Every morning and every night she dressed and undressed while he stayed outside. Today he wondered if she had bothered to put on a camisole under her blouse. He could swear the thin blouse was the only thing she was wearing, and baggy as her pants were, it did little to hide the shape of the slender hips under them.

He splashed himself for a few more minutes, needing to keep cool more ways than one. He wasn't sure why she seemed more tempting than ever today. Maybe it was that damn blouse. One more button and something would spill out of it. Was she really just hot, or was she deliberately enticing him? He got up and walked back toward the cave. He had to stop looking at her. "I'm going to dig a while longer, then quit for the night."

Allyson watched him walk away. His wet denim pants clung to his firm thighs and buttocks, and he looked darker than she had known him, from working so much out of doors with no shirt on. He turned and looked back at her, caught her staring. She blushed and looked away, wondering if he was suffering as much as she. Moments later she heard the rhythmic hammering of the pick. She began picking through the particles that had fallen into the cleats of the sluice, then straightened when Ethan suddenly shouted her name. "Allyson! Come up here!"

Allyson dropped everything and ran, her heart pounding. What had he found? When she reached the small cave, she noticed water trickling right out of the back wall where he had most recently been cutting. "Look here," he exclaimed. He walked out into the fading sunlight, his pants and skin and hair still a little wet from the creek bath. He held out his hand. "This is the biggest chunk we've found yet." He held out a huge chunk of rock that glittered in several places with what looked like gold.

"Maybe it's pyrite," she told him, afraid to believe it could be what it looked like.

Ethan pulled a pocket knife from his pants and opened it, then pried out one of the glittering particles. He stuck it between his teeth and bit down, then smiled. "It's gold," he told her, holding it out to show his teeth marks. Its softness told Allyson all she needed to know. She ran back into the cave and held up a lamp to study the fresh diggings. She saw more glitter.

"Ethan, this is the biggest chunk of gold I've found yet!

There must be a vein farther in somewhere. There has to be!" She set down the lamp and turned to hug him. "Oh, Ethan, thank you! I never could have dug in this far by myself. We'll be rich! We'll be rich! I just know it!"

Ethan ached at the feel of her breasts crushed against his bare chest. There was nothing between his skin and hers but a thin blouse. He moved his arms around her, laughed with her, carried her outside to whirl her around and celebrate with her. She flung her head back and their eyes met, and suddenly their smiles faded. "Maybe we've found more than gold," he said.

"Ethan, I—"

He cut off her words with a hot, demanding kiss, a kiss she welcomed, relished, returned with a burning passion she could no longer suppress. This was the Ethan she had truly been searching for. She wrapped her legs around his waist, never leaving his lips for a moment as he carried her into the cabin.

25

There was no right or wrong to it, no blaming for old hurts or wondering about ulterior motives. It was simply something that had to be. Allyson had never wanted a man this way. It was different from her wedding night, for then she had only resigned herself to submitting because she was his wife. Now the desire was there without the necessity of foreplay or words of love or even commitment. Now it was simply a ravishing hunger to be woman, to satisfy this man who had always been so helpful and forgiving, and whose very presence brought out a passion that she once was sure she would never feel for any man.

Nothing was said. She only knew she could not stop kissing him, could not get enough of the feel of his strong arms embracing her. She ran her hands over the hard muscle of his shoulders and arms, returning his kisses with a frenzy as he carried her to her cot, where she simply lay back and allowed him his pleasure, taking her own delight in return as he moved on top of her, caressing and licking her face, her neck. His kisses journeyed downward, his strong hands quickly tearing her thin blouse away from her breasts so he could take a pink nipple into his mouth and savor it with groaning satisfaction.

Allyson grasped his hair, arching up to him, feeling overwhelmed with an insatiable desire to feed him, powerful feelings of pure lust making her bolder than she thought possible. This was Ethan, the only man who had ever touched her this way, the only man who could awaken these womanly needs with such near-painful force. He was moving quickly, deliberately, ravishing her with a hint of forcefulness, yet she didn't feel forced. She only felt limp and submissive, aching for every touch, every soft movement of his tongue, every kiss.

Now he was pulling off her too-big denim pants, pants made for a man but worn by a woman trying to hide a firm bottom and soft curves. Right along with the denim pants came her drawers. Everything came off over her boots, and she lay there in all her nakedness, not even minding that his dark eyes drank in every inch of her before he took a moment to unlace and remove her boots and stockings so she no longer wore a stitch of clothing except her blouse, which lay open, exposing her breasts. She wondered herself why she didn't curl up and try to hide private places she should be bashful about. Instead, she only watched him, stretching her arms over her head. She bent one leg up and let it fall to the side, her whole body on fire, a terrible wantonness making her invite all that was man about him to invade her once more. She ached for it.

Ethan stood up and removed his boots, his pants, and longjohns. He stood there for a moment in naked splendor, and it was the first time Allyson had truly studied him fully. She felt a wave of mixed emotions, an odd, curious fear at the sight of how big he was, wondering how he had ever fit into her the first couple of times. Combined with that fear was a fiery desire to let him plant himself inside her again, surprised that she actually hoped it would hurt a little, for the woman in her realized now that such pain was also ecstasy.

Neither of them needed any further foreplay. He moved

on top of her, and she opened herself willingly, their eyes meeting in unspoken questions and promises. She closed her eyes and drew in her breath then when he pushed himself inside of her. He leaned down and licked at her mouth, then rested his elbows on either side of her and surged into her in rhythmic thrusts that made her moan with every breath she took. She leaned up and kissed at his chest, trailing her fingers over his muscled arms, over his firm chest, toying with his nipples.

His skin was so dark next to the fair skin of her hands. His long black hair brushed at her face and shoulders. She arched up to him, surprised and delighted to realize that this time all pain was gone. It had been replaced by an aching need to have all of him, to pull him into herself and never let go. Because of the long neglect of their sexual needs, it was over with quickly. She felt a dizzying climax that made her almost scream as she pushed against him with even greater force, and at almost the same time she felt his life rush into her, yet he did not stop the glorious, rhythmic movements.

"Enjoy it, Ally," he whispered, coming down closer to move his hands under her bottom, continuing to move until in only seconds she felt his maleness filling her again. She licked and kissed at his powerful shoulders as her own climax just seemed to go on and on. She realized he understood that once she experienced the wonderful, exotic explosion deep inside she needed to feel this ecstasy for yet a while longer.

Now she was lost in him, the room swirling with images only of Ethan Temple, his dark hair, those dangerous, exotic eyes, his handsome face, his beautiful lips that knew just the right ways to caress her, his dark skin and hard muscles. It made no difference what his heritage was. What mattered was the man himself, every perfect, handsome inch of him,

his goodness, his bravery, his skill, his worth as a total man
. . . and she knew she loved him, far more deeply than she
had realized before this moment.

They slept for over an hour, both of them weary from a
long day's work topped off with lovemaking so urgent and
passionate that afterward they were too spent even to get up
off the bed. They simply lay there naked together, wet with
perspiration from heated lovemaking combined with still-
warm air, even though the sun was setting behind the mountain, throwing the little claim site into the darker shadows of
dusk.

Allyson finally stirred, opening her eyes to see Ethan
watching her with a look of deep concern. "This wasn't supposed to happen, was it?" she said, more as a statement than
a question.

Ethan studied her blue eyes, hating himself for being so
weak when he was near her. "No."

Allyson sighed, resting her head in his shoulder. "Now
what do we do?"

Ethan kissed her hair. "If I had my way we would leave
today, sell out, and go start that ranch in Wyoming, start a
family."

Allyson felt torn between two worlds, two desires.
"Ethan, we've just found our biggest hit yet. We can't stop
now, and we can't sell out until we know for sure what's in
our piece of that mountain."

Ethan smiled sadly, a smile she did not see because her
head was resting against his chest. "Somehow I knew that
would be your answer."

Allyson felt his disappointment. "Ethan, surely you agree
with me." She kissed his chest, leaning her head back to

meet his eyes. "It doesn't mean I don't love you or that I don't want what you want."

"It just means that what *you* want has to come first."

"No. It means that we had a deal, remember? One year. It's only been six weeks. Just because we're up here mining a claim doesn't mean we can't love each other, can't *make* love or . . . or remarry." Was that too bold a remark? Maybe he wasn't even thinking of marrying again.

Ethan studied her blue eyes, a little part of him still not trusting her. It was so hard to know if her words were true, if even her lovemaking was true. She had taken him with such lust and eagerness. Was it just her way of making him want to stay, so that she did not lose her free help? "I'd take you to Cripple Creek and marry you tomorrow," he told her, "if I believed you would really give this up in a year and come to Wyoming with me, no matter how the claim turns out."

"I said that I would, Ethan, if we found love again. We have, haven't we? Please don't tell me that what just happened was nothing more than animal need. Please tell me it meant something."

He moved on top of her again, leaning down and gently kissing her lips. "It meant everything—to me. How about you?"

She closed her eyes against the hurtful distrust in his. "You still can't quite trust me or believe me, can you?"

He smoothed her hair back from her face. "Can you blame me?"

She caught his hand, kissed his palm. "No. I can only pray you'll believe me when I tell you that this time . . . this time was real." She felt her cheeks grow a little hotter, and for a moment she could not look him in the eyes. She had just flagrantly given herself to him, allowed him to drink in every inch of her nakedness, to invade her deepest privacy. "I wanted you, Ethan, just for the man that you are. It was the first time I wanted you before you even touched me, wanted you just for the sheer pleasure of being in your arms." Finally she did look at him. "I don't doubt that I love you, Ethan, or that I want to go with you to Wyoming. The problem is, it scares me. Everyone I have ever cared about has been taken from me. I have fought this all along because I'm afraid to care that much. I don't like thinking or saying that I need someone else. I've learned to get by on my own because that way there's no hurt when someone you care about dies. I don't like the realization that you're all I have in the world, that I need you, need your love."

He sighed, folding her into his arms. "Did you ever stop to think that it's the same for me? I lost my mother, my father, my grandmother, my wife, most of my relatives. I don't even know who I am or where I belong. At least you know that much about yourself. When you're brought up being tossed back and forth between two worlds, two races, never fully accepted by either one, it gets pretty lonely."

She ran a slender hand along his powerful arm. "I suppose it does. I didn't help much by showing my disappointment that day Cy Jordan said an Indian couldn't own land. I did a terrible thing, marrying you just to save my property, Ethan. I know that. I just wish you would believe me when I say I did also love you. I just didn't realize how much at first. Then after you left, it hit me full force what I had done, how much I wanted you with me; but you were so hurt and angry, I didn't feel I had the right to come and find you and beg you to come back. I deliberately convinced myself it was for the best, making myself believe I'd be just fine without you, that we didn't really belong together anyway."

Ethan kept stroking her hair. "Maybe we don't."

She traced a finger along the indentation between two

muscles on his upper arm. "All I know is I hate the thought of being without you, and when I'm near you, I turn into someone I don't even know, a wanton woman who wants to make love and just lie here like this in your arms. When we were apart, I couldn't stop thinking about you. Every night I wished you were lying beside me. That must mean something."

He moved his hand to lightly fondle one full breast. "It was the same for me. I hated you, but I loved you, too. Every basic instinct tells me I should never have come up here with you, yet here I am, back in your bed on top of it all."

She kissed his arm. "So now what do we do?"

"We get married, sell the claim, and move to Wyoming."

"Ethan." She met his gaze with a scowl. "You know that has to wait. That chunk of rock you just dug out of the mountain contains more gold than anything I've seen yet. We have to be sure what's in there."

He sighed and sat up. "And what if we hit a vein and find out there's a fortune in gold on this claim? How much will you need good ol' Ethan once you're a rich woman in your own right, just what you've always dreamed of? You won't need me or a ranch in Wyoming. You'll have your dream. Will you still be willing just to be a rancher's wife?"

"Ethan, we wouldn't even need a ranch then. We could live off the gold mine, maybe open businesses in Denver, build a home—"

He waved her off and got up, grabbing one of the blankets to wrap around himself. "I'm not made for that kind of life, Ally. No matter how wealthy I might become, all I want is a simple life, out in the open, away from the noise and filth and overcrowding of places like Denver. I like nature, wide-open land, working under blue skies and breathing clean air. I like animals, working with my hands, building things on my own, not hiring someone else to do everything for me just because I have the money to do it." He turned and met her eyes. "We're still worlds apart in what we want, aren't we?"

Allyson felt the desperate fear of losing him engulfing her again. "Not completely. We know we want each other, love each other. We had an agreement, Ethan. We didn't mean for this to happen, but it has, and we know why. In spite of our differences, each of us needs and aches for the other in ways no other man or woman can fulfill. All we have to do is find a way to come to an understanding about how we can each have our dream and still be together. Surely God means for that to happen, or He wouldn't have let me find you again. We have lots of time to decide what we're going to do, and for all we know, this claim never will bring us a real bonanza."

"But that's what you're hoping for, isn't it?"

"Of course it is. Aren't you?"

He smiled almost bitterly. "Partly, for your sake, though, not for me. I couldn't care less if it never pays off. The point is, Ally, if it doesn't, and after a year we sell the claim, if you choose to settle with me in Wyoming, to you it will be like giving up, like accepting defeat and settling for something less than you want in life. How do you think that makes me feel?"

Allyson sat up, keeping a flannel blanket around her breasts, suddenly shy about letting him look at her. "It wouldn't be that way at all, Ethan."

His eyes betrayed his pain. "Yes, it would." He turned away. "We're right back were we started, aren't we?"

"No! It's all different now, Ethan! I don't know what will happen, how this claim will turn out, what I'll want to do for certain if we strike it rich. But I *do* know I don't want to live my life without you. That's the *only* thing I'm sure of right now. Can't we just take a day at a time and not worry about what we'll do a year from now? We've only been here six weeks. If we're lucky, and there is a richer vein here, we're already closer to finding it and we'll know that much sooner."

Ethan walked to a stand beside the bed and picked up a bar of soap and a washrag. "We can't just start sleeping together, not being certain about whether a marriage would ever work. What if you get pregnant?"

Allyson felt herself blushing. Pregnant? She had not even considered it and was astonished that she hadn't. After all, that was the usual result when a man and woman mated. "Well, I . . . I guess then we would have no choice."

Ethan just watched her, thinking how different she was from most white women. In one sense she was more like an Indian, in her free spirit. She had made love to him because it simply seemed the right and only thing to do at the time, when most white women would never have allowed it. She did not think of herself as bad at all, just doing what came naturally. "I guess we wouldn't, would we?"

Allyson got up then, keeping the blanket wrapped around her. "Please stay, Ethan. Somehow it will work out if God wants it to."

He studied her tangled red hair, and one thing he could not deny . . . no other woman, not even his first wife, had made him this crazy. He had no business here, no business in her bed, no business risking the hurt that might lie ahead being in love with this unusual, independent, stubborn, misdirected, wanton, confused, money-hungry child-woman. Yet he knew he could not walk away from her. Would she give this all up and follow him if he did? If he had any sense, he would test her on that; but that would mean taking the chance of losing her forever, for if she did not follow him, his own pride would keep him from ever coming back to her. Somehow he could not take the chance of allowing that to happen. Staying here was a tremendous risk; yet he could not leave.

"Come on," he told her. "Let's go wash in the creek."

"The creek! It's freezing cold!"

"Good. Maybe it will help cool both of us off, in more ways than one." Before she could make another protest, Ethan let his blanket fall, then pulled hers away and lifted her in his arms, keeping the soap and washrag in one hand. Allyson let out a squeal of protest, but he kept a strong hold on her and hurried out of the cabin, running down to the creek and setting her in the cold water. She screamed even louder as he splashed her, then walked into the water himself, soap in hand. Allyson started to get out, but Ethan pulled her back in laughing, and he began lathering her with the soap. "It's not so bad once you get used to it," he told her.

Allyson's objections faded when he pulled her back against his chest and began moving his soapy hands over her breasts, down over her belly and between her legs.

"Kind of like it now, don't you?" he said, kissing her behind one ear. She groaned when he moved his fingers inside of her.

"You're a devil, Ethan Temple," she said, her voice gruff with desire. "Maybe I'm the fool and not you. Did you ever think of that? Don't think I've forgotten how you tricked me into letting you have your way with me that night in my tent back in Guthrie."

Ethan moved both hands to her breasts then, fondling her nipples, taut from the cold water. "Whiskey does work wonders, doesn't it?"

She turned, resting on her knees in the soft sandy creek bottom. She splashed water over herself to rinse off the soap, holding his gaze as she did so. Then she took the bar of soap from him and lathered her own hands. Daringly she reached down and began gently washing that part of him that once terrified her. "Maybe I didn't even need the whiskey. Maybe all I needed was a man who could show me how not to be afraid."

Ethan drew in his breath at the touch of her hands gently massaging him. "If I'm a devil, then you're a *she*-devil," he answered.

She held her chin proudly. "Maybe I am at that." She looked down at his manliness, splashing water over him to rinse off the soap. She was curious at how the cold water shrank it. He stood up then. "We'd better get back inside. Someone could come," he told her.

Allyson got to her knees, unable to resist a compulsion to touch him again, utterly fascinated by this part of man that had always frightened her so . . . until Ethan. It felt good to be woman, to enjoy these things, to feel so bold and daring and alive. She gently kissed him, and almost instantly the firmness began to return, exciting her, intriguing her. She kissed him again, caressing that part of Ethan Temple that held magical powers over her. She took the tip of it into her mouth, never even considering that it might be either a wonderful or a terrible thing to do.

"Ally," he groaned, grasping her hair. "We can't keep doing this."

She kissed him once more, slowly rose, moving her lips over his flat belly, his chest. He made no more protest, and he chastised himself for being totally without power or common sense around this woman. He picked her up and carried her back into the cabin. "We'll get the bed all wet," she protested weakly.

"We need to change it anyway. We have more blankets."

They exchanged hot, hungry kisses. "What about all the reasons . . ." Another kiss. "You gave for us for . . ." Another kiss. "Not doing this?" she finished.

Ethan laid her back on the bed. "What reasons?" He kissed her everywhere, trailing over her shoulders, her breasts, her belly-button, her thighs, her calves, her feet, back up to stop for a moment at the soft patch of red hair that hid private places that belonged only to him. He tasted, explored, enjoyed.

Allyson felt almost faint from the pleasure of it. She whimpered his name, gladly offering herself, until she felt the wonderful, pulsating satisfaction once again that only made her crave another mating with this beautiful man who satisfied her in so many ways. Again he invaded her. Everything was so perfect, so beautiful, so gratifying, such ecstasy when they were together this way. Surely there was a way for them to solve their other differences, and surely once she struck it rich Ethan would change his mind about what he wanted. Gold had a way of making men think differently. Somehow she would sway him to live the life of Denver's high society. She could fulfill her own dreams and have Ethan Temple in her bed on top of it all. It would be the ideal life.

Again he moved with power and rhythm, filling her to ecstasy, so much man. She arched up to him in sweet surrender, giving no more thought to anything he had said about wanting to settle in Wyoming. He would change his mind. She would make sure of it.

Wayne Trapp ushered a meek Trevor Gale into Roy Holliday's office. "Have a seat, Trevor," Holliday offered with a grin that betrayed his feelings of victory.

Trevor cast him a dark, distrustful look and moved to one of the leather chairs near the man's desk. He looked around the room before sitting down, noticing all the furniture was of fine mahogany. The whole room smelled of tobacco and rich leather, and his feet made no noise when he walked because of an Oriental rug. He eyed Holliday closely then, wondering why he had been summoned. Holliday must know he'd been trying to organize the miners to stand up for themselves against yet another pay cut; but since losing his job, he had been unable to get any work at all these last four months, and he knew damn well who was responsible. When the other miners realized he'd been blackballed, it had frightened them away from forming a union, fearful that Roy Holliday could also keep them from finding work anyplace else. The man damn well knew how to break people. He had him on his knees now. What was he going to do? Run him out of town completely?

"What is it you're wanting, Mr. Holliday?" he asked, determined not to beg. He could feel Wayne Trapp's eyes watching him from the side of the room.

"Just wondering how the wife and kids are doing, Trevor." Holliday sat down behind his desk, twirling a fat cigar and enjoying the look of embarrassment and anger on Trevor's face. His Irish blood came to the surface just under the skin, making him turn red instantly.

"You know good and well neither me nor my brothers has been able to get a decent job. We need miners' pay to take decent care of the little ones. We've found odd jobs here and there, but nothing that lasts, and nothing that pays anything close to what we were making. I've got one child with a club foot that needs operating on. My brothers, they don't have family, but I've got four little ones who need decent food on the table. Thanks to you makin' sure I can't get work, they're next to starving. I'm not one to go begging to others, but I will if I have to."

"You could have left Cripple Creek and gone to Denver or anyplace else."

"It's not easy movin' a whole family when you don't even know if you'll get work; and you know damn well there's a recession. The work just isn't out there. I've gone on my own to other mining towns, but I can't get hired. You've spread the word that I'm a troublemaker. Don't deny it. I'm the best damn explosives man you ever had, and because of one run-in with that damn Indian, you've got me black-balled all over the place."

Holliday shook his head. "Now, now, Trevor, you know yourself we had problems with your drinking more than that one time. That was just the climax of it all. I had to consider the safety of the rest of the men."

Trevor moved to the edge of his chair. "I can set powder better flat-out drunk than any other man stone sober, and you know it!"

Holliday held up his hand as though to calm him. "Of course I know it, but some of the men might not have. They might have resented me letting you go down. And, of course, the Indian didn't know it either."

Trevor snickered in disgust. "The Indian! That bastard humiliated me in front of the miners. I still get teased about it. I've been looking for that sonofabitch. I'd like to show the whole town that when I'm sober, that stinking redskin is no match for Trevor Gale!"

Holliday glanced at Wayne and grinned. He looked back at Trevor. "How would you like to have your chance at the Indian?"

Trevor scooted back in his chair, eyeing Holliday warily. "What do you mean?"

Holliday sighed deeply, then set his cigar in an ashtray, leaning forward to rest his elbows on his desk. Trevor Gale thought how the man always stood out in this town filled with sorry-dressed prospectors and miners like himself, whose hands and fingernails were always dirty no matter how hard they scrubbed. Holliday was always dressed in the finest fashion.

"I have an offer for you, Trevor. You do this job right, and I'll see that you get your old job back, with a dollar an hour raise. Of course, I don't want you telling the other miners what you're making—it will just be between you and me. Nobody will know why I hired you back. They'll just figure I've decided to give you a second chance."

Trevor frowned with curiosity. "I don't understand. What's this about the Indian? I thought he worked for you."

"Not anymore. We had a little run-in of our own. He hasn't worked for me for over three months now."

Trevor shifted his big frame in the chair, making it squeak. "And now for some reason you want him out of the way, and you want *me* to do it for you?" The man glanced over at Wayne. "What's wrong with your henchman over there? Not up to it?" He laughed lightly at the look of embarrassment and fury that came into Trapp's eyes. Wayne started to rise.

"Stay put, Wayne," Holliday warned, keeping his eyes on Trevor. "Wayne's a good man, but for what I want, you're the best man. You're the one who knows explosives."

Trevor rubbed at his square jaw. "Why you asking me? I'm just a man who once worked for you. I've even tried to organize the miners. I'm the enemy, remember?"

Holliday smiled. "We only make enemies through misunderstandings and disrespect, Trevor. I think you and I understand each other, and I respect you for your talents. You in turn respect me as a man who can destroy you, or make you a rich man. Which would you rather it be?"

Trevor watched Holliday's dark, threatening gaze. Yes, the man was right. Why not take the easy way? "Like I said, I've got a family to provide for. I'd just as soon be rich."

Holliday laughed again. "You're a wise man, Trevor. You'll not only be richer, but gain the sweet satisfaction of getting back at Ethan Temple for the way he humiliated you."

Trevor breathed deeply with a growing excitement. "I'm to use dynamite?"

"Whatever works best." Holliday toyed with his mustache. "Ethan Temple is helping a woman work a claim up on the mountain, a claim I've been trying to get her to sell. A convenient accident would put an end to Temple, and if the woman dies, too, all the better. If not, losing her help and the devastation an explosion would cause will break her. She'll come crawling, begging me to buy that claim."

Trevor thought a moment. "Woman? You mean that little redhead the men have talked about, the one who came here a few months back to take over the claim that John Sebastian had been mining?"

"Same one."

"She's living up there with the *Indian?*"

"She's a goddamn slut," Wayne put in. "Don't be worryin' about the men bein' behind her. They're not anymore—not since she went off with the Indian, especially when we've learned she used to be *married* to Temple."

Trevor kept rubbing at his jaw. "I'll be damned." He eyed Holliday closely. "I don't know. Slut or not, I don't like the idea of hurting a woman."

"She made her bed, let her lie in it. Maybe there will be a way around it, but if not, I don't want you to worry about it.

Wayne will take you up, and you can scout around the area, but stay out of sight. Set up something that will look like an accident—maybe a landslide, big enough to bury the mining site and destroy the cabin, preferably while they're both in it. People hear explosions up on that mountain all day every day. Hearing one more won't cause a bit of excitement. When the 'accident' is discovered, we'll just spread the idea that an explosion inside one of the bigger mines must have triggered a landslide, killing the poor woman and the Indian working that claim. I put my bid in to buy the site, and we're in business."

Trevor rose, paced a moment, and shook his head. "I don't like it. If it's discovered it was deliberate, I could be in a lot of trouble. Everybody knows I have a hatred for that man, and they know I'm the one who knows how to handle dynamite." He turned and looked at Holliday. "If you're so anxious to get that claim, it must be worth a lot of money. I want a share of it," he announced boldly.

Holliday's face darkened with surprise and anger at the man's effrontery. He started to protest, then thought better of it. At least he was agreeing to do the job. He could get rid of Ethan and the woman, get his hands on the claim, and at the same time stop Trevor Gale from organizing the miners. The man would be working for him, and once the job was done, he would have a strong hold on Trevor. The man's trouble-making days would be over. He could put a man of Trevor's size and influence to good use. "All right," he answered, surprising Trapp. "Five percent of the profits." He could feel Wayne's resentment.

"I want to be able to inspect the books," Trevor added, strutting with an air of cockiness as he walked closer to Holliday's desk again.

"Only the figures that apply to that site. You've no business seeing anything to do with my other mines."

"I don't give a damn about the others—only the one I'm going to own a share of. I want something in writing. I'm the one taking the big chance here. I want a legal piece of paper that says I own five percent of the mine, once you get your hands on it."

Holliday nodded. "Fine." He stood up and opened a drawer, handing five ten-dollar bills toward Trevor. "This should get you by for a few days until I decide how and when we're going to do this. I'll have Wayne get in touch with you when we're ready. In the meantime, you just pretend you're still looking for work. I don't want anyone to know yet that you even work for me. That way when you leave to go up to the mining site, you can tell your wife you're going to some other town to look for work. That will be your alibi. After it's done, I'll hire you back, but the deal we've made about your pay and a percentage of the mine will be just between us. You are not to tell your wife, and certainly not your brothers."

"Will you give them jobs, too?"

Holliday buttoned his silk suit jacket. "If it makes you happy."

"How do I explain the extra money when it starts coming in from the mine?"

Holliday shrugged. "I'll make an announcement to the other miners that I've given you a new job—promoted you. You'll be in charge of traveling around to all my mines, inspecting the handling of explosives, something like that. The men will think you've been bought off to keep you from organizing a union, but who cares? You're the one who'll be raking in the money and putting your wife and kids up in a fancy house down in Colorado Springs. As one of my supervisors, you'll have power over the other men, a different kind of power than you have now, much more control, a man of importance. You'd like that, wouldn't you?"

Trevor took the fifty dollars and counted it, grinning. "Yes, sir. I'd like that just fine, Mr. Holliday." He met the man's eyes. "From here on I'm your man."

Holliday laughed, a deep laugh of evil satisfaction that came from the gut. *You're just where I want you,* he thought, putting out his hand. "Welcome back, Trevor."

Trevor shook his hand, then glanced at Wayne with an air of haughtiness. "Looks like you and I are on the same side now, Trapp." He laughed lightly, shoving the money into his pocket. He looked back at Holliday. "I'll be waiting to hear from you then." He walked out, and as soon as the door closed, Wayne walked closer to Holliday.

"Five percent of the mine? You've never made *me* an offer like that!"

Holliday chuckled. "Relax, Wayne. You'll be taking him up there, remember? When the job is done and the Indian is dead, you shoot Trevor Gale. Everybody in town knows the man hates Ethan Temple's guts. It will be no problem at all convincing them that Trevor went up there to kill the Indian, especially when they find out the job was done with explosives. It's been a few months since that confrontation between you and the Indian and Allyson Mills. People won't think much about it anymore. We'll just convince them that since it has been several months since we made our first offer, and since Miss Mills apparently still hasn't found her bonanza, I sent you back up there with another offer, and the explosion occurred while you were there. You caught Trevor running away from the scene and you shot him. Everyone will put two and two together. Trevor tried to kill Ethan Temple and got caught. Right now no one knows he's working for me. As far as they know, he still hates my guts for firing me, so they won't link it with what he did to me at all. We're rid of the Indian and the woman *and* Trevor Gale, who is the only one who could link us to what happened. We get the mine, and we're off the hook at the same time. Trevor will have done our dirty work for us." He reached out and put a hand on Wayne's shoulder. "And for *your* part in this, I'll give *you* that five percent share."

Wayne blinked, thinking, letting it all sink in. Then he slowly grinned. "You're one smart man, Mr. Holliday."

Holliday grinned. "That's how men like me get to be rich. You do your job right and stay loyal to me, and you'll be rich yourself."

Wayne grinned even more broadly, then broke into laughter. "Yes, sir, you're one smart man."

26

Ethan walked quietly over fallen pine needles, his moccasined feet soundless. He always wore buckskins and moccasins when he was hunting. It was easier to walk through forest or underbrush without making noise, and the buckskin clothing helped camouflage him, as long as the wind did not blow in the wrong direction and carry his scent to his prey.

He had decided to take a day away from mining to hunt for rabbit and maybe a deer. The aspen leaves were beginning to change to their autumn yellow, and it was time to store up some meat for the long winter ahead. He thought how much happier he was doing this than picking away at a bunch of rock inside a cave. He liked the sound of the wind in the pines, of rushing waters, birds singing. He breathed deeply of the smell of pine trees, stronger today because everything was still damp. This morning was the first time in three days he and Allyson had not awakened to torrential rainfall. Pans of every size and sort were scattered over the floor of the sorry cabin, set there to catch leaks in the roof. When he was through hunting, he would have to take another day to cover the roof and sides of the cabin with tar paper, which he still had to go back to Cripple Creek to buy. On top of that there was wood to chop and stack, and he wondered just when he *would* be able to get back to hacking more gold out of the mountain. There was a lot to do to get ready for winter.

He still was not sure that what they were getting out of each day's hard work was worth it. He was finding bigger chunks, but getting to them was a miserable, unending, tedious chore. He hated being inside the small cave he had created, often thinking about how much happier he would be making his living on a ranch that was all his own. Every chunk or flake of gold he retrieved thrilled Ally, but he got no pleasure from it. He would be glad when the promised year was up, but he still feared that when the time came for Ally to leave all this, she would not be able to do it. The last thing he wanted was to be away from her again, but when he was through up here, he was getting off this mountain and going back to the real world. It would be Ally's decision whether or not to go with him.

He stopped for a moment to get his bearings. He'd never been up this way, above the cabin. He couldn't see it now, so he decided maybe he had better not stray too far in case Ally needed him. After all the rain they had had the last couple of days, he cherished the feel of the sun's warmth on his shoulders as here and there tree shadows gave way to openings where the sun could get through. That warmth did not amount to much, as up here in the mountains winter was already pushing at the door. Nights were much colder again, but the days were beautiful, crisp, clear, cool.

He sat down on a rock, hoping that if he sat quietly long enough, something worth shooting would stroll into his range. He had time to think for a few minutes, and all he could think about was Ally. He loved her, and there was no getting around it. How could he ever live without her after what they had shared up here on this mountain? He did not doubt her love for him, but he did still wonder if that love was stronger than her desire for wealth and independence.

Hell, he would gladly take care of her the rest of her life, but maybe what he had to offer wasn't enough for somebody like Ally. She was constantly afraid that she would lose him, that she would be alone again, left to survive by herself. She had been threatened and abused and abandoned too many times in her young life, and her experiences had left scars that maybe even the love they shared could not heal.

It was all so natural for them now, being together twenty-four hours a day, sleeping together, sharing their love through their bodies. It all seemed so right, but he knew deep inside that there were still many things wrong. There was still that little part of him that did not fully trust her, and there was still an eagerness in her eyes whenever he held up another gold nugget.

There was no sign of an animal, and he decided to move on to an area where the trees and underbrush were thicker. Rabbits and deer alike would prefer the cover. He turned to head toward a nearby stand of trees, then spotted an antelope lazily grazing on a rise above his own position. He slowly crouched down behind the rock on which he'd been sitting, then raised the rifle and took careful aim. It was then that he spotted something that took his attention away from his prey. It looked like a cave, the freshcut kind that a man would dig, similar to his own efforts below.

The antelope moved, and he reminded himself he was up here to get meat for the winter. He took aim again and fired. The antelope, a medium-sized female, collapsed, then tumbled down the hill, landing only a few yards from him. He quickly moved from behind the rock to check to be sure the animal was dead, then closed his eyes to say a quick prayer to the animal's spirit, thanking it for offering its body for food, an Indian tradition he had always kept. He took a piece of rawhide from the sack of supplies he carried over his shoulder and quickly tied the animal's legs together so he'd be able to pick it up and carry it across his back.

He rose then, looking back up at the cave-like opening. He decided to leave the animal where it was for a few minutes and go investigate. He kept his rifle in hand and made the steep climb, slipping a couple of times, then noticing it looked as though someone had made this climb before. When he reached the opening, it was obvious that the rocks and mud were remnants of someone's attempt to pile debris in front of the opening to hide it. The torrential rain of the last two days must have loosened everything, washing away the camouflage and leaving evidence that someone apparently didn't want anyone else to know about. Why?

He looked around, gauging his location. As far as he could tell he was still on land that would belong to Ally's claim. He ducked inside, wishing he had a lantern, glad it was still morning. The early-day sun was offering light at the entrance, just enough for Ethan to see that the dug-out area went about twelve feet back into the earth. The hole was almost big enough for him to stand up straight, probably big enough for a man of average height to work inside freely. He reached up and touched the surrounding walls and ceiling, digging into it a little with a fingernail. This was soft rock, an easy dig. Whoever had started it could probably have dug a cave this size in only a few weeks.

John Sebastian? His mind began whirling with the possibilities. Roy Holliday had been awfully anxious to get his hands on this supposedly worthless claim. Why? Was there something up here that held the answer? Someone had tried to hide it. Sebastian? Or was it Sebastian's killer who had attempted to keep it hidden? If it was the killer, then there was something here he didn't want anyone to know about, like maybe the reason Sebastian was killed in the first place . . . something the killer wouldn't want the new owner to find.

His heart beat with anticipation as he took a wooden match from a little pocket sewn to the sleeve of his buckskin shirt, striking its head against the rock. He quickly moved to the back of the diggings, then slowly held the match out to get a better look. Something glittered. "Jesus," he muttered. The match burned down to his fingers and he dropped it, then hurriedly lit another. There in front of him was a sparkling vein roughly four inches wide that looked like almost pure gold. He moved closer, pulling his hunting knife from its sheath. The second match burned down and he struck yet another, then quickly picked at the vein with his knife, managing to carve out a good-sized piece. It fell to the ground, and he quickly picked it up as the third match burned down.

He hurried outside with the rock so he could see it better in the sunlight. It looked so rich that it overwhelmed him for a moment. He moved to a boulder that jutted out from the earth near the cave and sat down, then took the knife and began digging at the rock, realizing quickly that what he held in his hand was an almost-pure nugget. This was not pyrite. This was the real thing, and there was a thick vein of it inside that cave. God only knew how much more there was if a man could just dig even deeper.

He squeezed the rock in his palm, all kinds of possibilities swirling in his thoughts. Had John Sebastian reported this find? Did Roy Holliday know about it? Was that why Sebastian had been killed? Maybe Holliday figured that since the co-owner of the site was a woman, he could easily convince her to sell the claim once the prospector was out of the way. Still, if Sebastian had reported the find, Ally would have known about it, wouldn't she? If Roy Holliday knew about this, then Sebastian *must* have reported it. Maybe the assayer was on Holliday's payroll. Hell, everybody else in town was. Maybe Holliday had paid the man to keep his mouth shut.

He opened his hand and studied the nugget again. He could just imagine how Ally would react if she saw this. She would scream with joy. She would be the happiest woman who ever walked . . . and she would probably forget all about Ethan Temple. A beautiful, young, wealthy woman could have her pick of any man. She could live like a queen in Denver, wear beautiful clothes, be courted by doctors and lawyers and politicians. The vein of gold inside that cave could help fulfill every dream Allyson Mills had ever had.

That was the hell of it. If he told her about it, he would surely lose her; but if he could keep this from her until she gave up and sold the claim, she would never know the difference. He could take her to Wyoming with him and she would be his wife and the mother of his children. Surely love and family were as important as all the gold on earth. At least that's the way he looked at it. But did he have any right to keep it from her? Did he have the right to keep her from her dreams, even if it meant risking losing her to a world he could never be a part of?

He had to think about this. He at least had to wait until he could get back to town and question Lloyd Hunt. What did he know about this? He hated the thought of what this find might do to Ally, how it might change her; but he hated even more the thought that men like Roy Holliday were trying to cheat her out of what was hers. She had worked and struggled too long—she deserved this. He held the nugget up again, and the sight of it actually brought an ache to his heart. Never had he felt so torn between what was the right and wrong thing to do. He could just let her go, let her give up and sell the claim, and take her to Wyoming; but then he would have been a part of the grand design to cheat Ally

Mills out of what belonged to her, a part of Roy Holliday's scheme to get rich off her ignorance, if Holliday even knew about this.

He got up from the rock and walked back to the small cave, pitching the nugget back inside angrily. Of course he knew about it, the bastard! Why else would he be so anxious to get his hands on this claim? The man had paid off Lloyd Hunt to keep quiet about the find, then had John Sebastian murdered. He had come up here and tried to hide the dig, hoping Ally would never find it and would agree to sell her "worthless" claim.

That had to be it. Nothing else made sense. The problem was, he could never prove any of it. Even to try would mean telling Ally about this find. In fact, Roy Holliday must be sitting down there in Cripple Creek right now worrying that it might be discovered. That meant Ally was still in danger. If the man had killed once to get his hands on the claim, he might try again. It was a damn good thing he'd come back up here with her after all.

He left the cave and began repiling the rocks that covered the entrance. Until he decided what to do, he was better off leaving it looking as though it still had not been discovered. It took nearly two hours to get everything covered again and another several minutes to carry a couple of fallen, rotted logs over in front of the rocks to shore them up. It was not easy to get it all looking natural, and to his own trained eye he would still know something was amiss, but someone like Ally wouldn't notice. It would have to do. If he didn't get down to Ally pretty soon, she would begin to worry. Besides, he had that antelope to clean. He'd already built a stone smokehouse, and he'd better get started curing the meat before the midday sun ruined it.

He walked back down to where he had left the carcass,

picked it up, flung it over his shoulder, and started down. He wondered what the vein he had just left behind was worth. Millions? God only knew, and maybe God would be the only one who would *ever* know. It wasn't worth a damn thing to him personally, not even his fifty percent of it, if it meant losing Ally.

Allyson stirred potatoes and carrots over a campfire, worried over what might have happened to Ethan. The days were growing shorter, and dusk was already falling. She had heard one gunshot, but that was at least three hours ago. She couldn't imagine that a man with Ethan's skills could have had an accident, but now she was beginning to wonder. A terrible loneliness filled her, along with a gripping fear, at the mere thought of Ethan never coming back.

This is why it isn't good to love and depend on another human being, she told herself. *Death takes them away, and then you have nothing but yourself.* It had happened to her mother, her father, Toby . . . Ethan had even left once. It was different then. It had hurt, but not like it would now. Now they had been together three months. She had slept with him, gladly offered him every inch of her body, had come to know and appreciate the joys of being a woman in Ethan Temple's arms.

She loved him. She just wished he fully trusted in that love. She didn't know how to prove her sincerity, except to sell her claim once their year of digging was over. After three months up here with Ethan, she realized more and more what she really wanted—to make a real home for him, to help him realize his own dream. They had taken a lot of gold out of the claim, enough to know they could get a lot more than the three thousand dollars Roy Holliday was offering, but not enough to make it worth slaving away all winter. She was considering leaving sooner, but she was afraid to tell Ethan, afraid to speak the words, for it meant admitting she was willing to go with him, depend on him, love him, give her life to him. She wanted all those things, but the fear of loving him that way and then losing him the way she had lost others she loved, made it difficult.

Maybe it was better not to care, but she was beginning to suspect she was carrying Ethan's baby. She was not sure enough yet to tell him, and she wasn't even sure how he would react. Would he think she was giving up the claim and going with him just because of the child? It was so important that he believe it was all for him and no other reason.

A baby. She touched her still-flat belly. Could it be true? She knew enough to realize that if a woman missed her time of month by several days, there was a good chance she was pregnant; and heaven knew they had made love often enough that she was surprised it had not happened sooner. Once they had fallen into each other's arms, it had been impossible to stay away from each other. There had even been days when they cut their work short because they wanted to make love instead.

She looked up when she saw movement in the distance. Ethan was coming back, some kind of deer or antelope hung over his shoulder. Her heart leaped with relief at the sight of him. "Ethan! I was beginning to worry. What took you so long?"

His dark eyes looked troubled as he came closer, almost as though he was angry about something. He dropped the antelope. "I followed a moose up higher," he lied, "and chased him all over but couldn't get a good shot. It wouldn't have done me any good even to have Blackfoot with me. The steep climb would have been too much for him."

Allyson noticed he looked tired, and his clothes and hands were soiled. "My goodness, you must have crawled on your hands and knees half the time."

Ethan looked down at himself, then began brushing himself off. "I tried crawling up a steep bank to get around the other side of him, but the damn thing outwitted me."

Allyson thought it odd that a man like Ethan couldn't get something as big as a moose, but then she supposed those things happened. "You look so tired. You can hunt another day, Ethan. Sit down and rest."

He took off his leather hat and set his rifle aside. "A moose would bring practically enough meat to last most of the winter. Now all we've got is this little antelope. I'll have to clean it pretty quick and start smoking the meat."

Maybe we won't need all that much meat. We might not be here all winter. Why couldn't she bring herself to say the words? She pulled a sweater closer around herself, thinking how quickly it got chilly up here now. The summer had seemed so short, but maybe it was partly because it had been spent with such joy, mining her claim, sleeping with Ethan, being loved and in love. She dished up a plate of potatoes and carrots. "At least I'll be able to mix a little meat with the vegetables next time," she commented, handing him the plate. She felt a strange chill at the way Ethan was watching her, as though she might jump up and run away any moment. "Ethan, is something wrong?"

You've hit your bonanza, Ally. You're a rich woman. He took the plate. "No. I, uh, I'm just disappointed I didn't get that moose, that's all. It would have made things a lot easier. If we already had enough meat, I could get around to other important chores, like chopping some wood and getting back to digging more gold out of that mountain."

"You're into a softer area now. I can do some of it."

"I don't like you being in the cave. It's getting more dangerous now."

"You have it shored up good. We get so much more out of there than by panning the creek. If that's our biggest find, we might as well make the most of it while we're up here. At least we know there's enough in there that we can ask at least five thousand for the claim if and when we sell it."

If? There was that word again, the one that made him doubt her love. Ethan struggled to get the words out again, but they would not come. He could just imagine her reaction. She would scream and dance, hug him, jump up and down . . . and right away she would start planning her future—a big house in Denver or Colorado Springs, fancy gowns, the best carriages, joining Denver's social elite. She could make history as the richest woman miner ever. Ethan Temple, her Indian lover, would be forgotten, no longer good enough for the fancy Miss Allyson Mills. She would consider selling now, but not if she knew about that vein farther up the mountain.

He finished the would-be stew, and Allyson was surprised at how little he ate. Something was not right, but then he did sometimes get a little moody and quiet. She attributed it to the Indian in him. She cleaned up camp while Ethan hung the antelope from a tree and gutted it. Once it was thoroughly cleaned, he climbed the tree and hung it up higher so wolves could not get to it. "It won't spoil overnight as long as the insides are cleaned out," he told her. "I'll skin it and finish cutting it up for the smokehouse in the morning. I'll show you how to clean a hide and stretch it out in the sun to dry. No sense wasting a good hide. There are a lot of uses for it, leastways if you're an Indian. Indian women could find a hundred uses for the thing."

Allyson wondered if he was comparing her to Indian

women, trying to say she was less capable. She was tempted to argue the issue, but then decided against it. Something would probably come out wrong and he would take offense. She had unintentionally insulted the Indian in him once too often, and she wished he understood just how proud she was of his heritage, not ashamed. There was a time when she thought it was terrible for a white woman to love a man like Ethan, but she hardly thought about his being Indian anymore. He was just a man—good, brave, handsome, gentle, skilled—everything a woman needed in a man . . . a woman, that is, who *wanted* to need a man.

Ethan scooped up the insides with a shovel. "They'd even find use for some of these guts, but I won't bother with it. I'll dump this farther away on the other side of the creek to keep the wolves away from the cabin."

Allyson carried plates and the pan to the creek to wash them, then returned to the cabin to get ready for bed. Their routine was to retire as soon as it got dark, then get up at the crack of dawn for another long day's work. She waited for Ethan, but he did not come right away. She lit a lantern, deciding that whatever was bothering him, she would let him brood about it alone. If he wanted to talk about it, he would come inside and say what he had to say. He still might. She took out a little book of Shakespeare she had bought back in Denver just out of curiosity, opened it, and began reading by the light of an oil lamp, wishing she could better understand some of the fancy prose. Maybe she could, if she could concentrate; but her mind was on Ethan and the way he had looked when he first returned, and the fact that he had hardly eaten. Now, for some reason, he was out there sitting alone. All that over not being able to bag a moose? Male pride was something she would never quite understand. It was different from her own stubborn pride, something a man took very personally, especially one as virile as Ethan Temple. She understood more clearly why the way she had used him back in Guthrie had stung him so deeply, and she supposed he would never quite forget it.

It was nearly an hour before he came inside, and he still had that look on his face. It was difficult to fully read it. One minute he looked angry, the next minute almost guilty, and sometimes he had almost a pleading expression. He wore only his longjohns, and he was clean—apparently he had washed in the creek. His face and hands and arms were still damp. He walked over and picked up a towel to wipe himself off. "I left my buckskins outside. I'll have to scrub them in the morning and lay them out to dry."

To Allyson's surprise he walked over to her chair and scooped her up in his arms, then carried her to the bed. She smiled when he laid her on it and moved on top of her.

"You'd better be naked under this gown, lady," he told her, moving his hand under it and along her thigh to her bare bottom.

"Always ready for my man," she answered.

Ethan took off his longjohns, then pushed up her gown, positioning himself between her legs. This was one of those times when all they needed was to be joined. Sometimes he was slow and deliberate, taking his time, taking her into a realm of ecstasy that made her wonder if she was even still in the real world. He would touch, kiss, taste every part of her, exploring her most secret places. He had taught her the glory of pleasing him and taking her own pleasure in all kinds of ways, bringing out a wantonness in her that amazed and sometimes even embarrassed her after it was over.

Tonight she knew there would be none of that. He simply needed to be inside of her, to quietly take his woman. "I love you, Ethan," she said, thinking that for some reason he needed to hear it tonight more than usual.

"Do you?"

She caressed his face, the high cheekbones, the perfect lips. "Why would you ask such a thing after what we have discovered about each other up here?"

He studied the blue eyes. *You're a rich, rich woman, Ally. I don't want to lose you.* "I don't know. I guess I just need to hear it sometimes."

"I love you more than I have loved anyone or anything in my whole life."

He kissed her lightly. "More than a fortune in gold?"

She laughed. "I don't think we're going to have to test that one. Our little bonanza didn't pan out quite the way we hoped it might. But if it had, I'd give it all up for you if I had to." *I'm going to have your baby, Ethan.* No, this was not the time. She wasn't sure of his mood tonight. He was very different.

Ethan wished he could believe she would give it all up for him. He knew deep inside that eventually he probably would have to test her on that. He couldn't keep what he had found today hidden from her forever. But he could keep it from her for just a little while longer. He met her mouth again, this time savagely, suddenly needing to prove to himself she belonged to him. After finding that vein of gold, he felt desperate to hold on to her, to make sure she knew she belonged only to Ethan Temple.

Quickly he was inside of her, probing deep, claiming her, eager to make sure she knew she could not get by without this, without Ethan Temple in her bed, allowing her the joy of being woman and loving fully. She had to understand that love came first.

Allyson groaned with a mixture of surprise and an excitement at the way he took her tonight. How could a man be almost brutal yet still gentle? It almost hurt this time, filling her to near-painful proportions. He surged rhythmically, pushing hard. He raised up to his knees, spreading them so that her legs were wide apart. He grasped her hips and pulled her to him, invading her with the look of a conquering warrior. It was both exciting and almost frightening. This was not the usual Ethan. Tonight he seemed almost a stranger, someone come to put his brand on her and make sure she knew he owned her. She closed her eyes, her breath coming in gasps as he pounded into her. He pushed up her nightgown so that her breasts were exposed. He studied her nakedness with unreadable dark eyes, until finally his life spilled into her.

The stranger in him gradually gave way to Ethan, and he looked apologetic. He lay down beside her and pulled her into his arms. "I'm sorry. Did I hurt you?"

"No." Allyson touched his chest. "What's wrong, Ethan?"

He sighed deeply, stroking her hair. "Nothing. I just . . . sometimes I imagine I'm still going to lose you, that's all."

"You aren't going to lose me. Don't you realize I worry about the same thing?"

"That's different. You only have to worry about losing me to death, because that is the only thing that could take me from you. I worry about losing you to something else."

"That can't happen, Ethan. There was a time when it could have, but not anymore."

How he wanted to believe that. He did not answer, but held her until sleep finally overtook them both. Ethan's last thoughts were of a secret, glittering vein of gold that lay waiting to make someone very rich. He just didn't want that someone to be Ally. He could keep it from her, but what about Roy Holliday? If he did know about that vein, he was surely going to do something about it before the winter was over. If they were in danger, Ally should know, but telling her meant letting her know what was up on that mountain . . . the fortune she had always dreamed of.

27

Allyson set down her coffee cup, ready to start a new day of digging. She worried the work might be too strenuous, now that she could be pregnant, but at least they were into softer rock now. Ethan needed to chop wood and do more hunting, and if she really was pregnant, that would mean they would have to leave the claim and get down to Cripple Creek before their year was up. She couldn't have a baby up here, where they could get trapped by snow. The cabin would probably be freezing cold in winter, they could run low on food, anything could happen. That meant getting as much gold as possible out of the earth before they had to leave. The more they had to show a prospective buyer, the more they could ask for the claim.

A baby. She should tell Ethan right now, tell him he didn't need to worry about storing up for the whole winter. In fact, the right thing to do would be to go down to the city and get married and make the baby legal. As soon as she was very sure she really was with child, she would have little choice but to tell Ethan and do the right thing. What worried her was that he might not believe marriage was what she really wanted, but baby or no baby, she would marry him in a second if he would just ask. The fact remained he had *not* asked, and she knew it was because he was not positive she really would choose him over her gold.

Last night had been beautiful. After that first almost-violent intercourse, Ethan had softened. They had made love again, slowly, intimately. Ethan Temple could handle a woman just as expertly as he could handle his guns and knife. The Indian in him gave him an almost worshipful attitude toward love and life, which helped her understand the deep hurt he'd felt over their disastrous marriage. It had meant everything to him, but circumstances had made it seem it had meant nothing to her. Finally they were getting back what they should have had the first time around, and she didn't want to do anything to make him doubt her again. She just wished she knew how he would react to her being with child.

She watched Ethan come toward her from the smokehouse, a small stone structure he'd built for curing meat. She was fascinated by how much he knew about such things, and she wondered how she ever would have survived up here without him. "Before long it will be so cold, all we'll have to do is hang our meat from the trees and let it freeze," Ethan told her as he came closer. He had gotten up extra early to cut down the antelope and skin it so he could get started curing the meat. "We're going to have to take turns checking the coals in the smokehouse," he added. "I probably should have built it bigger, but there wasn't enough time. I had barely enough room to hang all the meat."

"Are you hunting again today?" she asked, getting up from the campsite.

"Not today. I've got some digging to do."

"In the cave? I can do that. You said you needed to—"

"Not in the cave." He came around the fire and bent down to kiss her cheek. "I'm digging a tunnel, starting near the privy. I'll dig into the mountain, circle to where the cabin backs up against the mountain, and make a doorway at the back of the cabin that opens right into the tunnel."

Allyson rose, frowning. "Whatever for?" Ethan grinned,

but she got the distinct impression it was a false smile, the kind a person uses when they're trying to assure someone that everything is just fine when it really isn't.

"A lot of reasons. For one thing, come winter, the walk from the front of the cabin around to the privy is going to be damn cold, especially if it's the middle of the night, let alone having to trudge through snow. This way, you'll be able to just walk out the back side of the cabin through a tunnel that will be out of the wind and the snow, then take a couple of steps from the opening to the privy. Another reason is simple safety. What if that damn, flimsy excuse of a cabin should catch fire? We'll be using the wood stove a lot more once winter really sets in. If the front of that cabin was in flames, we'd be trapped. This way we have another escape." He gave her a wink. "Don't worry. I've checked the ground there, and it's soft in that particular spot, not all rock like so much of the rest. I only have to dig about fifteen to twenty feet. I'll be done in a couple of days. Then I'll get started on the wood. I'll spend half a day helping you dig and the other half cutting wood and doing a little hunting."

He turned and walked down to the creek to get a shovel. Allyson watched him, not at all convinced he'd told her everything about why he was digging a tunnel from the cabin to the privy. It seemed a strange thing to do, but then what he *had* told her did make sense. Should she tell him not to bother? She touched her belly. If she *wasn't* pregnant, they would probably stay up here most of the winter, in which case, she reasoned, the tunnel *would* come in handy. She shrugged it off, then headed for the cave to do another kind of digging. She reached for a pickax, noticing how dry and rough her hands had become. She looked down at herself, decked out in baggy denim pants and a common shirt. She hadn't worn lip color or rouge or a pretty dress in months.

How Ethan could find her attractive anymore, she could not imagine. Before long she would get fat on top of it all, but then to a man like Ethan, none of those things seemed to matter. That was what she loved about him.

Down at the creek Ethan picked up a shovel, then glanced up to watch Allyson heading for the cave. He hoped she had swallowed his story. The real reason for the tunnel was to have an escape, a way to hide and maybe sneak up on someone who might come visiting unexpectedly. That day Wayne Trapp had broken down the cabin door, Allyson had no escape. He didn't want that to happen again.

You've got to tell her, his conscience reminded him. *Show her the bonanza.* That was the honest thing to do. He could just see Ally's face if she saw that vein. The light in her eyes would no longer be there because of her love for him. Something would replace that love, something rich and golden. In his whole life, with all the things he'd been through, the dangers he had faced, nothing frightened him more than that vein of gold.

All night, after making love to her, he had argued with himself that it was best for them both if he didn't tell her. Somehow they had to get through the winter, then get to town and sell the claim. As long as she didn't know about that bonanza above them and it wasn't reported, Holliday would think they still had not found it, which meant he would probably leave them alone . . . but then he might try something because he was afraid that if they stayed up here too long, the secret *would* be discovered.

He jammed the shovel into the earth near the privy and began digging, his anger and frustration giving him more strength and energy and determination than normal. "God-damn antelope," he grumbled. If he hadn't spotted the damn thing, he never would have noticed that cave entrance. No. It was the rain that did it. If it hadn't rained so hard, the rocks and dirt piled around the entrance wouldn't have washed away.

He stopped digging for a minute, looking up at the sky. "*You* did it, didn't you?" he said quietly, speaking to God Himself. "Why? You know I can't tell her about it."

His only reply was a gentle breeze. He returned to his digging, feeling like an ass. Yes, he *would* have to tell her, but not yet. Just a little longer. He wanted to be with her this way just a little longer, because once she knew, he was going to lose her. He was as sure of that as he was that there was a sun in the eastern sky this morning.

Allyson awoke to a chill, feeling nauseated. September had given way to October, and already there was snow on the ground outside. "Ethan, I'm freezing," she spoke up. "Can you build up the fire?"

The sun was not quite risen yet, and the deep cold of a long, dark night had set in. Ethan stirred, kissing Allyson's hair and rubbing a big hand over her belly. It seemed to him she'd gotten a little thicker in the waist, and he considered teasing her about it but decided against it. Women were so easily offended by such things. He grinned as he got out of bed, then hurriedly pulled on his denim pants and buttoned them. "Damn, it's cold!" He rubbed at his arms as he moved to the stove to throw in more wood.

Allyson studied his dark skin, the way his muscles rippled when he worked, the dark hair that hung down his back. She remembered the first time she had met Ethan Temple, running right into his horse back in Arkansas City. That seemed a lifetime ago, and the Allyson she was then was a stranger to her now. Back then a man was the last thing she had wanted in her life. She'd had such big plans for wealth and independence. When she ran into Ethan, she had seen only an Indian—handsome, yes—but an Indian, something to be afraid of, maybe even ashamed to call a friend. Now she saw only the man, the father of her child. Suddenly the words came easily, perhaps because now she was certain.

"Ethan, I'm going to have a baby."

He'd been standing bent over the stove and had just thrown on another piece of wood, about to close the door. Allyson noticed he seemed to just freeze right there. Finally he closed and latched the stove door, then turned, his smile gone. He didn't even seem aware of the cold any longer. He walked a little closer. "You sure?"

"As sure as any woman can be. If I'm not pregnant, then there is something terribly wrong, because I haven't had . . ." She blushed. "It's been over two months."

Two months. Ethan turned and reached for the top half of his longjohns. He pulled it on, then pulled on a flannel shirt and began buttoning it. He came over to the bed and sat down on the edge of it. Two months. That meant she'd gotten pregnant before he found the vein of gold . . . the bonanza he still hadn't told her about. This could be his out. The baby was an excuse to give all this up, sell out and just leave, but that meant letting Roy Holliday get away with murder. He still hadn't figured out what he could do about that. Now there was a baby to consider. He met her eyes. Did she love him enough to marry him just for himself, or would she only be marrying him now because of the baby? If she did, she would always resent him, blaming him and the baby for taking away her dream. Still, she had certainly very willingly shared her bed with him.

He braced his arms on each side of her and leaned closer. "Ally, you know what this means to me. At first I wasn't sure

I wanted to get remarried, but within days after coming up here with you, I knew that was what I wanted. You didn't seem to want that. You're still bent on getting rich—"

"No! Not anymore, Ethan. You have to believe that I had decided before I even knew I was with child that no matter what we found up here, I'd sell out and go to Wyoming with you come spring. I swear it. I love you, Ethan. I just want to be with you."

He closed his eyes and breathed in a deep sigh. "I wish I could believe that's true, that you aren't just saying it because of the baby." He looked at her pleadingly. "I don't want you that way, Ally. I want a wife and family more than anything in the world, but I don't want a woman who feels she's been forced into it. You've always wanted things I can't give you. You want to live in a world I can never be a part of."

She touched his face. "Not anymore. I'm tired of it all, Ethan, tired of running, tired of being afraid to love. Yes, maybe it *is* partly the baby that has changed my mind about things, but I don't feel forced into anything. All the baby has done is show me even more vividly how much I love and need you, how much I want the same things you want, want to be a mother. The baby hasn't forced me to love you. It has only made me see more clearly how *much* I love you. You're my baby's father, and all of a sudden I want to give you *lots* of babies. I want a big, sprawling house on that ranch in Wyoming so there will be room for all the children. You have to believe me, Ethan, when I say that this baby is a joy to me because it's yours. You have to believe that I truly want to go with you to Wyoming, no strings attached, except that I'd be your wife. We've gotten enough gold out of here to buy all the land we want, build a nice home—"

Ethan rose, feeling sick at not telling her about the bonanza. "You don't know what you're saying." If she found out now, she'd still have to marry him because of the baby, and she'd never be able to use her fortune in the way she'd always planned. She'd hate him for that. They would be miserable together, pretending for others and for the sake of the child, but living a life she would hate because she'd know she could have had something much better.

"What are you talking about, Ethan? Why won't you believe me?"

"I *do* believe you, but you might not be saying these things if—" He hesitated, sure he heard a voice somewhere far off. He put up his hand for her to be quiet as he listened with a trained ear to things few men would ever notice. Quickly he pulled on his knee-high winter moccasins.

"Ethan, what is it?"

"I'm not sure. I heard something." An explosion rocked the cabin then, and caused Allyson to scream in surprise. A loud rumbling followed the explosion, and the cabin continued to shake, the noise growing to almost deafening proportions in a fraction of a second. In one swift movement, Ethan grabbed Allyson from the bed, dragging a blanket along as he hurried her out the back and into the tunnel. They had barely made it when it seemed half the mountain came down around them.

Allyson screamed again, and Ethan pushed her toward the outer end of the tunnel, then fell to the ground with her, covering her with his body as dirt and debris sifted over them. Ethan prayed the shoring inside the tunnel would hold back what he knew must be dirt and snow and boulders showering them from above. One thing was certain—the landslide was not a natural one. Someone had started it . . . someone who knew how to use explosives. Did Trevor Gale still have it in for him? He had thought it would be Holliday or one of his men who tried something like this. He had nearly forgotten about the confrontation with Trevor, but then he wasn't the only man who knew how to use explosives. Holliday could have hired anyone to do this, then decided to make it look like an accident.

"Ethan! My God, what's happening?" Allyson screamed, staying bent over with her arms wrapped around her head.

"I'm not sure yet," he yelled, trying to keep his voice above the continued noise of an avalanche that seemed to go on forever. "Maybe it's from one of the mine explosions," he lied, hating to have to tell her someone might be out to kill them.

"That was right here by us!" she screamed back.

"Just hang on!"

Allyson had never been so terrified, yet the feel of Ethan's strong arms around her, the closeness of his face, his voice, calmed her. They both hovered there for several minutes, until finally the noise stopped. Ethan finally pulled away from her and felt behind him.

"The tunnel to the house is blocked. We've got to try to get out by the privy. I think we're in luck. I can see some light on the other end."

"Oh, Ethan, get me out of here! I feel like I'm buried alive!"

Ethan bent back over her for a moment. "Maybe somebody *wants* us to be buried alive."

"Why? Ethan, what's happening?"

"I know you hate it in here, but for safety's sake, stay put for a few minutes. I'll go out first. And keep your voice down. If someone was trying to kill us, it's better to let them think that's just what they've done."

"*Who*, Ethan? And why? What aren't you telling me?"

"Not now, Ally. And keep your voice down."

"Who's going to hear us when we're practically buried alive?"

"Do you still have the blanket I grabbed?"

Allyson felt around in the dark. "Yes."

"Let's get to the end of the tunnel. Wrap the blanket around you if and when we get outside, then stay out of sight if you can. Are you all right?"

"I think I am."

"We'll have to find something for your feet. I wonder if there is anything left of the cabin."

"Ethan, I don't understand any of this."

"I think somebody tried to stage an accident, get us killed, and call it a landslide."

Allyson gasped, then realized who it had to be. "Roy Holliday?"

"Most likely. Follow me. You'll have to crawl over some dirt."

Ethan headed toward the light at the end of the tunnel, and Allyson prayed the earth remaining above them would not cave in before they could get out. She struggled not to cough or let terror overcome her at being confined in what seemed like a tomb. She made her way through the debris, crawling over a fallen support log, all the while trying to grasp what Ethan had told her. In a sense, it almost seemed as though he had expected this to happen. She thought about the fact that he had worked for Roy Holliday. Did he still? Had all this been a ploy to get up here and see what was really going on so he could report back to Holliday on her progress? Was that why he had looked at her so strangely rather than with joy when she told him she was pregnant? Was that why he hadn't remarried her yet? Maybe that whole thing back in Cripple Creek with Wayne Trapp had been staged. Maybe Holliday knew Ethan had been married to her once, so he figured she would trust him.

No! There had to be some other reason why he had acted so strangely the last month or so. Ethan wouldn't do such a thing. He was too good, too honest. Not her Ethan! Besides, he had just saved her, when he could have left her in the cabin to die. But what if . . .

A terrible grief overwhelmed her, unlike anything she had ever experienced. Not Ethan! Not Ethan! Did he hate her that much? Was this his form of revenge, to win her trust like she had won his, then turn around and throw it in her face? They were almost to the end of the tunnel when she reached out and grasped at his foot. "Ethan!" she groaned.

He reached a spot where he could stand up, then grasped her arms and pulled her against him. "What's wrong? Is it the baby?"

She looked up at him, able to see him a little in the closer light. She gasped in a sob. "Tell me I haven't been set up," she whimpered. "Tell me you don't still work for Roy Holliday."

Ethan was both astonished and disappointed. "My God, Ally, when will you ever learn to trust? How could you even begin to think such a thing?"

She sniffed, pulling away. "You knew! Somehow you knew something was going to happen. You've been acting strangely for nearly a month."

Ethan sighed deeply. He shook dirt from his hair, brushing at his shirt and pants. "Not for the reasons you think. My God, Ally, after all we've been through together, how could you even begin to think I would betray you?"

"Because that's how it's always been for me. But you . . . you were different. You made me feel loved, and I loved you in return."

"That's right. We *do* love each other. I love you so goddamn much that I *did* betray you, but not because I wanted to hurt you. I did it because I love you and I'm scared to death of losing you again!"

"What do you mean? How have you betrayed me?"

Ethan moved to the end of the tunnel, peering over a huge boulder that had landed at the entrance but left enough room for a man to crawl out. "I found out why Roy Holliday would be willing to kill for this claim, Ally. When I realized what I had found, I knew Holliday would never let us last the winter up here. It was just a matter of him figuring out how he could get rid of us without his being implicated."

Allyson's heart rushed with confusion and excitement. "What did you find?"

Ethan looked at her. "The bonanza, Ally. I found a vein of gold that would make you faint. It might be worth millions, for all I know."

Her eyes grew wide, and Ethan was sure he had lost her forever at the look of excitement as well as anger in them. "Where?"

He turned to watch what was going on beyond where they were hiding. "Higher up on the mountain," he answered, keeping his voice low. "John Sebastian must have found it. He'd dug a small cave into the mountain. Maybe he reported his find, I don't know. The assayer down in town might be on Roy Holliday's payroll. He probably told Holliday, and Holliday had Sebastian killed, then covered the entrance to the find, figuring you being a woman, you'd never bother coming here to work the claim. He'd just buy it from you and that would be that. At any rate, the day I went hunting for that antelope, it had rained a lot and must have caused a washout that pulled the rocks and mud away from the hidden entrance. I spotted it. When I went inside and saw what was in there—" He hesitated, then turned to face her. "I knew it meant losing you. Your dream is up there on the mountain, Ally, not with me."

Tears began to stream down her face. "How can you say that? I'm carrying your *child!*"

He looked back out to watch for whoever might come for them. "By accident, not by choice. You came up here for a different reason, and everything you have ever wanted is up there in that cave."

She choked on a sob. "How can you talk to me about trust, when you think I would so easily throw away what we have together? Everything I have ever wanted is *not* up there on that mountain! Everything I've ever wanted is standing right in front of me, and living inside of me! Nothing else matters anymore."

He looked back at her again, a strange sadness in his dark eyes. "You haven't seen what's up there, Ally."

"I don't need to see it!"

He closed his eyes and breathed deeply. "We have a lot to talk about, and now isn't the time. Come here."

Allyson wiped at her eyes with the sleeve of her nightgown, then pulled the blanket closer around her shoulders, walking on bare feet to where Ethan stood. She drew in her breath at the sight of the cabin totally collapsed under huge boulders.

"*Now* do you believe someone wants us dead? If I was working for Holliday, you'd still be inside that cabin."

Allyson covered her face. "I don't know what to think about anything anymore."

Ethan embraced her. "Just hang on to that baby right now, and keep still. Someone is coming. Whoever it is probably wants to make sure we're dead."

"Ethan, I'm scared," she whispered. "We don't even have a gun with us."

He gently pushed her aside and strained to see. Two men on horses came around to the front of what used to be the cabin. They dismounted and began inspecting the cabin site.

"They must be dead," one of them said.

Now Ethan could see them clearly. One of them was Wayne Trapp, just as he had suspected, but he was astonished to realize that the other was Trevor Gale. Holliday had fired the man a long time ago. How had he managed to get him back on his payroll? He must have offered a lot of money. Here was a former union organizer working for the very man he used to hate. Maybe he had himself been set up. Everyone knew he had it in for Ethan. Maybe this was Holliday's way of getting rid of him and Ally without looking guilty. He had no doubt who had set the explosives.

"One of them is Wayne Trapp," he told Ally. "Whatever happens, you stay right here."

Wayne Trapp! How she hated the man. Now he was out there with a gun, and she and Ethan were trapped in here with no weapons of any kind. They were surely going to die today, and neither one of them would realize their dreams, never hold their baby.

"I won't feel comfortable about this till we find the bodies," Trapp was saying. Allyson could hear his words.

"Who's the other man?" she asked.

"An Irishman I beat on in front of several other men. He never forgave me for it, but I didn't think he'd stoop to murder."

"They have to be in there. It's barely dawn," Trevor was saying. "They were still asleep. We've watched them long enough to know their habits. There's no way out of that cabin but the front door, and nobody got out that way."

Ethan looked at Ally, and she knew now why he had dug

the tunnel. She loved him for it, but hated him at the same time for not telling her about the bonanza. She thought she had earned his trust.

"Try to find their bodies," Trapp was telling Trevor Gale.

Ethan watched as Trevor began rummaging through the rubble. Then to Ethan's horror he saw Wayne Trapp raise his six-gun. "Turn around, Trevor. I don't like shootin' a man in the back."

Trevor hesitated, then slowly turned. "What the—"

"You don't really think Roy Holliday would leave you alive to get drunk and tell the whole town what happened up here, do you?"

Trevor's eyes widened, and he backed away. "What the hell are you talking about?"

"I'm talkin' about you bein' blamed for what happened up here today. I'm talkin' about me comin' up here to make Miss Mills an offer on her claim, only to hear an explosion. I seen you runnin' off and shot you down. Everybody knows you hate Ethan Temple. You came up here to kill him, and I caught you, but too late. Holliday is rid of Temple and the woman, and you, too. You get blamed for what happened up here, and Holliday gets his hands on this claim. It's a rich one, Trevor. There's a vein up there that's probably worth millions, and you just helped Roy Holliday get it."

Trevor's face turned almost purple with rage. "You bastard!" he fumed. It was then he saw a movement. Someone was quietly walking toward Wayne Trapp, his moccasins moving through a blanket of snow and freshly turned earth from the avalanche.

Trapp chuckled, his fat face glowing with sweet victory, unaware that Ethan was approaching him from behind. "You should have realized how it would be, Trevor. Roy

Holliday is a smart man. He's not about to leave somebody like you, who used to hate his guts, alive to tell the truth." He cocked the gun. Much as Trevor had hated Ethan Temple, for the moment he had to be grateful the man wasn't dead. Before Wayne could fire the six-gun, Ethan plowed into him from behind, sending him sprawling to the ground. The gun went off, and Trevor ducked, then scrambled to try to help Ethan as he and Wayne wrestled in the snow for the weapon.

Allyson watched in terror, shivering with the cold, her feet frozen, her mind whirling. Suddenly Wayne Trapp's gun went off again, and Ethan went limp. "God, no! No!" she whimpered. She watched in sickening terror as Wayne got up. "Ethaaaan!" Allyson screamed. In that moment she knew for certain that Ethan Temple was all that mattered to her in life. He was worth more than all the millions her bonanza might yield, but she had lost him, too, just like everything else she had ever loved.

It had all happened so quickly. Trapp turned and fired at Trevor Gale, who cried out and fell, grasping at his thigh and cursing Trapp. By then Allyson had run out from behind the boulder, wanting to get to Ethan. She stopped when Trapp turned on her, pointing the pistol. "Well, little bitch, I guess it's just you and me now, ain't it?"

28

Allyson was not even aware that her feet were still bare. She watched Wayne Trapp come toward her, while Ethan lay curled and writhing, and the other man Trapp had shot was still rolling on the ground yelling that the bullet in his thigh had broken the bone. Wayne Trapp seemed oblivious to all of it. His puffy eyes gleamed with something Allyson well understood. Inside she was screaming at the thought that Ethan could be dying, and a new determination overcame her, this time not to protect herself or her fortune, but to protect the baby growing inside of her. It might be all she had of Ethan before this was over, and Wayne Trapp was not going to make her lose it.

He still waved his gun at her. "This whole thing has been messed up, little girl," he growled. "Wasn't any of this supposed to happen this way, but as long as it has, I might as well get what I've got comin' from you before I kill you, too, and get the hell out of Cripple Creek. I'll just leave the dead bodies and let everybody else try to figure out what happened." He grinned. "Come on, now. It won't be so bad." He came closer, and Allyson kept backing away, looking around for something to use as a weapon. "Maybe you'll even like it. Maybe I'll take you along when I leave here."

Allyson had never known such anger and hatred. He'd shot Ethan! Ethan! How was she going to live without Ethan? Why had she even come up here again, and made

Ethan come with her? Why hadn't she just gone to Wyoming with him like he'd wanted?

"You'll *have* to kill me, Wayne Trapp," she spit at the man, "because I'd *rather* be dead than to go off with a fat, ugly, coward of a man like you!" She turned to run then, her feet numb from the cold, her mind full of thoughts about how she could hurt or kill this man so he couldn't go back and put a bullet in Ethan's head. She didn't even care what he intended to do to her. She could bear all of it if Ethan would live.

The blanket slid away as she ran. She could feel Wayne Trapp's lumbering body close behind her, but she was sure he could never catch her because of his age and weight. She was more frightened of what the cold and the running might do to the baby than she was of Trapp catching her. Suddenly her foot caught on a fallen branch hidden by the snow, and she cried out as she plummeted forward, trying to brace herself with her arms. She had already been in such a fast-forward motion that there was little she could do to cushion her fall. In a split second she saw a rock in front of her face and closed her eyes feeling her head hit it.

Everything became hazy and unreal. Someone jerked her up, lifted her, carried her somewhere, and literally dropped her into a snowbank. "Snow's as good a bed as any," a man's voice said. She felt her gown being pushed to her waist and heard a comment about the fact that she wore no bloomers. "Keep yourself naked for your Indian buck, I see," came a voice near her ear. "If you can let an Indian between these legs, you can let *any*body between them, you little whore!"

Allyson opened her eyes, trying to see the huge figure hovering over her more clearly, but he was a blur. She felt around for something to hit him with, but now her whole body was going numb from the cold, her fingers, her legs, mostly her feet and toes. She thought for a moment that maybe if she was half frozen, she at least wouldn't feel the horror of Wayne Trapp raping her.

She tried to scream, but nothing would come out of her mouth. She felt hands prying her legs apart, felt something wet run down past her eye. Blood? Then she thought she saw another figure loom over them, but still she could not see clearly. Suddenly Wayne Trapp grunted, as someone wrapped an arm around under his chin and literally lifted him off of her. Allyson sat up slightly and blinked. A big man with long, dark hair was choking Trapp so that the fat man was quickly losing consciousness.

"Ethan," Allyson muttered. Her vision cleared more, and she wiped at the blood on her face with her hand, then pulled her flannel gown down over her knees, bending her legs so she could also wrap it over her feet. Ethan had gotten such a grip that Wayne Trapp had quickly lost his breath and couldn't even get his gun from its holster. Ethan did that for him, ripping it out and letting the breathless Trapp fall backward into the snow.

"You fat, stinking rapist!" Ethan growled. He kicked the man viciously between the legs, and Trapp groaned and curled up. Allyson was surprised at Ethan's strength, for blood covered the front of his shirt and was beginning to also stain his pants. He pulled Trapp to his knees, then shoved the gun up under his double chin. "I ought to blow your fat head off," he growled. "I *need* to blow your head off, but I'm going to *save* you, Trapp, for the miners down in Cripple Creek! I'm going to save you and Trevor Gale *both*, so you can tell everybody down there what happened here—tell them how Roy Holliday paid the both of you to come up here and *murder* us—how he paid *you* to turn around and kill Trevor so he could be blamed for all of it!"

Trapp's eyes were wider than Allyson had ever seen them, filled with fear. "You goddamn redskin," he said, the words coming weakly from a coward trying to act brave. "Why don't you just . . . scalp me . . . skin me alive. That's what your kind does, ain't it?"

Ethan cocked the six-gun and jabbed it even harder against the man's chin; Trapp gasped and began to shake, looking down cross-eyed at the weapon. "That isn't the half of what I'd do to you if I didn't need you to talk when we get to Cripple Creek," he growled. "If I had my way you'd be chewing on your own balls right now!" He pistol-whipped the man, sending him sprawling motionless. He shoved the gun into his belt, then turned and half stumbled over to Allyson. She could see he was losing blood, realized he must still have a bullet in him. In the distance Trevor Gale was actually weeping from his own miserable pain.

Ethan reached Allyson and began removing his shirt.

"Ethan, no! You'll freeze!"

"Don't worry about me. You're carrying. Put this on. I'm going to get something to put around your feet." He reached down and put the shirt around her shoulders, watched her a moment, touched the blood on her face. "What did he do to you?"

"I'm all right, Ethan. It's you who's hurt the worst. My God, you've been shot! What are we going to do?"

His breath came in pants, and in spite of his dark complexion, Allyson could tell he was growing paler. "I don't think . . . the bullet hit anything vital. It just took the breath out of me for a minute. When I saw him bending over you . . ." He drew in his breath. "I've got to hang on . . . get you and both of them to Cripple Creek . . . let the law take care of this." His dark eyes burned with rage. "Or the miners themselves. There just might be a hanging in Cripple Creek before this day is over!"

"Ethan, you can't get all the way to town in your condition!"

"We have to try. There's no shelter up here now, and . . . this time of year a storm could hit at any time. Besides . . . what else are we going to do with Trapp and Gale?"

"You know that other man?"

"It's a long story. You sit tight. I'm going to find something . . . to wrap around my middle . . . something to put on your feet. I've got to figure out a way . . . to get you and both of them down this mountain." He touched her face again. "What about the baby?"

Allyson put a hand to her belly. This was not the time to tell him that cramps were beginning to stab at her insides. He would have enough on his hands getting them all into town. He didn't need something else to worry about. "I think I'm all right. If I could just . . . get warm."

Ethan nodded. "You just stay right there and let me do everything."

"Ethan, you can't—"

"I'll manage . . . if it means getting you to a doctor in town." He watched her eyes, a rather pleading look in his. "We have a lot to talk about, Ally. I should have told you . . . about the gold."

"Why, Ethan? Why didn't you trust me enough to tell me?"

He just shook his head, then managed to get to his feet. He walked to where the two men's horses stood packed with supplies. He untied a blanket, rummaged through a saddle bag, and pulled out a knife. Then he cut a length of rawhide from one of the horse's reins and carried everything over to the smokehouse, which had been undamaged by the landslide. He took the antelope skin from where it was laid out to dry on top of the smokehouse, then managed to rip the knife through it to cut it in half. He came back over to Allyson.

"I've got to use some of your gown to tie around my middle . . . help stop the bleeding." He glanced over at Trapp and then to Trevor Gale. It was obvious neither man was going anywhere for the moment. He took the knife and ripped off some of Allyson's gown, then tossed the material aside while he wrapped the fresh blanket around her. "Put out your feet," he ordered.

Allyson obeyed, and Ethan wrapped a piece of the antelope skin around each foot, then tied each one snugly with the rawhide to fashion a crude kind of shoe. "I knew this antelope skin would be good for something," he said. "See how handy it is to be Indian? We can make just about anything out of an animal skin." He looked at her sadly, and Allyson realized he probably heard Wayne Trapp's remark that if she slept with an Indian, she must be a whore.

"Ethan—"

"No time to talk now. You just wrap up in that blanket and wait until I get things situated. Do you think you can ride Blackfoot down the mountain?"

"I think so."

Ethan rose and pulled up the shirt of his longjohns. Allyson grimaced at the ugly hole in his lower left side. It looked like it was not bleeding so badly now, but she realized Ethan had to be in terrible pain. He began wrapping the flannel material around the wound. "I don't like the idea of you having to walk any of the way down," he was saying, "but on the really steep parts, we'll have no choice."

"Ethan, I'm afraid for you. You could be hurt worse than you know."

He winced as he tied the cloth tightly. "There are times when you just have to keep going," he answered. "Hell . . . you know that as much as anybody." He pulled his shirt back down. "We'll make it." He left her then, and Allyson forced back a need to groan at the pain that moved through her belly. She closed her eyes and said a quick prayer that she would not lose her baby. Not now. What if Ethan died? If she lost the baby, too, what would she have left? Her gold? Gold couldn't hold her in the night. Gold couldn't feed at her breast, or give her hugs. Gold couldn't love her, or give her the joys of being a wife and mother. She had never realized more clearly how much she wanted those things.

Ethan took the gun from where he had shoved it into the waist of his pants and walked back over to Wayne Trapp, who was groaning as he regained consciousness. He grasped the man by the neck of his jacket. "Get up, Trapp! We've got a little trip to make! You can either cooperate and walk down, or I can tie you by the ankles and drag you over the rocks and brush and through the cold snow like a sack of potatoes. Makes no difference to me."

Trapp seemed to be in a daze. There was a gaping cut across the right side of his head where Ethan had ripped across it with the barrel of the man's own pistol. Ethan quickly jerked off Trapp's fur coat before the man even realized what was happening. "You've got enough fat on you to keep you plenty warm," Ethan sneered. "*I* need this."

Trapp began rubbing at his arms. "Hey, you can't take my coat. I'll freeze." The words were spoken slowly and somewhat slurred.

"Right now I can do whatever I want, including cutting you open from your balls to your throat," Ethan growled. "That's what I would prefer!" He gave Trapp a shove. "Get over there by the horses!"

Allyson tried to rise, thinking she should help, but the cramps deep in her belly made her sit back down. She glanced at the cabin; rather, at where the cabin used to be. It had been flattened by boulders, and she realized that if not for Ethan's tunnel, they would both be dead, which had apparently been Roy Holliday's original plan. She shivered even more at the realization that someone had tried to murder her and Ethan today, but thanks to Ethan's keen hearing and sense of trouble, and his quick action once the explosion occurred, they were still alive to tell about it.

"Ethan! Ethan, please . . . help me," the one called Trevor Gale was yelling. "My leg! I can't stand the pain!" The man had managed to crawl a little closer to where Ethan and Trapp and Allyson were.

"You'll get your turn," Ethan grumbled. He gave Trapp a kick in the rear. "Get moving, you fat scum!" He shoved the man over near Allyson, then handed her the six-gun. "Keep that on him. I'll only be a few seconds. He makes one wrong move, blow his guts out! We've still got the other man to testify."

Allyson took the gun, cocking it and pointing it straight at Trapp. "I'll gladly pull the trigger," she answered. "Please do give me a reason, Mr. Trapp," she added.

Trapp stood still, fully convinced she would kill him if he gave her the slightest excuse. At the level at which she held the gun, the bullet would go right into his belly, and every man knew there was no more painful way to die than being gut shot. He wished the bullet he'd put into Ethan had been just a little higher. Apparently it had not done near enough damage. Still, maybe it was enough that the damn Indian would pass out before they reached Cripple Creek. Then he could still find a way to get the hell out of this mess. Roy Holliday was going to be furious when he learned how he had botched this.

Ethan went to get something more from the gear on the horses, and Trapp went to his knees again, still in pain from being kicked in the groin, and dizzy from the blow to his head. He glowered at Allyson. "How in hell did you two . . . escape bein' hurt?"

Allyson refused to show any sign of her pain. "Ethan had dug a tunnel behind the cabin to the privy. As soon as we heard the explosion, we ran in there. It held up enough for us to escape through it."

Trapp leaned over and groaned. "Goddamn Indian. I told Mr. Holliday . . . he never should have hired him to begin with."

Ethan returned with a length of thin rope. "You two brought along some handy supplies," he told Trapp. He grabbed one of Trapp's arms and jerked it behind his back, quickly wrapping some of the rope around his wrist.

"What are you gonna do?" Trapp asked, grunting with pain.

"Make you wish you'd never tried this," Ethan answered.

Allyson noticed Ethan was beginning to perspire in spite of the cold. She knew it was from the bullet wound.

"Get on your feet," Ethan ordered as he finished tying Trapp's wrists together.

"I ain't goin' nowhere. I'm in too much pain."

Ethan took his knife and cut the remaining length of rope. "You'll cooperate or I'll tie you by the ankles to the back of one of those horses and drag you all the way to town! We don't have a lot of time! I want to get Ally down to a doctor!"

Trapp managed to get up and half-stumble over to the horses. Allyson watched as Ethan tied more of the rope around the man's neck. Trapp protested with a string of curses when Ethan tightened it just enough to cut off a little of his air. Then he tied the other end around a saddlehorn. "You'll have to keep up or choke to death," he told Trapp. He left the man standing there practically crying, walked over to where Trevor Gale lay nearly unconscious. He bent over to check his leg, and Trevor groaned when he touched it.

"It's broken, all right," Ethan mumbled, wondering if he would make it all the way to town without passing out himself. The only thing that kept him going was knowing he had to get Ally down from the mountain to a place where she could be warm and where a doctor could tend to her. He prayed the ordeal wouldn't make her lose the baby.

He stumbled over to the fallen cabin and dug through the debris to find a wide piece of wood that had once been part of a wall. Two more pieces of wood were still nailed crosswise to it. He pulled what would be a makeshift sled over to where Trevor Gale lay with what strength he had left, he managed to scoot the man's body onto the wider board. Gale opened his eyes wide and watched him. "You . . . going to kill me . . . Indian?"

"I'll get more pleasure out of letting the whole town know the kind of man Roy Holliday is," Ethan answered. "Lie still. I'll tie you on this thing so your leg doesn't get moved around. The crossboards should keep it from tipping. I can tie some rope around the crossboards and then to one of the horses. These boards will have to act like a kind of travois to get you down to town where a doctor can look at your leg." Ethan started to rise to go get more rope, and Trevor grabbed his arm.

"You . . . saved my life . . . risked your own. Trapp . . . was going to shoot me . . . so he and Holliday . . . could say it was all me."

"I already figured out what the plan was. You just didn't bank on me and Ally surviving."

Gale still clung to the sleeve of Ethan's coat. "But . . . you already knew I'd . . . tried to kill you. Why did you . . . keep Trapp from . . . shooting me?"

Ethan pulled his hand away. "Because you're the only one who can tell the real story. I'll do what I can to keep you from being hanged, Trevor, as long as you do what *you* can to put Roy Holliday behind bars, or better yet, see him hang from the end of a rope! I think he's the one who had John Sebastian killed, and Wayne Trapp probably pulled the trigger!"

He rose and left, grabbing a canteen from one of the horses and taking a long drink. Thirst was beginning to overwhelm him, and he knew it was from the bullet wound. He rounded up Blackfoot, tying his horse and all the mules together. He tied Trevor Gale to the pieces of board and brought a horse over to tie ropes from either side of the makeshift travois to the saddle of the horse. Wayne Trapp remained connected to the other horse by the rope around his neck, still cursing and crying.

Ethan brought Blackfoot over to Allyson and took the gun back from her, noticing a strange look on her face. "Are you hurt worse than I thought?"

"I'll . . . be all right," she answered.

Ethan helped her to her feet. "It's the baby, isn't it?"

She shook her head but could not stop the tears. "Ethan, I'm scared."

"Let's just get down to Cripple Creek. Can you ride Blackfoot without a saddle? I don't think I can even lift one to put it on him. I'd let you ride one of the others, but I've got Trapp tied to one and Gale to the other. I'll have to keep an eye on both of them. I'll kneel down. You can step on me to climb up. I don't think I can lift you right now."

Allyson nodded, wondering if they would both die before they got help. She sniffed back her tears and used the blanket to wipe them from her face. Ethan crouched down, and she heard him grunt when she stepped on his back to climb onto Blackfoot. Her own pain was getting worse, but she refused to let Ethan know how bad it was. She noticed it was difficult for Ethan to even get back on his feet. He stood beside Blackfoot for a moment to take a few deep breaths, and Allyson suspected that of all the things he had been through in his scouting days, and whatever other injuries he might have suffered, this was probably the hardest thing he had ever done. He was hanging on for her sake alone, and she loved him even more for it. When he looked up at her his face was bathed in sweat.

"Ethan, maybe we should wait—"

"We can't. It's now . . . or never." He clung to the horses as he made his way to the one that had Wayne Trapp tied to it. He picked up the reins, then with a great deal of effort managed to mount the horse that had the travois tied to it. "Hang on," he called to Allyson. "Blackfoot will follow. You don't need to give him orders. Just hang on to his mane."

Allyson nodded, and Ethan got the horses underway. The rope pulled at Wayne Trapp's neck, forcing the man to follow. He tried to scream curses at Ethan, but the tight rope soon taught him to conserve his breath. Trevor Gale lay passed out on the travois, and Ethan prayed he would not die. The man's testimony would be vital, but then none of it would mean anything if he and Ally didn't make it. Never had he struggled so hard against pain, and he knew it would be a miracle if he made it to Cripple Creek before he collapsed from loss of blood. The most important thing of all was to get help for Ally. She was losing their baby, and as far as he was concerned, of all the things that had happened this morning, that was the biggest tragedy of all.

Miners and businessmen who happened to be milling about Cripple Creek noticed the sad procession. An Indian walked beside a saddled horse, clinging with one hand to its mane, keeping his right arm around a young, red-headed woman wrapped in a blanket and sitting in the saddle. Both looked ready to pass out. What could be seen of the Indian's denim pants beneath his fur jacket was bloodstained, and the woman looked white as a ghost. Her horse pulled a heavy-set man by the neck, and many recognized Roy Holliday's right-hand man, who wore no jacket and looked close to passing out himself. A second horse, linked by a rope to the first, dragged a travois with someone tied to it, and behind that came a bare-backed buckskin horse, a rope around its neck, leading a string of mules.

It was a strange sight indeed, and at first people just stared in wonder. Finally a man ran up to the Indian to ask if he could help.

Ethan just stared at the man a moment, hardly aware they had finally made it to town. Allyson had gotten worse along the way, and he had put her on one of the saddled horses so she could hang on better, then decided to walk along beside her to stay close by in case she should start slipping from the saddle. He knew deep inside what was happening to her. She was losing the baby, and it was his fault. If he had told her about the bonanza, they could have come into town a month ago, registered the find, and decided then whether to sell the claim or mine it. The confrontation with Holliday's men could have been avoided.

"Somebody . . . get the sheriff," Ethan told the man who offered help. Others were approaching now, some of them recognizing Ethan and Allyson, most of them knowing who Wayne Trapp was. "Have him . . . hold Roy Holliday . . ." Ethan turned and pointed to Trapp and the travois. "These two, also. They work . . . for Holliday . . . tried to kill me and Ally . . . so Holliday could steal our claim."

A mumble of disbelief circulated through the small group. "I don't believe it," one of them spoke up.

"*I* do," said another. "We all know the kind of man Holliday is. We've just never had proof, till now."

"Ask . . . Trevor Gale," Ethan told them. "On the . . . travois. Trapp . . . shot him. Holliday had him set dynamite . . . try to kill us. He was going to kill Trevor . . . blame it all . . . on him . . . keep Holliday's name in the clear." He looked back at the first man, grasping his shoulder. "Need a doctor. Ally's carrying . . . losing the baby. I've been . . . shot myself." With those words he slipped to the ground.

Someone ran for the doctor, another for the sheriff. Some helped Allyson down from the horse and others untied Wayne Trapp at the neck but left his hands tied behind his back. Trapp also fell to the ground, exhausted from having to keep up and not being able to get enough air. Some of the others dispersed to spread the word, heading for the saloons.

"Come on, Indian. We'll get you and the woman to Doc's place," someone told Ethan. He managed to get to his feet again, with the help of two men. Another man carried Allyson.

"Trevor Gale . . . don't let him . . . die," Ethan told the man helping him. "Bring him . . . too. He's my witness."

"Don't worry. We'll get to the bottom of all this."

Ethan could hear shouting, knew how fast word could spread in a little town like Cripple Creek. "Somebody get Holliday!" someone yelled. "He'll answer for this!"

"Holliday tried to kill that perty little woman!" added another voice.

Ally. What was going to happen to Ally? Would he lose her *and* the baby? Even if he didn't lose her to death, he had surely lost her another way—she would blame him for losing the baby. On top of that, she had her bonanza. She would be rich woman, just like she had always wanted. And just like back in Guthrie, she didn't need him anymore.

Now it seemed there was running and shouting everywhere. He heard Wayne Trapp yelling some kind of protest, shouting that "it was all Roy Holliday's doing."

"We'll let a judge decide," someone told him.

"Maybe we'll hold our own court right here in Cripple Creek!" someone else yelled. "A hanging is what they deserve! Everybody knows the punishment for claim jumpin', and that's exactly what Holliday tried to do!"

Ethan grasped the jacket of the stranger helping him. "Lloyd Hunt . . . the assayer . . . get him, too. He knew. I think . . . he knew."

"Knew what?"

Ethan struggled to keep from slipping into unconsciousness. "Bonanza. Allyson Mills . . . a bonanza on . . . her claim. That's why . . . Holliday wanted it. I found it . . . vein of gold . . . bonanza."

"They hit it!" someone yelled. "There's a bonanza on the woman's claim! Holliday knew about it!"

More shouting. Ethan turned to look at Ally. Pale! So pale! The picture stayed in his mind as a blackness enveloped him. He heard more voices, felt hands lifting him, then everything went dark and silent.

29

Roy Holliday picked up a fountain pen to finish signing some papers, wondering why Wayne Trapp wasn't back. The deed should be done. In fact, he was sure he'd heard the explosion himself early this morning. It had a different sound from the explosions in the mines deep inside the mountain. This one was louder, less muffled. He had breathed a sigh of relief when he heard it, while still lying in his bed. Now it was getting dark, and he was beginning to worry. Wayne was supposed to shoot Trevor Gale and be back in town by now, spreading the news of what he had found up on the mountain. Trevor Gale had gotten his revenge, and Wayne had caught him in the act.

He signed a few papers, then heard a commotion in the street below. He turned to the window, put the pen back in its base, and rose. There was a lot of shouting going on below, and he thought he heard his own name. Was Wayne back with Trevor's body? An intense excitement gripped him. At last he could get his hands on Allyson Mills's bonanza! He had no doubt it was worth millions. They might as well rename Eagle Mountain Holliday Mountain, because he would own most of it now!

He walked to the window to look out. Men were running about, shouting, some carrying torches, others heading toward the hotel with guns! He frowned and glanced down the street as far as he could see. They were helping someone

. . a woman and an Indian! "My God!" he muttered. Some-
hing had gone wrong! Now he could see Wayne. The man's
ands were tied and they were herding him toward the jail-
ouse! "That stupid, fat sonofabitch," Holliday snarled. "I
nould have hired a professional!" By now Wayne Trapp
nould *be* a professional. And what about Trevor? He was a
nan who knew explosives better than anyone in Colorado.
low could he have failed? And where was he?

He turned away from the window and rushed to his desk
o pull out a pistol. He shoved it into the waist of his pants,
nen hurried to a wall safe and scrambled to remember the
ight numbers. He could already hear footsteps and voices in
ne lobby below, then the sound of men heading up the
tairs. He grabbed wads of money from the safe and
rammed it into his pockets, then headed for a back way out
f the office, but too late. The main doorway burst open,
nd a mob stormed inside. "Hold it right there, Mr. Holli-
ay!" one of them warned.

Holliday turned and faced them, standing a little
traighter, putting on an air of authority. "What the hell is
oing on here? You have no right barging into my office this
ay!"

"From the looks of things, you already knew we were
omin'," one of them answered. "What you runnin' from,
1r. Holliday? Attempted murder? Claim jumpin'?"

Holliday could not control the flush that suffused his face.
What are you talking about?"

"Wayne Trapp spilled it all while he was bein' dragged to
ne sheriff's office," another told him. "Ain't nothin' left to
ry to cover up, Mr. Holliday. You've got some explainin' to
o to the U. S. Marshal. In the meantime, you can come with
s and wait for him over at the jail."

Holliday backed up slightly, then pulled the pistol out

and waved it at all of them. "I'm not going anyplace with *an...* of you!"

"Use your head, Holliday." The owner of a nearby supply store stepped forward. "You'd better come peaceful-like and maybe everybody will just wait for the marshal and le... this be handled the right way. You can get yourself a lawye... and all. If you try to shoot one of us or get away, this mol... will just get angrier. Think about it. Most of these people are miners who already have some grievances against you. wouldn't piss them off any worse. I've seen lynch mob... before. It's not a pretty sight."

"You had John Sebastian killed, didn't you?" one of the others shouted.

"You tried to kill that little lady up there who was mindin... her own business, tryin' to work her legal claim. Ain't non... of us much approve of her bein' up there with the Indian... but we know he's a good man, and it looks like he saved he... life today; and no matter what we think of folks workin' ... claim, ain't no man got a right to try to kill them and stea... it."

Holliday slowly lowered the pistol, then reached out t... lay it on his desk. "You're all crazy, and Wayne Trapp is ... liar! I didn't have anything to do with trying to kill anyone!"

"It's four against one, Holliday," another answered. "Th... Indian, the woman, Trapp, and Trevor Gale. He's still alive too. We know Trapp tried to kill him so's he could say it wa... all Trevor's doin'."

Holliday went white. He'd thought that at least Trevo... was dead. Then maybe somehow he could say Wayne wa... angry with him about wages or something and had staged al... of this for revenge. With Trevor alive to verify the plan, an... most certainly furious at realizing he'd been used an... tricked, there was no escaping the truth. He took a dee... breath, trying to keep his composure. "I'll go with yo...

eacefully, but I want a telegram sent to my attorney in Col-
rado Springs. I want him here at once!''

"We'll be sure to do your bidding," a man answered sar-
astically. Holliday recognized him as one of the miners who
ad joined Trevor Gale in trying to organize a strike. The
nan reached out for him. "Let's go."

Holliday jerked away. "Keep your hands off me!"

"Hey, what's that bulgin' in his pockets?" another put in.

In seconds Holliday was surrounded and searched. Men
ulled wads of money from his pants pockets and from in-
ide his jacket, then pulled the jacket completely off. "Stop
t! Give me back that money!" Holliday protested, but to no
vail. Men whooped and hollered and cheered. Paper
noney in bills of large amounts was tossed into the air and
egan raining down for the men to grab as they could. Holli-
ay was tossed about, his vest torn off, his gold watch ripped
rom its cord. It was impossible to see which man had taken
vhat or how much. The rings came off his fingers. Some of
he more respectable businessmen tried to stop the melee,
ut it was too late. All they could do was try to protect Roy
Iolliday. They got hold of him and rushed him out the door
o escort him to the jail, while some of the men remained
ehind to ransack his office for more money and valuables.

"Look here! A silver cigar box!" one of them shouted.

Holliday was forced out into the street, his hair a-tumble,
is shirt hanging out and torn. Men who had once called
hemselves his friends hurried him over to the jail, while
nore miners gathered around, shouting that he ought to be
anged.

"There's trouble coming," one of the men escorting Holiday observed. "These miners are ready to explode.
They've just been looking for an excuse, and now they've
ot one."

"It's gonna be one hell of a night," another replied.

"You just keep those worthless sonsobitches away fro
me!" a frightened Roy Holliday demanded.

He was whisked inside the jail and thrown into a cell. H
heard the iron door slam shut, then heard the bang of
thick, wooden door also being closed, muffling the noise o
the shouting. He turned, and in a rage he grabbed the thi
mattress from the cot in his cell and growled as he whirle
with it and tossed it against a wall. That was when he no
ticed someone sitting in the cell across from him, a heavy-se
man with a swollen, bloodstained face. His dark eyes wid
ened with hatred and disgust. "You!" he seethed. "You fa
worthless bastard! You messed up, didn't you? I should hav
known! God *damn* you!"

Wayne Trapp knew there was nothing left but to tell th
truth. There was no reason to try to please Roy Holliday
and he'd suffered his last insult. He rose, going to the fron
of his cell and staring at Holliday for a moment. Then h
took a deep breath, reared back a little and spat at the man,
wad of tobacco juice landing on Holliday's pant leg. "Go
damn *you*," Wayne sneered.

Allyson awoke feeling weak and spent. She studied th
flowered wallpaper in the small bedroom, taking severa
minutes to gather her thoughts and realize where she wa
She remembered someone carrying her in here, remem
bered the pain, the awful pain, and a doctor telling her ther
was no reason why she couldn't have more children. "Th
shock of what happened up on that mountain, probabl
mixed together with the fact that you have been working fa
too hard for a woman of your slender stature, made you los
the baby," he had said. "Maybe if you hadn't had to mak
that trip down the mountain on top of it all, you might hav

ung on to it. Who is to say? But you are so young. You will
ave more. And, after all, you weren't married to the baby's
ather. Maybe it's best this way.''

Best this way? The tears came again. How typical of a
nan not to understand how she was feeling. Didn't he know
hat the baby had been the most precious thing she had ever
ossessed? It had been a part of her and Ethan. No matter
ow tiny was the life she had aborted, it was still life, her
hild, her hope for love. Now that hope was gone, just like
verything else she had ever loved. Maybe even Ethan was
one. She had no idea if he was even still alive.

After all, you weren't married to the baby's father. What a
rude remark to make! Did that mean she was supposed to
ove her baby less? That its existence didn't matter just be-
ause Ethan wasn't her husband? In her heart he was still
ust as much her husband as when she had married him back
n Guthrie. She put a hand to her belly, wondering if losing
he baby was God's punishment for how she had hurt Ethan
ack then, or for lying with him after having the marriage
nnulled. Surely not, for that would mean He was punishing
than, too, and as far as she was concerned Ethan had never
one anything wrong.

Still, there was the gold . . . the gold he had never told her
bout. Part of her wanted to hate him for that. Would he
ave let her sell the claim for pennies when it might be
vorth millions, just to try to keep her? Did he trust her so
ttle. If he could not forgive her for hurting him over that
narriage . . . maybe all the love in the world would not
hange the fact that they could never stay together. Yet liv-
ng without him was an impossible thought now. Maybe she
idn't even have any choice. Maybe he had died! How
ould she go on living if he had?

She struggled to control her tears, realizing it seemed to

be early morning. The doctor had given her something fo her pain and told her to rest. Had she slept through th night. Had Ethan died without her being able to touch hi once more, tell him she loved him? "Ethan," she whispered She wanted to yell his name, but to her amazement she ha only enough strength for a whisper. She couldn't even mov her arms. Even taking a breath was an effort.

She closed her eyes, trying to think, remembering all tha had happened. A bonanza! Ethan had said there was a vei of gold up on her claim that could be worth millions! Holli day had apparently known about it. What had happened t Roy Holliday? To Wayne Trapp and that man called Trevo Gale? What had happened to Ethan? She tried in vain t rise, but could not even get her head off the pillow. She re membered being told she'd lost a lot of blood. Was it reall only yesterday she had finally told Ethan about the baby Now there *was* no baby. She felt so empty, and more alon than she ever had as an orphan. Strangely, the knowledg that her claim might be worth millions brought her no joy a all. She would gladly trade it all to have her baby back.

She sensed a quiet movement to her left, and turned he head to see the door opening. "Ethan!" she whispered. Sh watched him step inside. He still wore the blood-staine pants, but he was shirtless. Gauze was wrapped around hi middle, and she saw a small spot of blood on it at his lowe left side. Rather than his usual glowing bronze color, his fac looked more gray, and there were dark circles under hi eyes, eyes filled with a deep grief. He closed the door an came toward her; it looked to Allyson as though it took a the strength he had just to move a wooden chair near th bed.

Allyson managed to reach out her hand. "I was afraid yo were dead," she told him, forcing a voice loud enough fo

im to hear. More tears slipped from her eyes. "Thank God
ou're alive!"

Ethan took her hand. "I'm not so sure you should be glad
f that, after the way I kept the truth from you." He sighed
eeply. "How do you feel?"

She couldn't speak at the moment. She could only cry
gain. Ethan squeezed her hand, leaned over, and brought it
p to kiss the back of it. "I'm so damn sorry, Ally. It's all my
ault." He pressed the back of her hand against his cheek
nd just sat there for a few minutes with his eyes closed
hile she wept. Finally he kissed her hand again, then
eached for a small towel lying on the stand beside her bed.
Ie used it to wipe the tears from her face, then placed it in
er hand. He rested his elbows on his knees, holding his
ead in his hands.

"I wouldn't blame you if you wanted to just forget about
s," he said softly. "With the baby gone, and you being a
ch woman in your own right . . ." He sighed deeply. "If I
ad told you in the first place, we'd already have been down
ff that mountain a month ago and would have sold the
laim or had someone else mining it. You wouldn't have
tayed up there working so hard. It's my fault you lost the
aby, Ally. I was so damn afraid to tell you about what I'd
ound, afraid that once you knew you had struck it rich, you
vouldn't want or need me anymore."

Allyson held in a sob. "It's really . . . my own fault," she
nswered.

Ethan met her gaze. "How can you say that?"

Allyson studied the tragedy in his dark eyes. "I'm the one
. . who betrayed *your* trust in the beginning." She took a
noment to get her breath again. "You . . . had every right not
o trust me. All you've ever known about me . . . is that I was
o bent . . . on what I could possess, what I could own. All I

have ever talked about . . . is finding that bonanza . . . being rich woman . . . having something no one could take awa from me." She closed her eyes. "Ethan, once I knew I wa carrying your child, I knew what my most important posses sion was. It was life . . . your life . . . the baby that lived ir me." More tears slipped quietly out of her eyes.

Ethan sighed and got up from the chair, walking to loo out a window. "There's no going back for either of us, and I'm not sure now how we're going to make up for all the hur and misunderstanding."

Allyson studied him, remembering how he had suffered trying to get her to town for help and bring in Wayne Trapp and Trevor Gale at the same time. "I don't know either Ethan. I just know I'm glad . . . you didn't die."

He rubbed at his neck. "I was damn lucky. The bulle apparently didn't hit anything vital. The biggest problem was loss of blood. The doc says he doesn't know how I made that trip down without passing out long before I did." He turned to look at her. "But *I* know how I did it. I had to ge help for you. That was all I could think of."

She sniffed back more tears. "Maybe neither one of u . . . realizes how much we're loved by the other. After Okla homa . . . I tried so hard . . . to forget you, Ethan . . . but never could."

He did not reply. He turned to look back out the window and Allyson realized then that she had been hearing a lot o shouting somewhere in the distance. "This whole thing ha started a real mess," Ethan told her. "Wayne Trapp is blab bing like a baby. Apparently a former employee of Holli day's, Joe Carson, I think his name is, killed John Sebastiar on Holliday's orders. The man has since fled Colorado Once the miners found out about Roy Holliday's under handed schemes, they've gone wild. The doctor told me thi morning they have all gone on strike up at his mines wrecked parts of the processing mill, even blew up part of one mine. The U.S. Marshal is on his way up here, along with some army troops, to restore order." He looked at her and smiled rather sadly. "You sure do know how to stir up a ruckus anyplace you go, don't you?"

She wiped her tears again. "I never mean for any of it to happen. All I ever wanted . . . was just to be left alone . . . allowed my independence and to have something of my own. Why is that . . . so forbidden . . . just because I'm young and a woman?"

Ethan watched her for a few seconds. "I guess because men aren't used to such things in a woman." He walked closer again, leaning over her bed. "But that's what I always loved and admired about you, Ally, your strength and determination. That's partly what made it so hard for *me* to forget *you* after Oklahoma. We have a lot in common, you know. We both lost everyone who mattered to us, we both have pasts that hurt. We each admire strength and courage, value our ability to survive on our own. The one difference is that I have always known I wanted someone else in my life. I'm able to recognize that I *can't* do it all alone. Without a woman I love at my side, I'm only half a man. You could never quite admit that you needed anyone but yourself, and that's because you're so damn afraid to care, because you don't want to hurt anymore. Besides that, there's a little part of you that could never quite decide if it was right to love an Indian." He sighed deeply, turning away. "Now the whole town knows you've lost a baby. They know what we were doing up there, and that we were no longer married. We'll have to testify against Trapp and Holliday, and none of it is going to be easy. You'll have to face a whole town full of men who are never going to understand what we've been through. They're only going to see it one way."

"It doesn't matter, Ethan. All that matters . . . is that I love you and you love me . . . and we don't feel in our hearts . . . that we did anything wrong."

He looked down at her. "And what about now? I lied to you. You've lost the baby because of it. There are a lot of things for you to think about, Ally. My being Indian, the fact that you could be a very, very rich woman; and there is a lot for both of us to forgive about each other. Whatever you do, I want you to be really sure this time. Until this mess is cleared up, maybe we're better off not seeing too much of each other. I'll find someone who will be fair about it to go up to the claim and give you a true estimate on what that vein of gold is worth, then I'll let you decide what you want to do about it, and about us."

"Half of it belongs to you, Ethan. That was our deal."

He shook his head. "I don't want any of it, not if you aren't part of the package, and that's something you've got to make up your mind about."

"I . . . already have. I'd trade that claim right now . . . and whatever millions it might be worth . . . to have our baby back."

He leaned closer again. "But what if there hadn't *been* a baby? I wouldn't have wanted you to stay with me because of a baby, Ally. Now it's down to just me and the gold, and your dreams. I don't want you coming with me if you feel like you have to give up your dreams to do it. I don't need that gold. I never told you, but I have a thousand dollars plus interest waiting for me in Colorado Springs, reward money for capturing that gang of railroad outlaws I told you about when I met Roy Holliday. That and the money I saved while working for him is plenty for me to get started ranching. The Indian in me just wants that simple life, Ally. I'm not cut out for hanging with Denver's high society, running some kind of fancy business. I love you enough to take you without any extras. I'm just not sure you love me enough to do the same. You'd trade all that gold for our baby, but what about for me?"

"Are you saying . . . no matter what it's worth . . . I should just give it all up?"

Ethan leaned down and kissed her forehead. "No. All I'm saying is, would *I* be enough, if you *didn't* have the gold? If that claim had turned out to be worthless, would you have finally given up searching for happiness in money and possessions and come to Wyoming with me? There are a lot of ways to be rich, Ally. I just want you to understand what's really important in life."

Another tear slipped down her face. "But I do, Ethan. I just want to be with you."

Ethan's eyes began to tear. "You wait until you feel strong again. Wait until you find out just what that claim is worth. Follow your heart, Ally. I won't blame you for whatever decision you make." He touched her cheek. "I'll stand by you through the trial and all. I imagine we'll have to go to Colorado Springs for that. It's going to take a couple of months to get everything settled. We've got some time to think."

She grasped his hand and kissed it. "Please hold me, Ethan. The only time I feel really safe from the world . . . is when you hold me."

He sighed deeply, sat down on the edge of the bed, and reached down, pulling her into his arms. They both wept over the loss of the little life they had created. "We've been through too much together, Ethan," she whispered. "I don't see how we could ever be apart again. I could never, ever forget you now, or live without you."

He kissed the red hair he so loved. "I just want you to be sure." He thought about how rich the vein of gold he had seen had to be. He had a feeling she still had not grasped the full reality of what belonged to her. When she did, especially once she was stronger, this all might change again. He told himself he must not fall all the way into the deep river of love that beckoned him. He just might drown after all, but then who was he kidding? He had already willingly dived into those menacing waters when he agreed to go up on that mountain with this woman. No matter what she decided to do, it was not going to change the fact that he loved her more than his own life.

Ethan finished packing. He was leaving in the morning for Wyoming, and Ally damn well knew it. She should have been back by now.

Had she done it again? The trial for Roy Holliday was over. He and Wayne Trapp and Trevor Gale had been sent to prison for murder and attempted murder. Riots up at the mines had caused a lot of damage, and army troops were helping to clean up the mess. He hadn't been back up to Cripple Creek himself since coming to Colorado Springs for the trial. He never *wanted* to go back, but Ally had had no choice. A wealthy mine owner from Denver was interested in her claim. She had gone back with him to see the vein for herself and discuss a sale price.

That was what worried him. They had decided they would remarry when she came back. She was going to Wyoming with him, or so she had promised. But this was the first time she had seen the bonanza for herself. Knowing Ally, that could change everything. She was stronger again, fiestier. She had sailed through the trial and the rude remarks about a woman "living up on that mountain with an Indian." Like the Ally he knew, she had held her chin high and shown no sign of crumbling. By the time she finished testifying, few people were concerned with whether or not she had been living in sin. She had drawn their attention to the simple fact that she owned that claim and Roy Holliday and his men had tried to kill her to get it. She had rallied the whole town of Cripple Creek behind her, as well as half of Colorado Springs. The trial had been a sensation, and he did not doubt that the headlines about Roy Holliday's life sentence made the papers not just in Colorado but all over the country. Little orphaned Allyson Mills, who had run away from that train with her brother over two and a half years ago, was now a famous woman. Famous and rich. She had a way of charming the worst of them, and now she had the world at her feet, and she damn well knew it. She could have anything she wanted, and once she saw that gold . . .

He tied the rawhide strings of his leather bag. Who was he kidding? He was a half-breed nobody, with just enough hard-earned money to get himself to Wyoming and buy up enough land for a small ranch. He and Ally didn't have a damn thing in common. During the trial, there had been little chance to be together. For the sake of appearances, they had taken separate rooms; and because he felt Ally needed time to think about what she wanted, he had stayed away, let her alone. She had become the center of attention for everyone else, the subject of interviews and picture-taking. Some had depicted her as the poor young orphaned woman who had big dreams. Yes, she had strayed, with an Indian man who had somehow made her dependent on him, but the public had forgiven her. After all, she was young and alone. The poor girl had stood up against one of the richest men in Colorado and had won! There had not even been much mention of what he himself had gone through to protect Ally the day of the explosion, how he had almost died getting her down from that mountain, risking his life when Wayne Trapp had attacked her.

He smiled bitterly to himself and packed one more bag.

He couldn't care less that Ally had taken all the attention. He hated publicity, and he didn't consider himself any kind of hero. He had just done what he could to help the woman he loved. His anger was not at the press or the public, or even at Ally. He was angry with himself, for ever having gotten himself into this mess in the first place. All he would have had to do was never get involved with Allyson Mills back in Guthrie. It would have been so easy. At the least, he should never have gone back that second time. Why hadn't he just stayed away? And when he had seen she was successfully running that rooming house, knew she was doing just fine, why hadn't he just gone on from there and stayed out of her life?

Because no matter how angry she made him, he loved her, that was why. Now he'd gone much too far. Now, no matter what she decided to do, he would never forget Ally Mills or get her out of his blood.

He finished packing the second bag, then rolled himself a cigarette and lit it, walking to a window to look out at the snow-covered mountains above Colorado Springs. Her dream was up there, not with him. He wondered if the pain in his chest would ever go away, or the aching need to have her back in his bed. They had not slept together since coming down off that mountain. Maybe he would never know that pleasure again.

Someone tapped on the door to his hotel room then, and his heartbeat rushed with a mixture of dread and anticipation. If it was Ally, she had probably come to tell him good-bye. He took a deep drag on the cigarette and walked to the door, feeling an ache deep inside at the sight of her when he opened it. She stood there wearing a deep burgundy velvet and taffeta dress with a matching velvet cape and hat. She looked every inch the sophisticated woman of the world, a far cry from the dirty-faced girl in baggy pants he'd seen every day up at the mine; certainly far removed from the wide-eyed woman-child in hand-me-down clothes he'd met back in Guthrie.

This was the real Allyson Mills. She had been through more than most women went through in a lifetime, and he had shared half of it with her. Yet at the moment he felt almost like a stranger. She was more beautiful than he had ever seen her. She literally glowed, and he knew it was because she had seen that vein of gold. He wished he could read her feelings better. She looked too damn happy to have come here to tell him she couldn't go with him. Surely it hurt her some to do this.

"Hello, Ethan," she spoke up.

Why did he feel like he had never even met her before? He stepped back to allow her inside. "I wasn't sure you'd show up in time."

She smiled and shook her head, stepping into the room. "Or show up at all, you mean." She turned to look up at him as he closed the door, wondering if a more wonderful, more handsome man existed. Going back up to the claim without him had told her all she needed to know. It had brought a flood of memories, of nights snuggled close to his powerful body, feeling so warm and protected . . . and loved. Never would she forget how it had felt to know she was carrying Ethan Temple's baby. She wanted to know that feeling again. "If I am going to be your wife, Ethan Temple, you simply must have more faith in me."

She watched the doubt in his dark eyes turn to a flicker of joy, then disbelief. "You sure?"

"Very sure, but I'm not giving up *everything*, Ethan."

He frowned, taking another drag on the cigarette. "What does that mean?" He walked past her and put out the cigarette.

"It means that we can both have our dream, *and* each

other." She untied her cape and removed it and her velvet gloves. A little snow still clung to her leather boots as well as to the ruffled hem of her dress. Taffeta and petticoats rustled as she moved to lay her cape and gloves on the bed, a bed she noticed was still unmade. She turned to face him. "You were right about one thing. The sight of that vein nearly took my breath away. Mr. Benjamin feels he can probably get millions out of there, but like all such situations, it will also cost him a great deal to mine it right. He's the one with the know-how and equipment, and since I am going to marry and move to Wyoming with my new husband, I won't have time for such things, so I sold him the claim."

Ethan frowned, leaning against a wall to watch her, thinking how much more a woman she was. The way she filled out that dress . . . "You did?"

She smiled again. "You're surprised." She sighed and folded her arms. "Ethan, what am I going to do with you? You really thought I'd keep it and become some wealthy mining mogul, maybe buy up half of Denver, didn't you? That I'd just totally forget you even exist once I saw that bonanza." She shivered with delightful memories when his eyes moved over her in that way he'd always had of disarming her defenses.

"I know you pretty well, I'd say. You can't blame me for thinking the worst."

She turned away. "No. I guess I can't. All I can tell you is that I'm here because I *want* to be here. None of the things that used to matter to me make any difference any more. When I went up to that claim without you, so many memories came flooding in, not just from up there, but all the other things we've shared. Something keeps bringing us back together, Ethan, and now we've lost a child." She turned to face him again, studying the high cheekbones and full, tempting lips. His very presence made her feel safe and loved. "I want more babies, Ethan. That's the only thing I know for sure now. I want lots of babies to love and to love me back, and I want you to father them. I want to sleep in your arms at night. I hate being away from you. I—"

He put up a finger to stop her. "You said something about a compromise. Let's hear it all."

She dropped her gaze and sat down on the bed. "I told you I sold the claim, but just because I'm not going to mine it myself doesn't mean I'm not a rich woman. Mr. Benjamin gave me one hundred thousand dollars for full rights to the claim."

Ethan moved away from the wall, dropping his arms and whistling softly. "A hundred thousand!" He turned away. "A hundred thousand," he repeated. He shook his head. "Damn." He turned to face her. "And you still want to get married and go live on a ranch in Wyoming? Do you know what you could do with a hundred thousand dollars?"

Allyson scooted farther back on the bed. "I know exactly what I'll do with it, and we'll both have what we want."

Ethan frowned questioningly. "And how is that?"

"Oh, you're going to buy that land, all right, only you're going to own the biggest ranch in Wyoming, stocked with the best beef cattle and the finest horses. You're going—"

"Ally, I don't want to get into all the headaches of being that big. All I want to do is—"

"All you want is to be able to ride out on the open range, to feel free, to be with nature, work with animals. I know what you want, Ethan, and you can have it. *I'll* handle the figures and the headaches. Don't you see? It's what I love to do. We can be together, and you'll be doing what you love, while I'll be doing what *I* love. I'll be managing something—a business we can share. I'll do all the paperwork, and you'll be out there riding under the sky, taking care of the cattle and horses, doing what *you* love best. At night you'll come home to me, and we'll have time for just each other . . . and all the children we're going to have." Her smile faded, and her eyes misted with tears. "Of all the things I have lost, Ethan, the baby hurt the most. I want another, lots of sons for Ethan Temple. And if we're going to have a lot of children, we'll *need* lots of land, so that some day when they inherit it all, there will be plenty to divide up among them."

She rose from the bed and walked closer to him. "Ethan, we can have everything we both want. That hundred thousand dollars is yours. I had Mr. Benjamin make the check out to you, not to me. Doesn't that say something for how much I trust you? Love you? You can throw me by the wayside and take the money and run if you want. I wouldn't blame you if you did."

He grasped her shoulders. "It isn't the money, Ally."

"Of course it isn't. With you it never has been. And that's how it is for me now. I've fought what I know is really important only because I'm so afraid to love you and risk losing you to death. Now I know I have to take that chance, because I can't possibly go on with life and be happy without you. It wouldn't matter if I owned all of Denver. I don't need those things anymore, Ethan. I'm willing to take the chance. At least if we can have children, if I do lose you, I'll always have something left of you to love forever." She touched his chest, enjoying the feel of his soft buckskin shirt. "Ethan, I chose gold, land, possessions, because those things are easy to love. They can't die. Even if you lose them, you can find a way to get them back; but you can't get back a human life, and that's why I didn't want to care so deeply, why I allowed myself to believe all I needed was material possessions and money. But after spending all that time up there on the mountain with you, it was like you became a part of me. Letting you go now would be like cutting off an arm or a leg. The baby I lost was yours, too, and married or not, when you put your life into me it was out of love, and it was right. No one can tell me it wasn't. I just want to be loved that way again, Ethan, forever. I never knew that kind of love, and it frightened me."

She rested her head against his chest, breathing in the soothing, familiar scent that comforted her in the night and told her everything was all right, that she was loved. "Let's get married, take our money, and go to Wyoming, Ethan. I think it's exciting to think of what we could have together. I'll manage everything. All you have to do is—"

He grasped hold of her chin and made her look up at him. His dark eyes were scowling, but there was a teasing glitter, too. "Why do I get the distinct impression that you're manipulating me again?" He rubbed her chin with his thumb. "I'm going to be working *for* you, aren't I?"

She felt a flush come to her face. "I didn't mean it to sound that way. It wouldn't be like that at all, Ethan. We'd just be sharing something, both of us doing what we like."

"And you'd have the security of the ranch, in case something happens to me. It's that security you're always after, isn't it?"

She watched him boldly. "Maybe it is."

He suddenly broke into a handsome grin. "I also have a feeling that if we went broke and lost the ranch, you'd find some other way for us to survive."

She reached up to put her arms around his neck. "That won't happen, because you know the land, you know about horses and cattle, you'll love what you're doing."

"And you'll love balancing the books."

She smiled. "It will be exciting for both of us."

He frowned. "Just don't get *too* bossy."

"I'll try not to." She leaned up and kissed his lips lightly. "Besides, in certain parts of our marriage, you'll *always* be the boss."

He began pulling the pins from her hat. "Oh? What parts are you talking about?" He tossed her hat aside and began nudging her toward the bed.

"Well, I'd say during the hours of around nine P.M. until morning. During those hours I will be totally under your control."

He moved his hand into the neat bun into which she had wound her hair, wiggling his fingers until all the pins fell out and her hair fell down her back. "I prefer that you be totally under my control twenty-four hours a day." He picked her up and laid her on the bed, moving onto it beside her. He met her lips in a hot, hungry kiss, rubbing at the taffeta bodice that so beautifully displayed her small waist and full breasts. He cupped a breast in his hand, a little annoyed by the feel of stiff undergarments. "One order is that you don't wear these damn stiff things under your dresses."

She smiled, feeling fire move through her veins. "I'll wear them only on special occasions. After all, you'll be one of the richest ranchers and landowners in Wyoming. We'll have to go to socials once in a while."

He watched her blue eyes warily. "Why do I get the feeling I won't just be pushing cattle?"

Allyson touched a finger to his lips. She loved the way they were shaped, the way he kissed her. "Don't you know that women have a way of making a man feel like he's in complete control, when he really isn't at all?"

He grinned. "Maybe a man just enjoys letting the woman *think* she's putting one over on him."

Her eyebrows arched in surprise. "Ethan Temple, I thought I could fool you again."

He kissed her eyes. "Not anymore, Miss Mills. Two can play at that game, and I'll do it, as long as I can have you in my bed at night and call you my wife."

Allyson reached up and pulled away the rawhide tie that held his long hair back. It spilled over his shoulders. "You like my hair long and loose. I like yours the same way."

He began unbuttoning the front of her dress. "You mean you don't want me to cut it like a white man's?"

"Never," she whispered. She grasped his hand then and smiled. "If we're going to get started on another baby, shouldn't we find a preacher first?"

He kissed her throat. "There are plenty in this town. We'll find one later. First things first."

He met her mouth then, and Allyson returned his kiss with a passionate hunger. She knew what she wanted now, more than gold, more than her independence. She finally had something to call her own, and his name was Ethan Temple. This was one possession she was never going to lose again, and for the first time since her mother died, she was not afraid to love.

There is no fear in love . . . perfect love drives out fear.

I John 4:18

I hope you have enjoyed my story. For more information about me and other books I have written, send a #10 business-size, self-addressed, stamped envelope to 6013 North Coloma Road, Coloma, Michigan 49038. I will send you a newsletter and bookmark. Thank you!

About the Author

ROSANNE BITTNER is an award-winning author, specializing in books about Indians and early settlers of the American West of the 1800's. She is well known for her touching love stories, as well as for using authentic, well-researched historical fact in her novels. She has traveled extensively for this research, and is a member of the Council on America's Military Past, the Nebraska State Historical Society, Romance Writers of America, Western Outlaw-Lawman History Association, and the Oregon-California Trails Assoc. Her other Zebra books include *Shameless, Caress, Sioux Splendor, Sweet Mountain Magic, Prairie Embrace, Arizona Bride*, and the *Savage Destiny* series.

Rosanne and her husband have two grown sons and live on several wooded acres in a small town in southwest Michigan. Rosanne welcomes comments from her readers, who can write her at 6013 North Coloma Road, Coloma, MI 49038. Be sure to include a business-size, self-addressed, stamped envelope.

ROMANCE FROM ROSANNE BITTNER

CARESS   (0-8217-3791-0, $5.99)

FULL CIRCLE   (0-8217-4711-8, $5.99)

SHAMELESS   (0-8217-4056-3, $5.99)

SIOUX SPLENDOR   (0-8217-5157-3, $4.99)

UNFORGETTABLE   (0-8217-4423-2, $5.50)

TEXAS EMBRACE   (0-8217-5625-7, $5.99)

UNTIL TOMORROW   (0-8217-5064-X, $5.99)

FROM ROSANNE BITTNER:
ZEBRA SAVAGE DESTINY ROMANCE!

#1: SWEET PRAIRIE PASSION   (0-8217-5342-8, $5.99)

#2: RIDE THE FREE WIND   (0-8217-5343-6, $5.99)

#3: RIVER OF LOVE   (0-8217-5344-4, $5.99)

#4: EMBRACE THE
     WILD WIND   (0-8217-5413-0, $5.99)

#7: EAGLE'S SONG   (0-8217-5326-6, $5.99)

Available wherever paperbacks are sold, or order direct from the Publisher. Send cover price plus 50¢ per copy for mailing and handling to Penguin USA, P.O. Box 999, c/o Dept. 17109, Bergenfield, NJ 07621. Residents of New York and Tennessee must include sales tax. DO NOT SEND CASH.

SAVAGE ROMANCE
FROM CASSIE EDWARDS!

#1: SAVAGE OBSESSION   (0-8217-5554-4, $5.99)

#2: SAVAGE INNOCENCE   (0-8217-5578-1, $5.99)

#3: SAVAGE TORMENT   (0-8217-5581-1, $5.99)

#4: SAVAGE HEART   (0-8217-5635-4, $5.99)

#5: SAVAGE PARADISE   (0-8217-5637-0, $5.99)

ROMANCE FROM FERN MICHAELS

DEAR EMILY   (0-8217-4952-8, $5.99)

WISH LIST   (0-8217-5228-6, $6.99)

AND IN HARDCOVER:

VEGAS RICH   (1-57566-057-1, $25.00)

PASSIONATE ROMANCE
FROM BETINA KRAHN!

HIDDEN FIRES   (0-8217-4953-6, $4.99)

LOVE'S BRAZEN FIRE   (0-8217-5691-5, $5.99)

MIDNIGHT MAGIC   (0-8217-4994-3, $4.99)

PASSION'S RANSOM   (0-8217-5130-1, $5.99)

REBEL PASSION   (0-8217-5526-9, $5.99)